ALSO BY MIKE HOLST

The Last Trip Down The Mountain

Back From The Ashes

The Magic Book

Justice For Adam

No Clues In The Ashes

Nothing To Lose

A Long Way Back

AN
ABSENCE
OF
CONSCIENCE

Mike Holst

iUniverse, Inc.
Bloomington

An Absence Of Conscience

iUniverse books may be ordered through booksellers or by contacting:

iUniverse
1663 Liberty Drive
Bloomington, IN 47403
www.iuniverse.com
1-800-Authors (1-800-288-4677)

ISBN: 978-1-4759-0610-3 (sc)
ISBN: 978-1-4759-0611-0 (e)

Printed in the United States of America

iUniverse rev. date: 4/2/2012

ACKNOWLEDMENTS

To my good friend, Glenda Berndt, my wordsmith and editor. Thank you for your tireless efforts to make this story as good as it can be.

To Kitty, my soul mate, who encouraged me and talked me through the rough spots. Thank you so much, sweetheart.

Christian Heeb Photography took the cover photo.

Author's Note

Many of us have, over our lifetime, experienced someone who seems to be without a moral compass, or a guiding conscience—a person so self-centered and depraved that they laugh at any sense of ethics and morality. These are people who seem to justify all of their selfish evil actions, and fiendish deeds, as simply normal behavior. These are people who live completely outside man's law, and above God's law.

This story is about such a man. Mathew Halsworth Junior. Hal was sheltered throughout his life, by his father, from all consequences of all the trouble he spawned. A father who, in himself, was the epitome of hypocrisy for the way he lived, and the example he set for his namesake.

Hal did him one better, and then some, by far exceeding his father's bad behavior. There was nothing that would stop him from getting what he wanted. Not even murder.

Then along came Torch Brennan. A rugged, seasoned old homicide detective who "never said never." Who could not forget about the murder of a young woman that hit very close to his heart. Thwarted in his first attempt to try young Hal for his crime, but knowing he was guilty, Torch was given something detectives rarely get, a second chance.

Justice comes in many shapes and forms, and sometimes it takes twists and turns no one expects, but in the end, some semblance of justice always comes. Enjoy the story.

The Author

CHAPTER ONE

December 23rd, 1989

The sporty yellow Camaro cruised slowly away from the sprawling University Of Minnesota campus. The car hesitated for just a second at the first semaphore, even though the light was green, and then made an overly cautious, almost tentative, left turn onto University Avenue, staying in the outside lane. Then, as if it had finally caught its breath, the sporty car quickly accelerated, and just as quickly leveled off at or near the speed limit. The windows inside the car were smoked except for the windshield so that, coupled with the darkness of the cold December night, made it hard for others to distinguish anything inside the car. There were just the shadowy outlines of two people inside, one driving, and one seemingly asleep, leaning against the side window.

The campus grew smaller, and then slowly faded away through the rear window, as the driver drove warily up the street. The structures outside the car window slowly changed, from a bustling college campus, to a residential neighborhood made up of one hundred year old duplexes. Most of them with rooms for students to rent—advertised on hastily-made signs hung on dilapidated porches—or nailed to the front of the house. Cars seemed to be parked anywhere there was an empty piece of land. A few houses had even converted, what were once small front yards, into smaller parking lots. White smoke rose lazily from chimneys on some of the houses, and seemed to just lie there in a thin translucent layer. The light from a narrow slice of crescent moon filtered itself through the permeable cloud cover, reflecting briefly off the dirty snow and ice banks, but was then quickly enveloped by the darkness. The night air was completely calm, giving off an eerie feeling. At least it felt that way to Hal.

He reached for the heater controls, turning the fan on high and trying to coax some warmth from his still-cold automobile. His breath was fogging up the windshield, but his passenger didn't seem to be having the same effect on the other side. Hal reached over and turned the radio down from its normal pitch of heavy metal music. It was distracting him, and right now, he didn't need that.

Hal was trying very hard to pay attention to what he was doing. His mind was whirling with so many details and cautions, but there was no sign of panic, and he was completely focused on the job at hand.

The passenger's head bounced gently against the window as he hit a few potholes and ruts in the broken and patched asphalt. She was wrapped in a blanket with just a rooster tail of hair, forming her ponytail, showing out the top. There were few other cars on the road to contend with; mostly some drunks going home from the bars closing.

Hal saw, in the rear view mirror, red lights flashing behind him and pulled over as a large fire engine roared by and disappeared into the night. It had frightened him at first, but it had all happened so fast he hadn't time to get that excited. The semaphore at University and Washington was showing green ahead, so he slowed and then turned left again. The bright lights of downtown Minneapolis lay straight ahead. There were more discreet ways to get where he was going, but something told him not to try them. This was faster and he didn't want to drag it out. He was always extremely impatient but he was also tired and nervous and wanted to get this all behind him.

The car eased onto the bridge over the Mississippi, staying in the left lane away from the sidewalk. He could see the dark waters flowing below them when he looked across the roadway and the water looked cold and forbidding. Downstream in the distance, the lights from St. Anthony Falls glowed through a layer of thin fog, caused by the cold air and warm water. A young couple leaned lazily against the bridge railing, bundled up in heavy clothes, their backs to him. As Hal drove by, the red glow of a cigarette could be seen in the man's mouth as he turned to look. The young man's arm was around his friend's shoulders and he pulled her close once more, turning his attention back to her and the river.

In front of the Camaro, the covered Metrodome stadium loomed out of the night, looking like a giant mushroom from some far-off fairytale land, bathed in all of its white lights. Downtown, just off to his right, the tall skyscrapers, with their tops shrouded in misty vapors, stared down at him.

He would stay on Washington Avenue all the way to the freeway—yes, that was the plan. Hal took a sharp right and headed north, past the loop, and past the warehouse buildings that lined the streets north of there. There were more people here, but they paid scant attention to him. A few homeless winos were standing around a fire they had built in a barrel in the back of a parking lot, silently passing around a bottle in a brown paper bag and warming their hands.

As Hal turned the last corner, his passenger started to slide to his side of the car, and his hand instinctively reached over and steadied her. The lifeless body slid down in the seat a foot or so, and seemed to settle into a new place, and he put his hand back on the wheel.

He drove just under the speed limit, not slow enough to look suspicious, but not fast enough to be stopped for speeding. Everything had gone well so far, and now was not the time to get pulled over for anything.

Just past the downtown loop, the car went over a small rise in the roadway, caused by a short steel bridge over a railway crossing. The bump was just big enough to, once again, dislodge the body from its place on the seat and now it slid to the floor. It was not a terrifying event, but it did unnerve Hal for a second. Now her head leaned against the door instead of the window, and the blanket had fallen down around her hips so she lay there, nude from the waist on up. Hal checked his mirror, and there was no one behind him who could have seen her disappearing act, so that was good. She could just stay down there for the rest of the ride.

He breathed a sigh of relief, and turned the heater down as the temperature was getting warm inside, and it was accentuating a dislikeable odor coming from her body that suggested her bowels had let loose. He reached over and tried to pull the blanket back up over her to hold the stink in, but it was stuck and difficult to do while he was driving. It angered him that, even in death,

3

she had shit in his car. He cursed and pounded the steering wheel, but then quickly composed himself. Now was not the time for a hissy fit. Still struggling with the blanket, he finally gave up, managing to get it only partway up. One bare breast and shoulder still showed, and he caught glimpses of her each time he passed a streetlight. The dash light on the radio glowed just enough to keep her faintly visible. He reached down and felt of her breast to see if she was getting colder. The breast was small, and in life it had been much firmer. Now it felt flaccid—almost droopy. He heard his tires scrape the curb and corrected his steering, getting back onto the roadway, with both hands back on the wheel. Now was not the time to be feeling up a dead girl.

Hal rubbed the back of his neck to try to drive away the tension that was knotted up there. He was getting more tired by the moment, and the sooner this was over, the better. He took the off-ramp at Dowling Avenue and was on the I-94 Freeway now, heading north.

It wouldn't have to have ended like this. She'd brought it on herself. Stacie had called him a week ago and told him about her pregnancy. At first, Hal denied he was responsible, but unconscious or not, she knew better and had threatened to go to the police. "A simple paternity test would soon settle that question," she said, "and as for the act itself? That was rape, and would not be hard to prove if he wanted it that way." Putting drugs in her drink was also illegal, although he denied he had done it.

Hal had backed down, despite his denials, knowing she was right about the paternity tests. He had tried to talk her into getting an abortion. He offered to pay for everything, and even offered to go with her for the procedure.

Stacy was a devout Christian and would hear nothing of that—it was against her values. She might be a farm girl from Wisconsin, and maybe some people thought she was somewhat naïve, but she wouldn't take the easy way out and she was emphatic about that. There was only one thing for Hal to do, and that was to admit publicly what he had done, pay her expenses and the long-term costs of raising the child. She had made a mistake in trusting him and letting him drug her drink. Now she was prepared to pay for her consequences and he needed to do the same.

His mind wandered back to the past. This was not the first time he had impregnated a girl. Hal had only been fifteen when he knocked up the fourteen-year-old neighbor girl. That one had cost his parents a fortune. Then, when he was eighteen he had scored again, and again his father paid, but he had warned Hal, "You get one more girl in trouble and you will never see another penny from this family for the rest of your life." Hal was not about to see if he meant it.

He remembered what Stacie had said over the phone to him. Her voice still reverberated through his head.

"I am going to tell my parents at Christmas break next week, Hal, and I expect that you will come with me sometime in the future and meet them. I don't love you, and I don't think I ever could, so marriage is out of the question for now, but we will leave that as it is for the time being. I despise the fact you drugged me. I hate the fact you violated me. You are a despicable human being, Hal. You need to pay through the nose and maybe then you'll grow up."

Hal turned off I-94 and headed north on 252. He could still see the river off to his right, through the houses and buildings. He looked down at the body, which had slid even lower on the floor. *Who's paying through the nose now, baby,* he thought. *I'm not going to ruin my life just because you couldn't take care of yourself and take a simple pill. Things happen at frat parties and you knew that before you came over and started drinking and leading me on. I have big plans for my life and no prick-teasing girl who screws up is going to keep me from them.* Hal slammed his hand down on the steering wheel once more to emphasize his anger.

I need to stay cool, he thought, and rubbed his neck some more. He needed to watch for street signs now as the turn was somewhere just ahead. He had been here only once before, and he was only about fourteen then, but the image of the quiet park still burned in his mind. The picture that was the strongest, though, was the river flowing right alongside of it, and the concrete boat ramp that led down to the water.

He slowed suddenly, almost missing the turn, then made a hard right and then a left on the frontage road. It wasn't far now.

The body didn't move again as it was now wedged tight in its confining place on the floor. The stench was getting worse and Hal lowered the window on her side of the car. *Oh, how it pissed him off that she had done that in his car.*

The Camaro seemed to be the only vehicle on the road right now, so Hal slowed down to about fifteen miles an hour so he wouldn't miss the street sign. Once, he almost turned, but at the last minute realized that it was not the right place but at the other end of the park, and he swerved back onto the road. Then, a block down, he saw the sign and an arrow, just like he remembered it.

The parking lot had one car in it, but it appeared to be empty. Someone had met somebody, and left his or her car here. *They were probably getting it on somewhere behind a bar, and unlike Stacie, she probably knew how to take care of herself,* he thought.

Hal parked for a moment, on the edge of the lot, dousing his lights. He needed to get acclimated a little and check out the surroundings. There were lights in the homes across the river, but it was a long way over there and he was confident they would never see him. He lowered his window. It was cold, but he didn't want that stink to get stuck in his car. Hell, better yet, he needed to get her out of here. He slid the car back into gear.

Suddenly, there were headlights coming down the road into the lot, and as the vehicle passed under a streetlight, he saw the black and white paint job and the lights on the roof.

Shit, a damn cop. It had gone so good up to now and now this jerk was coming to ruin everything. He was reaching for the shift lever when the light bar on the roof lit up like a disco club, and for a second, Hal's heart lurched. There was nowhere to run, the squad was in the middle of the damn road and still coming straight at him. He could see the officer in the car, and then he saw him look over his shoulder, spin the wheel and do a one-eighty in the road—heading back up the hill where he had come from, his siren now wailing.

Hal pulled ahead to the middle of the lot. His heart was still racing from this close encounter and he was getting rid of her, here and now. He backed down the ramp, and then, about six feet from the river's edge, stopped. Putting the car back in drive, he turned and drove down along the frozen sandy riverbank.

There were some ice chunks on the bank, but it was mostly sand, so the going was easy. It was almost like a beach down here with the water levels seemingly down. The Camaro was hidden from the park by a high grassy bank and a row of old trees. He just hoped no one was around, as he hadn't had time to check the area out as well as he would have liked.

Hal got out and went around the car and opened the door. Stacie's head clunked on the doorplate, but she still laid there, a virtual puddle of flesh. Her tongue had come out between her teeth and her glazed eyes were half open. Hal tried not to look at her, and held his breath against the smell. He got his right hand under the blanket and then under her, and with his left arm between her back and the seat, he lifted her out. Her head fell back, unbalancing her body, and Hal had to quickly adjust or drop her. She was heavier than he remembered when he had put her in the car.

He stumbled under the load as he carried her to the water's edge, and then laid her down on her back. Hal wrestled the blanket out from underneath her and threw it angrily behind him. He had gotten something wet and slimy on his right hand, and he washed it in the frigid water flowing by her head, completely grossed out. Then, on his hands and knees in the sand, he rolled her over and into the water.

The body just stayed there in the shallow water, lying on the bottom, half submerged. The moon shone off the white skin of her buttocks like a theater spotlight.

Hal went back to the car and took off his shoes. He had been afraid he might have to do this, and had not wanted to, but he couldn't leave her there. He rolled his pants up to his knees and then waded into the river, grabbing her foot and pulling her with him. The cold water made him gasp, and he stopped to look around to make sure he was still alone. The water was no deeper a few feet out, so Hal went in farther, pulling the body behind him. Then, he stepped backwards into a drop-off. Instantly, he was in water six feet deep, still pulling her with him. Letting go of Stacie's body, he hit the bottom and came up sputtering. Then, pulling himself up on the ledge where the water was shallow again, Hal ran for shore and his car.

He was shivering violently now and he turned the heater on full blast. His first impulse was to put the car in gear and get out of there as fast as he could, but he had to retrieve that blanket. Backing up, he turned his lights on so they would shine on the water. He got out of the car and looked. Stacie was gone, and so were his problems.

Turning off the car and the lights, he walked behind the car, opened the trunk, and holding his breath again, put the blanket inside. The cold air felt like dry ice on his wet exposed skin. He could not get that stink out of his mind and he quickly closed the trunk. Getting back in the car, he backed up to the concrete ramp and across it, and then he put the Camaro in gear. With a squealing of tires he was gone, heading back to where he had come from. He had been in trouble many times before and weathered the storm. He was not going to stop now.

CHAPTER TWO

The ride back was uneventful, and uncomfortable, as Hal was very wet and very cold. No matter how hard he ran the blower, the condensation from his wet clothes continued to fog up all of the windows, so he found an old t-shirt in the back seat and constantly cleaned them off as he drove along. He couldn't wait to get back so he could get in a hot shower to warm up, and find some booze to help heat up his insides.

He had no remorse, but then, Hal had left remorse behind him a long time ago. You had to have a conscience to have that, and there wasn't a trace of one in him. Stacie was gone, and that was all there was to it. In Hal's world, there were a lot more Stacie's where she came from.

It was two a.m. when he pulled back into the same parking place he had left an hour ago. You could hear music coming from an upstairs apartment. Otherwise, the place looked deserted. A lone streetlight lit the lot on the opposite side from where he had parked. Almost all of the students had gone home for Christmas break, and those who hadn't were asleep, most of them after a night of partying.

Hal popped the trunk, and carefully rolling up the stinky blanket so as not to dirty his hands, he walked over and opened the dumpster at the end of the lot. There was a large black garbage bag right on top, and he stuffed it inside of that, being careful to let the lid down quietly.

His apartment was on the ground floor and had an outside entrance. Hal slipped his key in the lock and turned it as he turned the knob to the right. It was locked. Damn. That meant it must have been unlocked when he left. He slammed his fist against the door. A stupid mistake, yes, but not necessarily trouble. The chances of someone coming over this time of the night to see him were slim, but there was enough evidence to hang him in there, and he knew it.

He was shivering again, and the first thing he did was strip off his clothes and get in the shower. The warm water felt good, and for a few minutes he just let the heat soak in, and then he started to scrub himself. There was evidence from her on his genitals. *Yes, he had sex with her right after she passed out again, but not after her killed her. He was not that much of a low life,* he thought. Hal laughed out loud at his interpretation of his redeeming qualities, his voice echoing in the shower.

He could not believe she had been that stupid to let him slip her ecstasy again. He had given her a large dose so she would go down quick. Stacie had felt it coming on, but never made it off the bed.

"You filthy bastard," were the last words she uttered.

Hal had taken off all of her clothes after she died; while her body still lay on his bed. He already knew what he was going to do with the body; he had thought that out last night. The day before, her roommate had gone home for the holidays. Stacie had told him that when he asked her to come over and talk about the predicament they were in. Hal had made coffee, with a touch of chocolate in it, for both of them, and laced hers with the drug before giving it to her. She had been skeptical at first, smelling of her coffee before drinking it. *Fool me once, shame on you. Fool me twice, shame on me.*

He had given her so much ecstasy that he thought that alone would kill her, but she kept on breathing away while he raped her twice. Then finished, and his sexual appetite fulfilled, he had simply held her nose shut and stuffed her socks in her mouth. It had been so simple.

Warm again, Hal came out into his small living room and had a triple shot of Johnny Walker Red. He tossed it down in two gulps.

Gathering up all of her clothes, he laid the jeans on the bed and stuffed everything else inside of them, including her shoes and purse. He did remember to open her purse, and right on top was the positive EPT test. *She had brought the proof with her, had she? What a gutsy little bitch,* he thought. Hal took the money that was in her wallet—all fourteen dollars—then stuffed everything back in the purse, and shoved the purse inside a pant leg. He had taken her charm bracelet off her wrist, along with a watch and friendship ring. These he stuffed in the toe of one of her shoes and pushed her socks in behind it; the same socks she had suffocated on. Then, putting everything into a brown paper bag, Hal set it by the door. He would take it to his parents' place tomorrow, when he went home for Christmas, and burn everything. Hal washed the coffee cups and flushed the rest of the ecstasy down the toilet. He had bought it from a stranger on Cedar Avenue in Minneapolis. They could never trace it if they found out about it.

He sat in a recliner chair in his underwear while he went through his mental checklist once more. *That should be it*, Hal thought, and filled his glass with scotch one more time before dousing the light and going to bed. It had been a long day.

Oscar Morrison had farmed, just outside of the little community of Willow, Wisconsin, for forty years. That was ten years before he met Thelma, and thirty years after they were married. The farm had been in the family for three generations and it was his hope that Todd, the youngest son, would carry on the tradition once he graduated from school.

His oldest son, Jacob, had no interest in the hard-working life of a Wisconsin dairy farm, and had told Oscar that on the day he left for Minneapolis. He was now married and lived in the suburbs. His wife was expecting a baby in the spring. Oscar and Thelma's only other child was Stacie. She was Oscar's pride and joy, and a junior at the University of Minnesota. Today, as soon as the chores were done, he was going to go get her and bring her home for Christmas. Both Oscar and Thelma were looking forward to seeing their little girl again.

"Guess I will be heading out as soon as I clean up," Oscar yelled at Todd, over the noise of a clanging gutter cleaner.

Todd walked over to his father. "Drive careful, Dad—the roads are slippery." Oscar smiled. For a seventeen year old, Todd was pretty grown up.

The old man walked to the white clapboard house, about a hundred feet from the barn, and took off his overshoes in the porch. He would wash his hands and face and then he was ready for the drive to Minneapolis.

He was standing at the white porcelain kitchen sink with his sleeves rolled up, washing, when Thelma came in from the living room.

"I made you both some lunch to eat on the way back, Oscar. It's on the table. Call Jacob while you are town and see what their holiday plans are. He said they would be coming home, but I don't know when. I can't wait to see Stacie."

"I can't wait to see her, either," he said.

Thelma hugged Oscar and then held him at arm's length. They'd been through a lot together over the years, raising a family and working the farm. The wrinkles were showing on both of them from long days in the sun planting, cultivating and harvesting crops. They loved each other deeply, and Oscar was thinking, *he would have to pick Thelma up some of that Fanny Farmer candy she loved so much, while he was in Minneapolis.* He kissed her tenderly and hugged her once more, but said nothing. Oscar was a quiet man of few words.

Hal was headed to his parents' home. He had slept well, but awoke with a touch of a hangover from the scotch. A line of cocaine had cleared his head just fine and he was feeling good. Christmas at home was not the way he wanted to spend it, but his mother and dad still held some important purse strings and he didn't want to jeopardize that. He skirted the downtown area, heading west on 394 to Wayzata.

The Halsworth home sat on the west end of Lake Minnetonka, in an elite gated community reserved for the rich and famous. Hal's father, Mathew, was one of the more prominent attorneys in the Twin Cities area, and had made a fortune in corporate law. Now his hope was that his only son and namesake would follow in his footsteps. Young Mathew had never been called 'Mathew' by anyone but his parents. He hated the name, and preferred his nickname; even going so far as to sign his legal papers as Hal Halsworth, and this infuriated his father.

His father wouldn't be there today when he arrived. He had called his mother this morning and she said he was out of town until Saturday, Christmas Eve day.

The yellow Camaro hugged the road, and cornered around the curves on the frontage road like a sporty roadster. To his left lay the frozen lake; to his right, more mansions set into the hillsides. Hal had driven this road a thousand times, and had been ticketed more times than you could count. His father had always, somehow, had them taken care of. He still drove like he was in the Grand Prix and today was no different. It might be his last drive in this Camaro. He had always been given a new one for Christmas and his mother had hinted that this year was no exception.

Today, he was lucky no police saw him, and soon he was at the metal gates that cut their prestigious little community, of about ten homes, off from the rest of the world. He hit the button on the car's visor and the gates opened.

Hal was off again with a squealing of rubber. He took the first right and pulled up into a large circular cobblestone driveway, in front of a white two-story house. The house looked like it had been the house pictured on the cover of the book, "A House of Seven Gables." The cobblestone drive continued around to the back, behind the house and out of sight.

Three large-windowed dormers, with four windows in each one of them, graced the upper front of the house. The windows looked festive, filled with fluffy white curtains and red wreaths with candles in them. On the right end as you faced the house, there was a huge brick chimney covered with naked vines, which had now shed their foliage for winter. On the right, the house had a one-story building that looked almost as if it had been an addition.

The oak double front doors, trimmed in brass plates, were in the middle of a large rounded foyer, with numerous windows that extended almost to the driveway. As you drove up, you captured a glimpse of a shimmering crystal chandelier hanging in the middle of the foyer.

Hal left his car running in the drive. Lamont, the butler, would put it away for him.

Oscar drove by the farm homes of the neighbors he knew so well. Most of them had been there as long as he had or longer. God had blessed him so much, letting him live in this wonderful country. He had blessed him with Thelma, his wife and soul mate, and three wonderful children. Well, Jacob had been a little problem, but all in all, he was still blessed. He passed the little white Lutheran Church he had gone to all of his life. It sat on top of a hill nestled in pine trees. Behind it was a small cemetery where Oscar's parents and many friends had found eternal rest.

The red Chevy pickup was almost new, and he had put several bags of shelled corn in the back to give him traction on the slippery country roads. He even opened up a new air freshener, shaped like a pine tree, and hung it on the radio knob so it would smell nice for Stacie. She had said, "The truck always smelled like a barn, and so did she, if she sat in it long enough."

Stacie was a little bullheaded about stuff, but she loved her parents. When she finished college, she was going to come right back to Willow to teach in the same school she had gone to for twelve years. She was not going to live on a farm, though. She had been emphatic about that.

There was about thirty miles of icy blacktop ahead, as he had now left the gravel roads, and then he would hit I-94. After that, it was about a hundred miles to St. Paul and Minneapolis.

Oscar burped in his hand and thumped his chest with his fist; his morning bacon and eggs were talking back. He tossed the toothpick he had been chewing on down on the floor mat. He reached for his coffee mug, taking a long slug to wash the taste down, while wiping his mouth with the back of his calloused hand. Squinting, Oscar reached for his sunglasses, clipped to the visor in the cab, and pushed his stained green John Deere cap higher on his forehead. The fresh white snow on the ground was reflecting the bright rays of sunlight beaming down from behind him.

On the radio, the Six Fat Dutchmen were pounding out a tune called "Apples, Peaches, Pumpkin Pie" and Oscar's left foot was tapping rhythm on the floor. He hated driving in the city, and the sooner he got there, the sooner he could get out. Maybe next year, if milk prices held up, he would be able to get Stacie her own car.

Maybe next time he could see Jacob. There would be chores to do at five, and he could not expect Thelma and Todd to do it all, and tonight was Christmas Eve. He had called Jacob and it made him angry that Jacob had told him that, this year, he and his wife were spending Christmas with his wife's family. *Too good for us,* he thought.

The body had moved downstream, but not very far before it settled to the bottom once more. With no clothing on, it was almost buoyant. It would take a few days for the stomach contents to ferment and create gas. Then it would rise and float to the surface. It took longer in the winter because of the cold water, but it was still thirty-six degrees on the bottom, warm enough to help the process along.

On the surface, another process was taking place as each day became colder and colder. The volume of water decreased, and the current was slowing. The surface water, a few degrees colder than the bottom, was freezing, and gradually it would ice over. Stacie's body would still float, but it made the trip downstream much slower, as it would bump and slide along under the ice sheet. However, all of that would still be a few days away.

Hal's mother had met him in the foyer. She hugged him, but not closely, as the white pantsuit she had on cost too much to get soiled brushing against his dirty jeans.

"I am so glad you are home, dear. Have you had brunch?"

"I'm fine, Mother."

"It would be no trouble for Noreen to make you something. Perhaps an omelet?" She fingered her diamond necklace while she questioned him. It was hard to tell what sparkled more—the diamonds hanging on her neck, or the rings that adorned almost every finger.

"I think I will just go up to my room for a while and rest, Mother. What time are the festivities this evening?"

"If you are referring to gift-giving, it will be about 10 or so, I suppose. Did you do any shopping for anyone?"

"No, Mother…with what? The money you guys give me barely covers my expenses at school."

"My goodness, Hal, I would think you would have plenty left over." He was walking away from her as she talked.

Hal's room looked just the same as it had the day he had left home, except for some Christmas decorations. Posters were everywhere, and the shelves still held trophies and model planes that actually flew. A plush rug, in the shape of a football, was on the floor by his bed, and the bedspread matched it. He had been gone, for all practical purposes, for four years and this was his mother's idea of hanging on to the past.

Next door, his sister Becky's room still looked the same way, too, and she was out east going to college for God knows what? Ten years she had been gone. *Damn spoiled rotten brat,* he thought.

His brother Ralph's room was also untouched, and he was older than

Becky. *Married with one on the way. Oh yes, Ralph the Doctor.* Ralph was his parents' pride and joy and his mentor, chosen for him by his father. *How many times had his father whined to him, why can't you be more like Ralph?*

Hal sat down at his desk and poured out a line of coke on the glass top. He heard footsteps in the hallway. *Must be Noreen. He'd better lock his door,* he thought. Walking across the room, he pushed the button, but not before he looked out and saw her going into Becky's room with some bedding. *Was the brat going to be here tonight, too?*

The coke took the edge off and he lay down on the bed. That was a long night last night. He needed a nap to refresh himself.

Outside, Lamont started up the Camaro and pulled it around to the garage. He was under orders from Mrs. Halsworth to clean it out, and to put all of Hal's stuff in the new yellow Camaro parked next to it. On Monday, someone would be coming from the dealership to pick the old car up.

The car had an odd smell to it, like someone had crapped in it, but he dismissed it as Hal just farting before he got out. *It wouldn't be the first time,* he thought. Lamont parked it and closed the door. He would clean it out later. Right now he had to finish decorating the poolroom.

The poolroom was a large glass enclosure that covered the heated pool behind the house. On one end was an enclosed gazebo that would put most people's living rooms to shame. That was where the Christmas tree sat, waiting for him to decorate it. *Maybe he could get Noreen to help him,* he mused. *Damn lazy white bitch didn't do much around here. It wouldn't hurt her at all, but first he needed a little pick me up.*

Lamont, unlike Noreen, stayed on the premises all of the time. He lived upstairs, above the garage, in a small apartment Mr. Halsworth had built for him. Noreen went home to her cats each night. For many years there had been a nanny, also. *Elsa.* The thought made Lamont smile. *He and Elsa had got it on lots of times in his little apartment. My, my, they had, had lots in common, hadn't they? They were both black and came from poor families in Mississippi. They were about the same age. They loved the same kind of whiskey, and Elsa loved to rock his world.* He grabbed his crotch. *Yes sir, she loved little Lamont, didn't she. Poor little guy, he doesn't get out much anymore.* Lamont smiled as he took a pull out of his whiskey bottle from under the sink, and then popped a mint in his mouth. *Wonder whatever happened to her?*

Oscar was just getting into St. Paul and was still on I-94 heading west. The red pickup almost seemed to be in everyone else's way in the middle of the city traffic. Oscar drove the speed limit and not one mile over it. Oblivious to the stares and rude gestures, he stayed right in the middle lane, watching the freeway signs closely. He paid taxes too, and this was a federal highway.

He drove by the Capital, and took his eyes off the road long enough to sneak a peek. The one in Madison, Wisconsin was much nicer. The people in Wisconsin were much nicer, and not a bunch of impatient idiots like this. He hoped Stacie would be ready, and he wouldn't have to wait long, and he could get back through here before rush hour. He'd been stuck in traffic once, and vowed never again.

Past Highway 280, he switched to the left lane, his exit was just ahead. His old-time music station had faded out a ways back and he had switched to a Twin Cities station but now, frustrated with that, he shut the radio off.

You could almost see the apartment building from the freeway, and Oscar had been there many times before. He stopped out in front of the building, and sat at the curb for a moment. Maybe she was watching for him. The building was a three-story, red brick building that catered to female students only. It was privately owned by the University and was listed as a dormitory. It sat in a neighborhood of many other similar buildings, all just a short walk from the campus.

Oscar had been there about ten minutes and still no Stacie so, frustrated, he shut the truck off and walked up the steps. Inside there was a small lobby, and then you needed a security key to get beyond that. A sign told you to **"pick up the phone and dial 54 for help if no one was at the desk."** Oscar dialed and a feminine voice told him she would be right there.

There was a small table in the lobby, and someone had put a small Christmas tree on it. Someone else had hung a beer can on the tree, along with the blue and white bulbs. Christmas carols were coming over a small speaker in the ceiling. A space heater on the wall clunked noisily as the fan blades hit the grill that someone had kicked inward.

She didn't look a day over eighteen, dressed in jeans and a maroon and gold sweatshirt with a golden gopher on the front.

"Help you, sir?"

"Yes. I'm here to pick up my daughter and I wondered if you could tell

16

her I'm here?" Oscar stood nervously holding his cap and rubbing his thumbs and forefingers together.

"What room is she in?" the girl asked, snapping her gum.

"I'm not sure. Stacie Morrison is her name." Then, as if an afterthought, he said, "I know it's on the second floor."

The girl smiled. "Stacie's room is two sixteen. Why don't you go on up and get her. Going home for Christmas, is she?"

"Yes, yes she is, or rather, we are," The door buzzed and Oscar walked inside. The stairs were right in front of him so, rather than take the elevator, he walked up. Two sixteen was on the far end down the hallway, and he remembered where it was now.

He rang the bell three times and there was no answer, so he knocked twice, but still no answer.

Oscar was perplexed. He didn't know if he was angry or worried. She had called the night before last and said she would be ready, and now where was she?

A door opened behind him and a thin redhead, smoking a cigarette and dressed in a bathrobe and frog slippers, stood in the open doorway. "Melody left this morning, if that's who you are looking for."

"It's Stacie I'm looking for," said Oscar.

"She's not there either. Melody told me this morning she left last night and didn't come home. She thought she went home to Wisconsin."

The girl closed the door and Oscar stood alone in the hallway. He had no idea where to go or what to do next.

CHAPTER THREE

Hal heard the car door slam outside in the driveway and slid off the bed, while peeking through the curtains, looking out the window. It was his father's white Cadillac and he was bent over and gathering things from the back seat. He stepped back from the window and contemplated his next move. *I might just as well go down and meet the old bastard,* he thought.

Hal changed clothes, washed up and then walked downstairs. Noreen was just leaving for the night. "Why hello, Hal," she said. "I thought I heard you in your room but didn't want to disturb you. How's school going?"

"School's okay, I guess, if you like school."

"You're a senior this year, right?"

"Right, and then I have law school if I can get in somewhere." Hal was at a loss to say anything else so he just stood there.

"Well, Merry Christmas," Noreen said. "I'll see you on Monday."

Hal just smiled and nodded, but he was thinking...*The hell you will.*

His parents were in the poolroom with Lamont when he walked in. His father stopped talking to Lamont and turned to face him. "Well, well, well. Our little prodigal son came home. How are you, Mathew?"

"I'm fine, Father, and you?"

The elder Halsworth didn't answer his question but turned back to

18

Lamont and said. "Things here look good—why don't you take the rest of the evening off. Mathew, come on in here and let's catch up. Your brother and sister will be here shortly, and so will the food."

His father was holding a brandy snifter, in his right hand, with about two inches of brandy in it. "Drink, Mathew? You are twenty-one now and it's Christmas. Any new girlfriends we should know about?"

"No, Father." *Oh, there was one, but I killed her.* Hal smiled at the thought. "You know what? Maybe I will have a beer."

There was a dining table in the gazebo that was set for the family. A serving table for the food had been set up a few feet away.

His mother, who had been silent until now, smiled and said, "Hal, we are having leg of lamb for supper. You do like that, don't you? I know your sister does and she should be here any minute. Her plane gets in at five."

She had no more than said it, than Becky walked into the room. Their mother ran to her and threw her arms around her. The elder Halsworth waited his turn and embraced her warmly.

Oscar had just sat in the hallway for a while, and then the girl who had let him in found him, and tried explaining what might have happened.

"I bet she just went with some friends somewhere. You know how we girls are sometimes."

"You don't understand," Oscar said. "She was expecting me. We called her the night before and she hasn't been home for over a day? That's just not right. Can I use your phone?"

"Sure, if it's local," she said.

Oscar looked in his old weathered billfold, overflowing with cards and papers, until he found Jacob's number. There was no answer at work, so he tried Jacob's home. No answer again. *They might have already gone to her folks for Christmas Eve,* he thought.

"I need to call my wife in Wisconsin," he pleaded. "Here," he said, as he gave her five dollars. "That should cover it." The girl just shrugged her shoulders and stuffed the bill in her pocket.

Dialing his phone number, he waited as it rang several times before Thelma answered. "Thelma…Thelma, can you hear me? Thelma…she isn't here. What? I don't know where."

He listened for a moment and appeared to be getting more upset by the minute. "No one knows where she is, Thelma. She left last night and never came back."

He paused, listening to Thelma again, and then said, "Ok, I'll ask her again."

He turned back to the attendant. "Do you have a phone number for Stacie's roommate?"

"Here at the dorm?"

"No—her home or her parents' home. Didn't she go home for Christmas? I need to talk to her."

The girl looked through some files, and then said, "I'm not supposed to give this out, but I suppose under the circumstances…" She wrote the number on a piece of paper and handed it to him.

Stacie's roommate told Oscar almost the same story the girl across the hall had told him. She had left last night and said she would be back in a little bit, but she never did come back. "When I left this morning," Melody said, "I just thought she'd maybe caught a ride home early. She hadn't packed anything, but then, sometimes when she went home she didn't take much."

Oscar was sitting on a chair by the phone. He didn't know what else to ask her.

"Well, if you hear from her, will you ask her to call us?"

"I will. I hope nothing's wrong, Mr. Morrison."

"I hope not, too. Thank you."

Oscar sat there, holding the phone until it made a shrill noise from not being hung up. He stood up and replaced the receiver.

"Can I call the police?" he asked.

Lamont had planned on ushering in Christmas with a new bottle of Jack Daniels he had saved for just that purpose. But first, he had to clean out that car for Mr. Halsworth. *They probably won't pick it up till Monday,* he thought, *but if I let it go I might forget.*

He set the bottle by his bed and slipped his coat back on and went downstairs to the garage. There were four stalls in the garage, and Mr. Halsworth's Cadillac was in the first one. The next one was empty, and in the next two stalls, the old and the new Camaros sat right next to each other. They looked identical.

Lamont transferred all of the glove box materials, just stuffing it from one to the other. He looked in the back seat for Hal's car blanket but it was nowhere to be seen. There were a few things clipped to the visor, and some coins in the ashtray. Otherwise, that seemed to be it. He sat for a moment, behind the wheel, and tried to think of anything else to take. *Damn but it smelled like shit in the car. That is disgusting,* he thought.

He took a while to rearrange everything in the new car. *I love that new car smell,* he mused, feeling the soft leather seats with the palm of his hand. He had a car once, but couldn't afford one anymore.

Lamont stood outside the new car and went over a mental checklist. *What was he forgetting? The trunk! Yes sir, don't forget the trunk.* He pulled the keys from the ignition on the old car and walked around back. *The square key,* he thought.

The lid popped up and the light in it flickered on, showing an empty trunk except for some beer cans and a brown bag with some tennis shoes on top. *Wow, it smells like shit in here, too,* he thought. *What the hell does that kid do with his cars?*

There was something that looked like mud smeared on the mat in the trunk. Lamont stuck his finger in it, and putting his finger up to his nose, smelled it. *No damn wonder this car smells like shit—that is shit!*

Lamont grimaced, and wiped his finger off on another part of the rug. He took out the bag with the shoes in it, and set it on the floor of the garage. He didn't have the keys for the new car so he couldn't swap the trunk contents. *Hell, I'll just set it on the front seat.*

He picked it up by the side of the bag and it tore. The contents spilled out on the floor—the shoes and a pair of blue jeans stuffed with a sweatshirt. *And what the hell was this?* he thought.

Panties and a bra…what the hell did he do…take some girl's clothes and not give them back? Damn kids are nuts these days. He picked up the shoes last, and hearing something jingling in the toe of one of them, Lamont pulled the sock out and tipped the shoe back, and some jewelry slid to the heel. The ring was worthless, and the watch was a cheapie, but this charm bracelet was sterling silver and had some small diamonds set in it. He needed a gift for his niece for Christmas. *Hell, why not?*

He stuffed it all back in the bag, as best he could, and set it on the front seat and closed the door. He had a date with Jack Daniels and he was dry.

21

The University Police were not much help to Oscar. They, too, felt she would show up soon and everything would be fine. The officer was impatient and wanted to get out of there.

"If I was you, Mr. Morrison, I would just go back home for tonight. We'll send a car over tomorrow to check if she came back. If she isn't back, then we'll take the next step."

"That is?" asked Oscar.

"File a missing person report," the officer replied.

The words shocked Oscar. He couldn't think of anything better to do, so he walked out of the building. It was two p.m. He sat in his truck for another hour and then, reluctantly, he gave up, put the truck in gear and drove away. *What was he going to tell Thelma?*

It was chores time when Oscar drove into the yard. The house was dark, but there were lights on in the barn and that's where he headed.

When he came in the barn he saw Thelma right away, washing udders on a cow. She stood up and walked towards him, the white porcelain pan in one hand, and a washcloth in the other. Her lips were trembling. "You didn't find her?" she asked.

Oscar took Thelma in his arms and held her.

"No, I didn't find her." I talked with her roommate and she didn't know where Stacie was. I talked to people in the building and they didn't know. I talked to the police and they told me to go home."

"Did you call Jacob?"

Todd had walked over when he saw his mother crying. "What's happened, Dad?"

Once again, Oscar explained the situation. Todd just stood there with his mouth open. "Let's go back, Dad. She has to be somewhere. I'll go by myself right now." He was taking off his coveralls.

"Let's finish chores and we will all go back," said Oscar. Thelma agreed.

Like all Christmas Eve's at the Halsworth house, this was no exception—extravagant gifts and lots of good food. Hal's brother and family, and his sister, seemed to enjoy everything and the folks spent most of their time talking to them. They just didn't have anything to talk about with Hal.

So, at about eight-thirty, Hal excused himself to go look at his new car. His father had also given him a gas card for one thousand dollars, good at any

Amoco station. He knew better than to give him money. This was the fourth year in a row they had bought him a new car—always yellow—and always a Camaro. Maybe next year he would ask for a Corvette. His father had spent all evening talking with Ralph about stocks and bonds and ignoring Hal. His mother and sister had disappeared somewhere in the house, and he was getting a buzz on from all of the booze.

It was cold outside and he pulled his collar up as he walked to the garage. A few snowflakes were filtering down and covered the driveway with a half inch of powder. The doors to the garage were down so he went in the service door and flicked on the lights. He walked down to the two yellow Camaros parked at the far end, and sat down in the new shiny one. It smelled so fresh and clean. He turned the key on in the ignition and it roared to life. He pushed the opener and looked over at the old car as he waited for the door to go up. That's when he saw the bag.

"Son of a bitch," he screamed. He had forgotten about the bag in the trunk, and that dammed Lamont. He looked in the bag. The side was ripped out but it looked like it was all there. There was no time like the present to get rid of it. He hit the throttle and the rear tires squealed as he backed out and dropped it in drive. Then he roared around the house and out to the road, the back end of the car fishtailing in the slick snow. *They could sit there and make small talk without him,* he thought. *To hell with them, he had things to do.*

Lamont had heard the door open and had stumbled to the window. He saw the car back out and rapidly drive away. He was drunk, but his mind still worked enough to think, somewhat rationally, *you rotten little spoiled bastard.*

In no time at all, Hal was back on the freeway, headed for Minneapolis. He needed to find his drug dealer; his stash was almost gone. He tried his contact on his cell phone and was told, by the woman who answered, that he would meet him on Cedar in the usual location. Business was business, even on Christmas Eve.

He stopped at a gas station on Penn and 394 to fill his tank. It was cold outside so he sat in the car brooding while the tank filled. There seemed to be very few stations open tonight and this one was packed with customers. The lone attendant was too busy to watch much of what was going on outside.

When Hal heard the hose click off he stepped outside the car to hang it up. The bag of clothes was in his hand, and after grabbing a handful of trash from the can first, he stuffed the bag in the trash can by the pump, placing the trash back on top of the bag. Then he went inside to pay for the first part of his free gas, using the gas card he had received for Christmas.

It was six p.m. before Oscar, Todd and Thelma headed back to St. Paul. Oscar had called his brother, who lived a few miles away, and was widowed and retired. He would take care of the farm until they returned.

Thelma had found Jacob's in-law's phone number, and Jacob said he would meet them at the University Police Station at nine p.m. He was less than happy about it, as he felt his sister was just out horsing around. He had been to the same college and he knew what kids did there.

Todd was driving now, so the return trip went a lot faster. Both Oscar and Thelma kept cautioning him to drive carefully, but he tuned them out, driving eighty miles an hour.

"I just know something is rotten here," Todd said. "I talked to her day before yesterday, and she was looking forward to Christmas and getting away from the pressures of school and the big city. She didn't run off and forget about us."

His pessimistic talk upset Thelma even more than she already was, and Oscar held her closer, his face grim and bewildered.

The University Police Station was almost deserted. With most of the students gone for the holiday, they had no reason to have anything more than a skeleton crew. A lone officer was sitting at a computer when they walked in. He got up and walked to the counter to meet them. Todd stood, with both hands on top of the counter, looking all of his six feet four inches, but with that still-boyish face a seventeen year old would have.

"Look, I know my father was sent home this afternoon, and was told to come back in the morning, but you don't understand. My sister isn't at some party and she didn't run away!"

"Whoa, whoa, son. I have no idea what you are talking about so let's just back up here a minute. Who are all of you?" The older, paunchy, graying officer had picked up a pad and pencil and pointed it at Todd.

"My name is Todd Morrison, and my sister's name is Stacie, and when my dad came here..."

"This is your dad, I take it?" the officer interrupted.

"Yes," Oscar said, taking his cue. I am Todd and Stacie's father and this is my wife, Thelma...Todd and Stacie's mother," he added.

"Stacie is missing?" The officer looked concerned.

"Yes," Oscar said. "I came to pick her up this morning, for the holidays, and she wasn't there."

Todd wanted to say something else right now, but Thelma had grabbed his arm and held her forefinger to her lips.

The officer went over and unhooked the swinging door that led to his side of the counter. "Why don't you come in and sit down, and we can try to make sense of all of this. Can I get you some coffee?"

Todd shook his head no. Both Oscar and Thelma said, "That would be nice."

"By the way, my name is Wally," he said, and shook hands all around.

Wally was back in a few minutes with two cups of coffee, and a tray of condiments, and they all sat down around his desk. Another officer, with a red face, came in stamping snow off his feet, complaining about working Christmas Eve, and then disappeared into the bathroom.

First, Wally asked Oscar to explain things, and then he talked to Todd and Thelma. A half hour later, and with a page full of notes, Wally looked up at the family and said, "I tend to agree with you...that something is not right here. What I would like to do right now is turn this whole thing over to Minneapolis Police. We do keep law and order on this campus, but we have our limits and in cases like this, they usually take over."

"Is there a phone number where you can be reached?"

"Yes," Thelma said, and handed him Jacob's phone number. "We will be staying at our son's house. He should be showing up here any minute." She looked at her watch. It was nine fifteen.

CHAPTER FOUR

Hal bought his drugs and headed home. He knew that the atmosphere at his parents' house was not going to be much better than when he left, but at least he could put himself in a better mood. He also knew that he was going to have to control his drug usage a little better because this was getting to be an awfully expensive habit, and his father was going to be asking questions. In fact, he'd already hinted at that.

The new car ran great and he was glad to get rid of Stacie's belongings. He seriously doubted they would ever catch him, he had been too clever for that, but he didn't need to keep anything around that was that incriminating.

At one thirty a.m. he pulled around the house and put the car back into the garage. The back door was open so he quietly made his way through the house and up to his room. As he passed the poolroom he could see his father and Ralph, still sitting by the fire in the gazebo, and talking. *Probably talking about me*, he thought.

Torch Brennan had been on the Minneapolis police force for over twenty years. The last ten as a homicide detective, but at age forty-two, he was still the bottom man on the totem pole. Because it was Christmas Eve, Torch and one other detective were handling, not only the homicides that they usually handled, but tonight they were also taking missing persons calls.

It was nine forty five, when the call from the University came in.

"Brennan, Homicide," he answered the phone.

"Well, I certainly hope it's not a homicide but I do have a missing person's report. By the way, this is Wally Tomlinson over at the U."

"Whatcha got?" Torch asked. "We're handling everything tonight, that's why you got me."

"Torch, we have a missing female—twenty years old. White, five foot two, with brownish blonde hair. She's been missing since last night and I know that's not long, but this one sounds a little suspicious. Not a party gal."

"What's her name?" Torch said.

"Stacie Morrison. Her parents live in Wisconsin and they came to pick her up for Christmas. She seems to have just disappeared. I can fax you over what I have if you want it, or would you prefer to come over?"

"Tell you what. Why don't I run over? There is nothing happening here tonight. Even the shitheads on the street have taken the night off!"

Wally laughed, "I'll be here till midnight, Torch."

"See you in a half hour or so."

Torch turned to his partner, Theresa, who was doing a crossword puzzle out of the paper. "I have to run over to the U. Hold the fort down, huh?"

"Gotcha, Torch." She never looked up.

It was ten thirty when Torch got over to the University Police Station. He and Wally sat down at a desk and went over the facts. There were a few things that were going to make investigating this difficult. First of all, her roommate and most of the rest of the students were gone for Christmas, so there weren't a lot of people to talk to. Second of all, they needed to get a warrant or the roommate's permission to search the room. Torch also knew, the sooner they could get on it, the fresher the trail would be.

Wally had the phone number for Stacie's parents, and that was going to have to be where he would start.

Jacob had gone back to his family at his in-law's house—leading Oscar, Thelma and Todd to his house first. When the phone rang, Oscar almost tipped his chair over when he reached for it, and Todd jumped up, startled, from where he had been napping.

"Is this Mr. Morrison?"

"Yes, yes," Oscar answered. His obvious concern was evident in his voice.

"Mr. Morrison, this is Torch Brennan. I am a detective with the Minneapolis Police Department. I just wanted to ask you a few questions about your daughter, if I could."

"You know, it would be best if we did this face-to-face instead of over the phone. I realize the hour is late, and it's Christmas, but could you come down to police headquarters?"

"Tell us where to go."

Torch could hear Oscar tell his wife, "It's the police and they want to talk to us. Get your coat."

With directions in hand, Oscar, Thelma and Todd, who was driving, were on their way. It was snowing lightly, and the streets were greasy in the ten above zero temperature, but fifteen minutes later they were at police headquarters. They parked in a ramp across the street. Five minutes later, they were sitting in a meeting room talking with Torch, and his partner, Theresa Cross.

Torch and Theresa listened quietly as Oscar told them about their Stacie. Not the kind of girl who would ever miss a commitment, especially Christmas with her family.

"When you last talked to her did she seem concerned about anything? Did she have a boyfriend? Do you think she was into drugs or alcohol?" Torch and Theresa asked all of these questions and more, but all Oscar could say was, "No, no, no. Something is wrong—terribly wrong." Thelma was crying and shaking her head no, and to every question, Oscar answered with a "No." Todd stood in the background, defiant but quiet.

They gave Torch a wallet-size picture of Stacie, and after an hour of questioning, Torch stood up and put his hand on Oscar's shoulder.

"Look, tomorrow morning we will go over to her apartment and start looking for her. If there is any contact from her to you, let us know right away. It would be best, however, if you went home to Wisconsin. That is where she would try to call you, obviously, and you need to be there. We will call you tomorrow night and tell you how things are going."

"Why can't you start looking tonight?" Todd said. These were the first words he had said outside of "hi" when they had come in.

It was Theresa who answered him. "It's the middle of the night, Todd, and it would be very difficult to get ahold of anyone. If we had any evidence that something had happened to your sister we would go, but right now, she is just a missing person. There is probably a good explanation for her not wanting to see her family right now."

Todd just shook his head no, and walked out of the room.

By 2 a.m. they were home, exhausted and despondent. Oscar's brother was asleep on the couch. They woke him up to talk to him about what they had found out, and to ask him if she had called.

"No one's called."

Todd took his aging uncle home, and they all went to bed when he returned. The Christmas tree was dark; the brightly wrapped gifts lay unopened under it. The dining room table was still set for dinner with Thelma's best china. There were untouched plates of lefsa and Krumkaka on the table. The turkey was thawed and laying in the sink. It was all a stark reminder of Stacie's absence.

On Christmas day, Darren Mosley showed up for work at the gas station on Penn Avenue. Darren was seventeen and lived with his grandmother in a poor black neighborhood, north of the station. His job was to clean the bathrooms and empty the trash. Then there would be shelves to stock, floors to mop, and rugs and mats to change. Normally he came in at six, but today being Christmas Day, he was told to come in later.

After cleaning the bathrooms, he went out to empty the trash from the garbage containers in front of the store and by the pump islands. It was cold outside and the bags were frozen in the containers, so this morning, Darren just lifted the containers and dumped them into a large gray cart, with wheels, that was made for just that purpose. From there, it went to the dumpster in the back. Not being able to dump this cart in the dumpster, he would be forced to shovel it out, but he had done that many times.

The station was busy so he had to wait his turn to get at the containers and not disturb the customers, but eventually, he had everything and headed out back.

Darren was happy today, despite having to work. His grandma had given him a new Oakland Raiders starter jacket for Christmas and his girlfriend had given of herself last night…three times. He was proud of his sexual prowess and could not wait to tell his friends.

Shoveling out the cart into the dumpster, he came across some clothing that looked like it was in good shape. First, a tennis shoe, and then a pair of blue jeans rolled into a ball. Darren reached in, took the jeans out, and set them aside. One tennis shoe would do him no good, and he hadn't seen the other one. Maybe his girlfriend would like these designer jeans, though. She had been so good to him last night and he had no gift for her.

He unrolled the jeans and held them up, noticing a bulge in one pant leg. He reached inside the leg and found a small leather purse. Damn. Christmas was getting better by the minute.

There was a billfold in the purse but no money. "Shit," he said out loud. Then, looking in another pocket, he found a credit card and a student identification card for someone named Stacie Morrison.

We might be able to use the credit card, he thought, but the I.D. card showed a picture of a blond girl. *My black girlfriend could hardly pass for her, but I do know some blond chicks.* He stuffed both cards in his pocket, and threw the purse and jeans back in the dumpster. *Shit, he would buy her some new jeans and maybe she would get hot again for him.*

By noon, Darren was done working and headed home—his big find in his hip pocket.

With the help of some drugs, Hal managed to be a little more congenial on Christmas Day. He stayed home with his family all day, and went swimming with his sister in the afternoon. His mother and dad sat proudly by the pool, enjoying some wine and hors d'oeuvres, happy to see their two children socializing for once.

Lamont was cleaning up from last night's festivities, despite a terrible hangover. He wanted to go over to his sister's this afternoon and give his niece a little Christmas gift—a nice charm bracelet. Noreen had the day off.

It was after nine a.m. when Torch got over to the University dorm where Stacie lived. He was alone and was actually working out of his shift time. He just wanted to get an early start on things. Something was not right with this case. Maybe it was a just a gut feeling, but after all of these years in police work, his gut feelings were right more often than they were wrong.

The same young woman, who had let Oscar in the day before, now confronted Torch as he rang the bell to be let in.

"My name is Torch Brennan." He held the badge up for her to see. "I would like to get two things. I need the phone number for Melody Krants, and I need to look in her and Stacie Morrison's room. I must tell you, I need a warrant to search that room without Miss Krants' permission, which I intend to get."

The caretaker wasn't sure if he was talking about the warrant, or Melody's permission, but she didn't comment.

"It's not illegal for me to take a cursory look in the room, but you will need to accompany me for that. Could we do that now?"

"I guess so," she said. "Let me get the keys."

The shades were down in the room, so Torch turned on the lights. The caretaker stood in the doorway behind him. Both beds were made and both desktops were clear of any clutter. There were the usual banners, posters, and pictures displayed. From the look of the picture on her nightstand, showing Stacie with her family, Torch guessed that to be her bed. The bathroom door was open, and a white bathrobe hung on the back of it. He moved the shower curtain back and the tub enclosure held the usual toiletries. It gleamed white and clean in the fluorescent light.

Torch came back out and told the caretaker to not let anyone else in the room without his permission. He gave her his card, and went back out to his car to think about his next move. What he was supposed to do was to turn this all over to Missing Persons, but this case intrigued him for some reason. Maybe he would just get it cleared with his supervisor and see if he could stay on it.

There was no answer at Melody's parents' home in rural Minnesota. He needed to get a warrant. He was going back to the office to call a judge.

By nine a.m. on Monday, Darren Mosley and his love-starved girlfriend were walking into the nearest Best Buy store to try their luck with their newfound credit card.

There were long lines at the return counters, as shoppers were bringing back Christmas gifts for exchanges or refunds. The store's security team was closely monitoring any problems that come with the usual arguments of no receipts and ruined packaging. Usually, one of these people would be stationed at the registers.

Darren had used stolen credit cards before so he knew they had to be cautious with it. There was a chance it had already been reported as being stolen.

"Let's just get a couple of music disks and see if it works," he told his girlfriend. "If it does, we can go elsewhere and try for something bigger."

He gave her the card and sent her through the express line. The clerk asked her to sign the slip. Then, the clerk compared it to the signature on the back of the card and frowned. But she bagged the disks up, anyway, and wished her a "Happy Holidays" and they were out the door.

Torch Brennan was at work early Monday morning, warrant in hand, and he went back to the University. He had his supervisor's permission to look into things, but if he didn't find evidence of foul play, he was to turn it over to Missing Persons. He also had Wally, from the University Police, with him. The warrant had forbidden them to search through anything that was obviously Melody Krants' possessions, and they still hadn't had any luck in getting ahold of her.

The initial search turned up little of interest—mostly clothing, school notes and papers, and a checkbook showing an account at a local Wells Fargo bank. The only thing missing seemed to be her purse or billfold. The medicine cabinet had the usual over-the-counter drugs, and two prescriptions she had taken for allergies. Two suitcases were sitting empty at the end of her bed. An examination of her checkbook showed no unusual activity, but it did show checks that had been written for monthly bills from Visa and a cell phone provider. Neither a phone, nor a credit card, had been found.

After further examination, digging through some papers, Torch found a file full of receipts. "Hey, Wally...look at this." It was a receipt to a Walgreen's drug store for an E.P.T. kit. "Do you think our missing girl was pregnant?" He looked at Wally.

"Well, if she was, that could be a clue to her disappearing. Her parents seemed to be pretty straight-laced people, and maybe she was afraid to go home for Christmas."

"But running away? I'm not so sure she would have done that. I think I

32

need to talk to her parents' some more, and also, I am going to call Visa and see if there has been any activity on her credit card that isn't here. Let's tag this room to keep everyone else out for a while. I'd like the print boys to come over and look around."

Back at the office, two things happened that made Torch more convinced something was wrong. First, there had been activity on her credit card at several stores. In a conversation with Visa, Torch asked them to send out a code, which asked that the cardholder be identified and taken into custody, if possible, but not to refuse or seize the card right now. They needed that person.

Secondly, Oscar and Thelma assured him that Stacie had not told them anything about being pregnant, and as far as they were concerned, their daughter was not even sexually active. The more Torch questioned them, the more distraught they were getting. It was evident that they had never felt more helpless.

On Monday, Jacob and his family came out for the day, but Jacob didn't appear to be worried about his sister. This made Todd angry, and they had words that only added to Oscar and Thelma's grief. Thelma sat in her rocking chair with her Bible lying in her lap, and watched out the window as if she was expecting Stacie to show up any moment. Oscar went to the barn to be with the animals, and to think and pray.

CHAPTER FIVE

By Monday evening, both Minneapolis and St. Paul newspapers had printed news of the missing coed and they both ran a small article. The Minneapolis paper even had a photo, and a quote from Detective Torch Brennan that, "although they had no evidence to back it up, they were very suspicious of her disappearance."

A student group at the University announced plans to distribute flyers as soon as the students came back from break. A few could already be seen around the campus.

Late Monday afternoon, Torch did get ahold of Melody and she was on her way back to Minneapolis to talk to them.

On Tuesday morning, Darren Mosley and his girlfriend made one shopping trip too many. They went to a Target store in Bloomington, a suburb south of Minneapolis. They had already, in two days, charged over four thousand dollars' worth of merchandise on the card.

There were still a lot of shoppers returning Christmas gifts on Tuesday, so Target had hired off-duty Bloomington police officers to assist with the crowds. Darren had seen one of them, but didn't feel threatened because the cop was over at the return counter, and he was taking out, not returning.

With his girlfriend hanging on his arm, they decided to see if there was enough left on the card to buy a big screen television set. They looked at several of them before making a decision; even going so far as to haggle with the clerk over a coupon they had seen in the window when they came in. One good thing they had going for them—they were paying for their purchase right in the television department and not up front where the cops were.

When he entered the credit card in the register, the code came up but the clerk didn't understand what it meant, so he called his supervisor. The supervisor read the screen and then told the clerk to go ahead with the purchase. Meanwhile, he disappeared around a wall and called Security. A minute later, the supervisor came back with a cart to help them load the television on. They would do anything to stall them.

With the television on the cart and his receipt in hand, Darren and his girlfriend started to leave, but before he could push the cart ten feet, he was approached by police, front and rear. Dejected, he sat down on the cart next to the television set. He knew he was busted.

On Tuesday morning, Hal left for the University. He had breakfast with his mother and sister and told them both, in his most sincere terms, how much he had enjoyed Christmas. Now he needed to get back to school to study, and for once, he wasn't telling a lie.

Hal had been doing some soul searching, and knew he was on a fast train to nowhere if he continued the way he had been living. He had come out of his drug-induced haze long enough to be logical, and had made some decisions. He needed to get his grades up so he could graduate in May. Then get his father's help to get him into a law school somewhere—anywhere but the University of Minnesota. His grades were not that far off, but if he continued sliding he would be in trouble and his father would cut the ties completely, and with them went the money.

Hal hadn't thought much about what he had done to Stacie last Friday. For him, the "out of sight, out of mind" cliché fit. His twisted mind just didn't see any connection with what he had done as being that wrong. The thought had run through his mind that he had taken her life, true, but she had wanted to ruin his life, too. Turnabout was fair play.

A couple of things had happened though, and they were making him feel a little bit like a fugitive. He had seen the story in this morning's paper—just a small article on the metro page about her being missing—and the search that was being organized. There had been nothing on the television news, but it bothered him just the same. He also wondered how much Lamont had seen in that bag, and what he was thinking. But confronting him might be suicide.

Hal was smart enough to realize that the worst thing he could do was change his lifestyle, or move away. He had to play the part of not knowing and not caring—but not overplaying it. Maybe he would help with that search "even if he had never known Stacie." *Yea, then I would be privy to all of the talk and information. Good idea,* he thought, smiling.

His apartment was cold when he got there. He had been overheated on drugs when he left, and he had turned the heat off and forgot to turn it back on. So, after adjusting the thermostat, he went over to Stub and Herb's for a burger.

There weren't a lot of people in the restaurant, so he had his choice of a place to sit. The waitress had followed him to his seat, and Hal ordered a burger and a beer. He selected a booth by the window and while he ate, he watched the cars and trucks inching by on the icy streets, their tires throwing little rooster tails of gray snow that fell back to the street, only to be run over and tossed again by the next vehicle. Across the street on the sidewalk, a man stood holding his dog's leash and talking to another man. His dog pissed on his bicycle wheel, and he kicked at the dog, shouting something. Hal smiled at the scene.

He turned his attention back to a young lady at a table for two. She smiled at him and raised her hand an inch or so in a reserved greeting, but then went right back to the magazine she was reading. She was a petite brunette, and for a second, his eyes wandered from her crossed legs and bouncing foot, to her hands that were perfectly manicured.

Then his eyes were looking outside again, looking at a poster nailed on a light post right by the window.

Hal left his half-eaten burger, and most of his beer, and went outside so he could see the poster better. **Missing. Stacie Morrison. University Student. Last seen 12/22.** There was a grainy picture of Stacie in a sweatshirt. **Call Minneapolis police with any information.**

Hal's pulse had quickened. *Last seen 12/22. Where and by whom?*

He was parked across the street and around the corner and he needed to go think.

The apartment was warm when he returned, and Hal spent a few minutes tiding up before he went into the bedroom. Looking at the bed, he could still see Stacie lying there, staring at him through those half-closed eyes. He remembered how limp she was when he tried to undress her and how she had almost slid onto the floor.

Why did she have to do this to him, he thought. He turned to go back out of the room when he saw something halfway under the bed, glinting in the overhead light. Hal dropped to his knees and picked it up. A phone—Stacie's cell phone! *How the hell had he missed that? It must have been in her jeans pocket and fell out when he undressed her.*

He examined the phone, not sure how to operate it. It was off and he couldn't figure out how to turn it on. *Shit. What was he doing? Leave it off and get rid of it,* he thought.

But where to get rid of it? Throw it in the river where she was. Yes, that's it. He could just toss it over the rail when he drove over the bridge after dark. He needed just one small line of coke to calm down. True, he had made a resolution to lay off the stuff for a while, but right now just wasn't a good time to stop.

He measured out two lines and sniffed them up. Then he sat back to wait for the rush. It felt warm and the lights in the room were suddenly brighter. He was getting calmer and more collected.

Darren sat in the detective's office while they waited for Torch to show up, as Bloomington Police had handed both Darren Mosley and his girlfriend over to the Minneapolis authorities. Darren's girlfriend had then been handed over to juvenile authorities for the time being. Technically he, too, was a juvenile, but Torch wanted to talk to him before anyone else got the chance.

When Torch arrived, he took Darren into a private office. It would be more congenial, and right now, Darren was disturbed enough. He had been alternating between crying, and begging for his grandmother, since he arrived.

"What's your name, son?" Torch looked stern as he talked to him.

"Darren. Darren Mosley." He wiped his snotty nose on his shirtsleeve and looked at Torch out of red-rimmed eyes.

Torch looked at the driver's license they had taken from Darren, when they arrested him, to confirm what Darren had just told him.

"Quit your damn crying, Darren. No one here is going to hurt you and we haven't charged you with anything yet. We have called your grandmother and she is coming down here. She should be here any second."

"Where is Rhonda?" Darren asked.

"Your friend that was picked up with you?" Torch asked.

"Yes. She didn't do nothing wrong, it was me that used the card."

"Darren. Rhonda is fine and she hasn't been charged with anything, either. Let's wait until your grandmother gets here to ask or answer any more questions."

A young woman came in and handed Torch a note. "That's all we have." she said.

Torch had asked for a background check on Darren. For all practical purposes he had been a good boy. Oh, there was a shoplifting charge when he was fourteen, and a couple of speeding tickets, but nothing unusual that would make you think he was a criminal.

Torch talked to him about school and sports, trying to put him at ease. He even had him smiling about a couple of things. Then his grandmother was showed into Torch's office.

"What the hell you think you doing with this boy." She shouted. "He ain't no damn crook. He's a good boy who works hard and goes to school every day. Just because he's black you people think you can haul his ass in here for nothing."

Torch held his hands up in a defensive pose. "Mrs. Mosley?"

"No, it's Carter. Mrs. Joann Carter. I am a law-abiding citizen and I am here to tell you that this is not Mississippi, and this is not nineteen fifty-six. You got no call to pick this boy up and…"

"Mrs. Carter," Torch interrupted. "You're right. Darren is a good young man—we checked—so if you will just calm down and take a chair, we'll let Darren tell you why he's here."

Mrs. Carter sat down in the chair next to Darren, holding her big black purse in her lap with both hands. She looked at Darren with unblinking eyes, and he shrunk down and to the other side of his chair.

"I'm sorry, Grandma," he said, and then he started crying again.

"Sorry for what, boy? You going to be sorrier if you've been stealing, or what else. Is this about that no-account girl you been running around with?"

"No, Grandma," Darren sobbed. "I found a credit card and I used it."

"For what? God's sake, child…I have bought you everything you ever needed on God's green earth."

Torch, who had been sitting quietly, taking it all in, held his hand up and interrupted again.

"Mrs. Carter. We haven't charged Darren with any crime, and maybe we won't. The card he found belongs to a missing person and it might help us find her."

"Darren, where did you find that card?" Torch was asking the questions again.

"In the trash. At the station."

"What station, Darren?"

"The Quick Stop where I work."

"Where is this station located?"

"Penn and 394."

"Is that all there was, just the card?" Darren hesitated a moment, looking at his grandma.

"Tell the man the truth, boy," she said, shaking her finger at him.

"No, there were some clothes and a purse."

"Darren, this is important. Are those clothes still there?" Torch had come around his desk and was now squatting in front of Darren.

"I think so. I didn't take them; I just put them back in the dumpster."

"The purse, too?"

"Yes."

"If they were in the dumpster, what were you doing digging in there?"

"I wasn't. I was emptying the trash."

"So, they were in the trash, and you were emptying the trash when you saw them? Where was this trash from?"

"The cans by the pumps."

Torch patted his knee. "Thank you. Please stay here until I come back. I need to do something." Torch left the office in a hurry.

At the receptionist's desk, he was emphatic with his directions. "Ask that a car be dispatched to the Quick Stop on 394 and Penn immediately. Tell them to secure the trash dumpster."

Coming back in the office, Torch sat down, and leaned over the desk. "Darren, describe the purse and clothing."

"The purse was light brown, not very big."

"What else was in it?"

"Some other cards and some papers."

"What kind of cards?" Torch asked.

"An I.D. card." Darren said.

"Is it back in the dumpster?" Torch was getting more serious by the minute.

"No, Ronda has it."

Torch collapsed back in his chair, smiling. He picked up the phone and dialed a four-digit interoffice number.

"This is Torch Brennan, over at Homicide. Do you have a Rhonda there that was just brought in for questioning? Black girl about fifteen?"

"No. I don't need to see her, but ask her for the I.D. card Darren gave her."

There was a pause, then Torch's eyes widened. "Please read me the name on the card."

"Thank you...so much," Torch said. "Yes, please send it over to me right away."

Torch sat still for a moment. He had caught a break for now.

"Mrs. Carter, you can take Darren home now. Stop down at the end of the hall at the Juvenile Office and get Rhonda, too."

"Darren, I want you to gather up all of the merchandise you two bought. I will be sending a car over to get it. You are free to go, and thank you."

He shook Darren's hand, and also his grandmother's, who stood with a bewildered look on her face, saying nothing.

There was a knock on the door, and an older woman handed Torch Stacie Morrison's I.D. card. Smiling, Torch said, "Thank you, Doris."

He grabbed his coat and hat from the chair where he had left it, and picked up the phone. "I'll be going to 394 and Penn," he said to Doris. "You can get me on the radio."

Torch had been on a little bit of a roll and things were falling in place. But now, things were not going to go his way. When he drove up to the Quick Stop, he could see the black and white parked out back. The lone officer saw his car and got out to meet him.

"Hey, detective. You think we don't have better things to do than watch an empty dumpster?"

Torch walked over and lifted the lid. Inside the dumpster were just a couple of empty boxes.

"Sorry about that," he said. "Thanks for the help."

The officer didn't answer him, just got back in his car, gave a little mock salute and drove away.

Torch kicked a frozen clump of snow, sending it skittering across the parking lot. *What to do next,* he thought.

He walked around to the front and went in the store. There were two women working the register so Torch got in line and waited his turn.

The young girl didn't really say anything—just looked at him and said, "Yes?"

"Manager around?" Torch asked.

"Yes, I think he's in back. Who shall I say wants to see him?"

"Tell him it's the police."

She disappeared through a couple of swinging doors and came back with a man in his middle thirties. He looked annoyed. "What's up?" he asked.

"Not a lot," Torch said showing his badge. "Say, I noticed you have surveillance cameras outside and I wondered how long you keep the tapes."

"Forty-eight hours," the manager said. "We put them in to catch drive-offs. They work pretty well for that, but don't show much else. Why, what you got?"

Torch didn't answer his question but followed it up with one of his own. "The tapes that are in the camera right now…do you erase them or just copy over them?"

"I don't erase anything, so I would say they just copy over."

"They started copying over when?" He was getting a blank look. "Look, the tapes that are running right now today. Would it be safe to say they might have information on them from yesterday and Sunday?"

"I guess so. You can have them if you want. Who are you looking for and what makes you think what you want is on them?"

Torch thought for a moment. He didn't want to get Darren in trouble here, so he had to be careful. Darren had said he found the card on Sunday morning. *Sunday to Monday to today,* he thought. He shook his head no, slowly. *I guess I do owe the man some kind of explanation.*

"We believe a person who committed a crime was in this station sometime

41

on Saturday or Sunday, but those tapes aren't going to help us with that. Who picks up your trash?"

"Waste Haulers, Inc."

The store manager could only scratch his head and wonder what this was all about, and how come his garbage was so interesting to the police, but he preferred to stay out of it.

Torch offered his hand without any further explanation. "Thanks anyway, for everything…it was worth a shot. Happy Holidays."

Torch sat wearily in the cruiser's seat. An hour ago he had been cooking with Crisco, but someone had shut his burners off. He reached in his pocket and took out the picture of Stacie that Thelma had given him the other night. He'd glanced at it, but then, he hadn't really looked at it. She was pretty in a tomboyish-looking way. That blond ponytail with a few stray hairs hanging out, and just a hint of freckles on a suntanned face. Dimples that accented a carefree smile filled with perfect teeth. *Where are you Stacie?*

He eased the cruiser back onto the freeway and headed downtown. He saw thirty, maybe forty murders a year, but it was a case like this that tugged at his innards. He was hoping against hope she hadn't met with foul play. Torch knew, when personal effects start showing up in dumpsters, not a lot of good came from it.

Maybe his sudden interest was because he could not forget another young girl who would have been about Stacie's age. She hadn't gone missing, but she went away one cold November night just the same, never to come back. A drunk driver, and Susan and her boyfriend had been taken away in the blink of an eye. Torch wiped a tear from his eye. Christmas always made it bad. Not just the loss of Susan, but the loss of his wife, too. Oh, she was home, home physically, but her mind just floated from one bottle of gin to the next.

He lowered the window to get some air and lit a cigarette. He didn't smoke a lot, but he did when he was troubled.

As he drove, he dialed his cell phone and called the office.

"Hey, Doris. How are you kid?"

"Fine, Torch. What can I do for you?"

Call Waste Haulers, Inc. and ask them where they dump their trash from the Penn and 394 areas. I'll be in, in a few seconds, to see you.

CHAPTER SIX

There was a message for Torch to call his supervisor when he came in on Wednesday morning. There was also a message to call Stacie's parents. They had worked late last night at the recycling plant, digging through the trash, but there was no way they were going to find what he was looking for in that mountain of garbage. Most of the trash that came here was burned, and most likely, it had already gone through the furnaces by the time he got there. Things were going nowhere fast.

He knew what the first message was about as he had heard on the news, coming in to work this morning, of a triple homicide in North Minneapolis, so he sat down and called Oscar and Thelma first.

Oscar looked tired and defeated as Thelma handed him the phone. She had started crying the minute Torch told her who he was. Something in the tone of Torch's voice told her that it was not good news and "she didn't want to hear it," she said, "Here, talk to Oscar."

"Oscar, I wish I had more to tell you but let me tell you what we do have. Are you listening?" He had not acknowledged to Torch that he was on the line.

"Yes, I am listening."

"Oscar, we have found some of Stacie's belongings...her clothing, her purse and her credit card. I have to tell you we don't have the clothing right now, but we are doing everything we can to get it. It was found in a dumpster and the person who found it put it back, taking only her credit card and identification card."

"Why would they do that?" Oscar asked.

"Because he was a thief, Oscar, but we have no reason to believe he had anything to do with Stacie's disappearance. He's just a kid. But we are checking further."

"This means something bad happened to her, doesn't it?" He ended the sentence with a choking sobbing noise.

"Not necessarily Oscar, but you're right; it's not a good sign. However, it does give us a place to start, and a reason to take this case very seriously. We are going to launch a full-scale investigation right away. I wish I had better news, and I'm so sorry for you and your family." Torch didn't know what else to say, and there was an awkward silence.

"What kind of an investigation have you had that wasn't full scale?"

The bluntness of the question took Torch by surprise.

"Missing person reports come in here every day, Oscar, and most of them turn out to be nothing. I think this case is not just about a missing person any more. I hope and pray that I'm wrong."

Oscar said nothing, but Torch could hear his ragged breathing on the line.

"I will call you as soon as we know more."

Torch said goodbye and hung up. He felt sad that he had been unable to do a better job of consoling Oscar.

Now to see what the boss wanted.

True to form, the boss pulled him off what he was doing, and sent him to North Minneapolis. "Before you go, turn the file on what you were working on over to Missing Persons, Torch."

He shook his head yes, and walked back to his office. He had known this was coming, but it made him mad just the same. Now this wouldn't get the attention it deserved, while he chased some drug dealers, who had killed other drug dealers.

On Tuesday night, Hal had gone home to his parents' house. Being at the University made him extremely uneasy. He felt that everyone was looking at him with suspicion in their eyes. He wanted to try and cut down on his drug consumption and keep his mind sharp—something that was hard to do when you were in a constant state of paranoia.

Hal also wanted to talk with Lamont about the bag of clothing in the car, but had no idea how to bring the subject up without creating more of a suspicious atmosphere than he already imagined.

He had waited until late so there would be fewer people around when he left, and as he crossed the Washington Avenue Bridge, he lowered the window on the opposite side of the car and tossed Stacie's cell phone into the river. Had he been standing on the bridge, watching it go over, he would have seen it fall and then disappear into a drift of snow on the ice. The river had appeared to be open from his point of view.

His mother was happy to see him return and accepted, without question, his reasoning that he needed a quiet place to study. His father looked at him with skepticism.

The minister from their church had come over to try and console both Oscar and Thelma. Right now, they all sat drinking coffee at the dining room table. Todd had removed the Christmas tree, and had put all of the gifts on the front porch under a blanket.

Nothing the young clergy could say, or read from the Bible, seemed to make a dent in their grief. This wasn't like a death they were grieving for because it had so much uncertainty embedded in it.

Thelma sat, holding her balled-up handkerchief to her face, dabbing occasionally at the steady stream of tears.

Oscar remained stoic, showing little outward emotion, but it was obvious he was deeply troubled.

"We must have faith that God will help us get through this." The minister's words seemed unconvincing to both of them, but they nodded their heads in agreement.

"Everything happens for a reason, and it's not up to us to question God."

Oscar stood up from the table and said, "You think she's dead, don't you? Do you know something we don't?" The minister remained quiet, listening to him but not knowing what to say in return.

Thelma had collapsed forward on the table, her head in her arms. Her back was convulsing with hysterical sobs. Her coffee spilled all over the table and Todd, who had been standing in the corner of the room, came running with a towel. He was crying, too, but it was not evident if he was crying for his mother or his sister.

"I think it would be best if you just left for now," Todd said. "I know you mean well but…" He didn't know what else to say.

The minister closed his Bible, and stood with his hand on Thelma's back. He turned, put on his hat and coat, and Todd walked him out to his car. Oscar murmured, "Thank you for coming," from the open doorway, and then disappeared back inside.

By Wednesday morning, Stacie's body was starting to move downstream. It was still not buoyant enough to float, but it was getting there. Her stomach was swollen and distended. The rigor that had come soon after death had now left, and her arms moved slightly in the current as if she was trying to propel herself. The front of her body was dark from the blood that had settled there while she remained face down for three days on the river bottom. For now though, her body had turned over and she was face-up, bouncing from time to time as the current tried to grab on to her, while her corpse fluctuated around rocks and eddies and moved a few inches at a time.

Her eyes were wide open, but completely clouded over, like an advanced case of some kind of horrible cataracts. Her long blond hair floated ahead of her like sea kelp in an ocean current.

The soles of her feet and the palms of her hands were shedding loose skin, and small fish nibbled at the shreds from time to time.

Overhead, a thickening layer of ice was forming and trapping her below the dark surface. If she were to stay floating and emerge, it would not be here.

Hal had told his mother that he was studying and didn't want to be disturbed. He would come down at six for supper with her and his father. Right now, he was lying on the bed and staring at the ceiling, while going over every step he had taken from the time Stacie had called, until now. *Where had he slipped up…if he had?* The bag of clothing and Lamont came to mind. *How could he explain that away if someone asked?*

His thoughts were very deliberate. *His sister had been here. Could he say she had gotten sick and wanted him to get rid of the clothes? No, why would she ask him to do that when she could just throw them in the trash right here. That was the kind of stupid shit I better not say. What if Lamont had looked deeper in the sack and found the purse.*

Maybe it was a girlfriend he had taken to the municipal pool, and yea, she got hurt and they took her to the hospital. He had retrieved her clothes and belongings from her locker, and he was going to bring them over to her as soon as she was released. Yea, that might just work. Let's see, what was her name? Shelly. Yea, that's a good name, Shelly Anderson. There must be a million of them in Minneapolis. What else is there that I am missing?

Thinking of nothing else to worry about right now, Hal actually studied for a couple of hours. There was just one class that he was having trouble with, and he had a term paper that was due in a few days that he hadn't even started writing. Maybe he would have to buy one from somebody. Tonight, at supper, he was going to level with his father on his grades. He might have to eat some humble pie, but maybe his father cared enough to help him out.

Hal heard Lamont outside, shoveling snow in front of the house, so he grabbed his coat and went out to talk to him. It was getting bitterly cold outside, as the temperature seemed to be dropping a few degrees each day. The nights had been well below zero. He had noticed, as he drove down yesterday, that Lake Minnetonka was dotted with little clusters of fish houses so the ice must be safe to drive on now.

When Lamont saw Hal coming, he stopped shoveling, and leaned on the end of the shovel for a few minutes to rest. This was hard work and he was not getting any younger.

"Lamont, you got a minute?" Hal was stamping his feet, his hands buried in his jacket pockets and his head burrowed in the collar of his coat.

Lamont smiled a suspicious smile. *What did this little prick want now? He never talks to me unless he wants something.*

"Mr. Hal, good to see you. Sure I got a moment. I got lots of moments."

"Lamont, I wanted to ask you about something. Do you remember the night you cleaned out my old Camaro and put all of the stuff in my new car?"

"Oh shit, he knows I took the bracelet. "Yes, I remember doing that. Was there a problem? I was just doing what your mother told me to do."

"There was a bag with some clothes in it and you put it on the front seat of the car."

"I remember doing that. The bag ripped when I was taking it out of the old car, but I tried to keep everything together, Mr. Hal." *Shit! Now he's going to ask me about that bracelet that I gave to my niece. What am I going to say?*

Hal could see that Lamont was extremely nervous, and just stared at him for a second. *This old bastard knows something he's not talking about.*

"Lamont, those clothes belonged to a girlfriend of mine. We had gone swimming at the pool over at the university. She got hurt diving, and they had to take Shelly to the hospital in an ambulance. I got her clothes out of her locker and was going to take them over to her house when she was released but one of her shoes was missing. I just wondered if you had seen it."

Lamont was stumped for a second. He had been expecting something missing, but not a shoe. "I put both shoes right on top of the bag, Mr. Hal."

"Could one of them have been put in the bottom of the bag, Lamont?"

"I never emptied the bag, Mr. Hal. I don't know what was in the bottom…I told you it ripped, but most everything stayed in the bag."

"Well, it's not a big thing, Lamont. I was just wondering if you had seen it. Thanks for your help."

Hal was freezing so he hurried back in the house. Lamont stared at him as he left. *He had dodged a bullet it seemed. Or had he?*

With the information Torch had given them, Wes Blackstrom, from Missing Persons, was now sitting at his desk going over the file. *One thing he needed to do for sure was question this Darren Mosley some more. He seemed to be the only connection to Stacie right now. Maybe he would talk to the store manager, too, and find out what he thought about the kid. In his report, Torch seemed to be ignoring him. Wonder why that was?*

At first he thought, as he read through the file, that Torch had overreacted to a missing person's report. They usually didn't get that worried about women this age for a week or more, and this one had only been missing for six days. The University was no stranger to missing students, who ran off for one reason or another.

The fact that they had found some of her belongings, though, did put it in a different light.

He called the manager of the Quick Stop and told him he would be coming out, and wondered if Darren Mosley was working today.

The manager told him that Darren would be working today until noon.

The day was brutally cold—somewhere under ten below—and the wind was kicking up out of the north at about fifteen miles an hour. The roads were icy with a lot of black ice, caused by condensation from the exhaust of cars, but despite all of that, Wes pulled into the Quick Stop at eleven fifteen.

The detective, Darren, and the manager met in his office in the back of the building, but not before Wes first met with the manager to tell him what this was all about. The manager knew nothing about the clothing, or Darren's involvement, but now things were starting to make sense from yesterday's conversation with Torch.

"Darren, I'm Wes Blackstrom, from the Minneapolis Police Department." Darren stood just inside the office door. He had been called in from outside, where he had been cleaning up. He had a puzzled look on his face and a good idea what the cops were here for.

The manager sat behind his desk, bouncing a pencil off the blotter, and staring at Darren. This was the trouble with trying to give these kids a break by giving them a job. *What else had he taken from around here?*

"Darren, I want you to tell me what you found in that trashcan out front…when you found it, and why you took those cards instead of turning all of this stuff in to the police, or your boss here at the store."

"I told a detective yesterday that I found a bag full of clothing that someone had thrown away. When I went to put it in the dumpster, a purse fell out, so I looked inside for some identification and I found an I.D. card and a credit card. I took the cards, and my girlfriend and I used them, and got caught. We were wrong to do this and the police know all about it."

Wes was amazed at his frankness. The kid was almost cocky about it but not disrespectful.

"These objects you are talking about, Darren," Wes hesitated for a second, turned, and was now talking, facing the manager, but directing the conversation to Darren.

"Those so-called objects belonged to a coed, from the University, who has turned up missing. This is starting to smack of foul play, and they would have been very important pieces of evidence. Had Darren done the right thing here, we might have had something to go on. As of right now, we have nothing, except we know someone left her clothing and possessions here.

He turned back to look at Darren. "Darren, was that bag of clothing close to the top of the trash container?"

"I think so. There were just some cigarette butts dumped on top of them, and a few papers."

"Do you empty those cans every day?"

"Not always, but I had emptied that can the day before because I worked that day. If I work, I empty the cans."

"Darren, you can go," Wes said.

He turned to leave and the manager said, "Don't go home until I talk with you."

Wes sat down across the desk from the manager. "Would you do me a favor and talk to the people you had working the night before Darren emptied those cans. Maybe someone saw somebody dumping a whole bag of something. It's a long shot, that's for sure, but if they do know something, give me the employees' names and phone numbers so I can talk with them." Wes reached across the desk and handed him his card. "You can reach me anytime, night or day, with those numbers."

Before Wes left, he said to the manager. "As for your employee, Darren, I'll leave that up to you, but I wouldn't go too harsh on him. A lot of kids his age would have done the same thing."

When Wes had left Darren's manager called him back in. He was waiting for the words, "You're fired," but instead he said to him, "I like to trust my employees to do the right thing around here, Darren, but you don't seem to be up to doing that. When you come in tomorrow we will discuss what we are going to do about this. If you have anything to say in your defense that makes sense, I would have it ready when you come in. Do you understand? You may go," he said.

That night, the Star Tribune carried a one-column article on the missing coed, with the new information about the personal items found in the trashcan. Maybe someone else had seen whoever dumped the clothing, so the police had decided to get the information out there; it was worth a try. No one had called by Thursday morning, but it had someone's interest, and that someone was Hal Halsworth.

He would never have seen the article if his father hadn't left the newspaper lying on the breakfast table, where he had his morning coffee, before going to work. Hal, enjoying a bagel with his coffee, had caught the **Missing Coed** title over the article.

The four-inch article simply said that, "Stacie Morrison, a University of Minnesota student, had been missing since last Friday night, and foul play was not being ruled out." The article went on to say that some of her clothing had been found in a trash receptacle at a convenience store in Minneapolis, along with a credit card and an identification card. There was no mention of Darren and the part he played in it, and there was also no mention of the fact that the police didn't have the clothing.

The news article had an unnerving effect on Hal, and he tore it from the paper and pushed the rest of the paper into the trash. Taking the article with him, he retreated to the pool area to think. He poured himself some vodka, mixed it with orange juice, and went to sit in a deck chair next to the pool. An overhead fan noisily removed humidity from the room, and Noreen was running a vacuum in the gazebo. Hal eyed her suspiciously as he studied the article again, and then slipped it into his shirt pocket.

He was deep in thought again. *Was it possible he had left prints? Why hadn't he searched her purse more closely? Why did he throw it away in a public trash receptacle?* Hal smacked himself in the forehead with his palm in an act of disgust.

One of the things he had studied in school were the obvious mistakes criminals make because they don't take time to think things over and cover their butts. *Hal Halsworth, the law student, had not done much better. He had let the drugs foul up his thinking, and he had panicked. Now he had to try and rectify the damage.*

He needed to go back to his room at school and act as normal as possible. He had to quit shooting from the hip every time he saw a poster on a pole, or a bulletin board or a newspaper article. He needed to act like he would have acted if none of this had happened.

By Thursday morning the body had reached buoyancy, and was now floating downstream under the ice. The body had flipped again, and the glazed-over eyes were searching the murky bottom, and the tongue now protruded from the mouth like a miniature rudder from some macabre vessel.

It floated in the usual position, upside down with the arms and legs hanging down. Small fish still picked at it from below, and there were open sores in the skin. If they were too successful digging into the flesh, they would cause the body to vent, and lose some of the gas that had built up in the inside, and it would once again go to the bottom.

From time to time, the body would get lodged on shards of ice that were hanging down from the sheet above. It would stop momentarily and then, usually after spinning one way or the other, it would bounce away. The water was deep here and the only thing that would really stop it was if it ran into shallow water, and lodged between the ice and the bottom. The prevailing currents of the big river had a way of steering floating objects into deeper water, so for now, that wasn't going to happen.

The ice on the river, in this area, was about six inches thick in most places. That is, until you got to the industrial area of North Minneapolis, where a clear channel was still being maintained by barges that had a grain port there. The body, however, would not be that far downstream for a while.

CHAPTER SEVEN

Mathew Halsworth Sr. was the owner and C.E.O. of the law firm that bore his name. He had several senior partners in the firm, but they had no vested interest and they all answered to him. His corner office was on the thirty-fourth floor of the Newman Building, with an impressive view of the Minneapolis skyline, and the river flowing below. The Newman Building held another law firm that owned the building, and Halsworth Sr. was currently working on a merger of the two law firms. He planned on liquidating the older firm as soon as he could acquire it. It would be the third one his firm had swallowed up in the last few years. His main reason for this merger was, like the others, to get rid of them, but the building itself would be frosting on the cake.

He was in his mid-sixties now, but hadn't slowed down much. His usual work week was still seventy hours, and he expected as much from the other members of the firm—some sixty of them in all. He was usually at work by seven thirty in the morning, and seldom left before seven at night. There were very few weekends that he didn't work, but he did work just a partial day on Sundays.

He was robust and in good health. He worked out daily in the Sports and Health Club on the second floor, and he ate and drank a sensible diet.

He drank sociably, but in moderation, and allowed himself a good Cuban cigar on special occasions.

His wife, Melinda, and he were rarely together. They had slept in separate beds, but in the same room, for some time now. He had not been in her bed or in her body in quite some time. He had no time for that, at least not with her, and that was fine with Melinda. She dwelt on her social schedule, and her children and grandchildren.

Today was a special day in the firm, and his once a week meeting with his most trusted partners. It was the time when they would go over strategy and the performance of their subordinates. Mathew rarely got involved in litigation of any kind, anymore. His focus was to run the firm and not to practice law.

With a few minutes to spare before his scheduled meeting, he turned his attention to the report in front of him. This particular report had nothing to do with anyone in the firm. It had to do with Mathew Junior, and it was troubling to say the least.

Mathew had one real dream in life and that was to have his children take over when he was done working. The dream had been dashed twice already, and young Mathew was his last hope. Ralph, his oldest son, had elected to become a doctor. An honorable profession for sure, but doctors and lawyers were oil and water, so they had little in common anymore. Becky, his daughter, was studying to be a teacher and spent all of her time, outside of school work, writing articles for newspapers and political action committees. Oh well, she would have been a bad fit, anyway.

The people he had hired to watch Hal had found out the following things.

Number one, his grades were not where they belonged, and although he might graduate, those grades were not going to get him into the law school of his choice, no matter what his father did to persuade them.

Number two, he had been seen in the company of known drug dealers, and Mathew had seen evidence that his son was a user. The large amount of money he spent was proof in itself.

Mathew walked to the glass wall that looked out over the Mississippi River. Far below he could make out the University Campus across the river on the far bank. That had been where he started all this years ago, but he had been serious about it. He'd had to work his way through school, driving a delivery truck at night. No one had given him the free ride Hal was getting. Maybe that's why his success was so precious to him.

His phone rang behind him and he picked it up. "Mr. Halsworth, they are waiting for you." His secretary said.

"Thank you, Jenny," he said. "Tell them I'll be right in."

He stuffed the report in the middle drawer of his desk. He would deal with Hal tonight when he got home.

Oscar Morrison was so confused he no longer knew who to talk to about Stacie's disappearance. Thelma's overwhelming grief also bore heavily on him, and although he wished he could support her better, he could barely function within his own grief. Only his beloved dairy cattle gave him some semblance of escape, twice a day.

Oscar talked softly to them while he washed their udders and made them ready for the milking machines. Some of these cows had been with him for ten years or more, and they were like family to him. He could tell you, off the top of his head, how many calves they had produced and what their milk production was. He would sit on his little three-legged stool, his head against their soft sides, and could feel the calves moving inside of them. That sign of life in their wombs only brought on more grief as he thought about the fact that Stacie's life may have been taken away. Oscar would sob against the only warm body that seemed to understand what he was going through right now.

Thelma, on the other hand, refused to leave the house, waiting for news from anyone. She would not even close the bathroom door, as the phone was in the kitchen and she was afraid she wouldn't hear it. They were old-fashioned people and Oscar had never changed their phones to cordless ones, or for that matter, even installed a message center. "That wasn't the way to treat people when they called," he said.

Now Thelma sat at the kitchen table, stuffing sausages with some pork they had left over from butchering.

Todd had left for the campus and was on a crusade to find out anything he could about Stacie's last movements. With Stacie's roommate's permission and the colleges, he was staying in the room until she returned from break on January third. Then he planned to bunk with Jacob and his wife for a while.

The same hindrances that had frustrated the police were also there for Todd. For the most part, people had gone back to their families for Christmas, and there was no one to talk to. But the students he did find were sympathetic to his cause and those that were around told him all they knew.

The triple murder in North Minneapolis had been just as Torch had thought; a turf war over drug territory by rival gang members. No one was talking and no one would talk, so all they could do is wait for a break.

With not much going on today, he had wandered over to Missing Persons to talk with Wes Blackstrom about Stacie's case. There were things about that case that still bothered him, and he felt that the answers were there if they just dug a little deeper.

The two detectives grabbed their coats and headed over to Whitey's for lunch. Whitey's was a deli that catered a lot to cops, and was located about two blocks from the main police station.

The loop was crowded despite the absence of holiday shoppers. Maybe they were getting ready for New Year's celebrations tomorrow night. The weather had mellowed a bit, and the temperatures had rebounded enough that the young girls who worked downtown had shed their heavy coats. The snow that hadn't been removed was melting during the day, and refreezing every night, making the whole area a slippery mess. People stood back from the curb to avoid the splatter from buses and cars passing by.

Whitey's was packed, but they managed to find a booth in the back that hadn't been cleared yet, and took possession anyway.

"Sometimes, I think it's ironic that I work in Missing Persons, and this damn world is so full of people you can hardly move. Maybe a few more need to go missing." Wes smiled at his own attempt at humor and tossed his jacket in the corner of the booth.

"Well, at least people talk with you," Torch responded. "The scum I have to deal with kill each other in their own private wars. Then we get called and no one knows anything, no one sees anything, or hears anything. We should just go home and say, 'call us if you have something, otherwise, quit calling us'."

An older lady in a blue uniform, with coffee stains down the front, pushed the dirty dishes into a gray bussing tray and slid a wet rag around the table.

"Someone will be right with you," she said, giving them a yellow-toothed smile.

"Have you talked to those people in Wisconsin about their daughter yet? I take it that nothing new has come up?" Torch looked at Wes, the question mark showing on his face.

Wes drummed his fingertips on the tabletop. "No, and no," he said. "I was going to call them…maybe tomorrow. Their son, Todd—I think he said that was his name—called and left a message for me to call him back. I haven't been able to get ahold of him. I guess he's here in the city looking for her. I should talk to him and see if he has stumbled onto anything. Whole case is going to just be the shits if she is screwing around with her family."

"I don't think that's the case," said Torch. "Just a gut feeling I have. You want me to call the parents? I did talk with them a couple of times."

The old lady had been replaced by a young girl with braces who stood, holding her order pad in front of her, and smiling a metal grin. "Special is meatloaf, gentlemen."

"I ate the meatloaf once," said Torch to Wes, "got the shits. Give me a Rueben, sweetheart, and tell them to use pastrami instead of corn beef. We could also use a couple of beers." Torch pointed to an advertisement for Budweiser, saying, "Those will do. Take this fat man's order here, too, and put it all on my tab."

Wes, smiling, said, "I'll take the meatloaf, honey. I could use the shits."

The girl gave him a sick grin. "Back in a moment with the beers," she said.

"Yea, Torch. If you want to call her family, go ahead. I did talk to the manager at the Quick Stop, but I'm at the same dead-end you were at. We were able to cut the timeframe, when the clothing was dumped, to sometime Christmas Eve, for what that's worth." He shrugged his shoulders and took a good pull on his beer that had arrived. "Tomorrow will make one week since she disappeared so I think we're going to need a break here pretty soon, or this case is going to get cold in a hurry."

Torch's pager beeped. He pulled it from his shirt pocket and studied the number. He put it back in his pocket and said nothing, but the concern was showing on his face.

By Friday morning, a couple of things had happened. Wes had found out, from a tip that had come in from a Bruce Baldwin, that Stacie had been seeing a boy for a few weeks. He was sure it wasn't serious, because he knew firsthand, he was that boy. He agreed to meet with Wes and came down to the office.

"Mostly, we just studied together," he said. "Lately, she was hard to get close to. It was almost like she didn't want to get close to anybody, anymore; like someone had wronged her somewhere along the line. I had known her only a year or so and something had changed her dramatically in the last two months. She was definitely not the same fun-loving girl she had been."

But in another part of the city there was something even bigger that had happened. Actually, it had happened on Wednesday, but the real meaning of it didn't become apparent until Friday morning.

Two young boys, on Christmas break from school, had wandered out on the ice under the Washington Avenue Bridge. They got as far as the first set of pillars when one of them stuck a foot through the ice, and both of them sat down and started screaming and crying, afraid to move. Passersby, on the walkway above, told them to stay put on the pillar ledge and they would call the Fire Department.

When the Fire Department arrived on the scene there was too much ice for a boat, and too little to walk on, so they elected to lower a basket and hoist the kids up and over the side of the bridge.

A group of spectators had formed and now they stood watching over the edge, laughing, joking and encouraging the boys. That's when one of them spotted a cell phone in the snow, not five feet from the boys, and mentioned it to the fireman. The fireman that had gone down to assist the boys into the basket retrieved it, and shoved it into his pocket. For now, he had a job to do, and that was to get these boys off the ice.

Back at Station Two, firefighter Carl Keller had forgotten about the phone in the pocket of his bunker pants. When he pulled out his wet mittens to exchange them for dry ones, it fell out on the floor.

"Hey Tom," he said to another fireman. "Look at this phone I found down there on the ice where those kids were at. What in the hell makes someone throw a good phone like this in the damn river?"

"Probably some angry girlfriend took it away from her boyfriend and tossed it. My loose screw of a wife would do something like that if she got pissed off. Hell, she would do worse than that. She would probably throw me in the damn river." They both laughed at their banter.

"Battery's dead," Carl said, pushing some buttons.

"Looks like the same kind Tookis has," Tom said. "He always has his charger in the office. All he does is talk on the goddamn phone. I think he's a fricking pimp or something."

Carl walked into the office. The charger was empty while Tookis and his engine company were out on a medical. He slipped the phone into it and the charger light came on. He'd tell Tookis about it when he came back.

When the engine returned, Tookis told Carl he didn't need the charger so leave it in there for a while. It was there until shift change Thursday morning.

When Carl pulled the phone from the charger, it lit up and seemed to be fine. *Maybe he would give it to his daughter,* he thought. *She had been nagging him for her own phone for a while, but in the meantime, he would do the right thing and call the owner whose number was on the display when he turned it on. No, wait—that was this phone's number, wasn't it? That wasn't going to solve anything. Maybe he would have the cops trace the number. Yea, that would tell him who it belonged to.*

Carl walked into the office, called Police Dispatch, and asked for a car to stop by.

On Friday morning, the body was still making slow progress down the river. The January thaw had increased the river's volume and the current was getting more aggressive by the day. For a brief moment this morning it had entered open water, and floated unobserved until the ice closed the river again. It hung there on the lip of the ice for a while, then gradually, the current tugging at the arms and legs hanging down from the torso won out and it disappeared under the ice sheet once more.

Decomposition was now taking place at a more accelerated pace. The back, which had been exposed to the ice and the air, was now a mass of jagged cuts and large blisters of gas trapped under the skin. The stomach underneath was grossly distended, giving her the appearance of a malnourished child in some faraway country. The skin was changing color, and her once-fair complexion was now turning black, except for the soles of her feet and the palms of her hands. The calloused skin there had turned snow white.

Fish had bit and pulled at parts of her body, leaving chunks of flesh exposed. Most of her protruding tongue, the nipples of her breasts and the ends of her fingers and toes had been chewed away. It was just a matter of time until the gas that was making her body float would escape through some orifice in her flesh, and then the body would return to the bottom to finish rotting away.

She no longer resembled, or for that matter, was no longer Stacie. Her body was just a mass of putrid flesh.

Hal had taken the call from his father on Friday morning around ten a.m. He wanted to meet him for lunch downtown, and wondered if Hal could make it.

"I can be there, Dad. I was on my way back to the University, anyway. What's up?" he said.

"Nothing really, Hal. I just wanted to talk for a while. Nothing has to be up."

Spoken like a true lawyer, Hal thought. His father never wanted to talk unless something was up. But he would show up as, after all, his father's money was essential to his lifestyle.

Hal had been to the Newman Building a few times over the years. Mostly, to be present at what he called his father's "Rah Rah" parties. The gala events when he invited all of his friends and associates over to do a little showing off.

He took the elevator to the top floor, riding up with two female paralegals that were mean-mouthing their boss. The younger of the two gave him more than a cursory glance, and smiled shyly at him. Hal smiled back but said nothing. The last women on earth he wanted anything to do with were people who worked for his father.

The corridor was empty as Hal walked briskly to the end, and the glass door that simply said, **Offices of Mathew Halsworth.** He needed no title, at least not in this building.

Jennifer Calon, Mathew's receptionist and secretary, rose to meet Hal as he came in the door. "Why Hal, what a pleasant surprise. Did you have a nice Christmas?"

Hal took her hand loosely in his. "I did, Jenny, thank you for asking."

"Well, your father is expecting you, so why don't you just go right in."

Mathew Senior was bent over his desk when Hal walked in.

"Hal, this is great that you could come. Let me get my coat and let's go someplace where we can talk a little. How's that new car running?"

"Fine, Dad. It's new—it should run great—right?"

Laughing, Mathew slapped his son on the back, ignoring his sarcasm.

They had reservations at Demonicas, an upscale Italian restaurant in the warehouse district. There was a long line waiting to be seated, but as soon as they entered, they were ushered to the front of the line by the Host, who greeted Mathew enthusiastically. Hal fell in behind the two men as they threaded their way through the red table-clothed tables to a quiet corner. The smell of basil and oregano was everywhere, and somewhere, the sound of string instruments playing Italian music could be heard.

So this was the way the rich and famous get treated, Hal thought. *Not too shabby.*

When they had ordered and had their drinks, Mathew Senior spoke softly, but very emphatically. A look of seriousness had come over his face.

"Hal, it's always refreshing for me to have some time alone with you, but I am not going to bullshit you. I brought you here for a reason today, and I hope you'll listen to reason, and let me help you."

Hal squirmed nervously in his chair. He unfolded and refolded his napkin, and then rearranged his silverware. All of the time, avoiding eye contact with his father.

Here comes the third degree, so let's just stay cool.

"Hal, I have worked hard in life to get where I am. One of my hopes was that this would all continue after I am gone. Tomorrow we are merging with one of the bigger firms in Minneapolis, and we are purchasing the building where we now reside. It has been my dream, from the time you children were small, that you would be part of this firm. Your brother Ralph, although successful, has decided to go his own way and that was disappointing to me. Your sister too, although I never could see her here anyway, so be that as it may...you are my last hope, Hal."

The waiter had arrived with the food they had ordered, so Mathew suspended his conversation until he had left, appearing irked at the interruption.

"Hal, you know I have access to your grades at school. You are not doing that great, son."

Hal was chewing his food slowly, and now was staring at his father, who could sense he had gotten into sensitive territory. He would soften his tone.

"School is hard, son. I also had trouble in some areas, and that's all right. You just need to ask for some help before it's too late."

Hal washed his mouthful of food down, and wiped his mouth, still saying nothing.

Mathew stared at his son for a second. This one-sided conversation was not what he had hoped for. He didn't have any idea how to approach the drug subject so, for now, he wasn't going to.

"Hal, when you graduate this spring your grades will need to be better to get into law school. There is just so much I can do for you in that area, so I am asking you…how about this…I have arranged for a dear friend of mine, in the firm, to tutor you. She knows just what you need to do and how to get there. Do we have a deal on that?"

Hal shook his head yes.

"Great. This is her phone number. I want you to call her tonight and she will help you set up a schedule. This is great, son, you and I talking like this. Hang in there and it will all work out, I assure you."

Mathew Halsworth snapped his fingers, and called for his check, even though he hadn't touched his veal cutlet.

"I have a one-thirty meeting, Hal, and I need to rush off so finish eating. Hell, eat this too, if you want." He pushed his plate across the table. "I hope you don't think I'm rude."

Hal just smiled. He hadn't said one word since they sat down.

Finally, he said, "Thanks for lunch."

"You're welcome, son, and don't forget to call her, okay?"

He shook his head yes, as his father came around the table, squeezed his shoulder and left.

He had his father's uneaten dinner boxed up, and left, walking back to the Newman ramp to get his car. He needed to digest what had been said here, and what had been left unsaid, as well as what had been eaten. His father knew something else. He was sure about that.

It was a ten block walk back, but the day was nice and the streets, although busy, seemed to be orderly. No one was honking horns or seeming to be in too much of a rush. A police officer, with his whistle in his mouth, was standing in the middle of the intersection. He bowed deeply as an elderly lady, in a white Lincoln, crawled through the intersection as if she was driving on a bed of nails. Despite the irritating pokiness, he was laughing at her.

Hal was deep in thought as he walked. *His father was right about his grades. His father was always right about his life. He knew every move he made and was watchdogging him every step of the way. I do have a secret you don't know, father, and you will never find out.* Hal smiled at the thought.

He had thought little about what he had done to Stacie. Clearly, there was no remorse in him; just the fear of getting caught and even that was starting to subside. He was too damn smart to get caught.

CHAPTER EIGHT

It was three p.m. when Wes returned from the University, where he had been interviewing people in the building. There was a note on his desk, "Call Carl from the Fire Department." The subject line on the pink "**While you were out**" slip said simply, "Cell Phone." Carl was out on a call when Wes called the Station Two office, but the man who answered the phone said Carl would be back any minute, and he would have him call back.

"I'll be here for about another hour," Wes replied.

The interviewing at the University today had gone all right. Stacie, he had found out, was kind of an enigma to most of her fellow classmates. She was a loner who rarely talked to others and socialized little. Her grades were above average, and her school record was clean. She was just a good kid.

Her brother, Todd, was at her apartment when Wes got there—preparing to head to his brother, Jacob's, place. He had been playing detective for two days and was totally frustrated by the lack of cooperation he had received. Brother or no brother, people were very reluctant to talk to a seventeen-year-old kid about this, and especially in an all-girls dorm.

"I wouldn't have to be out here making an ass out of myself if the police would do their job," Todd had said to Wes. He was mad, and made it clear that if someone wasn't going to get busy on this case, he was going to go to the papers, the mayor, and the goddamn Governor, if he had to.

He went on to explain the suffering his family was being put thorough. "You people treat her like she is some prostitute, or a whore who is just out screwing around for a few days. Well, you don't know my sister. She's a good girl, and she didn't run away. She hasn't run away from anybody or anything before and she isn't now, either." He was red in the face—almost shouting at Wes. His eyes were full of tears, and Wes finally just took his hands, and sat down with him on the edge of the bed.

"I am here today to find out what I can, Todd. With Christmas, and all of the students being gone, it hasn't been easy to talk with anyone. We will find your sister. You should go home and be with your parents. I'll tell you what...here's my card. On the back is my home number. Call me anytime you want to talk about this. Hell, reverse the charges if you want. I want you to know everything we know, son. Okay?" Wes had put his arm around the crying boy.

Todd nodded softly and blew his nose. Then he stood up to leave and said, "Thank you. You have to understand—I love my sister very much."

His cell phone's ringing startled Wes, snapping him out of his train of thought. He reached for it and nearly dropped it. "This is Blackstrom," he said.

"Yea, this is Carl over at Station Two, Minneapolis Fire. Hey, on Wednesday we pulled a couple of stupid kids off the ice, under the Washington Avenue Bridge. While I was down there, I found a cell phone on the ice. I didn't think much of it for a while, but then I charged the battery up and the number of the owner was on the display. I thought I would do the right thing, and get it back to them, you know."

"This has something to do with me?" asked Wes, somewhat sarcastically.

"No, not you, but the owner of the phone," Carl said.

"This number is registered to a Stacie Morrison, and one of the boys at the station said that just might be the girl from the University that was missing—is missing," he corrected.

Wes was speechless for a moment. "You going to be there for a while?" he said.

"Yes, well, unless we get a call."

"I'll be right over," Wes said.

He grabbed his coat and was headed out the door, but decided to first run down the hall to see if Torch was in...he was.

Torch listened intently as he explained the situation.

"I knew she had a phone," Torch said. "I found one of her past statements. What I didn't do, and I should have, was check her past call records. Maybe this phone can help us with that. Hang on, I'm going with you."

It was only a few blocks to the fire station and the weather was nice so they walked over, talking as they went.

"You know Torch, I might not be able to do anything with this until Monday. My old lady made reservations for New Year's Eve, along with some friends, at a hotel upstate. We're leaving tonight. I usually get laid once a year—on New Year's Eve if I need it or not—so I would hate to screw that up."

Torch smiled. "I would hate to spoil that for you, my friend. I have a date myself for New Year's Eve, but my friend is always with me, so I can be much more flexible."

"That just might be the way to go," Wes laughed.

"Never been turned down yet," said Torch.

The phone lay on the counter in the fire station office, with Torch, Wes, and Earl looking at it. It had no leather case—it was just a shiny silver cell phone.

"Anybody except you touch this?" Torch asked Earl.

"I'm not sure. I had it in the charger here in the station for a day or so, and anybody could have grabbed it, I guess. I could ask."

"No...no...you don't need to do that right now. How did you find out who it belonged to?"

"Through the police dispatcher. They called the cell phone company."

Earl fished a piece of paper out of his billfold. "This is the name and address she gave me."

Just then the klaxon sounded and Earl held his hand up, asking for silence.

"Engine Two, Ladder Six. We have smoke showing from a building on Thirteenth and Portland. We'll update the address in a minute."

"I've got to go," Earl said.

Torch waved him on and reaching into his pocket, pulled out a small baggie, and using his pen, slid the phone into it. They stood on the sidewalk outside for a second, and watched the big rigs roll out of the station and head east, sirens blaring and air horns echoing off the big buildings as if they were in a canyon.

"That's what I should have done." Wes said. "Those guys are always everybody's heroes. No one calls them pigs and spits at them."

"My brother is on the Department in Chicago," Torch said, the smoke from the cigarette he had just lit streaming from his nose. "Says it's hours and hours of boredom, interrupted by brief periods of incredible violence. My ass is flat enough."

"Look, I'm going to go back and have the lab take a look at this," Torch said, holding up the bag with the phone. But first I have to go and pick something up. "Happy New Year, buddy." He slapped Wes on the back.

As Torch walked back to the station, his thoughts went back to Susan once more. Christmas had lost all of its meaning when he had lost her. His wife and he had the perfect family at that time, and it was made all the more precious because Susan had been the only child they could ever have. Now, home was a living hell, and he avoided it as often as possible.

Torch stopped at a drugstore and going in, stood at the counter just inside the door. An old woman in front of him was digging in her tattered bag for a few more coins, while the young male clerk held out his hand impatiently.

She had on a long black coat and had a kerchief wrapped around her head. Her face was a road map of wrinkles and her eyes looked tired and scared at the same time.

"I thought I had some change," she said. "Could I maybe have part of the prescription and I will come back tomorrow for the rest?"

"I can't do that. You need fifty-nine cents more, or I will have to put it back in the box until you get more money."

She turned and looked at Torch, her eyes pleading. Her chin was quivering, and she was on the verge of tears.

Torch reached into his pocket, and taking out his money clip, peeled off a ten and gave it to her. "Here," he said.

Now the tears were coming and Torch laid his hand on her shoulder. "Take the change and get yourself something to eat for New Year's," he said. "Happy New Year."

"God bless you," she said. Taking the change, she started to say something else but a middle-aged man behind them shouted, "Come on, let's get going."

Torch whirled and stuck his finger in the man's chest. "You wait your turn, asshole," he said, through clenched teeth.

Turning back to the clerk, he said, "Give me a carton of camels." The old lady had disappeared.

It was four-thirty before he returned to the station. The night shift was coming in, but they were used to Torch being there at all hours. Theresa stopped on her way in and sat down by his desk.

"Busy day, Torch?"

"Same old shit," he said. "Going out to celebrate tomorrow night, kid?"

"Have to work," she said. "Otherwise, yea, we would like to. Lester and I don't get much time to do anything anymore, with me working days and him working nights."

Theresa sat with her hands in her lap, turning her wedding ring around on her finger. Her hands were chapped and red, and she looked tired. She was three months pregnant and had a three-year-old at home. She and Lester worked opposite shifts because they couldn't afford daycare. He was a nurse at the county hospital and they had met one night—four years ago—when Theresa had brought a rape victim in for treatment.

"Let me cover for you."

"Geeze, Torch, that's nice, but I owe you two days now."

"You owe me nothing. Go and have fun."

She reached across the desk and took his hand. "You're the best, Torch. I really mean that."

He shook the phone out of the baggie and onto his desk blotter. His plan was to have it printed, and looked at for any other evidence such as hairs, but first he wanted to see something.

Torch reached into his middle desk drawer and pulled out a yellow lead pencil. Using the eraser end he pushed buttons until the display lit up. It showed the phone's number. He wrote it down on a scrap of paper. Then he scrolled down through the menu to the history. There were ten phone calls listed; the last ten calls she had made. One by one, Torch wrote them all down, noting that all but three of them were to the same number. He reached for his notepad in his pocket, and flipped back until he found what he was looking for. Oscar Morrison's phone number in Wisconsin, and the number that matched seven of the calls.

The other three calls were all local numbers. One was the oldest call on the list, one was the last call on the list, and the other one was next to the last.

Torch pushed the phone back in the baggy, with his pencil, and walked down to the lab. "I need this checked for prints and trace evidence," he said.

"Give me a couple of days, Torch?" The middle-aged clerk looked at him over the top of his reading glasses."

"Yea, that will work."

"Hot case?"

"Not yet buddy, but it's getting warmer. Happy New Year!"

"Yea, you too, Torch."

Hal hadn't gone back to his apartment; instead he had gone to see some friends of his, on campus, that were having a little pre-New Year's Eve party. There were five men and two young women, and right now one of the women and two men had disappeared into one of the bedrooms right behind him. From the sounds coming through the wall behind his head they were not sleeping. Hal was engaged in a serious discussion about cars with a guy named Chip. Chip had called his Camaro a compact car, and Hal had insisted it was a sports car.

One thing for damn sure, he wasn't going back to his parents' house for a while and listen to his father's bitching. He would call the woman who was going to tutor him in the morning, but that was as far as he was going to go. He did recognize that he had to get his grades up.

Right now, he was well on his way to getting a good buzz on, drinking Mexican boilermakers. It was a drink they had invented with Corona and tequila. Half of a picked-over pizza was on the coffee table in front of him, and the other men, besides Chip, were throwing darts across the room at a poster of a naked girl.

Chip, who was a lot more sober than Hal, got up and joined the dart throwers. It was impossible to have a sane discussion with Hal, anyway. Especially when he was drunk and belligerent like right now. Although, as far as Chip was concerned, Hal was belligerent most of the time. *Hal was just a spoiled rotten rich brat,* Chip thought to himself.

Hal busied himself at the table, mixing a fresh drink, and returned to the couch to brood over it. Just then, the bedroom door flew open and a naked girl came running out, laughing. She ran around the room, and then back into the bedroom with both boys, also naked, chasing her.

Hal grabbed his coat off the coat tree by the door and left. He needed something stronger than beer and tequila, and he wasn't going to get it here.

Torch called the oldest phone number on the list first. The girl's name was Anita Carlson, and yes, she had talked to Stacy, about a week before Stacie disappeared. She and Stacie were not friends, but they were classmates and she knew very little about her. Stacie had called her about some books she had lent her, and they had only talked for a few minutes.

"Is there any news about her?" she asked.

"I'm afraid not much," said Torch. "It's almost as if she dropped off the face of the earth."

"There sure is a buzz on campus about this—lots of rumors going around."

"Yea. Well, unfortunately they are just that, rumors. Look, if you hear anything that sounds like it might help us, give me a call. Just call Minneapolis Police and ask for Torch Brennan."

"I will," she said. "Happy New Year."

"Happy New Year to you, too, kid." Torch hung up the phone.

The next to the last call on the list was to her brother, Jacob, and Torch explained that they had found her phone and were going through the history on it.

"Where was the phone?" Jacob asked.

Torch hesitated for a second, but he had gone this far so he might as well say it. "On the ice under the Washington Avenue Bridge."

There was an uneasy silence, and then Jacob said, "Do you think she jumped?"

"You know about the clothing, don't you?" Torch asked.

"Yes."

"Well, no—I don't think she jumped off that bridge."

"Was she thrown off the bridge?"

"That's a possibility, but usually when that happens, we would have a body by now."

There was some confusion on the line for a second, and Jacob could be overheard talking to another man.

"Sorry," he said. "My brother is here, and he wanted to know what you said."

"Look, Jacob is it?"

"Yes."

"I'll get back to you when we find out anything. How are your parents doing?"

"Not good," said Jacob. "They are very, very, distraught."

"I'm so sorry. I'll be in touch."

Two calls and two dead-ends to show for it. He looked at the last number and then lit a cigarette. Stacie's picture, that Thelma had given him, was lying on the desk. He opened his wallet and put it inside—right behind Susan's. He had to go find a toilet.

When he returned to his desk, Torch dialed the last number on the list. It rang four times and then went to an answering machine. "This is Hal. Leave a message and I will return your call when I get a chance." The voice sounded brash and impatient.

Torch dialed another two-digit number.

"Dispatch," the voice answered.

"Hey, Brennan here at headquarters. Do me a favor and look up this number in the cross directory." Torch gave them Hal's number.

"Hang on," the dispatcher said.

When he came back on the line he said. "Brennan, the number lists to a Mathew Halsworth Junior. Do you want the address?"

"Please."

Torch sat looking at the address and the name. He knew of a Mathew Halsworth who was a big shot lawyer downtown. In fact, the asshole had won a case from him a few years back. *Don't suppose they are related, do you? This one is Junior—could be his kid, couldn't it?*

Torch reached in his pocket for his reading glasses, while he pulled a Minneapolis phone book off the bookshelf behind him. There were about twenty Halsworth's, but only one Mathew Halsworth Senior, at 16601 Island

View Circle; South Lake, Minnetonka. In parentheses it said, (See Halsworth Ltd under Attorneys).

He closed the book and put his glasses back in his pocket. It was five thirty and time to call it a day, but maybe he would take a little drive first. Hell, he hadn't been out to Minnetonka in quite some time. He grabbed his coat and hat and was out the door.

Torch drove down Hennepin Avenue and then cut over in front of the Basilica to get on the ramp to 394. The Basilica was still adorned with decorations from Christmas. Next to the church, a small wooden building had been built to look like the manger in Bethlehem had looked, on that special night two thousand years ago. As he waited for the light to change, his mind went back to when he was a young man, growing up in a strong Catholic family. He had even gone to Catholic school for the first eight years of his formal education.

As he looked at the figurines that depicted the Holy Family, he wondered what had happened to him to make him lose that faith that had been so important to him way back then. He still believed in a God, he just didn't have time for one right now, and he felt guilty about that.

The light changed and he merged into traffic, gunned the car down the ramp, and headed west on the freeway. About a mile down the road, Torch passed the Quick Stop where Stacie's clothes had been found. Although he noticed it, the significance of it didn't register right then. He was thinking of Susan and Stacie.

Before long, he was passing through the inner ring suburbs of Golden Valley to the north and St. Louis Park to the south. The commercial buildings and strip malls had given way to streets filled with fifty year old two-bedroom expansion homes, and an occasional shopping center. Just beyond that, he entered the City Of Minnetonka—named after the great lake it surrounded.

The freeway ended and turned into a two-lane highway that would go west across the state, if you stayed on it, but Torch turned south towards the lake and Mathew Halverson's estate.

It was pretty driving around the lake, despite the fog that had formed from the cold ice meeting the unusually warm air. It gave the surrounding homes an eerie look in the near darkness. Fish houses, out on the lake, sat in little villages. There was an occasional pickup truck or snowmobile parked outside, and a faint light glowed through their little windows.

The traffic, that had been so heavy on the main roads, was now reduced to an occasional car. Torch slowed down considerably as he scanned the street signs, looking for the address he had written down.

He made a right turn into the access road for the rich community, and soon was stopped at the wrought iron gates. He got out of his cruiser and walked over to read the sign that was blurry in the fog. **FOR ADMITTANCE CALL THE PARTY YOU WISH TO SEE. ALL DELIVERIES MUST TAKE PLACE DURING DAYTIME HOURS OF** 7-5.

Back in the car, he dialed the number of Mathew Halsworth Senior. After the fourth ring, an out-of-breath male voice answered. "Halsworth Residence, this is Lamont."

"Lamont, my name is Torch Brennan. I'm a Minneapolis police officer. Can I come in? Will you activate the gates?"

There was no answer, but the gates opened and Torch drove in. *Cobblestone streets,* he mused. *So this is how the rich bastards live.*

Torch pulled up in the circular drive and parked. The house was lit up and he could see a man looking out from behind the drapes. Police coming to the house was not a rare occurrence by any stretch of the imagination. They'd been here many times, and always, looking for young Hal.

Lamont made him ring the bell, anyway, but opened the door almost immediately.

"Are you Lamont?" Torch asked.

"I am sir, and you are who?"

Torch offered his hand. "Lamont, my name is Torch Brennan. I work for the Minneapolis Police Department, and I am here to see Mathew Junior, if I could."

"I'm sorry sir, but young Hal has gone back to school. He left this morning. He might be back. I never really know for sure what he is going to do. Nobody tells the butler much around here. Is there something I could help you with?"

"Not really. I just have a couple of questions I wanted to ask him. Are his parents' home?"

"No, no. Mr. Halsworth has not come home from work yet, and Mrs. is at a social event."

Torch could see that Lamont was being inquisitive but didn't want to appear that way. "Look, if young Hal should come home, have him call me, would you?" Torch handed Lamont his card.

"I will sir," he said.

Lamont watched Torch, through the sidelight window, until he drove off. Then he sat down and looked at the business card he had handed him. The words literally jumped out at him. **TORCH BRENNAN, HOMICIDE.** *Young Hal had done a lot of bad things in his day, but murder? No, wait; maybe he witnessed a murder or something like that. He was a mean little bastard all right, but murder?*

Lamont studied the card again. The image of the bag of clothes in the car came to mind. *No, no…he had said those belonged to his girlfriend. But I still have that bracelet and watch. Maybe I should go see my niece tonight. No sense taking chances.*

Lamont picked up the phone and called her. "Clarice…hi, honey. You know I wanted to come and see you at Christmas, but one thing led to another and well, you know how that goes. Can I come over tonight? I have something for you."

"Uncle Lamont…how nice of you to think of me. Sure, come on over. I'm not doing anything tonight."

Lamont hung up the phone and then, picking it back up, called a cab. If he hurried, he might have time for a good stiff drink before the cab came.

Torch was going to call it a night. He headed home the same way he had gone to the Halsworth residence. He wasn't drawing any conclusions right now, but there were some troubling questions that needed to be answered, and he intended to get those answers. *First of all, was Stacie thrown off that bridge where her phone was found? If so, why her clothes were found someplace else didn't make sense. There was ice where the phone was found. How could she be under the ice, and not her phone, if she was in the river? Why had she called Hal?*

He passed the Quick Stop once more on the way back. This was too much of a coincidence for this store, where the clothes were found, to be right on Hal's way home. He was coming back here tomorrow to talk to the manager once more. He might have another card to play.

CHAPTER NINE

By Saturday morning, Stacie's dead body had emerged from under the ice sheet north of Minneapolis. It was floating down the middle of the river, surrounded by chunks of breaking-up ice. It had passed the 694 bridge about an hour ago, and was fast approaching North Minneapolis. From here to the Ford Dam, the river would be open.

The temperature was getting colder again and hung in the mid-twenties. Snow had been coming down for an hour or so, and already there appeared to be an inch or more on the ground, and on the exposed back of Stacie's corpse floating downstream. Her back, and the surrounding chunks of ice, looked remarkably alike.

The current was getting swifter from all of the snowmelt of the past few days. That, and the fact that there were no more obstructions for the body to get hung up on, and no ice sheet overhead to rub against, was making for fast travel right through the heart of the city.

Torch worked around home on Saturday morning, while his wife got an early start on New Year's Eve.

"Damn it, Evelyn, you would think you could at least wait until the middle of the afternoon before you start in on the sauce again. Don't you have any goddamn clothes to put on? All I ever see you in is those baggy ass pajamas."

She stood glaring at him, her ever-present drink glass in her hand. "What do you give a shit about what I look like, Torch. You never take me anywhere to eat where I don't have to unwrap my goddamn food. You're never home; you're married to that god-forsaken job of yours. You do everything you can to avoid me."

She tipped her glass up and finished up about two inches of straight gin.

"It's New Year's Eve tonight, Torch. Let's go out and celebrate." She was hanging on his arm, trying to be conciliatory, while he tried to wash dishes at the kitchen sink.

Torch turned and stared at her. By the time New Year's Eve comes around, you will be stiff as a poker, Evelyn. Besides, I have to work tonight. I'm covering for Theresa.

Evelyn walked across the room and refilled her glass. "I might be 'stiff as a poker' like you say, Torch, but it will be the only thing that will be stiff in this house. Speaking of pokers, you poking that little friend of yours? You seem to do her a lot of favors."

"You're despicable." Torch wiped his hands, and went out to the garage, slamming the door behind him. It was cold out there, but at least it was quiet. He sat in the car and fumed. Evelyn was right about one thing, there had been no sex in this house for a long time—not since Susan had died. He reached for his wallet and took out Susan's picture, propping it up against the speedometer. "I love you so much, my princess," he said. Torch lay down on the seat and pulled his coat over his head. He wanted to cry in privacy.

Hal woke up on Saturday morning with the mother of all hangovers. He wasn't sure if it was the beer, the tequila, or the two lines of coke he had snorted before he passed out. Right now, he had a case of the dry heaves that would not quit. The only thing that felt good on his forehead was the cold tile floor of the bathroom.

Finally, the nausea subsided long enough for him to make his way to the couch. He tried to focus his eyes and looked at his watch. It was nearly noon and he had another party to go to tonight. He'd better get in shape soon.

He tried to call his father's pick for his tutor last night, but there was no answer, so he left a message for her to call him. Right now, maybe a beer would help him think again, as much as it didn't sound that appealing.

Hal shuffled to the kitchen and opened the refrigerator door. The light was blinding him so he held his finger over the button while he looked for a beer.

The phone's ringing startled him, and he dropped to his knees before realizing what it was. *It was probably his father's friend—I better get it.* He picked the phone up from the end table and said. "This is Hal."

"Hal, good, you're home. Torch Brennan, from the Minneapolis Police Department. Are you going to be there for a while?"

Hal had no immediate response. This was what he had feared would happen, but he had prepared himself for it.

"Can I ask what this is about?"

"Why don't I come over and then I can go over it all with you. 3302 Uclide...right?"

"Ah...right."

"I'll be there in half an hour."

Hal did not answer, but heard the phone hang up. He'd better get dressed.

Torch had called from his garage in South Minneapolis. He should tell Evelyn he was leaving. He walked to the house, and before turning the knob, looked through the window. She was passed out on the couch—one hand still wrapped around a bottle of Beefeaters.

He watched for a minute to make sure she was breathing, but made no attempt to go in. As much as he despised her drinking, he did still care for her. Did he love her? He wasn't sure he had ever loved her the way he should have. She was Susan's mother though, and although he didn't have Susan anymore either, well, that wasn't her fault.

The drive over to Hal's took only fifteen minutes, so he drove around for a few minutes so as not to appear early. The last thing he wanted to do was to piss someone off that he was trying to get answers from.

The streets were narrow here, and cars seemed to be parked everywhere. Several students could be seen, walking along the sidewalks with their books and backpacks. As Torch turned the corner once more, something was familiar, and he slowed almost to a crawl. That was the building where Stacie lived. Yes, that was the building he had come to the other day when he looked in her apartment. It was less than a block from Hal's address.

Hal seemed irritated when he opened the door, but he did ask Torch to come in. "I have to apologize. I have the flu or something so I'm not feeling all that good."

He motioned to a chair at the kitchen table. "Can I make you some coffee?" he asked.

"That sounds good. But you don't have to make it just for me."

"No…no…I could use some myself." He was wearing a pair of sweatpants and a plain white tee shirt and was barefoot.

While the coffee was brewing, Hal sat down across the table from Torch. *What was this man thinking? What had he found? I better be a better listener than talker here*, he thought.

Torch reached across the table and shook Hal's hand. "I guess I told you over the phone who I was, but I'd like to introduce myself, Hal." He pushed his card across the table at the same time. "As I said before, my name is Torch Brennan, and I am an investigator for the Minneapolis Police Department. Normally I work out of Homicide, as my card says, but for today I am just following up on a missing person's report. Stacie Morrison. Did you know her?"

Careful here—no lies, he thought. *Just answer his question*. Hal was still looking at the business card. "Ah yes, I did know her, but not well." We shared some classes together."

"You do know she was missing?"

"Yes, I did. I saw it in the papers and there are posters all over the place. I hope she's all right. She seemed to be a great girl from what I knew about her." Hal had gotten up and was rummaging in the cupboard for some cups.

Torch shifted gears a little. "I drove out to your parents' place last night, looking for you."

Hal had his back to Torch as he poured coffee. "Yes, I left yesterday morning. It was time to get back to my studies."

"That's what Lamont told me. Your parents sure have a nice place there." Torch saw the surprised look on Hal's face, as he was coming toward the table with the two cups of coffee, when he mentioned Lamont's name.

He talked to that old bastard. I better be careful here. What am I going to say if he asks about those clothes? Son of a bitch, I never should have tossed those clothes where I did. I know they found them. I saw it in the paper.

"Yes, my father has done well for himself in life. I hope I can only be as successful." Hal smiled a weak smile. "I'm sorry...did you need cream or sugar?"

"No, this is fine. Good coffee, Hal. Thank you. You know Hal, checking Stacie's phone records, we found the very last call she made was to you. Do you remember that call?"

Careful...careful. Where had they found her phone? He threw it in the river. Hal sipped his coffee slowly, looking at Torch over the top of his cup. If he took a gulp he was going to puke again, and he wasn't sure he wasn't going to, anyway. His guts were rolling.

"Yes, I do remember her calling me. I think it was the night before Christmas Eve." *No more now, make him ask the questions.*

"Any particular reason she called you? This is important Hal, because you seem to be the last person she talked to. Did she say where she might be going? Was she in a good mood or was she troubled?"

Torch's eyes never left Hal's. *Sometimes they didn't need to answer, it was written all over their faces,* he mused.

"No...she seemed fine. She just called to wish me a Merry Christmas and said she was going home to Wisconsin for Christmas. I think she said Wisconsin. I'm not really sure. Like I told you, we weren't good friends or anything like that."

Torch was quiet for a second; not really knowing what he should ask him next. He could feel Hal was being elusive, but that might be normal. *What the hell, he was a cop and that made a lot of people nervous. Maybe he should do some checking on a few other things. He could always come back to this.*

"Well, Hal, I think you've answered my questions. Why don't you call me if you think of anything else? My number is on that card."

"I'll do that. Sure you don't want some more coffee?"

"No, I had better get busy. I need to talk to a few more students who were home for Christmas and just came back. Thanks anyway."

He stood, putting his coat back on, and Hal walked him to the door. "Hope something shows up soon," he said.

"I do, too. And I hope that something is Stacie."

Torch sat in his car for a few minutes, gathering his thoughts. He wasn't sure how to take Hal. He was either being very honest or very smart. He needed to think about this conversation he had just had.

He drove over to the dormitory where Stacie lived and rang the bell.

Hal ran to the kitchen sink the minute the door closed, and threw up his coffee.

For Oscar and Thelma, each day without Stacie brought more thoughts that she had met with something terrible. Either at her own hands or an outsider's. They were gentle, peace-loving farm people that had heard all of the horror stories of what went on in the big city, and what happened to kids after they have left the safety net of their parents. Now, it seemed, it had happened to them. Thelma just wandered around the house, her handkerchief stuffed in her apron pocket within reach, because she never knew what picture or thought would bring the tears back again. She had no theories as to what had happened to her daughter. She refused to even think the worst.

Oscar was in the barn most of the day. If a cow defecated, Oscar was right there with the shovel to clean it up. He talked to all of them constantly, and fed them small handfuls of grain and hay. He groomed them until they all shined, and when milking time came, he asked Todd not to come down. He wanted to do it himself. He wanted to talk with each cow about his problems and he wanted to be alone. He blamed himself for not being there when she needed him. The pregnancy test kit the police had talked about was like a dagger in his side. He really believed that Stacy, if she was pregnant, had done something awful to herself to avoid the shame. For now, he didn't believe somebody else had harmed her.

Todd had come back home because he had to go back to high school, but he, too, was deeply troubled. His grief, however, had seemed to be more in anger than sadness, and was a wound festering inside of him. A wound he didn't know what to do with. He stayed in his room with his video games. He talked very little with his parents because his view was that someone had done something to Stacy. He didn't believe she would harm herself.

Clarice was getting ready to go out for New Year's Eve. She'd had a great conversation with her Uncle Lamont last night. Lamont and her mother had been as close as a brother and sister can get. Now, since her mom had passed away, Lamont was about all of the family she had. But she was a big girl now; she had a great job, a new boyfriend, and things were looking up.

She sat on the edge of the bed, in her underwear, and picked up the bracelet Uncle Lamont had given her last night. It had been an expensive bracelet and he admitted to her it was not new, but said a friend had given it to him. It just wasn't her kind of jewelry, but it was the thought that counted, so she would keep it and think of her uncle every time she looked at it. He had also given her a watch and she would wear that. She could always use another watch.

She looked at each charm on the bracelet; a tennis racket and a little dog that resembled a small poodle. There was a saxophone and an open Bible. There was also a pair of skates and what looked to be a diploma. She turned it over and right next to the clasp was some small engraving. It looked like **S.M. 1987.** She put it back in the box and finished dressing.

Earlier that afternoon, Torch had called the Quick Stop to see if the manager was in. He was told he wasn't there, but would be in this evening for a few hours. "Why don't you call after six," the young girl said.

"Thanks, I will," Torch replied.

For now, he was going to go back to the station and run some background checks on Hal Halsworth. No one at the University had given him much to work with, so he decided to give up on that.

CHAPTER TEN

Charlie Malloy was one of Mathew Halsworth's most trusted associates, and the woman he had talked with about tutoring Hal. She hated young Hal, even though she hadn't been around him a lot. As far as she was concerned, he was arrogant, selfish and downright mean. But her professional relationship with his father came first, and so she had relented, and against her better judgment, agreed to work with Hal.

Charlene, or Charlie as she preferred, was one of the most intelligent women Mathew Sr. had ever met, and a fierce litigator in the courtroom. She lost very few cases, because she always knew what she was doing, and where she was going. Very few lawyers did the preparation she did before going into battle.

She had just celebrated her forty-fifth birthday last week, but to look at her, no one would guess her to be over forty. Maybe even in her late thirties. She had taken care of her body as well as she took care of her mind. Charlie also took care of Hal's father, and had been Mathew Senior's lover for over ten years. Her intentions were not to screw her way to the top—she didn't need to—she was an accomplished lawyer in her own right. At first, she had been somewhat fond of the old man, and their lovemaking was consensual, but things were changing there. She was not so sure, anymore, that he wasn't using her in more ways than one.

She had talked to young Hal on Saturday morning, and she was going to meet with him on Monday at his apartment.

It was shortly after six when Torch pulled back into the Quick Stop on 394 and Penn. The weather was turning brutally cold again. Right now, the temperature hovered in the ten below zero range, with about a twenty mile an hour wind out of the west-northwest. He pulled his collar up and hunched down inside his warm coat, like a turtle seeking the protection of his shell, as he left the warmth of the car and headed inside.

The manager he wanted to see was behind the cash register, talking to a young girl he appeared to be training in. He recognized Torch and greeted him warmly in his Arabic accent.

"Ah, my friend, the policeman. Yes, they told me you had called. Let's go back here and we can talk." He led Torch back to his office and closed the door behind the two of them.

"Can I get you some coffee?"

"No, but thanks, anyway. I drank so much coffee today that I'm wired for two twenty right now."

The manager laughed, even though his look said he had no idea what that meant.

"The reason I'm here has to do with that bundle of clothing we talked about earlier...that was in your dumpster."

The manager had a question on his face for a second, and then laughing, said, "Yes, the clothing the boy found. He is no longer working here. I had to let him go because I felt that I could no longer trust him, you know."

"I wish you hadn't done that," said Torch but then, seeing he was getting into something he shouldn't be in, waved his hand and said, "That's not the reason I'm here, and I don't need to see him."

"Look, we established that those clothes were dumped in that trashcan sometime after noon on Christmas Day. Darren said he had emptied the cans that morning. So using that timeframe, I was wondering about something. Does your cash register show receipts? The one that shows all of your transactions for the day—does it have credit card numbers on it?"

The manager was still looking at him with a blank look. He didn't know what Torch wanted.

"Look, you have a master receipt tape for each day, do you not?"

"Yes. Yes, we do."

"What information is on that tape?"

The manager got up and went to a file cabinet and dug through it. "That would be the twenty-fifth, right?"

"No," Torch said. "The twenty-fourth."

He turned around, smiling; and holding a sheet of paper that had a cash register tape about three feet long folded up, and stapled to it, handed it to Torch.

Torch got up and walked to a table in the office that was full of papers. He pushed things around until the front of the table was clear, and then spread the tape out.

The tape appeared to record the time, the amount, the item, and cash or charge. If it was charge, it also listed the card by name, such as Master Card or Visa, but no numbers. Torch studied the tape until he found only the transactions for that afternoon, and drew a line on it with his pen. "I need this part of your tape for a while." He pointed to the part on the tape where he had drawn the line. "You will get it back, I promise you."

The manager smiled and shrugged his shoulders. He reached over, tore the tape in two, and handed Torch the part he wanted.

"Ok," he said.

"Thanks," Torch replied. "It's a shot in the dark, but I need to start somewhere."

Hal had stayed home the rest of the day. He still couldn't keep anything down that he had eaten, and he needed to think about just staying home tonight. Right now, the thought of more booze was revolting.

The meeting with Torch had troubled him somewhat. He could understand, with his phone number being on her phone, why they would question him. The thing that bothered him the most, though, was Torch talking to Lamont. He had wanted to ask him, in the worst possible way, what Lamont had said, but he was also smart enough to know that would only feed Torch's curiosity. The person he needed to ask that question of was Lamont.

His parents' home was not a good place for him to be right now, and for a while, he needed to stay as far away from his father as possible.

He would call his mother and ask what their plans were for tonight. Hell, it was New Year's Eve. They'd never been home on a New Year's Eve that he could remember.

"Mom…hi. Hal here." He was lying on the couch, trying to do something with his throbbing headache. "Say, I wondered if you guys were going out tonight or what? I thought I might stop by for a while if I could."

"We are going downtown to your father's work tonight, Hal. They're having a small party for all of the people in the firm. They're not only celebrating the New Year, they are celebrating the merger, also. You're welcome, I'm sure, but it will be a black tie."

What merger? Hal thought. *He won't be happy until he owns every damn law office in town.*

"No, that's all right, Mom. I do have some plans of my own for later in the evening, but maybe I will come out anyway, and stay the night. We can have breakfast tomorrow."

"That would be nice, Mathew. Your father would like that, too. Did you talk to Charlie?"

"He told you about that, huh?"

"Why shouldn't I know, Mathew?"

"No…no, you should. I didn't mean it like that. He makes a big thing out of everything."

"He just cares about you, Mathew."

No, Mom, he cares about his reputation and his glorious legacy. He doesn't give a shit about you or me. He wanted to say it so bad, but held his tongue.

"I've got to go, Mom."

"Bye, Mathew."

By the time Torch got back to the office, the background checks he had asked for, on Mathew Halsworth, were on his desk. Disappointingly, it was mostly the kind of thing that shows up on a lot of kids' records, except for one thing. In nineteen eighty nine, he had been accused of rape and terroristic threats, by a seventeen year old girl from Minnetonka. Her father had filed the charges that were later dropped. There was no explanation as to why they were dropped, but there must have been some kind of an out-of-court settlement. Juvenile records were hard to access without a judge approving it, and although he had been eighteen, she was not. This investigation had not risen to that level yet.

The only other things were a rash of speeding tickets and one charge of unlawful assembly at the University last year.

He turned his attention to the cash register tape. It would be possible to follow up on the charge cards that had been used on that Sunday, and there were a lot of them. But, if he eliminated all of the ones that were not for gasoline, that would cut it down. If he eliminated all the ones for over twenty gallons, that were most likely trucks, that, too, would help the chore. Whoever had put those clothes in the trash, while parked there at the pumps, must have bought gasoline.

After eliminating the ones that were for groceries and other items, he really only had four credit companies. Visa, Discovery, Master Card and Amoco. He would draft a letter to these companies, asking if they had a Mathew Halsworth, at such and such an address, as one of their members. They probably wouldn't give him numbers, but he felt they could, and would, acknowledge that he was a member.

Torch lit a cigarette, spun his chair around and typed out the letter on Police Department stationary.

Walking out in the office, he gave the letter to Amy Bridges, who was the night secretary.

"Hey, beautiful, I want you to look up the billing address for these four major credit card companies, and then fax them this letter."

Amy smiled. She was pretty, but she knew Torch and his mannerisms. Seriously, he was all business. "At last, something to do," she said.

"It has been dead around homicide, hasn't it? I've spent most of my time this week working a missing person report."

"You have a way with words, Torch." She looked up from her desk, smiling. "How soon do you need this?"

"A little while ago, kid. For now, I am going home, and if anything comes up they can page me...okay?"

"Happy New Year, Torch."

"Happy New Year, Doll."

When Hal got out to the house, the doors were locked and no one was home, but walking around to the back, he did see the lights on in Lamont's apartment.

Lamont's apartment was the upper level of one end of the garage. Below it was storage for lawn tractors, tools and pool chemicals. Actually, it was like a two-story small house, attached to a four-car garage. It had an outside set of stairs that went up to the entrance on the upper level and then, inside, there was another set of stairs that went down into the lower level and into the garage.

Hal hesitated at the stairway for a moment, thinking about what he was going to say, and then started up to the landing. He looked through the window and could see the back of Lamont's head as he sat in a recliner watching television. His hand, on the end table next to him, encircled a glass half-full of whiskey.

When Hal knocked on the door, the hand and the glass magically disappeared somewhere down in front of the chair, and Lamont rose and came to the door.

"Why, Master Hal, what brings you out on a night like this? Come on in. Too damn cold to be outside. Happy New Year to you."

Hal stepped inside the door. He hadn't been up here for a long time, and Lamont had made a lot of changes. At one time, this had been a recreation area for him and his brother and sister when he was growing up. He'd lost his virginity up here when he was fourteen, and so did the neighbor girl.

"Lamont, I left my house keys at my apartment and I need to get in. How've you been? And yes, Happy New Year."

Lamont smiled. *Why would this little bastard be caring how I been. He never gave a rat's ass about me before.*

"I'm fine, Hal, and the door by the pool is open. I just came from there."

"Oh, thanks. I never even tried it. Say Lamont, the police called me today and asked me some questions about a car wreck I was in. Not my car, my buddy's. The officer mentioned he had tried to find me here. Did you see him?"

"Yes, sir, I did." Lamont walked into his bedroom and came out with Torch's business card. "Man told me to give you this and have you get ahold of him, but I guess you already did that."

"Thanks. Did he have any other questions while he was here?"

"Nope. Just said to give you the card."

Hal stared at the card in his hand. "Okay. Well, thanks, Lamont. Sorry to disturb you. I have to get some stuff out of the house. If you see my mother tomorrow, tell her I stopped in but couldn't stay, and again, Happy New Year."

"You too, Master Hal."

Lamont stood to the side of the door and watched Hal disappear down the stairs, and through the back door of the poolroom.

He scratched his head, as he thought. *Hal had something else on his mind; yes he did, the little bastard. Something is going on here that don't pass the stink test, and old Lamont is going to find out what.*

He walked back to his chair and fell into it, retrieving his drink that he had set down. Lamont took a long swallow and wiped his mouth with the back of his hand. He should call Clarice and see if she liked the bracelet and watch.

Melinda Halsworth and her husband had parted company shortly after they had arrived at the party, which was being held in the ballroom on the first floor of the Newman Building, which was soon to be renamed the Halsworth Building.

She had found some old friends and was talking nonstop about some charity auction that was coming up, and how much work it had been to get everything organized.

Mathew had told her he had to go upstairs for a few minutes to take care of some business, and he would be right back. Right now, his only business included sexually abusing Charlie who sat, or more accurately, lay on his desk on her back, one foot in each drawn-out drawer on either side of him. She was leaning back on her hands, while Mathew, standing behind the desk and between her legs, engaged in nothing more than consensual rape, his pants and shorts around his ankles. His tempo was increasing and his face was cherry red. The erotic sight in front of him, and the thought of how she was being totally submissive to him, behaving like an animal showing its soft belly in a sign of defeat, was fueling his passion more than the sex act itself. He was the boss, always, in more ways than one. He gasped and suddenly collapsed, spent, on top of her, while Charlie, with her hands gripping his butt cheeks, tried to pull him closer to her if that was possible, or maybe she was simply trying to make him stop.

For Charlie, it was just another duty she had to fulfill, and now she rubbed his back and kissed his neck. "Happy New Year, Mathew," she whispered in his ear. Mathew separated himself from her and fell back into his desk chair, wiping the sweat from his brow, and then handed her the handkerchief. Slowly, he reached down and pulled his clothes back up.

Charlie rearranged her clothing and then, sliding off his desk, pulled her hose back on and reached for her purse on the corner of the desk. Walking across his spacious office, Charlie disappeared in the bathroom to freshen up. Mathew had not said one word since the episode started, but he seldom did.

When she came out, Mathew was standing in front of the window, looking over the Minneapolis skyline. He was feeling more powerful than he had ever felt in his life.

Charlie stood beside him and took his hand in hers. "What are you thinking?" she said.

"Just what a good year it has been and how, someday, I am really going to reward you for being such a good partner."

"Law partner?" she said, smiling."

He smiled back at her. "That, too, my dear. That, too."

CHAPTER ELEVEN

Torch pulled his car into the garage, shut off the engine, and sat there for a moment. It was a New Year, and with the New Year came new hope for a better life. He needed to work hard at making that happen for him and Evelyn. He was feeling bad about what had happened this afternoon. She was sick and he needed to do something about that.

Torch walked to the back door and looked in before he turned the knob. The kitchen was dark, but he could make out her outline on the couch in the living room. The only light was coming from the television set. Torch threw his coat and hat on the chair and went to the couch and sat down on the edge beside her.

Evelyn had thrown up on herself and was passed out. An empty gin bottle and glass lay on the floor. Torch stripped her nightgown from her, carried her into the bathroom, and laid her in the tub. Slowly, he filled the tub with warm water and Evelyn moaned and retched again, but there was nothing in her. She had abused herself for so long that her ribs were showing, and her hip bones protruded like a couple of hat racks. There was nothing sensual about her emaciated body.

He got a bar of soap and a washcloth, and kneeling beside the tub, Torch lovingly washed her body from one end to the other. His once pretty wife looked yellow and jaundiced, and her skin had a dry, flaky feel to it. The thought came to him that she looked like an Auschwitz survivor. Evelyn had lost so much weight, her once firm full breasts were all but gone, and now two folds of skin hung loosely were they had once been. Her pubis bone jutted out from the wasted body. She was skin and bones—nothing more.

Washed, Torch took her in and laid her on the bed, still unmade from last night. He put on new pajamas that he had gotten her for Christmas, and brushed out her thinning hair. Evelyn still gave no indication she was aware he was even there.

Torch lay down beside her for a while and held her; his tears mixing with her wet hair. There had been times he had been so fed up with her drinking that he almost wished she would go away. Now, he felt so guilty about those thoughts. Eventually, he sat up and turned on the bedside lamp. Taking the phone book out of the drawer, slowly he dialed the phone, while all the while, his other hand stroked her hair.

"Metro Ambulance," the dispatcher answered.

"Yes, I need an ambulance to 8809 Stinson. It's not an emergency."

He listened for a moment, and then said, "The ambulance is for my wife. She needs to go to a treatment center for alcoholism. I'm her husband, and I'm committing her."

Hal returned to his apartment for a while, and then, restless and feeling better, he drove over to the party he had planned on attending. His fears had eased somewhat, after talking to Lamont. He felt that Lamont had accepted his reasons for the clothing being in his car, and he really couldn't see him giving much of a shit about it, anyway. As long as he had his bottle, he was happy.

He had parked a block away, but even so, the noise from the party could be heard from the moment he got out of his car.

One of the fraternity brothers was sitting by the front door, checking on guests coming and going, but he was so drunk himself it was kind of a futile effort.

Hal brushed by him and went inside.

"Hi, Hal." A girl he didn't know was hanging on him before he had gone three feet.

"Hi." said Hal. "Look, I need to find someone, so let's get together later, okay?"

Hal turned and went back outside. This, he had suddenly realized, was the same house he had raped Stacie in, and he was not comfortable being here.

He drove back to his apartment and went to bed.

Stacie's body had gone under the Washington Avenue Bridge that night at about midnight. It picked up speed now as it reached St. Anthony Falls, and then emerging from the turbulence there, it continued on its trip downstream.

It had passed under the stone arch bridge, oblivious to the partygoers walking above, and still floated down the middle of the river. There were other bridges to pass under at Franklin Avenue, Lake Street and 35W. Couples were walking on the bike paths along the shore, some with their dogs, but the body floating amongst the ice chunks went unnoticed. It passed under the Ford Parkway Bridge about five a.m.

A strong current, that now took it closer to the eastern shore of the river, was pulling the body and it was now closing in on the Ford Dam. At about six a.m., it hit the dam, hesitated for a moment, and then spilled over the concrete and landed in the white water below. For a while, the water spilling over the dam kept the body submerged almost on the bottom, but slowly, it came back to the top. It had lost a lot of its buoyancy and it would not float much longer.

A whirlpool had formed next to the dam, and the yellow brick building fronting the river. It housed the electrical generators that had supplied power, for so long, to the automobile manufacturing plant owned by the Ford Motor Company.

Slowly, in a never-ending circle, the body turned, disappearing when it was close to the spiraling water, and reappearing on the far side of the circle. As long as the water rotated in this whirlpool it could go no farther.

Torch returned home from the hospital at about three a.m. Evelyn had awakened shortly after they got her to the hospital, and they gave her a sedative to calm her down for a while. The plan was for her to stay there, for only a day or two, and then to be admitted to Hazeltown Treatment Center for therapy. As soon as she had gone back to sleep, Torch left, telling the nurses he would be back in the morning. He was exhausted.

Sixteen-year old Tory Snyder stood, in the early morning light, on the east bank of the river. From his home in Highland Park, he had taken his dog out for a walk. It was always so nice and peaceful down here by the riverbank, and in the warmer months he would play fetch with his black lab, throwing a stick in the river.

There was fog coming off the river from the warm power plant discharge, so you couldn't see very well out over the water. Every so often, the wind would blow just right, and then he could see the water crashing over the spillway. Chunks of ice and debris were circling in the whirlpool that had formed by the bank. There was part of a log and some Styrofoam insulation that had come around a couple of times. He picked up a rock and threw it at the insulation but he missed. Maybe he would get it the next time around.

Suddenly, something almost totally submerged, came into view. It looked like part of an old air mattress or some kind of blow-up toy. He reached for another rock to throw at it. His dog, Max, saw it too, and started barking at it. Tory held Max's leash tightly to keep him from going in after it. It was then that he saw Max testing the air, and he knew that Max had not just seen something, he had smelled something.

A puff of wind cleared the vapors for a moment, and just then the body rocked in the current, and Tory ran for the guardhouse at the power plant. It was a corpse!

Kyle Stevens had worked for Ford for thirty years, and had watched them remove many bodies from that same whirlpool.

"There's a body in the river!" Tory nearly shouted the words at Kyle.

"Where?" Kyle asked.

"In the whirlpool."

He made Tory sit down in the guard shack while he walked down to the riverbank. He had to make sure. Once he had called authorities, and it was just an old half-inflated raft floating around. They had not been too happy with him.

The fog had come back, and Kyle squinted out over the water. He knew where to look; they always ended up in the same place. A couple of times he had even pulled them up in shallow water, but the water was too damn cold for that today.

After a couple of minutes, he was thinking that Tory was seeing things, and then it appeared out of the fog. He reached for his radio and asked the other guards to call the Fire Department. They definitely had a floater.

Going back to the guardhouse, he told Tory. "It was just like you said, pal. We called the Fire Department. They will bring a boat and go out there. You don't need to hang around if you don't want to; it's nothing to see, believe me."

Tory nodded his head yes, and grabbing Max, was out the door. He walked to the top of the bank and waited. Gruesome or not, he wanted to see it.

The call came into Station Six, one of three fire stations that had a boat. As many times as they had recovered bodies from the river, it was never a task they liked. Often, the bodies were decomposed, and the smell could be as bad as the sight. But, with all firefighters' duties, it went with the territory.

They put their boat in at a landing about a mile downstream, and worked their way back up the river. Three men were in the boat, and the front two wore cold weather wet suits, in case they had to go in the river. The other man was the operator, and he wore his turnout gear.

Tory heard the boat before he saw it, and then it appeared around a bend. He could see Kyle standing on the bank waiting for them. The boat stayed close to the shoreline, and proceeded cautiously in the treacherous current, with chunks of ice clunking against the hull.

The morning sun had burned off the haze over the river and right now, Tory could make out the body each time it circled. With Kyle pointing, the fire fighters saw it right away. They reached out with a short pole, with a hook on the end, and pulled it alongside of the boat. A tarp, that had weights and ropes tied on one side, was lowered alongside of the boat and then pulled up on the other side of the body. Shortly after that, the whole thing was lifted into the boat. It had taken less than five minutes. Stacie's trip was over.

The police department had been notified by the fire department about the recovery, and they would be sending someone down to the Coroner's Office to try and make identification. This was a routine procedure. Many of the bodies that were pulled out of the river were suicides. They kept a list of people who went missing throughout the year. Right now, the list included four people.

A despondent black woman, in her mid-fifties, had jumped last September, and two homeless men, who were thought to have fallen in the river in early December. Several suburban departments also had lists, and they would be checking those, too.

The detective who was sent down was Theresa Cross, Torch's partner in Homicide. It was a little after ten a.m. when she walked into the Coroner's Office. She had a headache from celebrating last night, and too little sleep. She was also nauseous from morning sickness.

The information they had given Theresa on the phone was that the body was that of a white female; probably under thirty years of age. Stacie was the only person they knew of that fit that description, but they had to be sure.

She knew Torch had worked on this case and had a burning desire to solve it, but she wasn't going to call him until she knew for sure. She had come to the Coroner's Office with Stacie's picture and description. The only identification mark the police knew about was a missing toe, from a lawn mower accident when she was twelve. Melody had told them that.

She had been here many times before, and every time she had dreaded it. Her father, also a Minneapolis cop, had always told her that the dead gave you nothing to worry about; it was the living you had to watch out for.

The Coroner's Office hadn't done anything with the body, except unbag it and put it in a refrigerated drawer. An autopsy would be scheduled for tomorrow morning.

The body was pulled out, and Theresa looked first at the feet. The little toe was missing on the left foot. That checked out. Then the sheet was pulled back and she looked at the face. Although the body had started to decompose, the face was in remarkably good shape. She looked from the face to the picture she held in her hand. There was no doubt it was Stacie.

Theresa went to the phone in the Coroner's Office and dialed Torch's number.

"Hey, out of bed, you lazy ass. You work one night shift stint and then you sleep all of the next day."

"Had a bad night," Torch responded. *Had to put Evelyn in the hospital.* "What you got, kid?"

"Torch, Stacie Morrison's body showed up this morning."

95

"Where?"

"In the river, washed up at the Ford Dam."

Torch was quiet for a second, while he thought about his next move.

"Look, kid. I need to go over to the hospital this morning and be with Evelyn for a while. Are you sure it's her?"

"It's her, Torch. The coroner is going to call her dentist just to make sure and have him fax her charts down, but it's just a formality. What's up with Evelyn?"

"Same old shit, kid, but it's time to put a stop to it so I'm putting her in treatment this afternoon."

"I'm sorry, Torch. Look, if you want I can call Stacie's folks as soon as the coroner is positive."

"How did you find her dentist?"

"We lucked out, Torch. There is only one in the small town she came from, and we told him to hold his tongue for now."

"Let me drive out there, kid. I want to tell them. Tell Wes Blackstrom, in Missing Persons, what you have so he can quit looking. This is our case now. Thanks for the call, kid." Torch sat in the kitchen staring at the phone. *What was he going to tell her family? Oh well, he had time to think about that on the drive over. Right now he had better get cleaned up and head for the hospital.*

CHAPTER TWELVE

The drive over to Wisconsin was a quiet one, even though Theresa had elected to go along with Torch to break the news. They took I-94 into St. Paul and then headed east over the St. Croix River, through the small town of Hudson. From there, it was about sixty miles to Stacie's hometown. Torch had called ahead, but only to ask if they were going to be home. Instinctively, they knew why he was coming. They already felt the worst had happened.

For Oscar and Thelma, the news was going to be devastating, but their faith would see them through it. Todd, however, would be another story.

The long ride over gave the two partners time to talk and socialize a little, although it was subdued. It didn't seem to be a time to talk business. They talked about Evelyn and her problems. They talked about Theresa's baby that was due. They talked about everything except Stacie, but right now, there was no hiding it that she was first and foremost in both their thoughts.

The car was warm, and soon Theresa was nodding off. It had been a long day for her, especially with being so far along in her pregnancy.

Torch tried to rehearse what he was going to say to the Morrison's, but many years in homicide told him that the best way was just to say it. There were no right words, and there was no way to color it. Life, out here in the country, seemed so simple from life in the big city. Oh, they had a bad ass or two around, but there was nowhere for them to hide, so everybody knew about them.

They passed through the town, and it looked almost deserted. Just a few kids walking home from school, throwing snowballs at each other. Then he turned onto the tar road that led out to the farm. Torch had been here once before, so he thought he remembered the way, but he made one wrong turn and then, realizing his mistake, he quickly backtracked.

Stopping momentarily, at the end of the driveway going up to the farm, woke Theresa up. Like a typical woman, she reached for her purse and mirror, and took care of her face.

"Shit, Torch, I am getting more damn wrinkles than I can hide."

"Comes from too much sex," Torch quipped. Theresa smiled, but didn't answer him.

Oscar was just coming up from the barn with Todd, when the two cops pulled into the yard. The two men, with pails and towels in their hands, stood watching the brown sedan come into their yard. They had just finished the evening milking.

When Torch got out of the car, Oscar recognized him, saying to Todd, "I wonder what they want?" His heart skipped a beat when he saw a female getting out of the other side. For a second his old eyes, in the waning daylight, thought it was Stacie, and then Theresa walked around the car and stood next to Torch.

"Oscar, how are you?" Torch shook his hand, while Todd stood about ten feet away. *Something bad had happened, he just knew it.*

"Stacie. Did you find her? Is she all right?" Oscar's eyes were searching Torch's face for answers.

"Oscar, this is my partner, Theresa Cross. Oscar looked at Theresa, but didn't acknowledge her. "Let's go inside where we can talk."

The kitchen was dark, even though a pot was bubbling on the stove. Oscar flipped on the lights and called for Thelma. When Thelma walked into the room and saw Torch and Theresa, she put her hand to her mouth, and a soft moan came from her throat. She, too, knew this was not a social call.

They all sat down around the kitchen table except for Todd, who stood in the doorway going into the living room. "Todd, why don't you sit down with the rest of us?" Torch said, but Todd ignored him. He was still clutching the galvanized pail, filled with wet towels, to his chest.

Torch wasted no time. "I have some very bad news," he said. "This morning, Stacie's body was found in the Mississippi River. It appears that she has been dead for some time. Tomorrow, the coroner will be conducting an autopsy to determine why she died."

At the word, autopsy, Thelma sobbed out loud and collapsed on the tabletop. Theresa left her chair to try and comfort the grief-stricken woman. Oscar was crying, too, but silently, the tears rolling down his weathered old cheeks. Todd stormed from the house. Through the window, Torch saw him throw the pail that he had been holding, clear across the yard, and then run to the barn, disappearing from sight.

"I can't tell you how sorry we are, Oscar and Thelma, but I promise you this. I will not rest until we find out what happened to her." Theresa was now sitting next to Thelma, holding her and crying with her.

"I know how difficult it is to lose a child," Torch continued. "I lost a daughter once, too." For a second, his voice cracked, and he was at a loss for more words.

Theresa, who hadn't said a word since they arrived, except "hi" to Oscar, wiped her eyes, and took Oscar's hand in hers. She was also still holding Thelma's hand. "We will call you as soon as we can release Stacie's body, so you can bring her home. It should only be a day or so. Is there someone we can call to be with you for a while; a friend or relative or clergy?"

"We'll be all right," Oscar said. Then he stood, walked around the table and took Thelma in his arms. They stood there, crying, and clinging to each other.

Torch's look to Theresa said it was time to leave, and they stood silently. "We will be in frequent touch with you," Torch said. "Again, we are so sorry."

Neither Oscar nor Thelma looked up. They wanted to be alone in their grief.

Outside, it was now completely dark. The barn lights were the only sign of life and Torch said to Theresa, "Hang on a second." He walked the hundred yards to the barn. Torch did not have to look far; Todd was lying in a pile of straw, just inside the door. He sat down in the straw and took the grieving young man's hands in his.

"Todd, I am so sorry for your loss. I just want you to know that I will find the truth, and you and your folks will be the first to know what happened.

You need to go back to the house and be with your parents, Todd. They have never needed you more than they need you right now, and whether you realize it or not, you also need them, son."

Somewhere in the barn, a calf bawled, and the sound of cattle eating and moving in their stanchions could be heard. A cat sat in front of them, licking her paws and cleaning her face. Torch had never been in a barn that he could remember, but it seemed like a quiet and peaceful place.

Todd stood up and Torch took his hand. They walked back to the house, not saying a word. At the house, Torch squeezed Todd's shoulder and Todd said, "Thanks," and went inside.

As soon as they had left the driveway, and were on the gravel road, Torch looked at Theresa and said, "This is the worst part of this job. Now I need to find the answers they need." Theresa nodded her head in agreement.

"I just hope those people don't let what happened to me and Evelyn, when Susan was killed, happen to them."

"Tell me about Susan, Torch. I know what happened to her, but you've never told me what Susan was like."

"She was my life, kid. She was just my whole life, and right now is not a good time to talk about it. But someday I will." Torch reached over and touched her arm. Theresa was disappointed that he didn't want to talk, but she didn't press the issue. He was right, it was a bad time.

For now, Torch would have to wait for tests and toxicology reports to come back. The coroner had promised him something by Wednesday. Torch was sure in his mind of one thing—even without the reports—Stacie had been murdered.

He had tomorrow off, and he was going to spend the day with Evelyn. So far, things had gone fairly well. At least she wasn't mad at him anymore.

He went with Wes to Whitey's for lunch, and this time he had the meatloaf. If he got the shits, he got the shits. He needed something hot and homey to eat.

It had been slow in Homicide. A couple of the guys were working on cold cases and two others were on vacation. That left any new business for him and Theresa. After dropping Wes off at the office, Torch decided to take a walk to think about all the things that were cluttering up his life right now. His mind seemed to jump from one subject to the next, as if it was in a fight with itself as to what was most important to tackle first. But for now, he was going to drive back over to the University.

He drove over to the University, thinking about what he was going to ask when he arrived. The campus appeared to be somewhat deserted, and what students he did see were scurrying from place to place to get out of the cold. Torch continued over to Stacie's apartment building, parking in a no-parking zone, and putting his visor, with his police identification on it, down. The building manager hadn't given him much time to talk with her the other day and he hoped she had more time now.

It was bitterly cold out, with a stiff north wind, and Torch pulled his head back in his collar as he headed up to the building, carefully avoiding the icy spots on the sidewalk. It felt good to get in the lobby and out of the wind. He stamped the snow off his feet, and punched the button for the manager. Somewhere in the building, two people were laughing hysterically, and it was getting louder. The two women, who were the perpetrators of the laughter, suddenly appeared around the corner, stopping the laughter long enough to brush by Torch and go outside. Torch grabbed the door before it locked and walked in to the narrow corridor and over to the manager's door.

She was just opening the door when he raised his hand to knock. He had his badge in his hand, and flashed it in her face before anybody said anything. She didn't seem to be surprised.

"I'm Torch Brennan, from Minneapolis Police. I wondered if we could talk a bit about Stacie Morrison."

"Sure, come in. I saw the papers today and wondered when you guys would be back. By the way, I'm Carla."

"Glad to meet you, Carla." Torch motioned to the table behind her. "Can we sit down for a minute? I need to write while I talk."

"Sure, I'm sorry, please sit. Can I get you a cup of coffee or pop?"

"Coffee would be great." Torch had slipped off his shoes and hung his overcoat around the chair back before sitting down. He took out a small yellow pad and retrieved his pen from his shirt pocket.

"This has been a frustrating case for us, Carla, because before yesterday, we didn't know if we were dealing with a missing person or something worse. That, and the fact that everybody was gone for Christmas, and we had no one to talk with, complicated things a lot. Now that the truth is out, we need to find some answers and fast. How well did you know Stacie?"

Carla set his coffee in front of him, and sat down across the table. "I'm not sure anyone knew Stacie very well. She kept very much to herself. She was a small town girl, out of her element here in the big city. But she did live here for three years, so yes, we talked from time to time."

Carla wiped her eyes. "She was just a good kid that didn't deserve getting hurt like this."

"Knowing what you did about her, do you think she could have hurt herself?"

There was still a question of suicide, which Torch did not believe she had done, but it had to be answered.

"Did she kill herself? No, no way. Do you mind if I smoke?"

"Not at all, if I can join you." Torch found his lighter and lit both of their cigarettes.

Carla blew a long stream of smoke toward the ceiling; her head slightly tilted back, her eyes closed, thinking. "You know, late one night, a couple of months ago, I heard some commotion out in the hallway. When I opened the door, it was Stacie with some guy I had never seen before, and he was dropping her off. She seemed to be very intoxicated, which was out of character for her. I guess that's why I remembered it."

"Did you get a good look at the guy?"

"Not really, but I do know he drove a fancy sports car, because I saw him drive away."

"Do you remember the make or model?" Torch was writing as he talked.

"No, I'm not much on cars and it was dark outside."

"Well, it might or might not be relevant. Let's talk about her roommate. Does she have any boyfriends that you know of?"

Carla put another cigarette in her mouth, stubbing out the other one, that had burned down, in the ashtray. Torch reached across and lit it.

"Melody is a carbon copy of Stacie; quiet and to herself. I never saw her with a boy. Some kids in the building thought they were lesbians because they spent so much time together and stayed away from the boys."

"That's not a possibility?"

"No. No way. Stacie did like boys; she just didn't want a commitment with anyone. She went to a party now and then. She was just shy and cautious."

"I spoke with Melody once. She did seem to be a good kid." Torch thought he would throw that out there, but it brought no further comment from Carla.

"Ever hear about a boy named Bruce Baldwin? We talked with him, and he seemed to know Stacie pretty good."

"Everybody knows Bruce. Yes, they studied together a lot. They would always go to the recreation room and sit and talk. I would be the most surprised person in the world if Bruce had anything to do with this."

Torch was running out of questions, and he could hear a baby crying in the next room. "I'd better go," he said. "I want to thank you for being so cooperative. You've been a great help." He stood, and reaching across the table, shook her hand. He reached in his pocket and gave her a card. "Call me if you hear anything or remember anything that you might think important."

"I will," she said. He drove around the block and passed Hal's building once more. Then he went into the alley behind the building, where the cars parked. In front of Hal's apartment door was a yellow Camaro without plates. It had a yellow registration slip in the back window, and Torch stopped and went over to read it. It was registered to Hal, and had been issued the day Stacie disappeared. He couldn't have had it two months ago.

Torch drove back by way of the Washington Avenue Bridge. He stopped a block before the bridge, parked in a drugstore parking lot, and walked along the walkway to the middle of the bridge. The cold wind was brutal, but he had to check something out. The river below looked as cold and forbidding as a river could. Fog, from the warmer water meeting the frigid air, hung over the surface and chunks of ice were floating everywhere. The east shore was frozen for several yards, about twenty feet out, but the barges had kept the rest of it open.

This was a busy highway. The chance of anyone being able to carry a body to the railing, and then throw it in the river, was remote, and you would have had to park in the traffic lane while you did it. He could not imagine anyone, in his or her right mind, even trying. But then, whoever did this was not in their right mind, or were they?

Torch concluded that the body, if it was dumped in the river, had to have been put in elsewhere. Cold and confused, he drove back to the office.

There were several things waiting for him when he got back. First of all, there was a message to call Evelyn's doctor as soon as possible. There was also another message to call the Coroner's Office, and there was a fax waiting for him from Amoco credit. It had been doubled over and stapled and Torch tore it open, eager to read what they had to say.

It acknowledged that Mathew Halsworth Senior did have an account with their firm, and had purchased a gasoline card in the name of Mathew Halsworth Junior on December ninth of last year, for the sum of one thousand dollars. It also gave him some information that he didn't think they would have received without a court order. It was a pleasant surprise, indeed.

The card been used three times since the first of the year, and the first time had been at the Quick Stop on Penn and 394. The date it had been used, was December 25th of last year.

It didn't prove anything, except that Hal had been there, but it was another piece of the puzzle. He dialed Evelyn's doctor and was told to leave a message. "This is Torch Brennan, and I will be there in about an hour," Torch said, looking at his watch while hanging up.

His call to Dr. Collin Lang, the County Coroner, went right through and the receptionist said, "Hang on, Torch, and I will page him. He really does want to talk to you."

Stacie's autopsy had been scheduled for early this morning, so they should be done by now. Sometimes, when they found evidence that could be useful in an investigation, they would call it over, even before the final report was issued.

"Torch, you old dog. I thought they fired you a while back."

Torch laughed. "Hey, how's my favorite butcher."

Collin laughed at his remark, but then his voice took on a more serious tone.

"That coed from the University that they brought in yesterday? Well, I got a few things for you. The toxicology tests will take a couple of days yet, except for one we already identified, but let me back up a second."

Her identity was confirmed, by her dental records, and by her older brother, who came down this morning and took a look. That was tough on him."

"I can imagine," Torch said.

"She had been in the water about nine to ten days, as best we could tell. The cold water in the winter makes it more difficult to judge when death did take place. Most bodies, lying in cold water like that, would still be lying on the bottom, but there are a couple of things that helped this one float sooner.

First, she was nude so there was no wet clothing to hold her down, and second, her last meal seemed to be something that gassed up in a hurry. Her bowel was empty also, so she was traveling light. Small girl like that was not that far away from being buoyant when she was alive." The doctor seemed to be thinking as he was talking, and he hesitated for a moment before going on. "Looking at the tears in the skin and flesh on the back, I would also say she must have floated around under the ice for a few days."

This was interesting, Torch thought.

"Torch, she was six weeks pregnant. I don't know if she was sexually assaulted, or not. We weren't able to determine that because of the water washing things away. I will say this; she had not been sexually active very long. We saved the fetal tissue and will be doing some more tests on it."

"Tell me this Doc...can you determine who the father is from that fetus?"

"Well, if you're talking a DNA paternity test here, right now I would say no. That science is not that advanced yet, but it's coming soon. We would need your suspect's DNA if you have one, to try and make a match, and I am not sure how difficult that would be for you to get. We can determine who was not the father by blood tests, but that isn't something that would you any good in court."

"How was she killed, Doc?"

"Well, that's interesting, Torch. She didn't drown, we know that for sure. She also had enough GHB in her system to be fatal if someone hadn't killed her first."

"GHB—the date rape drug?"

"That's right, Torch. This is the third one, in less than a year, that we've found that drug used on."

"But right now, Torch, if I was a betting man, I would say she was smothered while under the influence of the drug. I'll know for sure in a few days, and I will explain that better then. Just thought I would give you a heads-up on what I have."

"Thanks, Doc. I owe you one. Say Doc, anything on her last meal besides that it was gassy? She must have been at Whitey's, huh?" Torch laughed, ironically, at his little joke.

Colin, laughing, said, "Glad you asked about that. Best we can tell, she ate about two or three hours before she was killed. It looks like she ate

Mexican cuisine—tacos and that sort of stuff. Also, she had drunk some kind of chocolate drink that was most likely mixed with the drug. There was no alcohol involved that we could tell."

"Well, thanks again. Call me when the tests come back and I will buy you lunch."

"Not at Whitey's," chuckled the doctor.

"Chicken shit," Torch answered.

He looked at the clock on the wall. It was getting late; he'd better get to the hospital.

CHAPTER THIRTEEN

Evelyn was sitting in a soft chair, looking out the window, when Torch walked in. He had stopped to see the doctor first; to talk about a course of treatment. The doctor minced no words.

"She either quits drinking, Torch, or she will be dead in a year. The important thing is, she can't do this by herself—and you will have to be with her every step of the way. We need to get to the root of her problem, too, as to why she drinks."

"Hi, Evie." Torch wrapped his arms around her shoulders from behind, and kissed the top of her head.

She turned and looked at him. Her face was gaunt and sad. She looked much beyond her forty-six years. "Torch, you have to get me out of here, otherwise, I am going to kill myself."

"Let's take it one day at a time, Evie. I just talked to your doctor. Your liver is nearly gone. You have to stop drinking or you will, in effect, kill yourself anyway. I need you, honey—we need each other. If you can hang in there and beat this, we can have good times together again, just like we once had, kid."

Evelyn didn't answer; she just kept staring out of the window. "Give me a cigarette," she said.

"Here kid, I brought you a carton. Tomorrow I can bring you some clothes, but you have to tell me what you want."

Evelyn took the carton of cigarettes and then, turning to Torch, said, "I'll call you and let you know what I am going to do. It's my problem, Torch, not yours."

Torch didn't reply, and just then, a nurse came and told her she had to come downstairs with her.

"I'll see you tomorrow, Evie."

She looked at Torch with a bewildered look on her face, and said nothing.

As he drove home, his thoughts went from his troubles with Evelyn, back to Stacie's murder. He had a few things to look into, and then he was going to call Mathew Halsworth in for questioning. His dad was head of the biggest law firm in Minneapolis and they had butted heads before. This wasn't going to be easy.

On Monday afternoon, Hal had missed running into Torch by just a few minutes. He had walked home from his classes, and entered the parking lot, right after Torch had left. He didn't go inside but started his car and headed straight for Charlie's office.

This was going to be a lesson in pride-swallowing for both Charlie and Hal. She hated the little prick, as she referred to him, and he had no time for her, either. He had long suspected his father was poking her. His father gave him speeches about keeping it in his pants. *What a hypocrite he was, and what a conniving whore she was.*

Charlie knew that, if she wanted to be a senior partner in this firm and share other things besides Mathew Senior's carnal cravings, she had to do this.

As for Hal, his grades were at the point that, without her, he was not going to get into law school, and maybe even with her he wouldn't make it.

"We will work two hours each day, and Saturdays, when necessary. No absences and no excuses, Hal. Do you understand?" Charlie had a serious look on her face as she lectured him.

"Yes, mother," Hal replied

"You can also keep your smartass comments to yourself. Now, let's get to work." By six p.m. they had a plan, and seemed to be working together without too much tension. "Here are tomorrow's notes for your test. Let me know how you do. Or, should I say, how we do."

Hal shook his finger at Charlie. "If I can't be a smartass, teacher, neither can you." She smiled and said, "Get out of here."

As he walked out the front entrance of the Newman Building, the metal newsstand caught his eye. He walked over and looked at the front page of the morning paper.

BODY OF MISSING COED FOUND

Hal dug in his pocket for a quarter and took out the top paper. Then, as if he had second thoughts, he looked around and, seemingly alone, he took the remaining papers, too.

He walked briskly to his car in the ramp, started the engine and turned on the dome light. There wasn't a lot of substance in the article. It mentioned that the Fire Department had recovered the body from the river, but it didn't say where. It also mentioned that the County Coroner was conducting an autopsy and they would know more, later in the week, as to the cause of death.

It had Hal thinking, however. His one conversation with the police had been unnerving, to say the least. Just to know that there was a connection, from him to her, gave cause for a lot of concern. He had been over the details of that night many times in his mind, and although he knew he had made some mistakes, no one could prove he had killed her. *Piss on them—the ball is in their court* was his last passing thought, before he squealed out of the ramp and headed back to campus.

Torch sat at the kitchen table with a beer and his cigarettes. There was a smoky haze in the quaint little kitchen and he looked around at all of the knick-knacks and things that made it home. However, without Evelyn it seemed cold and empty. He blamed himself for a lot of her problems. He had not been there for her when she needed him the most, so she had taken refuge in the only comforting thing that was available to her—her one friend—her bottle of gin.

Two suitcases were on the floor next to the drawer full of her clothes. She hadn't called, so he did the best he could. He had found, and thrown away, over twenty gin bottles that she had stashed around the house and forgotten where she had put them.

His thoughts about Evelyn waning, once again he took the picture of Susan out of his billfold and sat staring at it, with tears in his eyes. Then he reached in and took Stacie's picture out, too.

Torch went out to the car and got his file on her case, and then came back in and set it on the table in front of him. *What did he really have? What did he really know for sure? He knew one thing; he needed to talk to some people at the University.* Theresa was going over tomorrow to talk with Melody. He also needed to go through Wes's notes better. He had already talked to some students and maybe there was something there that would help. Someone had to know Stacy better than what they had found out so far. Someone knew her good enough to impregnate her. Someone drugged her, and killed her, and then threw her in the river.

He had one suspect so far, if you could call him that. Mathew Halsworth Junior. Mathew was the last person Stacie had called. Mathew had been in the Quick Stop where her clothes were found. *Was he the last person to see her alive or not? Was he the reason Stacie was not alive anymore?* He needed to find out more about Mathew.

These were the two troubling questions that bothered him right now, and if he could find the answers, they would go a long way towards helping this investigation. *Who was the kid in the sports car Carla had seen? Why would anyone drink hot chocolate with Tacos, and where did she have that last hot chocolate, and with who?*

Torch picked up Stacie's picture from the table. He didn't put it back in his billfold, but stapled it to the front of the file. Only Susan belonged in his wallet and Stacie had to remain where he could see her. He went to bed.

Hal went through his apartment with a fine-tooth comb, until he was sure there was nothing that could connect him to Stacie. The only evidence he possessed that could connect him to her had been disposed of. Even the car he used was gone. He was smart enough to know that all the police needed was a hair or some spot of body fluid.

She had been pregnant, he thought. *Would they find that in an autopsy? Probably. But could they determine that the fetus was his? He would have to check on that. For now, he had to act normal and stay cool. Like he had said, the ball was in their court.*

Tomorrow he would go over to the library and do some checking on genetics.

110

Also, his buddy, Rocco, was studying to be a doctor. He could ask him. No...that was a bad idea. They might come and talk to Rocco. He would ask his brother, Gerald, who was already a doctor. Yea, that would be better. He'd already checked out Lamont and was convinced that he knew nothing.

The doctor had done a good job of talking to Evelyn, or she had had a change of heart. When Torch arrived on Tuesday morning, she was sitting in the lobby, smoking a cigarette and waiting for him.

"Hi, Evie," he said. "How you doing today?"

"What day is it, Torch?" She asked him, avoiding his question.

"Tuesday, kid. Tuesday all day today."

She gave him a slight smile. "Let's go for a walk, Torch. Can we do that?"

"Sure, baby. Where do you want to go? I got some stuff for you out in the car. I was going to bring it but I didn't..."

She waved her hand to stop him. "Leave it, Torch. You can bring it up later."

They walked down the corridor, and into a large room that looked to be a recreation area. There were pool tables and people playing cards. They walked over by the windows and Evelyn sat down, motioning for Torch to sit beside her.

"Torch, I am going to make you a deal. I will go through the treatment program here and give it a fair shake. In turn, you have to promise me you will never make me do this again. It didn't work last time, Torch, and I have my doubts that it will work again." She held her hand up to make a point. "I will try my best, I promise that."

Torch looked at her with an expression that was someplace between hurt and bewildered.

"And if it doesn't work, you will do what?"

"You won't have to deal with it, Torch. That's all I am going to say."

He was not clear what she was talking about, but he decided to drop the subject for now. "Want some coffee, Evie?"

"That would be nice, Torch."

He found a coffee machine and purchased two cups of coffee. When he returned, Evelyn was standing at the windows, looking at a vast snow-covered yard that disappeared into a spruce forest.

111

"I wish we had had more kids, Torch, don't you?"

"That would have been nice, but I really wish we had the one we lost." The minute he said it he knew he shouldn't have, but it was too late now.

Evelyn turned and looking at him, reached out and took his hand. "She's gone Torch, and I think, for the first time today, I realized it. I have to deal with that, also. You've got it worse, having to deal with that and this old drunk."

"I love this old drunk, Evie, but I don't want you to ever call yourself that again."

He stayed until dark. They played cards in the afternoon and then watched a movie on television. Evelyn was still getting some strong tranquilizers, so she fell asleep right after they ate supper. Torch brushed the hair out of her eyes, and kissed her goodnight. He was going home. He was exhausted, both physically and emotionally.

On Wednesday morning, Theresa was working with Torch, and had a few things to share with him. First of all, there had been a long interview with Melody, Stacie's roommate. Although visibly upset by her roommate and friend's death, she seemed much more cooperative and willing to talk about Stacie than she was before. Maybe it was just the fact that she was talking with a female detective that helped, but whatever the reason, they had met at the apartment and talked for a couple of hours.

Torch, in the meantime, met with the University police to see if they uncovered any leads, but it seemed that once the Minneapolis police had taken over the case, they had dropped the ball. They had their hands full with the day-to-day crimes and troubles that took place on campus.

The campus seemed to be rather quiet this morning, as he walked back out to his car. The weather was turning bitterly cold again, and Torch hurriedly unlocked the vehicle and sat inside, rubbing some warmth back into his hands. He might as well pick Theresa up and call it a day. They could go back to the office and regroup, and he also needed to call the Coroner's Office and see if the tests had shown anything else.

"You know, Torch," Theresa said, "it's pretty hard for a girl like Stacie to get herself knocked up; and no one on that campus knows anything about her having any kind of a relationship with a boy, including her best friend and roommate."

Torch rubbed the back of his neck to ease the tension that had been building all day. "What did her roommate have to say about the incident the housemother talked about? The one when Stacie was brought home, drunk, by the mysterious boy in the sports car?"

"Melody said she came home later that night, and Stacie was sleeping when she got home. She did say Stacie was upset the next day, but she didn't want to talk about it." I really think that incident, that night, ties in with something here."

"I do, too. By the way, Torch, What the hell is a housemother?"

Torch laughed. "You know what I mean. The woman who guards the front door at the apartment building."

The Coroner's Office didn't smell at all like the rest of the building. If you hadn't known better, you would have thought it was some kind of a business office. There was a sign on an inner office door that said, **Dr. Lang, Hennepin County Coroner**. Looking through the window, Torch could see him on the phone. Before the receptionist could say anything, the good doctor motioned for him to come in. The receptionist smiled, and said, "Hi."

"Place is kind of dead around here today," Torch said, and she smiled, a rather sick smile, as if to say "Haven't I heard that a few times before?"

Torch amused himself, paging through his notes, as he waited for the good doctor to get off the phone.

As he hung up the phone, he said, "Sorry about that. Sometimes this job sucks and that was one of the times." What he meant by that, Torch didn't know. He didn't elaborate.

"Bet you're here to talk about that young girl you guys drug out of the river the other day."

"Yea, I just wondered if you found out anything else."

Dr. Lang reached into a pile of manila folders, on the corner of his desk, and pulled one out, about three down from the top. "What did I tell you the other day?" he asked.

"That she didn't drown and was pregnant. Oh yes, and you found GHB in her blood."

Colin Lang turned over a few pages, and then showed Torch a photo he had taken with the body lying on her stomach. Her back was racked with cuts and tears that seemed to go deep into the flesh. There was also what looked like huge blisters that had formed under the skin. Many of them had broken open and torn flesh surrounded those.

"I think I mentioned this to you the other day, but I think that this body was under the ice for quite some time. Those cuts and tears came from the body bumping along under the ice sheet. The bottom of the ice sheet is rough and has sharp edges hanging down...especially in the river with the current. I only mention this because I would be looking for a site somewhere upstream, where I think the body was disposed of."

Torch looked at the other pictures while Dr. Lang talked about what else he had found out. The pictures didn't look anything like the picture he had on his desk of Stacie, in a better place, and on a better day. The river and decomposition had taken an awful toll on her body

"I see under 'cause of death' you have 'undecided'. Were you not able to determine one, or what?"

"I know this, Torch. There was no trauma that would indicate she was beaten, stabbed or shot. My best guess is that she was suffocated, but that's only a guess. She had enough GHB in her blood to kill her, but that wasn't what killed her. Her body never had time to absorb a lethal amount. There were marks on her neck that would indicate strangulation, but if she was in a coma from the drug, all anyone who did this would have had to do was close off her airway. Hell, they could have held a pillow over her face. She would have been defenseless."

"How far along was the pregnancy?"

Dr. Lang leaned back in his chair. "I would say about six weeks. We have the fetus in a jar of preserving fluid if you want to see it."

Torch gave him a squeamish look. "I think I will pass on that for today. Thanks, anyway."

Torch seemed puzzled. "Would you say she had been sexually active for a while or can't you tell that?"

"Well, not always, but in her case I would say she was relatively new at the game. There were still remnants of her torn hymen in her vaginal canal. They usually get removed with consistent intercourse."

"Has her body been released to her parents?"

"Just this morning."

Torch handed the folder back. There seemed only one thing to do at this point. Bring Hal Halsworth in for questioning. It was the only lead he had going. First though, he had a car dealer to talk with.

CHAPTER FOURTEEN

Midtown Chevrolet was one of the biggest new car dealers in the city, with cars and trucks—new and used—spread out over many acres. Torch parked in the visitors' lot and walked up to the gleaming glass and aluminum building. Outside the front door, a new car revolved slowly on a turntable, high in the air. A young man, wielding a broom, was cleaning snow from the cars just outside the door and didn't look too happy with his job.

There were several little glass cubicles scattered around the sales floor; most of them empty of any sales people. However, in one of the cubicles, four sales people were laughing at something someone had on his computer, but they quickly became aware of Torch approaching, and the seated one turned the screen away. Turning, they all smiled at him.

"Help you, sir?" One of the salesmen said, as he reached for Torch's hand and shook it enthusiastically.

"Well, first of all, I am not here to buy anything; I am just here to get some information. My name is Torch Brennan and I work for the Minneapolis Police Department."

At first, no one said anything, and then the salesman who had addressed him previously spoke up. "Something wrong?"

Torch ignored the question, but asked if any one of them had sold a car to Mathew Halsworth in the last month or so.

They all either shrugged their shoulders, or said, "Not that they could remember, but if he went to the sales office they could probably help him with that information." One of them pointed to an office area upstairs.

Upstairs, the lady who waited on him was about sixty years of age, and had a pair of small reading glasses—that she mostly looked over the top of—perched on the end of her nose. "The name is familiar," she said, and if Torch would bear with her for a minute, she could probably find what he needed.

She left the counter, and in just a moment was back with a folder. "Mathew Halsworth Senior did purchase a new automobile here, on the tenth of December last year. Joe Camp was the salesman," she said.

"Joe Camp here today?" Torch asked, as he tried to look at the papers she was obviously trying to shield from him.

"He should be. Let me try to page him." She was clutching the papers to her bosom while she dialed the phone.

"He will be right up. Why don't you have a seat, Mr. Brennan." She pointed to a row of chairs behind him.

Torch had barely sat down when the door opened, and an older gentleman in a gray pinstriped suit came in and walked to the counter. He said something to the lady Torch had been talking to. She pointed at Torch, who was seated behind him.

"Mr. Brennan, I am Joseph Camp and I own this company. I understand you are trying to get some information on one of our customers, and I want you to know that is not an issue we take lightly here."

Torch had been sitting while he listened to the man, but now he stood and looked him straight in the eye. "First of all, I think your secretary here, or whoever she is, neglected to tell you that I am a detective from the Minneapolis Police Department." Torch emphasized his remarks by flipping his badge holder out and dangling it a few inches from the man's face."

Camp, somewhat taken aback, stared at the badge as if he was looking at some rare piece of art, until Torch lowered it from his face. "I...I was not aware that you were...let's step into my office." Torch followed him down a narrow hall to an office with huge windows, which looked out over the large inventory of cars. He didn't sit behind his desk, but sat down beside Torch in one of the leather chairs that sat in front of the desk.

"Mr. Halsworth has bought many automobiles from us, detective, so you can understand our reluctance to get too personal with information." Camp was nervous and crossed and re-crossed his legs, picking at the crease in his trouser legs. "What kind of a detective are you?"

"If you are referring to what department do I work for, I work for homicide. If you are referring to my abilities, I think I am a damn good detective. But that is neither here nor there. I need some answers from you, and not statements about me. Now, I gather from your comments that this car was purchased in December by Mathew Senior. Am I correct?"

"Yes. That is correct."

"When did he pick the car up?"

Camp stared down at the papers in his lap. "We delivered it on the twenty fourth of December to the Halsworth estate. It was a Christmas present for his son."

Torch was counting days in his mind. Either way, the kid didn't have the car on the night that the landlady at the apartments saw Stacie dropped off, sick and confused. He sat, thinking about what else he had to ask Camp, when the answer hit him in the face.

"Was there a trade-in, Mr. Camp?"

"Yes. We took in his old Camaro. I'm not sure when we picked it up. This is the third or fourth year that they have done this."

"Any chance it's still here?"

"Let me check. Camp walked around his desk and picked up a phone."

While Camp checked the records, Torch walked over to the row of windows and looked down below. The young man who had been clearing snow from the cars when he came in, was now sitting on the trunk of one of the cars, smoking a cigarette and blowing in his hands to warm them up. Down on the freeway below, traffic was bumper to bumper in the westbound lanes. *Must have been an accident*, Torch thought.

Camp walked over to him. "The car is on the lot yet. Do you want to see it?"

"We will be confiscating it for a while, Mr. Camp. I want the lab boys to take a look at it."

Torch pulled out his cell phone and called the police lab, while Camp sat on the corner of his desk and listened. Finished with his conversation, he folded up his phone and turned to Camp.

"They shouldn't have it more than a day or so. Then we'll deliver it right back to you."

"Can I ask what kind of a crime you are working on, and how our automobile is involved?" Camp appeared irritated.

"Let's just say you will be the first to know when we find the answers. Thank you, Mister Camp. It's been a pleasure."

Torch turned, and walked to the door, and then hesitated. "I can get the keys where, Mr. Camp?"

"I will have the car waiting for them in service. The keys will be in it."

Charlie had never been more frustrated than she was today. She was a damn good lawyer, and loved to play the part, act the part, and now Mathew Senior was subletting her work out so she could tutor his prick of a kid.

For Charlie, it was if she was training the enemy because, although it was a long way down the road yet, someday this little bastard would be working here. That was a foregone conclusion, and when that day came, where would she be? Would she be a senior partner in this firm, as he had led her to believe, or would she still be just a depository for the old man's filthy penis and Junior's teacher. Worse yet, and she shuddered at the thought, she might be working for Junior.

She paced the carpet in front of her desk. She regretted the day, twenty years ago, when she had started working for Mathew Halsworth. She also regretted the things he had made her do. His cheating philandering ways were bad enough, but she was part of it, and that made her as bad as him. Charlie had been fooled into thinking he cared for her and believed in her. At first, Mathew had seemed so sincere, and she fell for him, big time. He had taken her, from a fledging lawyer in a dead-end job, and made her someone in the biggest firm in town. The firm everybody wanted to be a part of. As dumb as she had been in the past, she now saw through his shallow ways and manipulative actions.

Charlie had thought about quitting, but he made her sign a contract that kept her from practicing law for five years if she left his firm. It was a stupid, stupid move on her part and how much she now realized it. At the time, she had signed for the money he had given her, and it seemed like a dream come true. But, each and every day, it was proving to be a damned nightmare. Her career was in the toilet when she came here, but there had been other options at the time. Signing with Mathew had just seemed too easy at the time.

She could only hope now that someday, when he was grunting and poking around inside of her, that evil heart would burst and she would get the pleasure of feeling his dying quivers.

Hal had forgotten all about Stacie. He was confident that he'd committed the perfect crime, which only a perfect mind like his could conceive and carry out. There was one other thing that he possessed in his warped, twisted mind, and that was a total lack of guilt. What happened had happened for a good reason, and that's the way life went sometimes. Some days you eat the bear, and some days the bear eats you. Stacie had gone up against the wrong person.

Torch went to see Evie after work and they had had a good talk. No, it was more than that. It was the best day in a long time and it made Torch very happy.

He brought her some of her favorite Chinese food, and they had shared each other's food out of the cartons, just like old times. Rice and shrimp, and sweet and sour pork in an orange sauce. Then, stuffed, they broke open their Chinese cookies and Evie had laughed at her fortune. *Her handsome prince was on his way.* Torch thought that was pretty good, too, and he laughed, making a show out of combing his hair.

Tomorrow she was being moved to a less restrictive area, and if things went well, maybe in a few weeks she could go home for a visit. "A conjugal visit," Torch quipped, and they both laughed again. It had been a long time since that had happened. He tried not to think about the part of their past that had been so difficult. He just wanted her healthy again and maybe, someday, they just might go travel for a while, and get to know each other again. Torch shook his head. That was way too far off to think about now.

Stacie's funeral was held on Saturday morning at eleven, in the same little church she had gone to all of her life, and both Torch and Theresa made the trip over to Wisconsin. It had been the only time in his memory that he had gone to the funeral of one of his victims. Victim in the sense that all of the people he tried to help were victims.

Though they left early, they had run into traffic coming out of the big cities, and the funeral was nearly ready to start when they arrived in Torch's personal car. The last thing they wanted was for people to realize they were cops, although Stacie's family would know.

They slipped into the last pew, trying to remain as inconspicuous as possible. Theresa held Torch's hand, and a white lace handkerchief was intertwined around her fingers. Her long black coat hid her pregnancy.

Stacie's brilliant white coffin was placed right in the middle of the church, its brightness contrasting with the dark scarlet carpet. It sat just before the two steps that led to the altar. It was half-buried in flowers and wreaths, the lid sealed and closed. The local mortuary hadn't been able to fix her up enough to give her friends and relatives that last precious look they all wanted. Memories of a similar coffin in a small church, not that long ago, washed over Torch and he wiped tears from his eyes with the back of his hand—not really sure who he was crying for—Stacie or his lost child. Theresa pretended not to notice, but deep down, she understood why.

The small church was packed to overflowing. There were many of Stacie's college classmates standing along the side aisles, under the arching stained glass windows that let in some filtered sunlight. From time to time, the sound of someone's uncontrollable grief would leak out, making the whole scene sad, and even more pathetic than it already was. Stacie's classmates were huddled together for support, but for the most part they were bewildered by it all. For most of them, this was a new chapter in the book of life's lessons, and they didn't care for it very much.

The minister talked as if he had known Stacie all of her life, and that very well may have been the case. His stories were up-close and personal, as only life in a small community can be. But in the end, it did little to comfort the grieving people.

Oscar and his family were in the church, already seated, when Torch and Theresa arrived. When the family exited up that center aisle, at the conclusion of the service, their faces expressed their agony all too well. Thelma's eyes were closed, and she literately huddled under her husband's arm as he shepherded her to the back of the church. There would be a short service outside, at the gravesite, and then everybody would meet in the basement of the tiny church for lunch. Theresa would watch the crowd, while Torch paid his respects to the family, at the gravesite.

It was Torch's hope to be able to talk with Oscar, but the stream of well-wishers seemed to be impenetrable. Then, looking through the crowd, a bewildered Oscar saw him standing there. He walked slowly over to Torch, ignoring people who were trying to say something to him.

"Thank you for coming." His voice was thick with emotion.

"I wish I knew how to say how sorry I am, Oscar, but I don't." Torch fumbled with the ends of his worn brown scarf as he talked. "People say you'll get over it and time will heal; but I'm here to tell you firsthand that that doesn't happen. They loved you for all of their lives. Now you will continue to love them for the rest of yours. There are no words strong enough at times like this. I needed to say goodbye to her, too. I also wanted to tell you that we are making some progress on the case. I hope to have something positive to tell you soon. Finding Stacie's killer will never bring her back, but it might bring some semblance of justice to you and your family."

"We are grateful for that," said Oscar. "Can you come out to the house for a while? Have a cup of coffee or something?"

"I can't today, Oscar, but let me do this—if something breaks on this case, I will personally bring you the news, my friend, so you keep that coffeepot hot. May God bless Stacie and take her home with him, and may God bless you and your family, Oscar."

Oscar let the slightest hint of a smile come to his face. "God bless you, too, Mr. Brennan."

On the ride back to Minneapolis, Torch filled Theresa in on what he had found out at the car dealer. "The lab boys said the car had been detailed before it was put on the lot, so there was nothing inside they could find, but listen to this. There was a mat in the trunk that had a stain on it they thought might be blood. It wasn't, but it was the next best thing."

"What, Torch?"

"Shit, my friend. Human excrement, partner, and from that excrement they are trying to find some of Stacie's cells. Your body is constantly casting off dead cells and that is one place they are found. Let's hope it works. It will take some time for those tests to get back, but the lab people were pretty confident the cells would be there. In the meantime, I am going to bring Hal Halsworth's sorry ass back in here and question him again. He's hiding something, that's for sure."

"What if there are cells and they aren't hers?"

Torch was upset. "What are you saying, Terry? This guy shit in his own trunk? Of course it's hers."

"You know, Torch, don't you think we might be jumping the gun here? This guy has talked to us, so far, without screaming at us about his rights and all of that bullshit we usually hear. Maybe we should just bring him in quietly again, and tell him we really need him to help us in this investigation."

Torch was quiet, just staring out of the windshield.

"I know this funeral upset you, and I know that you still haven't begun to get over Susan's death, but you and I know that once these turkeys get scared and think we know what they did, cooperation goes out the window."

Torch looked at Theresa with a look that was somewhere between disgust and anger. "I also know that every day this case gets one day colder, dear, and I'm not talking about the weather, Terry. We need to act fast. I have lost more cases because I wasted time than I have ever lost jumping the gun, as you say. Every minute we wait, this asshole has more time to refine his lies, and concoct stories we will never be able to prove wrong."

Theresa knew she had touched a nerve. When he started calling her dear, and Terry, he had his dander up. It was best to let go of it for now. It was his case to win or lose, not hers.

"I hope you're right, Torch. I certainly hope you're right." She reached over and touched his arm, to see if he was over it. Torch smiled and patted her hand. She thought he might be sorry for the speech he had given her, but she knew he had not changed his mind about bringing Hal in.

CHAPTER FIFTEEN

Torch planned to bring young Halsworth in on Monday morning. The tone was going to be a lot different this time. The last time he had been questioned as if he was a witness to the crime. This time, he was going to be a genuine suspect.

Torch had gone over to the treatment center early this Sunday morning. He and Evie had had breakfast together, and then made plans to go to a non-denominational church service on the grounds. There hadn't been a lot of religion in their lives for quite some time, and they both thought they could draw some strength from the services. For Torch, it was his second day in church in two days, and that had to be some kind of a record for him.

For the first time since Evelyn had come to the Center, she seemed to be taking a genuine interest in her appearance. Another lady had done her hair for her on Saturday, and she had put on a dark blue pantsuit, that she purchased a while back for Susan's funeral, and never worn. She had called Torch last night, and asked him to bring it with him, when he came to see her. Maybe it would be appropriate now; she had thought it to be too festive at the time. She remembered why she had bought the suit, but for now, was able to get beyond that. It was time to get way beyond that, and it made her feel good that she could. Evelyn needed to see some progress in her life, too. It was a little baggy, but as Evie put it, "My ass will grow fast enough, Torch."

Torch could only laugh. "Your beautiful ass was the first glimpse I got of you, Evie. Remember—you were riding your bike in front of me on your way to school. I had such a woody on by the time I got there; I had to carry my books in front of me for the whole first hour."

"Let's get to church, you pervert." Evie grabbed his arm and walked him out the door.

Torch made himself a spam sandwich for lunch and now, as he sat at the kitchen lunch bar, he remembered why he didn't like spam, and he pushed it aside. His familiar yellow legal pad, with all his notes and comments, was in front of him. If he was going to bring this guy in tomorrow, he needed to have his ducks lined up. He knew the right questions, at the right time, had broken a lot of cases wide open.

Torch numbered the key points that made him think Hal Halverson was implicated in the death of Stacie Morrison. He listed them in a neat column, with side notes. Some of the things they had already talked about the first time he talked with Hal, but that had been off the record. This time was for keeps. If he could get this character to admit to at least one of these points, he would have enough evidence to convince the County Attorney to take it to a grand jury…maybe.

He looked at what he had written, starting with number one. Hal was present at the party, with Stacie, in November. There were witnesses that had seen them together. There were witnesses that had seen them leave together. He was being an awfully good Samaritan to take a sick drunk girl home, and by the way, they had a witness for that, also. Well, she could identify his car, anyway. He claimed he had never seen her before that night. Stacie was, coincidently, six weeks pregnant. She hadn't been sexually active before. In fact, the coroner said he believed she had very little sexual contact. The party was six weeks before she was killed. Coincidence? Torch didn't think so. He was going to ask Hal for a DNA sample.

Number two. Hal's phone number was the last number she called before she was killed. The phone was found right where he would have thrown it over the bridge railing, from his car, and so would not have seen the ice below. Had he thrown her naked body over the bridge railing there, too? That didn't make sense; if he had, he would have seen the ice. He had to work on that one. There were a thousand places upstream he could have dumped her in, but where?

What girl would call a boy she had met only once at a party six weeks before? That was bullshit, if he was sticking to that story. She had more to talk to him about that night than just wishing him Merry Christmas.

Number three. There was the credit receipt from Hal's card, at the store where Stacie's belongings had been found on Christmas day. A store that was conveniently located right on Hal's way home, and oh, yes, the stuff had been dumped in the very can, next to the very pump, where he had gassed up his car. This was new information that he had not discussed with Hal in their earlier conversation. *I'd better be careful here,* Torch thought. It still pissed Torch off that he didn't have all of her stuff that had been in the dumpster, but Hal didn't know that.

Last, but not least, the mat in the trunk of his old Camaro could also be a link. Especially if the lab could prove it was Stacie's waste. He better play that one close to the vest until the lab reports came back, but this one could be a big one.

Torch ran his fingers through his hair, and looked out the kitchen window at two blue jays fighting in the bird feeder. *What a simple life they had,* he thought. *Eat and shit and chase each other around every day. They didn't get hung up on family problems or work. If one of them got bumped off, well, that was just more room at the feeder, wasn't it.*

Back to his notes, and forget about the damn birds, he thought. *What was he missing?* He was going to have Hal located and arrested the first thing in the morning. Along with that, he would be getting search warrants for Hal's apartment, and his parents' house.

Theresa was out talking to drug snitches today, to see if anybody could remember Hal buying drugs. Funny what people could remember when you were willing to look the other way for them now and then. The only bad thing was, they made piss poor witnesses because of credibility problems. No judge in their right mind would let most of them get on the stand. No prosecutor in their right mind would want them there, either. But once in a while, they knew things you could prove in other ways.

Torch put his paperwork back in the folder, and threw his spam sandwich in the trash. He would have a bowl of cereal later. He went into the living room, stretched out on the couch, and turned the television on. There was something hard under the cushion, so he sat up and dug around under it. It was another full bottle of Beefeaters gin. He went to the sink and dumped it.

Hal had studied late into the night on Sunday. Charlie was demanding more and more of him, and he was more afraid of her lousy hissy fits than he was of his father's temper. She didn't seem to like him very much, but that was all right because he didn't like her, either. They just had to get along for the sake of both of them because school would be out in a few months, and then screw her for the summer—not literally—his father was doing that. He was going to Europe to one of those white sand beaches in Southern France. He would just sit there all day, and get stoned, while he watched those naked coeds frolicking in the surf. Then, at night, he would join them at the ever present parties.

He was still doing a little coke from time to time, but not the way he had been. He felt he had a handle on it and had nothing to worry about. No cocaine, no person, or anything else, ruled Hal Halsworth.

Theresa had had some luck with the drug dealers on the West Bank, but not a lot. Yes, they knew who Hal was, and yes, he had bought cocaine from them, but no GHB, at least not that they knew of. One thing was for sure. You didn't have to look far to find anything you wanted over there. If you wanted GHB, it was readily available.

Theresa was to meet Torch early tomorrow morning and brief him, and then she had three days off. She didn't want to be in on the questioning, and when they had gotten back from the funeral yesterday, she had asked Torch to be excused from it. She had told him she was just too stressed, what with her pregnancy and all.

The request for the warrants had been in Judge Susan Harris's hands for two days now, even before the funeral, and unbeknown to Theresa. On Sunday night, the judge released them. They had a warrant to search both Mathew's apartment and his bedroom at the Halsworth residence. The warrant specifically limited the search to Mathew's personal space in the Halsworth estate. Any DNA samples would have to be voluntary, and were not included in the warrant.

The last warrant was the one Torch was going to personally deliver—an arrest warrant for Hal for the abduction and murder of Stacie Morrison. The judge had been somewhat reluctant to issue this one, as she personally felt the evidence against Hal was sketchy and circumstantial. But a warrant for Hal's arrest was a far cry from a conviction in court, or an indictment, so she went ahead with it. She warned Torch, though. "No names or pictures in the papers."

Torch was pumped. He blew off the judge's criticism, and Theresa's cautiousness, and the disappointing report on Hal's drug purchases. He was more confident than he had ever been that they were on the right track. At 9 a.m. he left City Hall with two cops in blue uniforms, and all of the warrants in hand, except the one for Hal's parents' home. That warrant was being delivered to the Halsworth residence by the local police in that jurisdiction, who would secure the site until the lab boys could process it.

It took the three cops just a few minutes to reach Hal's apartment. There was no answer at the door, and a visual inspection through the undraped windows showed it was empty. His car was in its usual parking place.

Their next stop was the administration building, to find out which class he would be in if he was there.

Torch approached the desk and wasted no time. The only attendant was a student worker who seemed to be visually disturbed by the appearance of Torch, with his badge hanging in her face, and the two burly cops behind him.

"I'm from the Minneapolis Police Department and I need some information."

"What kind of information?" the young woman stammered.

"I need to know which class Mathew Halsworth Junior is in at this time."

At this, a half-opened door in the back of the office opened all of the way. The door was directly behind the frightened girl and a much older, stately-looking woman came out and approached the counter.

"Officers, my name is June Williams, and I'm the supervisor here in the Records Department. May I ask what this is all about?"

Torch was losing patience. "No, you may not. Just tell us where we can find Mathew Halsworth Junior."

For a second, she seemed to be speechless, but then, regaining her composure, she said. "This is highly irregular. The whereabouts of our students on this campus is not public information."

With that, Torch held the warrant directly in her face. "This is from a Hennepin County Judge, lady, and if you don't want to honor it you can come with him, when we find him, for obstructing justice." Torch lowered the document and looked at her with a sneer on his face. "We will find him if I have to look in every damn classroom on this campus. Now, quit your screwing around and give me that classroom."

"Find the person for them," she told the young lady, and went back to her office, slamming the door behind her.

Both of the "boys in blue" had grins that went from ear to ear.

The classroom was on the second floor of the language building, about a block away. The three men walked briskly between the buildings, saying nothing to each other. They skipped the elevator and walked up the stairs to the second floor. It was the first room they came to. The placard on the door said, **English for the Twentieth Century**, whatever that meant.

Hal's head was down, and he was writing in a book, when Torch opened the door. There were about twelve students in the class, and there was no instructor in sight at the time.

"Stay here," Torch said to his escorts. Hal raised his head at about the same time Torch entered the room. It was obvious he recognized Torch, and the detective stopped with a sneer, and motioned with his forefinger, for Hal to come with him.

All of the students were now looking at the two of them. Hal stood and walked over to him. "What's up?" he nonchalantly asked.

"Come outside for a moment," Torch said.

They were the only four people in the hallway, except for a lone custodian with a ring of about a hundred keys jingling on his belt, who was making an attempt to look busy, mopping the floor, while he watched them out of the top of his eyes. One look from Torch sent him walking away, and down the hall; leaving his mop pail against the wall and talking to himself.

"Mathew Halsworth. I have a warrant for your arrest for the abduction and murder of Stacie Morrison."

Hal was ashen-faced and speechless.

"Turn around and put your hands behind your back."

Hal had not moved, still standing there with a puzzled look on his face.

"Your way or our way, Hal, what's it going to be?"

The two boys in blue, who had been hoping for a scuffle, each grabbed an arm and cuffed him. They went out the same way they came in.

As soon as they were all in the car, Hal and Torch in the back, Torch turned to his prisoner and said. "As much as I hate to do this Hal, I have to read you your rights."

"I know my rights, fat boy."

Torch smiled, "Now, now, Hal, let's not get testy and starting calling each other names. I know you know your rights, but you're going to hear them again, like it or not." He had the Miranda card in his hand.

Hal turned, and looked out the window with a new expression on his face, as Torch read the card. He had gone from scared to defiant.

At the same time Hal was being escorted to jail, his father was being notified by the University Police that the Minneapolis Police had arrested his son. Torch had notified them, as it was a matter of policy for them to notify his parents.

Grabbing his coat and hat from the closet in his office, Hal's father brushed by his secretary, Jenny, who was just coming in for dictation. "Family emergency, cancel all of my appointments this morning. I will call you if it's longer."

"Mr. Halsworth, what shall I tell them?" The young woman was walking briskly down the hall with him, her steno pad in her hand.

"I don't give a shit what you tell them. Tell them I died for all I care."

She stopped in the hall, obviously exasperated, and watched him walk away and enter the elevator. "Horse's ass," she muttered, throwing her pad and pencil on the floor.

Mathew Senior was no stranger to City Hall, and no stranger to the Police Department. He knew exactly where to go.

Questioning of Hal was set for three in the afternoon. Right now,

Mathew Senior didn't want to see his son. First, he wanted to see the arresting officer.

Torch was sitting behind his desk, and was on the phone, when Halsworth came in without knocking. Torch put his hand over the receiver and said, "Have a seat. It will just be a moment."

Halsworth was not used to waiting for any man, but he did what he was told, balancing his hat on his knee and glaring at Torch.

Torch hung up the phone. "Mr. Halsworth, good to see you. We meet again. What the hell case was that, that you and I butted heads on?"

"I'm not here to reminisce with you, Brennan. Why have you arrested my son? This better be good or I am going to have your ass."

"You know what? You and your son both have a very nasty attitude, did you know that? Why did we arrest your son? He's charged with....what the hell was that?" Torch slapped the side of his cheek. "Murder, yea, that's it—second degree murder."

"Murder? Who is he supposed to have murdered? Are you people out of your goddamn minds?"

"Ever hear of Stacie Morrison, Mr. Halsworth?"

Halsworth looked at Torch, with a blank look on his face and at a loss for words.

"Stacie Morrison, Mr. Halsworth, to refresh your memory, was the young University of Minnesota coed, who was murdered, and her body thrown in the river. We have evidence that implicates your son in this. Do you plan on representing him in this case?"

Halsworth was thinking, twisting his hat around in his hands. "When are you questioning him?"

"At three this afternoon."

"His lawyer will be here."

"Good enough. Tell them not to be tardy. We run a tight schedule. Do you want to see him?"

"No." Halsworth turned and walked out of the office. He was furious. As if he didn't have enough on his plate right now, and now this. He had no idea what the evidence was the police possessed, but knowing his son, he would not put it past him to be in trouble again. It was just one problem after another with this jerk of a kid.

Charlie stood in front of her boss's desk. All she knew was that he had asked her to come to his office.

"Charlie, my son is in trouble with the law again." He stood with his back to her, looking out the floor-to-ceiling windows that looked out over the bustling Minneapolis skyline. Across the street, two window washers sat on their scaffolding, eating lunch as if they were sitting on a park bench, their feet dangling over twenty stories of nothingness.

Charlie did not comment, but stood staring down at a figurine of **The Thinker,** on his desktop. The same one she had gripped in pain as the old man violated her.

"I want you to do two things for me, Charlie." Halsworth had turned around and was now looking at her with a pleading look. "I want you to represent him in this, and I want you to tell me the truth about his actions. This lawyer client, confidentiality thing, does not apply here."

"Where is he?" she said.

"Minneapolis Police downtown. They question him at three, so rearrange your schedule."

Charlie could only shrug her shoulders and say, "okay." It beats doing his schoolwork for him.

"By the way, Charlie, my wife is going to Mexico with our daughter for a week next week. Maybe you could slip out some night."

"Yes. I guess I could do that." *So you can slip something into me, huh boss?* She winced at the thought. No wonder his kid was such a jack-off. The apple had not fallen far from the tree.

CHAPTER SIXTEEN

Charlie had asked for a room to interview her client in. "Something that wasn't bugged," was her exact request to the police.

Hal was brought in after Charlie was already in the room. She had been briefed by Torch as to the charges against him.

"Well, I'll be damned. Maybe I won't miss any school after all. Hi, teacher." Hal slumped down in the chair across from her, looking at Charlie with a shit-eating grin on his face. "Let me guess, you're also my lawyer."

Charlie looked at her watch, ignoring Hal's remarks. "We have one hour, hot shot, so let's talk."

"Talk about what?"

"Talk about what? Talk about what you have been arrested for. This is no damn game, Hal."

"Do you have any idea what evidence they have to tie you to this crime, Hal?"

"No."

"Look, Hal. It will help us both if you tell the truth to me, and if you are going to lie in the courtroom, at least let me know that you are lying. God, I hope this doesn't get that far."

"Have you said anything to the cops I should know about?"

133

"Not today."

"What do you mean, not today? When did you last talk with them?" Charlie had her hands on her hips, scowling at him.

"A few weeks back."

"You were a suspect a few weeks back, and we're just finding out about it now? Do you ever talk to your father about anything?"

"No...no." Hal waved his hand to emphasize his point. They were talking with everybody at the U about her disappearance. This was before her body showed up, and no, I don't talk to my father about things. What do you do with my father?"

Charlie glared at him. "This is about you, Hal. Not me and your father."

"Did you kill this girl?"

"How you talk."

Charlie stared at Hal. He was still slumped in his chair while she stood over him. She knew, right then and there, that he was guilty of something. In fact, she had suspected it before she even came here today.

Torch looked at his watch. He and Dave Jenkins, an old friend from Homicide, would be doing the questioning. Before he started, he had one more phone call to make that he had been putting off. He dialed the number, and rubbed his eyes while he waited for it to be answered. He was getting tired. He hadn't slept well last night.

"Hello." Thelma's voice was so faint he could hardly make it out.

"Is this Thelma?"

"Yes."

"Thelma, this is Torch Brennan. Do you remember me? I didn't get a chance to talk to you last week at the funeral."

"Torch, Oscar is right here. Why you don't talk with him. I'm not feeling very well."

Before Torch could say anything to Thelma, Oscar was on the line.

"Oscar, listen. I just wanted you to know that we have arrested someone for Stacie's murder. Who? Well, I can't tell you that now. We just arrested him today and we haven't finished with things yet, but I wanted to tell you before it hits the papers...if it does. Oscar, I do need to get over to the jail, so listen—I will talk with you later, okay?"

"Torch, can I ask you a question?"

"Make it quick, Oscar."

"Stacie had a silver charm bracelet that she always wore. We gave it to her for graduation. I talked to the funeral director and he said she didn't have it on when she came home." Oscar hesitated, and Torch could sense he was crying. "It was also not in the stuff that Jacob brought back from her apartment. I just wondered if you would look into that for us. It's kind of important to us, Torch."

"Sure, Oscar. I'll call you tomorrow and let you know what we found out."

"Thanks, Torch."

"You bet, Oscar. Talk to you later."

He scribbled himself a note on a yellow Post It and stuck it on his desk blotter. It said, **Charm Bracelet**. It was almost three, and he had to hurry.

Dave was waiting for him outside the interrogation room. *How many people had Torch tripped up in this room over the years?* He was good at it, and he knew it. But it was always good to have a partner in case you wanted to play some good cop, bad cop. They both went in and sat down. The clock on the wall said two fifty eight.

At exactly three, Charlie walked in and sat down. She was alone and had no papers, briefcase, or files of any kind. She had nothing but a serious look on her pretty face. She folded her hands in front of her, and sat down, prim and proper.

"Gentlemen, I wish to make a statement on behalf of my client. My client will not cooperate with any kind of questioning or testing, so he has elected to not appear. Any and all questions you have may be directed to me. As for my client, he says he is innocent, and if you wish to continue this charade, then go ahead without him. In other words, take it to the grand jury, and if you can get an indictment, we'll see you in court." Charlie finished with a sick smile.

Torch felt like he had been hit square in the face with a brick. Charlie had obtained a copy of what Torch had presented to Judge Harris. She knew the evidence was flimsy, but she didn't know everything. Right now though, he sensed she felt she knew more about what had happened than Torch knew. *Was she bluffing?*

135

Maybe he had screwed up—maybe he had jumped the gun and run with it before he had all of his ducks in a row. *Well, piss on it, he wasn't done yet,* he thought. *When the test results come back, from that excrement in the trunk of Hal's car, then we'll see who laughs last.*

He walked slowly back to his office and sat down in his chair. To hell with it, he was going home for today. Charlie was petitioning Judge Harris to have her client released right now. Jenkins had called and told him that. He needed to regroup. Slowly, he reached up for the switch on his desk lamp, and then saw the note he'd left for himself. He shrugged. *Might as well check it out.*

A quick call to the Coroner's Office confirmed there was no bracelet on Stacie when she was brought in. Maybe he'd better have another talk with the boy from the gas station.

Something went right for a change. Darrel had just come home from school when Torch pulled up to his grandma's house. Torch got out of his car, and walked over to the porch, where Darrel was standing watching him. "Hi, kid. How's your day going?"

Darrel shrugged his shoulders. "Ok, I guess."

"I need your help, buddy. Can I ask you a question?"

"Ok." He had a questioning look on his face.

"When you found those clothes and that purse in that dumpster, was there also a charm bracelet with that stuff? In the purse or in the pants pockets?"

Darrel shook his head no slowly.

"Look kid, we don't need the bracelet right now, but if you gave it to your girlfriend or sold it, just say so. Nothing is going to happen to you."

Darrel still shook his head no.

Torch looked at Darrel long and hard. "I believe you, son. Look, thanks for talking to me, and if you do recall anything about it later, here, call me." Torch gave him a business card with a ten dollar bill folded behind it.

"Something for your time, buddy."

"Gee, thanks."

Torch drove slowly away. If Hal took the bracelet off her, did he keep it? Naw, he's got to be smarter than that. He made a note to call and see what the searches turned up at Hal's parents' house and his apartment. But not today—tomorrow.

Hal was out. The judge who had reviewed the case would not even consider bail. It didn't, however, mean the charges were dropped. They were already a matter of record. Until the police department could bolster their case with something more substantial, they would remain in limbo, and at some point they would have to try and proceed with the case, or drop the charges against him.

Hal was cockier than ever. He had thumbed his nose at the establishment once more and came out on top. He celebrated his victory by throwing a party at his apartment complete with liquor, drugs, and loose girls. He got high, he got drunk, and he got laid, but not a word was said about his arrest by anyone. Hal made no excuses, nor gave anyone an explanation for what had happened. For once, he was doing what Charlie told him. Keeping his big mouth shut.

Mathew Senior also kept to himself. In a meeting with Charlie, she had told him, "I'm not sure if he is guilty or not. He wouldn't give me a straight answer. I do know this, though. The police are going to find the key to this case if they stay at it long enough."

They were sitting at a table at Winston's, a plush upscale café just off the Nicollet Mall downtown. Outside the window, the never-ending sea of humanity flowed by, all of them with a mission in mind. They were people with places to go, people to see, and things to accomplish.

Charlie's thoughts were depressing to her. She had wanted to be a lawyer from the day she graduated from high school, but never in her wildest dreams had she thought it would come to this. With every job there were things that went with the turf, but she had dug a hole that put her under the turf, and she hated it. The worst thing about it was, the only way out would ruin her career.

Mathew interrupted her thoughts. "Charlie, our firm is going to diversify. You have been in on some of the preliminary discussions. Some of the smaller firms we have acquired specialize in areas we have no expertise in. Personal liability, cases of income tax fraud, to name two of them. At first, I wondered if we were getting too many things on our plate, getting into all of these areas, but the more I have thought about it the more I now know we need to be a firm for all needs. You have been a good criminal defense lawyer, and for that reason, I am going to put you in charge of that part of our firm. We will also be moving other employees around, so you will have to get used to working with some different people."

"You are offering me a Senior Partner position?"

"Yes."

"When will this take place?"

"As soon as Hal graduates."

"Is that a prerequisite for the position? Hal graduating and my getting his ass through school?" She had blurted it out, and was now regretting the way it sounded.

"I wouldn't call it just that, but yes. You have enough going for you for now and I want you to finish it. I thought you would be elated with this news, and here you seem angry about it."

She didn't answer him, electing to stare back out the window. *It wasn't anger*, she thought, *it was disgust. No, to hell with it, it was anger but she would get over it. He knew it, and so did she.*

The news couldn't be worse for Torch. First of all, the search warrants hadn't turned up anything of interest in either location. Oh, there had been some trace amounts of cocaine in his apartment, but not enough to press charges of any kind. No evidence that Stacie had been there, no GHB, and no smoking guns of any kind. He waited for the lab results on the trunk mat now, and continued to look for the missing bracelet, but that was proving to be impossible to trace or find. The rest of the week was just a blur of trips to see Evie, and going over what evidence he had. Somewhere, though, there was an answer. He could just feel it in his gut.

On the following Monday, the roof fell in. The detailing of the automobile had used detergents that had, for all practical purposes, destroyed the evidence on the floor mat. It was useless.

But the real kicker was a letter from the County Attorney's Office that told him to drop the charges. There would be no indictment. No grand jury. He could re-file charges later if something showed up, but not for second-degree murder.

For now, it was a dead case. *As dead as Stacie Morrison,* Torch thought.

Theresa tried to encourage Torch to drop it for now, and get on to some other cases. He had been so consumed with this case it was all he could dwell on.

"Go spend more time with Evelyn, take a vacation, read a book in the park." She told him. "Sooner or later, the clue you need will show up. Hal will talk to the wrong person at the wrong time. These kinds of people always screw up and talk, my friend. Someone will remember something, but you have to let it come to you, Torch."

"As for me, the boss has given me a new assignment. I'm sorry, old buddy; you are on your own."

Torch gave her a hug. "Thanks for the help, Terry. Thanks for the friendship. Sometimes I can be a stubborn old bastard, and you're right, it will work out sometime. Knowing that bastard did this, and that he's laughing at us, makes it tough for me. I will never let go of this case until it is solved and I can see his smug, cocky, rich-ass face behind bars for the rest of his life."

They were still hugging. Torch reached down and kissed the tip of her nose. "I hope we work together again, kid. Good luck with that baby." He released her and walked out into the hallway and walked away. Maybe he would go see Evie. Maybe they could go for a drive.

He called the treatment center to tell Evie he was coming over. He'd stopped and bought some flowers, and her favorite Key Lime pie, at Perkins. This time, the operator didn't connect him to Evie's room like before. Instead, he got the Administration Assistant's office.

"Mr. Brennan, I don't know how to tell you this, but your wife walked away from the treatment center this morning. We have been trying to get ahold of you. We have no idea where she is."

THE REST OF
THE STORY.

July 24th, 1999.

CHAPTER SEVENTEEN

Torch Brennan had changed over the years. He no longer became as personally involved in cases as he had in the past. Time had shown him that it was just too rough on him. Not that he didn't do the job well; he did, and had solved more cases than any other detective in the history of the division. He just didn't take it so seriously anymore.

He was fifty-two years old now, and that once-mousy brown hair was now streaked with more gray than brown. The chiseled chin that had given him that look of firm determination was still there, but not as prominent as it had once been. His bright blue eyes still twinkled when he smiled, but the face had grown more fleshy and wrinkled. His shoulders were more stooped, making his clothes hang a little, and giving him a permanent tired look. All of this was not just happening from the ravages of the job. It was the slow erosion of time, making a once-handsome man into an old one.

It had been the kind of day that was just too good to stay inside, and Torch had taken his thoughts and walked over to the Third Avenue Bridge. He stood now on the sidewalk, half leaning over the rail, watching the calm waters flow quietly downstream. The water level was low from a summer drought and rocks and deadheads, that had lurked below the water's surface, now poked their heads above the current, creating little eddies of current around them. A flock of pigeons he had disturbed circled the bridge girders, waiting for him to leave. Traffic moved slowly by him on the roadway.

His stained fingers held what was left of one of the cigarettes he practically lived on. There had been so many changes over the years. Theresa no longer worked for the Police Department, having given it up to be a stay at home mom. Wes had retired, and now lived by a lake, somewhere in Northern Minnesota. Torch had gone from Sergeant to Captain, and was now in charge of the Homicide division. It was a job that had taken him away from what he had loved to do, and replaced it with endless employee issues and political bullshit that was coming out his ears.

The flowing waters had brought back subtle memories that he had tried to bury, but wouldn't go away. Instead, they kept bringing him back to this river and the memories of a beautiful girl whose killer still had his freedom. The case folder had sat on the corner of Torch's desk for a long time, but gradually, it went into the cold case files; buried there with so many other unsuccessful cases that he no longer opened. Nothing new had ever come up, and the efforts of the Halsworth law firm had stymied any efforts he had made to pursue the case.

Still, it was a case that would haunt Torch to his grave. He thought of her parents, Oscar and Thelma, often. Thelma had died two years ago. Oscar had told Torch she had never gotten over Stacie's death, and she wanted to join her daughter the only way she knew how. Oscar now lived in a nursing home in town, battling Parkinson's disease—still waiting for that phone call from Torch that would tell him justice had been served. Todd had taken over the farm, and after the funeral, Torch didn't hear from him again.

There were also memories of Evie, running away from her demons in those bottles of liquor that had haunted her so much. Running until she could no longer cope, and ironically, ending up in this same river, jumping from this same bridge that Torch now stood on. This river had brought so much life to the cities and towns that lined its banks, but it had also taken some precious lives away.

Torch had sold the house in the suburbs after Evie's death, and moved into a condo downtown where he could walk to work. His work was his life right now. He didn't drink, so bars were out, and he seemed to be content to be a loner. Oh, he'd had a few one-night stands, but they never went anywhere.

Few women wanted a man who was as married to his work as he was, but that was all right with him.

Torch flipped what was left of his smoke over the rail, and watched it hit the water below and float away. It was time to get back to work.

Mathew Halsworth Senior had also mellowed with age. He was the head of the largest law firm west of the Mississippi, and his ego had finally been satisfied. Most of his days were spent in his spacious office, gloating over his successes and overseeing the day-to-day operations. There was a board of nine senior partners that were the second level of administration, and he never dealt with anyone below that level. Each of the partners headed up a division that dealt with the nine branches of law the firm dealt with.

Some of the divisions were bigger than others, but none of them had less than a hundred lawyers in them. When you added to that the paralegals, law clerks, secretaries and support staff, the Halsworth firm had over three thousand employees working in the gleaming skyscraper they owned. The firm took up the top thirty floors.

Every Monday morning, he would meet with the senior partners and they would give their reports on what was on going in their divisions. Mathew would sit there in all his splendor at the head of the table and listen closely to what they had to say, smoking a cigar and nodding his head in agreement from time to time. He took careful notes and never criticized anyone at the meetings. They would be called into his office later, for more information, or an occasional ass chewing. He hated lengthy reports, and more than once, had asked someone to consolidate their notes before they came to the meeting, which never lasted over two hours.

As for his home life, his wife, Melinda, was in the late stages of Alzheimer's and now had a full-time housekeeper to watch over her. Noreen had long ago left the scene. Lamont, however, was another story, and the old black gardener still tended to the grounds faithfully, and still played the part of the butler when he was called upon. Little had changed with the estate in the last ten years. It was still one of the showplaces of the area, but it didn't, in any way, give credence to the vast wealth which the Halsworth family had now accumulated. Mathew Senior was rich, but he didn't live the lifestyle he was capable of.

His affair with Charlie seemed to be a thing of the past. At seventy-three, his waning sexual appetite had little need for her, in that capacity. She was in charge of the criminal law division at the company, the largest of all of the divisions, but outside of the weekly meetings they had very little contact. Most nights during the week he didn't go home, but stayed in his private quarters that had been added next to his sprawling office.

Mathew Junior, with Charlie's constant tutoring, had not only made it through college, but also three years of law school out east, and passed his bar exam six years ago. Since then, they had rarely spoken.

Immediately upon passing the bar, he had gone to work in his father's firm, which was now referred to, by him, as the family firm. No one had ever climbed a corporate ladder so fast, with so little effort.

He went from a junior lawyer to a senior partner in three years. There were those in the firm who had worked half of their lives away for Halsworth; that now could do little but express their astonishment at this travesty. Some had become too vocal, and were fired or forced to quit. Then there were those, like Charlie, that knew it was inevitable and just kept their mouths shut.

Mathew Junior was in charge of the corporate tax law division. He knew very little about what went on under him, but he lavishly rewarded those who made him look good so, from the outside looking in, he appeared to prosper. His father seemed to be content with his work.

After graduating from law school he had returned to Minnesota, and for a while, lived with his parents. Then, two years ago, he had married and almost immediately had a child. This time, he didn't try to get out of it. Stephanie and Hal lived in a downtown condo with their young son, Mathew the third. She seemed to be content to live the lifestyle of the rich, and not so famous, spending most of her time shopping and traveling. She had developed a gambling problem, and could often be seen at the Indian gaming casinos south of the Twin Cities.

As for Hal, he spent a lot of time after work at trendy bars in Minneapolis, and had been seen, more than once, in the company of a female that was not Stephanie. He still had the same cocky brash attitude that had been with him from high school, and he did pretty much as he pleased.

Charlie Malloy was no longer as miserable as she had been the last ten years. One thing that had helped was Mathew Senior losing sexual interest in her. That carnal act, if you could even call it that, had started out somewhat consensual, and then turned into the most repulsive thing she had ever had to do for anyone.

It also helped that she seemed to have found a new life far from the Halsworth law firm. Charlie was dabbling in politics. For a few years, she had gone to caucuses, and had been quite active in the Democratic Party. She had also been a key fundraiser and a large contributor. Then, four years ago, she had been named Vice Chairman of the Minnesota Democratic Party. This fall, Charlie had her eye on one more plateau. She was going to announce her plans to run for the Hennepin County Attorney's Office. Bob Harris, who now held the position, had said he was not going to run again, had recanted, and now was saying he planned to run again. This was an elected position in the most populated county in the state. She didn't like Bob Harris and she knew her chances of beating him, if she ran against him, were slim. Charlie was disappointed, but maybe two more years would give her time to be in a better position to beat him.

Charlie had one fear with her desire to run for any elected office. Mathew Halsworth Senior. Although they were still good friends, he had little time for politics, or for people who were disloyal to the firm. He would certainly see this as disloyalty, she was sure of that. If she were elected, she would have to leave the firm she had worked at for almost her entire career. She knew, in her heart, he wasn't going to look kindly on her leaving, and that bothered her.

As for Mathew Junior, she still loathed him and he despised her even more, but they had, for the sake of his father, kept a quiet truce. At the board meetings while in front of the old man, they would talk, but that was the only time words passed between them.

Charlie had never gotten too hung up on Junior's fast rise up the cooperate ladder. She had expected that. But two things still burned in her mind, and would always bother her. The first was his disguising himself as a lawyer. Oh, he had passed the bar and had a license, but he wouldn't make a good pimple on a real lawyer's ass and she knew it. The thing that bothered her most, though, was that he was as guilty as sin in the death of Stacie Morrison, ten years ago. This man, who sat on the managing board of the biggest law firm west of Chicago, had gotten away with murder. The thing that really bothered her about this, was not his getting away with it, it was the part she had been forced to play in it. A wrong she would like to make right someday.

CHAPTER EIGHTEEN

When Torch returned to the office, there was a voice mail waiting for him from the chief, and he knew damn well what it was about. Four women had been raped and murdered in the last eighteen months, and the media had made a publicity frenzy out of it. As of right now, they had four unsolved murders, but there was really nothing that suggested they were related.

The local paper last week, however, had capitalized on rumors of a serial killer, and the whole Southside community of Minneapolis was up in arms. He had been waiting for this call, but it would not be quite the way he had expected it.

"Chief. You called?"

"Torch, thanks for getting back to me right away. Say, listen; drop over to my office if you can. I have some people coming over I want you to talk with."

Ray Loftus had been Chief of the Minneapolis Police Department for three years now. He had come from New York with a promise to reduce crime, and hold the line on expenses. So far, he had not done well at either, and the hawks were circling. He had one year left on a four-year contract.

"Sure, Chief." Torch replied. "Anything special I should know about before I get there?"

"No, we're just going to go over a few things with the mayor, and some concerned citizens, on these recent killings. These women that were raped and killed are the issues they want to talk about. You know what to say to these people, Torch. I don't, and they're driving me crazy. I don't know what the hell to tell them, but we have to do something to squash these rumors."

"Any special time you want me, Chief?"

"They're here in my office now, Torch. Make it ten minutes while I blow a little hot air up their asses and try to soften them up."

"Gee, thanks, Chief. See you in ten."

Torch flopped down in his desk chair. He ran his hands through his hair and tried to think about what he was going to say. That was nearly impossible when he didn't have the foggiest idea what they were going to ask.

I need to tell them we are making progress, but these things take time, he thought. *As far as we can tell, people, we are not dealing with any one person here. What else would they ask?*

Do you have any suspects? Yes, we have suspects, but we don't have enough evidence to arrest them. Well, I take that back. We do have enough on one case, and we are going to arrest someone. As for the others, you can screw a case up early if you don't have enough patience.

A flashback shot through his mind. *Hal Halsworth. Yes, that's a damn good example. Where the hell did that thought come from?*

Do you have DNA? Good question, that's all the damn paper has been talking about lately. DNA, good old DNA. First and foremost on everybody's mind nowadays…like a magic elixir. Hell, we could find out who killed Hitler if we just had some DNA. These people watch too much damn television. Yes, we have some DNA on some of the cases, but not all of them.

Isn't that unusual?

No. There have been a lot of changes in the DNA testing procedure recently, but the bad guys also know this, and they are being more careful.

Are there more patrols being made in these areas?

Yes. Thank you for asking that. We have increased the patrols by fifty percent, but we can't be everywhere all of the time. Citizens need to be aware of their surroundings and…

He looked at his watch. Shit, he'd better hurry; it takes a few minutes to get there.

When Torch entered the chief's spacious oak-paneled office, there were four other people besides the chief and the mayor that he didn't recognize. They were all women.

"Ladies, this is Torch Brennan, head of the Homicide Division here. He has graciously volunteered to take some time out of his busy day to answer some of your questions." The chief was standing behind his desk, holding his right hand out in a gesture toward Torch.

Torch smiled and said, "Thanks, Chief, and I'm glad to meet all of you." *Just what I need today, to get grilled by these old prunes,* he thought.

One by one they introduced themselves. Hillary Causton, from the City Council's Fourth Ward, Jane Overbee, from something called "Citizens for a Safer Minneapolis," Cara Spencer, from "Women of Today," and Gail Larson, who appeared to be trying to stare a hole through Torch and didn't mention who she represented. *The combined age of the four women had to be close to four hundred,* Torch thought.

Torch sat down at the end of the chief's massive desk, at a right angle to the four women sitting in front of the desk. The mayor was sitting straight across from Torch, seemingly mesmerized by a stack of papers he was paging through.

"Torch, what I would like you to do today is bring us all up to speed on the four open cases. Tell these people where we are in each of the investigations. Now we all understand that there are some sensitive areas that you can't comment on, but help us all out here, if you can." the chief leaned back in his chair with his hands locked over his belly and a painful grin on his face.

For a moment, Torch was silent and looked at the chief, as if to say, *Thanks, you son of a bitch, for giving me the chance to go before this kangaroo court you have assembled.*

Quickly composing himself, and taking great strides not to look at Gail Larson, Torch looked down at the notes he had brought, and then looked back at the four women, who seemed to be waiting for him with baited breath.

"I understand your concern with these three cases, ladies. No, I'm sorry, four cases. I prematurely cut it to three cases because an arrest is imminent in the latest case." Torch glanced at the chief, who seemed satisfied by that remark. "The case I am referring to is that of Connie Walker, who was killed in June. Yesterday we issued a warrant for the person we think raped and killed her, but I cannot release the name yet. We believe the accused is in town, and it's just a matter of locating the person. We do have DNA that matches the

MIKE HOLST

accused; not only semen, but he also bled all over her. She got her licks in before he bashed her head in."

"Next is the case of Yvonne Nelson, who was killed last February. We have no leads, I'm sorry to say, and this will be a very hard case to solve. The victim was a prostitute and a meth addict."

"I'm sorry," the councilwoman interjected. She had been writing down Torch's every word on a steno pad. "What kind of addict?"

"Meth…Methamphetamine.

"It's a drug that's highly addictive and is getting very popular." Torch waited for her to finish writing what he had said.

She smiled at him to indicate she was happy with his answer.

"Was there DNA in this case?" the mayor asked, pausing for the moment, from rummaging through papers.

"Yes, too much, I'm afraid. The victim had had sex with several men before she was killed, and there were copious amounts of sperm in her body from at least four different people. The sex would have to have occurred almost simultaneously. It could indicate a gang rape, or it could just indicate a very busy woman. In any case, it will be hard to use the evidence, despite all we have of it."

Gail Larson had opened her black leather purse and taken out a white lace hanky. Torch felt she was about one gulp away from losing her breakfast.

"The third victim, which I believe was Bess…" Torch paged through his notes. "Yes, Bess Porter. Killed and raped on August eleventh, last year. This is also a very active case. We think that this was a drug deal gone bad and rape was just an afterthought. The reason we think this, was that the sex was anal and tore her up pretty bad. The perpetrator used a condom, so no sperm, and consequently, no DNA. We did have a witness in this case that gave us a statement, and then had his throat slit from ear to ear a week later. We have not been able to corroborate his statement, or find the people he implicated. By the way, we have not solved his murder, either."

Back to his notes, Torch continued, "The last victim was Sarah Moen; another prostitute who, by the way, had recently come down with full-blown AIDS. She might have the last laugh on the rapist in this assault. We have a sperm sample from her body, but no match, and it does not match any other sperm samples from the other victims. This has been another tough case to solve."

150

Torch looked up at the four women. The councilwoman had stopped writing and was using her steno pad to fan herself. She had also gathered her skirt around her knees and was holding them bunched together. Her legs were clinched together as if she was expecting something, or somebody, to crawl in there and assault her at any moment.

Old frail Gail was pale and trembling slightly. Torch touched her arm to see if she was all right, but she didn't respond. The other two wide-eyed women didn't seem to look like they needed, or wanted, any further explanation. The mayor was still digging in his papers, quite oblivious to what was going on around him. The chief was sitting perfectly erect in his spiffy blue uniform, with all of the stars and braids. His hands were folded in front of him yet, and he had a look on his face that would pass for a person who had tried to sneak one out and soiled his underwear.

Torch continued. "I apologize if I was too graphic, but I wanted you all to realize that these are vastly different cases. There are those in the media who would argue that they are all connected, but believe me, they are not." With that, Torch closed his folder and looked at the chief, and the mayor, who had given up his paper hunt and was now staring at Torch, too.

The four women all rose in unison, thanking the chief and the mayor for meeting with them. They pretty much ignored Torch, then turned and walked out. Two of them were holding Gail up, slightly, as she seemed a little light on her feet.

As soon as the door closed, the mayor rose and also thanked the chief. Nodding at Torch, he said. "Thanks for meeting with us, detective. What did you say your name was?"

"I didn't," said Torch, smiling. "It's Brennan...Torch Brennan."

"Irish?" said the mayor.

"It's an Irish name, but I'm pretty much a mutt." Torch gave him his best grin. The mayor smiled and left, leaving the door open. As soon as the mayor was out of earshot, the chief started in on him.

"Holy shit Torch, why didn't you just bring along a few morgue shots. I thought that old gal was going to puke right here on my brand new carpeting. My God, man, copious amounts of semen, and anal penetration that tore her up pretty bad. You have a way with words, don't you? You should run for office or give lectures somewhere."

"Bet they won't be back," Torch grinned.

The chief just shook his head.

"May I leave?" Torch asked.

"Please do, and close the damn door behind you."

Torch walked past the chief's young secretary, who handed him a note as he passed her desk, while she talked on the phone. She gave him one of those cute little finger waves and a flip of her hair. Torch smiled, and blew her a kiss.

The phone number on the pink slip was familiar, but he couldn't place it. There was no name. He had to go to a staff meeting, but he would call it when he got out.

He smiled, thinking, *All in all, the meeting had gone well, hadn't it?*

The early morning phone call had been a big surprise to Charlie. She was just walking out the door to go to work. It was David Rasmussen, the chair of the Minnesota Democratic Party.

"Hey, Charlie, got a minute? This is Rasmussen."

"David, good to hear from you. Hang on a second." She was trying to balance her coffee cup, her purse and keys, and an attaché case while she talked. Charlie dumped all but the coffee cup in a chair by the front door.

"You caught me just going out the door, and I had to set something down or drop the whole damn mess. What's up?"

"Charlie, Bob Harris pulled out of the County Attorney race last night. This guy changes his mind more than most of us change underwear, but this time, it's for real. He is going to run for the Senate. This is a late date for him to do all of this, with the election four months away, but that's another story for another time."

"I think you know why I am calling you, and especially now that you know what I just told you." He hesitated for a moment, and there was a short awkward silence. "Charlie, we need you to run for the County Attorney's Office. We have no one else so—if not for you—for the party. Look, I can assure you that you will have party endorsement, and we will launch one hell of a campaign for you. We will work our asses off to get you in that office, and the campaign money is there, my friend. We need you to be that candidate, but we have no time to lose."

Charlie had swept all of the things off on the floor that she had put on the chair, except her coffee cup. She sat down because she needed to sit down.

Her mind was spinning and she didn't know what to say right now. This was the position she had dreamed about and now that it was being offered to her, she was confused. She took a deep breath and bit her lip. She always did this when she was perplexed.

"David, this is very sudden. I really don't know what to tell you right now. I wish I did. This is all too sudden, as attractive as it seems." She ran her hand through her long auburn hair; her eyes were closed in a grimace, trying to think of what to say that would make sense.

"Give me the day to think about it, David. I'll call you back tonight. By the way, who else is running?"

"No one right now, Charlie. No one wanted to oppose Harris, but that might change if you run. I can't see it being an uncontested race. I would almost think the other party would have to put someone in the race, but right now, who that would be is anybody's guess. All I can say is, at this late date, if we hit the pavement running, I can't see anyone else being much of a challenge. I can't keep this quiet very long, Charlie. Harris is making an announcement for his bid for the Senate tonight, at the Sheridan."

"I understand, David. I just have a lot at stake here. I have a very good job and..."

David interrupted, "Look Charlie, let's do this. Let me take you out to supper tonight. No strings attached. My wife will make me be home by nine, anyway." He laughed nervously. "What do you say, my friend? Murray's at seven? My treat?"

Charlie smiled. That seed that had been planted a couple of years ago, was poking through the ground today, and she knew right now she was powerless to stop it. David was only the catalyst.

"Murray's at seven it is." She folded her phone and dropped it in her purse.

The drive to work was just a few short miles that normally took half an hour; half an hour that she always used to plan her day. When she pulled into the ramp, she hadn't had one conclusive thought. Her mind refused to be tied down to any one thing this morning. It was racing around helter skelter, not sure where to go, or what to do.

She stepped off the elevator and walked across the corridor to her office. The silver letters emblazoned on the frosted glass door saying, **Charlene Malloy and Associates**, seemed to leap out at her, and she wondered how they would remove them. She passed her receptionist's desk and muttered, "Good morning," but didn't make eye contact.

The other people in the room, coming and going, seemed to be a blur, and although several of them spoke to her, she could only smile like the cat that ate the canary.

At last, arriving at the refuge of her spacious office, she slipped inside and closed the door. She went right to the windows that looked out on Washington Avenue far below. How many times had she stood here, frustrated and in deep thought, trying to form some kind of one-way bond with those tiny characters walking way down there. Her work at this place had alienated her from ordinary citizens. Charlie loved people, and loved working with them, and that's what this job would be—a public servant trying to make this world a safer place to live in. For way too many years she had been on the wrong side of the criminal justice system, defending the very people she despised. All of her legal victories had been hollow meaningless victories; always tainted by the realization that she had helped keep someone who belonged in prison, out of prison.

Prosecutor. God, how nice that sounded.

The ringing phone on her desk snapped her busy mind back to reality. She looked at the I.D. on the phone. It was Mathew Senior. *Had he heard something already? He seldom talked to her anymore. Why now?* With trembling fingers, she pushed the button and left it on speakerphone. She preferred to be standing a few protective feet from the instrument.

"Mathew, Charlie here. What's up?"

"Charlie, good morning. Listen, I need to talk to you about something. Can you come up here in an hour."

"Sure, anything serious?"

"Just a change that's in the works, but we can talk more when you get here."

"See you in an hour, Mathew." She disconnected the line.

This had nothing to do with what was happening to her right now. She knew that for sure, and beyond that, well, she just didn't give a shit anymore, did she?

Charlie sat down in her big leather chair and spun around in circles, the way she used to play in her father's chair. She put her phone on "do not disturb" and walking over, locked her door. She needed to make this as painless as possible, so the first thing she had to do was write a resignation letter.

She was doing the right thing, right? She didn't think about it very long.

Right, she was doing the right thing and there was no turning back now. She had defended her last guilty felon. She had laid down with Mathew Senior for the last time, and she was through being nice to his asshole kid.

Charlie started to giggle. My God, she was almost giddy. She fired up her laptop and started writing.

Hal was late to work this morning, as he was most mornings. He had come home drunk again last night, but had lucked out, as Stephanie was out sowing her own wild oats. Her oats had been dropped on a card table in a casino somewhere, and Hal's had been spewed deep in the loins of a girl he had been seeing for some time now. But live and let live, right? That was Hal's philosophy, but things were coming to a head in the household. Propped up against the coffee pot this morning was a note to Hal from Stephanie.

Dear Hal. Tell me who you are sleeping with, and I will tell you how much of your money I have lost. Love, Stephanie.

He had crumpled the note and left it right where she had put it. It was none of her damn business who he slept around with. She was never available, and when she was, well, it was no good anyway. Marrying her had been the biggest mistake he had ever made, and some day it was going to cost her dearly. For now, he was going to cut off her credit cards and her allowance. They were going to have that talk tonight if she was home.

This morning, there had been a message from his father to see him as soon as he came in. He took the shiny chrome elevator up to the old man's office. He was in for another of his ass chewing's and he knew it.

Jenny had looked up from her desk, outside of Mathew's office, only long enough to tell Hal to go right in, he was expecting him. The old man had not looked happy today when he came in, and this guy was the main reason. Everybody knew that.

Hal walked over to the front of his desk, and sat down in one of the leather chairs.

"What's up?" Hal said smugly.

Mathew Senior took his glasses off and stood up, walked around the huge ornate desk, and made himself a drink from the liquor cabinet. He did not offer Hal one.

"Hal, when I put this firm together, it was always my hope that you would someday try and take over." He was talking somewhat calmly, but his face told another story.

"I knew this would be expecting a lot because, from the day you were born, you have been a bitter disappointment. Your life has been one big parade of unfulfilled dreams and bitter disillusionment to me. You have, in effect, been the epitome of failure to me."

"Yesterday, I received another report from your department that only seeks to emphasize how bad your leadership has screwed that department up. So I am taking the following action."

Hal looked up at his a father with a cynical smile that spoke volumes for his selfish, no-caring attitude.

"Do tell." He mocked his father.

Mathew Senior gulped the rest of his scotch, and with a look of utter contempt, lowered his voice. The tone was somewhere between a hiss and a loud whisper. He pointed his right forefinger at Hal.

"This is your last chance. You have embarrassed me, this firm and your family for the last time."

"Effective Monday, you will be relieved of your duties in the department you have been ruining. You are being moved to the Criminal Justice division, where you will be under the direction of Charlene Malloy. It is my hope that she can straighten you out and maybe, just maybe, someday you can take over that department. Hopefully, before I retire. Do you have any questions or comments that could be deemed constructive? I don't want to hear any of your useless lies and excuses."

Hal just continued grinning, and shrugged his shoulders. He had a hell of a hangover, and arguing with this old relic was not something he needed right now.

"If you have nothing to say, then fine, I will be notifying Charlie… Charlene…later this morning. One other thing I want to say before you go clean out your desk, is this…" He was now standing directly over Hal, and was talking in a normal voice with a stern, fatherly look on his face. "I know what you are doing, with your home life, to ruin it. Take responsibility for your marriage and your child, and for once in your life, behave yourself."

"Do you have any idea what my wife is doing in her spare time?" Hal looked up at his father.

"No, I have no control over that. You need to work things out. I don't want to know."

"Why not? You know everything else that is going on." Hal was getting angry.

"Look, I will take your changes and maneuvers here at work. It's your firm…for now," he added. "But you keep your goddamn nose out of my family's life and my personal life." Hal was standing now, facing his father and glaring at him.

Mathew Senior did not respond. He went over to his private bathroom, slamming the door behind him. He stood, palms down on the vanity top, looking at his face in the mirror. The veins in his neck were sticking out and his face was beet red and sweaty. He felt dizzy and disoriented and had pains in his chest. *Too much scotch, too early,* he thought. He turned and ran for the stool and vomited. Then he slumped down next to the stool and rested his head on the seat. Here was Mathew Halsworth Senior, the President and CEO of the biggest law firm around, at his wits' end. He got up, went over to the sink, and rinsed his mouth out. When he opened the door, Hal was gone. *Good,* he thought, *Charlie should be here any minute.*

CHAPTER NINETEEN

Almost any other time, Charlie would have dreaded a meeting like this, but not today. She had no idea what it was going to be about, and cared less. He had physically touched her for the last time. No more dirty jobs to get junior out of a jam. No more cooking the books to hide other things from the other lawyers. She was charting a new course and if it didn't work out she would chart another course, again and again, until she found what she wanted.

Last Sunday had been her fifty-fifth birthday, and Charlie had suddenly realized that she was in the last third of her life—maybe the last fourth. The middle third had been wasted, and now she had a chance to find some happiness and salvage the rest. Standing in front of the mirror in the bathroom last Sunday morning, she had preened naked and still liked what she saw. She still had a nice butt, and her breasts had drooped a little, but nothing bad. She might get a little face tuck to pull up some of the sagginess. Her hair was still full and vibrant, even though she used a tint to hide some gray. Not having children had helped, and the physical standards she had set for herself also contributed.

Charlie had found out early in life that she couldn't have children. She had come to grips with that, and it was okay. But not having a husband had not been something she had accepted. Maybe now some things would happen in her life. She was feeling good about herself and that was a great start in the right direction.

Mathew was not in his office when she walked in, but she could hear water running in the bathroom, so she sat down and made herself comfortable. He came out, wiping his hands on a paper towel, and then wiping his face with it before throwing it in the wastebasket. He didn't go behind his desk but took the other chair beside her. He put his hand over hers on the armrest before he started talking.

"Charlie, we have been through a lot together over the years, and I have asked you for many favors. Too many, I know. But you have been a good and faithful employee and you have gone the extra mile for me many times."

Like taking my panties off, she thought.

"What I have to ask you today is not going to sit well with you, but I have no other choice."

Charlie turned to face him, looking at him, curiously.

Not one more time for old time's sake, please! No...this was not his sex-begging speech...something else was up.

"Charlie, you know all too well what a disappointment my son has been, not only to me, but also to this firm. I should have washed my hands of him long ago, but I can't."

He paused to see if she had any comments, but Charlie said nothing. She was staring into her lap, playing with the crease in her pants.

"I am moving him to your department, Charlie. Because of him, the department he is in is in serious trouble. I want you to teach him how to be a good lawyer, and a good manager. He would never have made it through college, in fact, he would have never passed the bar without your help, and so you need to help him one more time.

Now, that being said, I know that you don't like Hal, which is understandable, but I have no choice in this matter, and neither do you, as far as that goes. Do you understand what I have just said? You seem awfully quiet."

"I have no comment," Charlie finally said. "You're the boss."

"It will all work out," Mathew replied. "Let's give it a chance." He reached over and put his hand on her shoulder and squeezed it. You know, it's been a long time since we have done something together. Maybe we need to take a few days off and fly down to Mexico this fall. Would you like that?"

Charlie smiled. "Let's see what comes." She patted his hand. "Now, if we are done, I have a meeting."

He stood looking out the window after she had left. *That had gone better than he had thought it would.* For a few minutes he thought about Charlie, and all she had done for him and the company. *The companionship she had brought him. Maybe he should try to think of something special he could do for her. She was already one of his highest paid employees, so money wasn't the answer.* He had to think about this.

He also had to think about this indigestion and pain he had been having in his chest. Maybe he should make an appointment with his doctor. It had been a while, and the pain and indigestion seemed to get a lot worse when he was upset.

Torch called Todd just before he headed home for the weekend. He picked up on the first ring, as if he was sitting, waiting for the call.

"Todd, Torch Brennan here. How are you doing?"

"Torch...thanks for calling back. Hey, I'm doing all right. Getting married in a couple of weeks and I just bought another farm. Guess I can't complain."

"That's great, Todd. How's your dad doing?"

"He's getting along, Torch, but the reason I called you was because he asked me to. You know the end of the year makes ten years since Stacie was killed. I guess both of us wonder why you guys seem to have given up on finding her killer?"

"We haven't given up, Todd, and you know what? I know who her killer was. I just never had enough evidence to put him away. But you're right, maybe it's time we took another look at things. Let me do this. We have a big caseload right now, but barring any more cases coming in that are difficult ones, as soon as I can I will try to reopen things here. Just a few more weeks, and hopefully, things will be better."

"You're not just giving me lip service, Torch?"

"No, I promise you, buddy. I'll see what I can do."

"Thanks, Torch."

"That's what we are here for, pal. Take care of yourself."

Torch hung up the phone, and looked down at the pile of reports and papers on his desk. Then, rising wearily, he went over to a file cabinet and sorted through a row of files until he found the one he wanted. Her picture was still stapled inside the manila cover that read, **Stacie Morrison**. He stared at the picture for a moment, while thoughts about the case ran through his mind; things he had tried to put out of his mind for a long, long time. Theresa, his good partner, and the warnings from her he had not heeded. That smug, female attorney from Hal's father's firm that had blocked everything he wanted to do. Yes, maybe it was time to look at this again. He put the file on his desk blotter. On Monday morning he would have another look. For now, he was tired and was going home.

It had been ten years since Stacie was murdered, and it had also been ten years since Evie had died. A lot of water had flowed under the bridge since then. Maybe it was time to try and do something about it—the murder and Evie's death. He was terribly lonely.

Murray's was not that crowded for a warm summer evening. David had reserved a table in the back, where they could have some privacy, and he was waiting in the front when Charlie showed up. She had taken a cab because she didn't like to drive after drinking, and she just might have a bump or two. After all, this was a momentous occasion. At least for her it was.

David looked so nice in his dark blue suit and red tie. It made her think, for a moment, what the lack of a man in her life had done to her. Then she got back to reality, and she quickly recovered. Smiling broadly, she said. "Hi, David. It's good to see you." Charlie kissed him on the cheek. He smelled so good.

"Charlie, damn, you look good tonight."

"What night was it that I didn't look good, David?" she said laughing.

He laughed with her. "Quit being a lawyer, Charlie—just for tonight, though."

They ordered drinks and relaxed with the usual chatter about work, friends and family. The subject matter, that had brought them here tonight, seemed to be taboo for the moment. Maybe they just wanted to enjoy each other's company a little before the serious talk came along. Maybe, at least in David's case, if the evening was going to be spoiled, let it be at the end.

Murray's was known for their steaks, and although they were both health freaks, they ordered and dived in anyway. This was as good as food got. There was little conversation while they ate, both of them preferring to just enjoy the ambience. They finished it off with a piece of German chocolate fudge cake they resolved to share. It was almost exotic, and they smiled and savored every bite.

At last, full and relaxed, it was time and Charlie knew it. David had reached for his attaché case to get some papers. In it was his presentation that he had worked on for most of the day. David feared this would be needed if he was to have half a chance to draw this powerful woman away from the firm she had worked at all of her life. This could be a threat to her security blanket, both financially and career-wise. He had little to offer her in return.

Charlie sat smiling, her hands in her lap, while David arranged all of his papers on the recently cleared tabletop. This was going to be fun.

David cleared his throat. Charlie's broad smile was making him nervous and he didn't know what to think of it.

"David." Charlie's voice was soft and almost seductive. "The answer is yes."

David's eyes registered his surprise at first, and then his entire face broke into a huge smile. "Yes! Yes! You mean you will do it?" They had drawn the attention of people at tables around them, who could only surmise that she had agreed to marry him, or something of the sort.

"Yes, David, I will do it, and you can put all of that crap away and order us each another drink."

He was ecstatic and pushed all of his papers into a pile and threw them on the floor. Charlie, you will not be sorry you did this." They both looked around at the stares and broke out laughing. They were not going to explain anything to anyone. Let them think what they may.

"David, I have one favor to ask you. None of this hits the media until the day after tomorrow. I have things that need to be done properly. I think you understand."

"You got it, my friend. But Monday morning, we are going to start the…" He lowered his voice. "…the campaign that will make you County Attorney of the most populated county in the state. He was quiet for a second, just staring at Charlie. "Tell me, Charlie, I'm curious. When did you make your decision?"

"About five minutes after you called this morning." She giggled at both the thought, and the look of astonishment on his face."

"You couldn't tell me then?"

"I wouldn't have gotten this supper date then, would I?"

It was David's turn to laugh hysterically, with his head down on the table.

Charlie didn't need that cab ride home. David walked her to her door, even though she hadn't had that much to drink. She was feeling a little euphoric, but it had nothing to do with alcohol. It had to do with a whole new outlook on life.

When she was finally in bed, the whole impact of what she had done finally sank in. She thought of some of the negatives—the comfortable lifestyle she had enjoyed and the huge salary that had made it possible—the people she had worked with for so long, and the friendships she had made. It was going to hurt a little, no doubt about it, but tit for tat, in the end she was going to be way ahead. For once, she would be the boss, and she would call the shots. Before this, she had all of the responsibility and none of the glory. Everyone needs some glory in his or her life. Everyone needs a chance to plot their own course.

Charlie was laying in her king-size, four-poster, solid oak bed, on her twelve hundred dollar sheets, staring at the gold ceiling fan revolving slowly over her head. The breeze felt good through her thin cotton pajamas. She clutched her pillow to her breast. This change was going to be good, but something was still missing. There was still an ache in her heart that she had suppressed for a long, long time. Someone needed to share this bed with her. For so much of her life, this had been her place of comfort. The only place where she had been truly happy; her refuge where she had cried when she was sad, and where she had screamed and pounded her pillow when she was mad. She had sat on this big bed and worked on legal cases in her underwear, while eating a smoked turkey sandwich, and drinking twenty dollar a bottle white zinfandel or anything else that tempted her palate.

She put the pillow back under her head, and rolled on her side, facing the empty part of the bed. *Please God*, she prayed, *bring me someone to love*.

CHAPTER TWENTY

Hal made the decision on Monday morning at work. He cancelled out all of Stephanie's charge cards. He had closed out their joint checking and savings account, and reopened one in his name only. He paid all of her bills off, and was absolutely incensed at the amount of money she had spent. He also filed legal papers to absolve him of any further debts she had. *The bitch will live by my rules now,* he thought. *Tonight the shit is going to hit the fan.*

There was another bitch he had to meet with today, to iron out the details of his switch to her department. His father had insisted they work it out together. As for the rest of the day, he was meeting with his successor, the man that would be taking over his office and responsibilities.

Despite all of his hate and animosity for Charlie, Hal fully realized that he was not going to succeed in this firm without her help. He was not going to be able to treat her the same way he treated Stephanie. He dialed her number but she wasn't at her desk. Her secretary said she had gone up to Mr. Halsworth's office.

Piss on meeting with her. They could meet tomorrow.

Getting off the elevator, Charlie held the letter in her clammy hand as she walked down the hall to Halsworth's office. She had lain awake late into the night, thinking about what she could say to soften the blow. She knew he was going to be irate, that was a given.

She stopped in the hall, once more, to read the letter.

Dear Mr. Halsworth,

I regret to inform you that I have decided to terminate my position with

The Halsworth Law Firm to pursue another venue. By the time you read this letter, my intentions will have been made public to the media. I plan on running for the County Attorney's Office in Hennepin County, and if I am not successful at that, well then, I will probably go into private practice.

I want to thank you for all you have done for me over the years. I have many fond memories of my career here at this firm. However, now it is time for a change.

I will do whatever I can do to make the transition go smoothly, but consider this my two weeks' notice.

Sincerely, Charlene Malloy

She thought about going back and rewriting it. It seemed cold and too business-like, but then she thought about the cold abuses he had made her submit to over the years. *He had screwed her over, both literally and figuratively. Why should she worry about his feelings? Let's get it done.* Charlie pushed open the door and walked to his receptionist's desk.

"Go on in, Charlie, he's expecting you." She smiled softly. She had seen and heard too much over the years when Charlie was in that office.

Mathew was behind his desk, working on some paperwork, when Charlie walked in. He set down his pen and looking up, smiled broadly. "Charlie, you wanted to see me. Sit down...sit down. Can I get you something?"

"No, I'm fine," she said.

She wiped her sweaty palms on her pants legs and sat down carefully, not sitting back but leaning forward, and handed him the envelope across his desk.

Mathew was frowning, "What's this, Charlie?"

"Read it, sir. It's self-explanatory."

Mathew read the letter, and then set it down in front of him on his desk, and stared at Charlie. It was as if he was thinking about what to say, but the words would not come. He picked up the letter and read it again. Then he crumpled it into a ball, and threw it on the floor.

At first, his voice was nearly normal, but you could tell he was making a great effort to keep it that way.

"I can't say that I am not surprised. I'm not going to question your wild aspirations here, but I do question your loyalty to this firm and me. I took you from a timid little bumbling lawyer and made you what you are today." His voice raised an octave. "This is the thanks I get?"

His voice rose again, and he walked around his desk, now hovering over her in her chair. "You have to be out of your goddamn mind to even consider this!" He waved his arms at her to emphasize his point.

He was quiet for a moment. Charlie was clearly uncomfortable. She met his angry eyes with her pleading eyes for just a fleeting second, and then stared back at the floor. Her heart was racing and she could feel tears, that she couldn't let fall, filling her eyes. She had to try and remain composed—she knew that was important.

Mathew had gone back behind his desk, and reached into a file. When he looked up, his angry face had been transformed into a cynical face. It was almost a sneer.

"Maybe you have forgotten about this, Charlene." He had never called her by her given name before.

He held the contract that she had signed, so many years ago, in front of her face. His hands were shaking so badly she could barely make out the words but she didn't need to. She knew what it said. She had a copy.

Now he was mad again and getting louder. "This contract says you cannot practice law anywhere else, for five years, if you leave this firm without my consent. How do you propose to be the head attorney for this county, and not be able to practice law?"

Now he was cynical again, his voice nearly a hiss. "That is if you get elected, and I might have something to say about that. I am a very powerful man in this community and I have ways to get things done you can only dream about. Wake up, Charlene!"

Charlie jumped up out of her chair. Now it was her turn to be mad. "That contract can be challenged, and I am not sure that I do have to practice law to administer that department. If I challenge that contract, a lot of dirty details will be brought out, I promise you that. Not just about the degrading filthy things you made me do, but also about your no-good bastard of a son. You don't think I have details about crimes he was accused of? Trust me, Mathew, it won't be pretty."

Now the tears were coming, but she was past the point of caring any longer. "That letter is final notice of my intentions, and I'm not going to sit here any longer and be abused by you. Copies have been sent to the other partners. If you have anything else to say to me that is constructive, I will listen. Otherwise, I am leaving."

"Get out," he shouted. "You don't have to resign. You're fired, bitch!"

"Great," Charlie said. "It works for me."

She held herself together until she got back to her office. Then she shut the door and collapsed on the floor sobbing, but only for a moment. This was a defining moment in her life and she was not going to ruin it by acting like a wimp. Slowly, she stood up and went to the bathroom; she washed her face and fixed her make up. Then, Charlie sat down behind her desk and pushed the intercom button.

"Sharon, will you have maintenance bring me up a couple of cardboard boxes I can put some things in. File size would be sufficient."

She opened her purse and took out a Valium she had saved for just this kind of occasion. She swallowed it, without water, and pushed the intercom again.

"Sharon, there will be a meeting of the entire staff at 1 p.m."

"What shall I tell them it's about?"

"My leaving, Sharon."

As soon as Charlie had left his office, Mathew collapsed in his chair. His face was beet red and he was having trouble breathing. He put his forefinger in his collar to try and make more room. His left arm and neck were aching, just like the other day. Nausea was coming in waves and he turned and vomited into his wastebasket. *What the hell was the matter?*

The vomiting finally subsided. It seemed to have relieved his symptoms somewhat, but for a long time he sat with his head down on the desk. The cold desktop felt good on his hot face. Then he rose and went to his closet and got his coat. His secretary looked up at him when he walked out. She could see his ashen color and trembling hands.

"Mr. Halsworth, are you all right, sir?"

"Just a touch of the flu. I am going home for the rest of the day. Cancel my appointments."

"Yes, sir. Is there anything else I can do?" She had gotten up from her desk to go to him. She could smell the stench of vomit on his breath.

He didn't answer her; he walked past her and out the door.

Torch had been in court all morning and didn't get back to his desk until after three. He sat wearily sorting through his notes. Most of them could wait, but the last one was the one he had left for himself. **Call Collin Lang**.

Lang was a fixture in Hennepin County. He was closing in on twenty years with the Coroner's Office. He was also recognized, in the state of Minnesota, as an expert in the field of forensic medicine. His work was well-known and hailed throughout the area. Many difficult cases had been brought to his laboratories to be worked on.

He had worked closely with Torch on several cases where DNA testing had been used, as conclusive evidence, in convicting criminals. Torch had not kept up on the science himself, but he was aware that great strides had been made in this field, and that was what he wanted to talk about with Lang today.

"Hey, Collin. How are things in the Rue Morgue?"

Collin laughed. Torch always had some sick joke for him about, what Torch viewed, as a ghoulish job. "Same old, same old, Torch. If you got time, we have an autopsy today on one that was floating in a lake for about three weeks, and should smell pretty good."

"Well, if it's all the same to you, I think I'm busy. Listen, you got time to jabber about DNA for a while?"

"You need to find out who your father really was?" Both men laughed at the banter.

"No, but I do need to find out who someone else's father was. Collin, do you remember a case, about ten years ago, involving a college coed that was murdered and dumped in the river?"

"Keep talking and refresh my memory."

"Her name was Stacie Morrison; U of M gal that hailed from Wisconsin."

Torch could hear Collin typing on his keyboard. "Yea, I have it here, Torch. Case was never solved—or was it?"

"Well, it was solved as far as I was concerned, we just never had the proof we needed to get an indictment."

"There was a fetus that was removed from Stacie's womb, and saved. You still have that...right?"

"Ah, yes. We would not have destroyed it without your permission. It's probably been frozen all of this time. Want me to check?"

"Yes. First though, answer my question. When I talked to you way back then, you told me that you couldn't determine the paternity of that fetus. That you could only tell me who the father wasn't."

"That's correct, Torch."

"Is that still the case?"

"No, no. We have been able to, for quite some time now, separate the DNA and determine the parents. We can do a reverse paternity test by separating the Y-chromosomes from the X-chromosomes. It's not totally conclusive because, if the suspect has a brother, he would also be a match."

Torch was thinking. "But it limits it to that particular family...right?"

"Right."

"You say you could have done this several years ago?"

"Yes, I would say at least five years ago."

"Damn it, Collin. This pisses me off. Here I have been sitting on this thing all of these years and...shit to hell!"

"Torch, I'm sorry, but we can't keep track of...."

"No, no, Collin." Torch interrupted. "It's not your fault." It was quiet for a few seconds. "Make sure you still have that specimen and I will get back to you. How long does it take to get this test done?"

"Well, once you get us the DNA, it might be a few months. We have to send it to a lab out east and they're pretty backed up. I'm going to send you over a booklet that will show you the proper way to collect and preserve DNA samples, but you should know this stuff already."

"Thanks. There's no way, once we get the DNA to you, to get this testing done faster?"

"They do make exceptions for emergencies, but I doubt they will see this in that light. Girl's been dead for ten years, and as far as they are concerned, what are another few months?"

"Thanks, Collin. I'll be talking with you."

Torch hung up the phone. He was still mad at himself for not making this call a few years ago, but that was going to have to wait. Right now, he was going to have to figure out how to get Hal Halsworth's DNA. It was a cinch he was not going to get him to come in and do it in a test tube for him. He'd better wait for that booklet. He had screwed this case up enough already. As for now, he was going to Whitey's for supper.

Hal had gone up to his father's office that afternoon to ask about the arrangements for moving from office to office.

"He went home sick, Hal. He really looked peaked." Mathew's secretary seemed quite concerned.

"Well, maybe I'll just stop out at home and check up on him. Thanks for the info."

First, Hal had other plans. He needed to go home and finish his fight with Stephanie. Before that though, he needed some courage, and he knew just the place to get it.

Hal made it to three of his favorite drinking establishments before he wandered into the house to face Stephanie, who was waiting for him with both barrels loaded. She had gone shopping today, and found all of her credit cards revoked. She was sitting at the kitchen table feeding their son, when Hal walked in, feeling no pain.

"Put the kid to bed," he said. "You and I have to talk."

Stephanie picked up the toddler and left the room. When she returned, Hal was leaning back in his chair with a bottle of beer in his hand, and his feet up on the table. He was smirking at her when she walked in and sat down. She reached over and pushed his feet away from in front of her.

"You mind telling me what the hell is going on? I was with my friends today, and all of a sudden, none of my cards are good and the checking account is closed. I have never been so damn embarrassed in all of my life."

Hal said nothing, just smirked at her.

"If you think, for one minute, that you are going to keep me penned up here in this hole all day..." Hal swung his foot from the other end of the table, where she had pushed it, hitting her on the side of the head and knocking her off her chair onto the floor.

As quick as a cat, he was on top of her, holding her sweater bunched up in his hands and pushed up against the side of her head. "You listen to me and you listen good, you no-good bitch. You have had your last damn shopping trip for a while, and you are going to stay home and be a wife and mother."

Stephanie tried to squirm out from under him, but he held her tight between his knees, sitting on her stomach and chest. She could hardly breathe, let alone move. Worse yet, she could feel his groin pressing against her. *The son of a bitch had an erection on. What in the hell was going on here?*

Hal was still grinning at her like he was berserk, and he let go of her sweater, with his right hand, long enough to reach up on the table top and grab his beer. He chugged down the rest of the beer, and then smashed the bottle against the table leg, and held the jagged top to her throat.

"I should just cut your miserable throat and get it over with."

Stephanie was truly scared now. She had seen him mad before, but never like this.

"Marrying you was the biggest damn mistake I ever made, and all because of that snot-nosed kid. Well, Hal Halsworth rules the roost here from now on, and you just better do as I say, and keep your goddamn mouth shut or I am going to gut you like a dead animal. Do you understand?" he shouted.

He backhanded her across the face, the broken bottle cutting open her forehead, and his fist breaking her nose. The pain was incredible. Blood was running down her face and she tried to scream, but it was all garbled. He slid down and pulled her sweater up over her head and ripped her bra off. She was trying to kick him in the back with her knees, but he was sitting on her legs just enough that she couldn't raise them. Then he reached down and bit one of her breasts so hard he tore it open, and she could feel blood running onto her chest. He was laughing like a savage. It was then she realized, if she continued to struggle he would probably kill her, so she went limp.

From there, it was all a bad dream, as she felt him rip off her jeans and panties. She tried some token resistance, holding her legs together, but he forced them wide apart and she felt him roughly enter her. Her head was banging against the wall, and each hit brought her closer to unconsciousness.

Let him have his way, her mind was saying. *It will be the last time.* Then he stopped. He was still sitting on her, his breaths coming in gasps, his hands still gripping the side of her bloody head.

Stephanie was not able to function at all. She was still aware of his presence, but she was powerless to talk, see or move. She felt his body weight moving off of her, and him withdrawing from inside of her. Then blackness robbed her of everything.

When she came to, Hal was still there. She could hear him walking around the house, smashing things. He was ranting and screaming, but she couldn't make out what he was saying.

Then his footsteps were coming back towards her again. She curled up in a fetal position, trying to protect her body as good as she could. She was lying in busted glass and she could feel it cutting her side. The footsteps grew louder, and then they were right beside her. Stephanie could hear his ragged breathing once more, and she was afraid he had come back to finish what he had started. Common sense told her to remain still.

She could feel his shoes against her back and then he stepped up on her side with one foot, and bending over, grabbed her hair and pulled her bloody face close to his. "You ever question me again, bitch, and you will end up in the river just like the other one. I never wanted you or that kid and you remember that, too." He slammed her head back to the floor and she passed out again.

When she came to it was quiet, except for little Hal's crying, in the other room. For a moment she lay still, listening for any noise that might indicate that Hal was still there. She was lying on her side in a puddle of blood. Struggling to lift her head, she tried to see and feel what damage Hal had done to her. Her forehead, nose, breast and her vagina were all bleeding. In the bedroom, the toddler's crying had changed to screaming. Stephanie tried to get up and walk, but her jeans and underwear were still tangled around one foot and she fell again, hitting her elbow. She kicked off the clothing and ran for the bedroom. Little Hal was standing in his crib, crying, but he looked okay. She wandered back to the kitchen, locked the door and dialed 911.

"Police and Fire. Do you have an emergency?"

"Yes, my husband tried to kill me."

"Do you need an ambulance?"

"Yes…I mean no… I don't know." She was sobbing hard right now. She dropped the phone and slid down to the floor. She suddenly realized that the door she had locked, for protection, was locked when he got here but, she thought, of course…he had a key.

As soon as Mathew arrived home, he went straight in to see Melinda.

The pain in his arm and neck had gone away, but he still had a heavy feeling in his chest and was very wound up. It was if his heart just simply wouldn't slow down.

Melinda was sitting up in bed, even though she was dressed. The housekeeper could be heard down the hall in the kitchen.

"Melinda." She turned to face Mathew, smiling softly, but didn't answer him. The disease had progressed rapidly in her, and right now, Mathew was not really sure she knew who he was, but he talked to her anyway. He sat on the edge of the bed, holding her hand while he talked.

"Charlie is leaving the firm and I am not sure what we are going to do," he said. Her soft smile told him she didn't comprehend what he had said, so he didn't carry on. He just patted her hand and taking a blanket from the end of the bed, went into his library and curled up on the couch. The pain in his arm was coming back and he had to lie down. He had called the doctor the other day and they had urged him to get in and get himself checked out. First thing in the morning he was going in if he still felt this lousy. He'd taken a sleeping pill and a Valium, and drowsiness was setting in.

Hal was on Highway Twelve now, heading for his parents' house. The tires on his car screamed as he drove down 394, hitting the off-ramp and heading east on the winding road around the lake.

CHAPTER TWENTY-ONE

Hal was sweating profusely. He'd hurt her bad, and he knew it. Would she call the police? He wasn't sure. It depended if she was scared enough or not.

His white shirt was covered with blood, part of his shirttail was sticking out of his fly, and the zipper was jammed up. As he always felt, after one of his anger fits, he was the victim here. She had provoked him into doing what he did. He was right and she was wrong, and sometimes with some people who wouldn't listen to reason, well, you just had to get a little more forceful.

The gates were open when he arrived at the community. Hal had been lucky on the road as a police officer had witnessed him speeding around the lake. Before he could turn around and pursue him, however, he'd gotten a medical call that was a higher priority. He did get his license plate number, and if he had time, he would follow up.

Lamont was cutting grass in front of the house when Hal drove in, leaving his car in front of the entrance. He'd not seen much of Hal lately, and that suited him just fine. He managed a glance at him as he left his vehicle, noticing the bloody white shirt. *Maybe someone was just teaching the little shit some manners,* he thought.

The police pounding on the door brought Stephanie back to reality, and she rose shakily to open it, and then realized she was nearly naked. "Just a moment," she yelled. She stumbled around the table and found her jeans and bra and put them on. She had no idea where her panties were. She went back and opened the door, collapsing into the arms of the police officers.

When she awoke again, she was being loaded into the back of an ambulance. "Hal," she cried.

"The attendant tried to calm her fears. "Shh," she said. "He's right here." She looked over, and sitting beside her was a female police officer, holding the sleeping toddler.

When they arrived at the hospital she was taken right into the emergency ward. The police officer accompanied them. While the doctors looked over Stephanie's injuries, she tried to find out what had happened to her. "Who did this to you, Stephanie?"

"Where's my baby?"

"In the Children's Center here at the hospital, Stephanie. He's fine, but let's talk about you."

The nurses had stripped off her clothing and they could now see the full extent of her wounds. Both of them could only look at her in astonishment. They had given her a sedative, which was taking affect and she was falling asleep.

A doctor finally worked his way into the cubicle. Her broken nose was still bleeding but it was just oozing blood now. Two big ugly clots of blood clogged her nostrils so she had to breathe through her mouth. The cut on her forehead had stopped bleeding altogether, but it would take a lot of stitches to close. It appeared to be about two inches long and white scull bone was showing through. The bite on her breast, however, was just plain ugly. He had nearly severed her nipple. There were teeth marks visible under the nipple, where he hadn't broken through the skin. A quick look at her genitals told him she was going to need stitches there, too, and she was going to need a pelvic examination to check for internal damage.

There were a few other cuts and bruises that were showing. They rolled her on her side, and her back appeared to be all right, except for a few small pieces of glass embedded there that they quickly removed.

"Let's get her cleaned up and then I will start sewing. Be real careful with that breast. I might have to take her to surgery on that one. Let's also get a CT scan as she might have a concussion." The doctor shook his head slowly, as if he could not believe what he was looking at. "Whoever did this is an animal," he said, to no one in particular.

Outside of the cubicle, the police officer talked to the doctor for a moment.

"This appears to be an assault and rape," she said. "We need a rape kit done for evidence, and some pictures of her wounds."

The doctor stuck his head back in the cubicle and relayed the message to the nurses.

Hal burst through the door just as Ellie, the housekeeper, was reaching for the knob to let him in. She tried to stifle something between a sob and a scream that was trying to get out of her throat when she saw him, but it was too late and it echoed in the foyer.

Hal only glared at her, and kept coming into the house, slamming the door behind him. That was when his father, who had heard all of the noise, arose from the couch and walked out of his library door. His face had a look somewhere between astonishment and concern.

At first, he didn't know what to think, but when the words finally came, he asked, "Hal, were you in an accident?"

"No, that bitch of a wife was in one. She got a short course in doing what she was told."

For a second, Mathew Sr. tried to say something, but nothing coherent came out and then, with his eyes pleading, his flailing hands grabbed his chest and his eyes rolled back in his head. He collapsed face first, in a heap on the tile floor, his forehead bouncing off the gray ceramic. Ellie ran to him, while Hal could only stare. The huge grandfather clock in the foyer, with its ornate pendulum and Big Ben chimes, rang out loudly five distinctive times. It was as if they were announcing the very moment that Mathew Halsworth's heart quit beating, for the first time in seventy-four years.

Lamont had seen and heard the commotion from outside and he burst through the door, stopping for only a second, before realizing what had happened. He ran for the phone in the kitchen and called 911.

The same police officer that had been heading for the Halsworth estate, to question young Hal about his driving, took the medical call. He was only a few blocks away.

When the officer arrived on the scene, a confusing display greeted him when he came through the doors. By now, Hal was bending over his father and screaming for him to breathe. Lamont, who was crying, was comforting Ellie, who held her hands to the side of her face and was sobbing hysterically.

In a few fleeting seconds, the officer took it all in, his survival instincts telling him to be careful, that "not everything is as cut and dried as it seems."

He called for help on his handheld radio, and then, pulling Hal off his comatose father, he rolled the elderly man onto his back and checked his vital signs. No pulse. No breathing. For a second, his eyes took in Hal's blood-stained clothes, but he quickly surmised it had nothing to do with the scene in front of him. Right now, his full attention went to Mathew Senior.

He quickly zipped open the pack he had brought in and took out a resuscitator. Holding the mask over the old man's face, the deeply concerned cop tried to fill Mathew's empty lungs with oxygen, but to no avail. He repositioned Mathew's head and tried again and saw the chest rise. Than he straddled him, and started chest compressions, stopping every so often to push the button that controls the oxygen and fills the lungs again with the air that he needed to survive.

With his motley-looking gallery anxiously watching his every move, he worked feverously, but to no apparent avail. Then the ambulance and paramedics arrived to take over for him.

For a moment, the officer stood and watched with the rest of them. Then, realizing he was no longer needed with the resuscitation attempt, he ushered Hal and the other two into an adjoining room.

"Who is this man?" he asked Lamont, but it was Hal who answered.

"My father." he said. "Mathew Halsworth."

"Were you in a fight?" he asked Hal.

"It's a long story," Hal said, wearily.

"A story I want to hear. Don't go away."

They all turned around, aware of another presence and looking up, saw Melinda. She was holding her dress up to her face, much in the way a little girl would do when upset.

Ellie ran to her, and took her in her arms, ushering her back the way she had come.

"My mother," Hal explained, "She has Alzheimer's"

"I'm so sorry," the officer responded.

The paramedics were preparing Mathew for transport. One of them continued with CPR as they rolled him out and into the back of the waiting ambulance. For several moments the ambulance just sat there, rocking with the activity that was taking place in the back. Then they slowly pulled away with the red lights flashing and siren wailing.

"I'll take you to the hospital," the officer said to Hal. "We can talk on the way."

Charlie sat at her kitchen table, drinking a glass of wine. This had been a difficult day and one that she didn't want to have to go through again. The phone was ringing and she jumped out of her trance to go pick it up.

"This is Charlie." She answered, her voice sounding soft and subdued,

"Charlie. David here. I hoped I could catch you. I called you at work and they said you had left for the day. How did it go?"

"It was brutal, David. Not unexpected, however. You would have to know Mathew to understand."

David seemed to not be too concerned about what had transpired, quickly changing the subject. "Charlie, I know this is fast, but there is a "Meet the Candidate's Forum" tonight. We need to get you introduced."

"David…already? I've barely had time to catch my breath, and now we're off and running?"

"That's the nature of the beast, Charlie. The one who runs the fastest gets the prize."

Both of them were quiet for a second. "Tell me where to be, and when," she said wearily."

"The Regency at eight."

"Dress up or casual?"

"Not dress up, but I think a business suit would be in order. There will be reporters there, so you will want to look nice. That shouldn't be hard for you."

"Thanks. You're sweet. See you at eight."

"Charlie?"

"Yes."

"You did see the paper this afternoon, right?"

"Ah, right. See you tonight, David." She had been embarrassed to say she had not seen the paper. In fact, she didn't even get the paper. It had always been on her desk at work. She slipped on her shoes and grabbed her coat. It was a short walk down to the corner store.

The sun was shining and it was a beautiful summer day. The world looked brighter somehow, and she had a silly impulse to skip or run.

While she waited for the light to change, she noticed a panhandler standing on the corner, holding up a crude cardboard sign that said, **Will work for food. Vietnam vet.** Charlie gave him a five out of her coat pocket and said, "Vote for me."

"Gee, thanks, lady. Whatcha running for?"

"Just keep your eyes open…you'll find out."

Walking into the store, she grabbed a paper and a coke, and after paying for her purchase, she went outside and sat down on a bus bench. It was on the front of the metro section. An article just a few lines long.

Charlene Malloy Running for County Attorney.

It was announced just this morning, by the Democratic Committee, that Charlene Malloy, a well-known local attorney of the prestigious law firm of Halsworth and Associates, is tossing her hat in the ring for the nomination to run for County Attorney on the Democratic ticket. David Rasmussen, the party chair, said that confirmation was certain. As of yet, no other candidates have surfaced for the seat held by Bob Harris, who is running for Congress.

Charlie read it twice. It had a nice ring to it, didn't it? County Attorney. She held the paper to her chest while she soaked it all up.

A bus was coming and she stood and waved it by. Then, she turned and ran for home.

Hal was sitting in the back of the squad as they raced for the hospital; the police officer was studying him in the rear view mirror. The cop wasn't buying into the fight story Hal had told him back at the house. There was not a mark on him; that was someone else's blood.

Hal had grabbed a light jacket, and put it on over his blood-stained shirt before they left, and it looked out of place on this warm day. Right now, he was looking out the side window, appearing quite emotionless. Not what you would expect for someone whose father was dying. But previous experience told the cop to withhold judgment on that for the time being. The questions could also wait until later.

Stephanie had been treated and released, and right now she was sitting in the back of a cab, making its way to her condo. She reached into her purse and took out a small mirror, looking at her face. Both of her eyes were turning black and blue, and she had a metal splint on her nose. Sutures showed above her eyebrow, and she had a few more in her breast and vagina. They had shot her full of antibiotics to control infection, and her breast and bottom were still numb from Novocain.

Hal was sitting on her lap, looking at her as if he wasn't sure if she was his mother or not. Poor kid spent so much time in daycare that he was used to strange faces, but not beat-up ones like this. She buried her face in his hair and cried softly.

The police had taken a statement from her at the hospital, and said they would follow it up with a visit tonight, when she had time to think longer about what had happened to her. For now, she wouldn't press charges, so they had made no attempt to go after Hal.

The cab driver, who seemed nonchalant about Stephanie's appearance, stopped in the driveway. Getting out, he offered to take Hal up to the house, but Stephanie said she was fine, and gave the man the last twenty she had. "Keep the change," she said.

When she walked into the house, she went straight to the bedroom, skirting the mess in the kitchen. Hal had fallen asleep on her lap on the way home and she laid the toddler, still sleeping, on her bed. She wanted to take a bath, then lie down and think for a while.

The Novocain was wearing off and her wounds were starting to ache. They had given her some pain pills and she took two of them. Then, returning to her bed after taking a bath, she laid down with Hal, covering them both up with a throw from the end of the bed, and she, too, fell asleep.

At 6:15 p.m. at Trinity Memorial Hospital, Mathew Halsworth Senior was pronounced dead. Hal stood and looked down at his father's body, showing no emotion. A member of the clergy stood by, but Hal told him he had no need for comforting, from the clergy or anyone else, and he should leave him alone.

Hal made arrangements with a funeral parlor to come and pick up the body and then left the emergency room to call a cab. The same police officer who had brought him to the hospital was still there, and he offered to take him back, but Hal refused the offer.

"Look, you have some explaining to do about a couple of things, and I just thought it might make things easier if we talked in the car. Otherwise, I can get a conference room and we can talk right here."

"Let's go in the car." Hal wasn't happy about the compromise, but he had no choice, or so it seemed.

The officer moved some stuff around and let him sit up front this time. They drove in silence for a short while, and then the officer initiated the conversation.

"Look, I am really sorry about your father." Hal just shrugged his shoulders and didn't answer him. He was staring out the side window, looking more mad than sad.

"You know, I saw you driving crazy earlier today. I clocked you at eighty in a forty five."

Hal gave him a defiant look. "That's what you want to talk about? My speeding down the damn road. My father was sick; don't you think that was a good enough reason?"

The cop was quiet for a second.

"I want you to explain the blood all over your clothes."

"I told you it was from a fight."

"A fight with whom?"

"Some guy in a bar."

"Which bar?"

"Look, if the guy presses charges then you can question me on this. I am a defense attorney and I know my rights. Now, please take me home."

They drove the rest of the way in silence, except for Hal saying, "Thanks for the ride," when he got out. The cop was silent.

He went straight up to his bedroom…he had to think. He'd yet to show any emotion about his father, but he thought maybe he should call his brother and sister right away.

His sister, who was in Rhode Island, screamed and dropped the phone when he told her about Mathew. When she had composed herself, Hal said. "Look, it was very sudden. He just had a heart attack and died. He didn't suffer any. You'd better come home so we can make funeral arrangements."

She just hung up the phone, sobbing.

Brother Ralph was another story. He didn't get emotional; he got angry and accused Hal of provoking the old man into a heart attack with his reckless behavior. He also flexed his authority over being the oldest son, and told Hal he would be over this evening to make all of the arrangements. Hal said he would contact the family attorney about wills and last wishes.

"Did you forget Mother is still alive, Hal?" his brother asked.

"She's a basket case, Ralph. She smiled when I told her Dad was dead." This was another lie; he hadn't said anything to her yet.

"We'll talk about it when I get there. Don't you do anything," Ralph said, hanging up.

There was a soft rap on the door and when Hal opened it, it was Ellie, tears running down her face.

"Mr. Halsworth, how is he?" She asked in her soft Spanish accent. Neither she nor Lamont knew what had happened yet.

"I'm sorry, Ellie, but he is dead. Tell Lamont for me, will you, and I will handle it with Mother."

Ellie put her apron to her face and walked away wailing.

CHAPTER TWENTY-TWO

Charlie had never shook, pressed, or patted so many hands in one day. They had hugged her, congratulated her, and were so overly enthusiastic about her being a candidate that you would have thought she'd already won the election. David showed her off like a new car, and introduced her to "everybody that was anybody," and was willing to listen.

The governor was there, and David told Charlie that his coattails were long and it was a good place to be. She met the Mayor of Minneapolis and several state senators and representatives. Bob Harris, the man she was trying to replace, was late, but David said she should get together with him, as he would have a wealth of information for her.

Charlie had worn a black pinstriped suit and a simple gray silk blouse. She had worn flats, to look less tall than she was. At five ten, she could be taller than some men, and she found that to be a disadvantage in social events, but not in the courtroom. She wanted to be dressed up enough to look the part of a lawyer, and to help her reach her goal someday, of top dog.

Bob Harris was flamboyant, and when he did arrive, all eyes were on him as he came in the door. This was the Democrats best opportunity, in a long time, to get a senator in Washington.

Bob knew Charlie well; she had filed many cases through his office over the years. But when he saw Charlie, it was with almost a look of astonishment, and he stopped talking to the people around him and rushed over to her.

"Bob. David says I need to hire you for a coach."

"Charlie, come with me." He took her hand and led her to a quiet area off to the side.

"You must not have heard or you wouldn't be here." His face was dead serious.

"Heard what, Bob?"

"Mathew Halsworth Sr. dropped dead of a heart attack late this afternoon. I just found out about ten minutes ago."

Charlie found the back of a chair, pulled herself around it, and sat down before she fell down. For a few minutes, she just sat there letting it sink in. *Had her meeting with him brought this on?*

"I need to leave," she said finally.

She held it in until she turned the key in the lock, and then the tears came in a torrent. Sure, he had abused her, and sure, he had taken advantage of her. But you don't work with someone that long and not get attached. She looked at her watch. It was ten p.m. *Was it too late to call the family?*

It was Ralph who answered the phone. Hal had gone to the airport to pick up his sister.

"Ralph…Charlie here. I am so very sorry."

"Don't be sorry, Charlie. As a doctor, I know how these things happen. It's life's fickle hand of fate. I think we all knew that Dad would work himself to death someday."

"I don't know what to say, Ralph. I met with him just this afternoon. He seemed fine when I left him." Her conscience was talking right along with her. *I just quit my job and told him that I was not going to babysit his son anymore, and actually, he was quite upset.*

"Listen, Charlie, I will call you with all of the funeral arrangements, and I think you can keep things going at the firm until we get things worked out, right?"

"Ralph, I no longer work for the firm."

"No? Since when? I didn't know that."

"Today, Ralph. I quit, just a few hours before your father's heart attack, to go into politics."

Ralph was quiet for a few seconds. "I'll call you, Charlie."

She lay in bed for a long time, but sleep wouldn't come. So many things had happened that it was hard to keep her mind on any one thing. But always, her thoughts came back to the guilt. She remembered him now, standing and shaking that letter in her face, and….and….

The letter. Who knew about that letter? Common sense told her it was just Mathew and her. She knew where he had thrown it. *No,* she thought, *not that letter—the contract letter. But to be safe she should get them both.* It could be serious if Hal or anyone else in the firm found it. That letter was a major threat to her ambitions.

Charlie was out of bed, and digging for her clothes in the chair where she had left them. She literally ran downstairs, and hopping in her car, headed for her old office. There was a pretty good chance her cards and keys still worked. He wouldn't have had time to get all of them un-encoded or locks changed after she left.

The car tires squealing echoed in the nearly empty ramp as she drove in and headed for the third level. That's where she'd been going in for all of the years she had worked there.

Charlie took the stairs into the main hallway and went right to the security desk. She had to play this by the book. The lone security guard was not someone she knew and that made her nervous as she gave him her card.

"Reason for going in?" he said.

"I forgot some papers that I need tomorrow."

He swiped the card and looked at the screen. "Good to go, Miss Malloy." He gave her a big smile that showed several teeth missing.

There were security cameras in all of the hallways, so she went to her old floor first. That would be the one he would be watching, if he watched at all.

Charlie only went as far as the receptionist desk, and grabbed an empty brown file folder out of the supply drawer. She went back out to the elevator and pushed the button to go up. At Mathew's office floor, she had to hope they weren't watching. The key Mathew had entrusted her with was held tight in her sweaty hand.

In a few seconds she was in the outer office, through the reception area, and into his office. The lights of the city, showing through the windows, cast enough light to see by. The drawer where he kept the files, and where she thought he might have put the letter, was locked and she had no key for that. How was she going to force it open? She looked around for some kind of tool.

Then she saw her crumpled letter, not on the floor but on the desk, and it had been smoothed out some. *Had Mathew picked it back up and read it again?* Lying in back of his desk on the floor was the contract letter. It wasn't crumpled up but he must have thrown it, too. Charlie grabbed the letters and stuffed them in her file folder while running for the elevator. She punched third floor and leaned against the back wall. Her knees felt weak and her heart was beating a hundred beats a minute.

The guard was still sitting behind the desk, half asleep, and she could see that the monitor was still panning her old office hallway.

"Elevators are all screwed up tonight," she said. "I pushed third to come back here, and it went up to the top. Then, when I pushed third again, it just sat there for a few minutes before it came back down again."

He gave her the same toothless smile, seeming to not even hear her quickly manufactured excuse.

"Find what you need?"

"I did, thank you."

Back in the ramp, and in the safety of her car, Charlie let out a sigh of relief. That was the first thing that had gone right for her all day.

Torch was scanning the morning paper for his own story when he saw the article on Mathew Halsworth's death. Ironically, it was on the same page as the article he was looking for. His article announced that the ten-year-old Stacie Morrison case was being reopened from the cold case files. The news clip went on to say that new evidence had come forth that warranted taking a second look at the case. It also went on to say that there was a reward of ten thousand dollars for information leading to the arrest and conviction of the person, or persons, who had killed Stacie Morrison. Anyone with any information was asked to call the Minneapolis Police Homicide Division.

Torch had skimmed by the story of Mathew's death, and now he returned to it, reading it again.

Mathew Halsworth, a prominent Minneapolis attorney, and the owner of Halsworth Law Firm, passed away at home. Doctors believe it was from a massive heart attack. His son, Hal Jr., and some servants,

were present at the time. His wife, Melinda, his three children and four grandchildren survive him. Arrangements are pending.

To Torch, it seemed to be a fateful coincidence that these two stories would appear on the same page. To the average reader, there were no parallels.

He was walking down the hall, to go to the bathroom, when he ran into one of the detectives who worked for him. "Hey, Sheldon, how's the Scanning case coming?" Torch was referring to a murder case they were working on.

"Great, Captain. We should tie things up pretty quick. Hey, by the way, I saw your news article on that Morrison case. Need any help on that? I love that cold case crap."

"Let's see what it brings. That's one I would love to solve myself, that's for sure."

"I also saw that old man Halsworth died yesterday. Wasn't his kid implicated in that case?"

"Yea, he was. We just never had enough on him to bring it to trial. You knew about that?" Torch asked.

"Yea," he answered. "I love to read about those old cases. You know, I talked to one of the cops on patrol yesterday. I was down at the hospital getting some evidence of ours. She had just taken a statement from his wife. Bastard beat the shit out of her and raped her. They had her in the hospital, sewing her up. Son of a bitch damn near bit her nipple off. Can you imagine doing that, and then raping your own wife?"

Torch nodded his head to the affirmative. "With him, yes. Is she pressing charges?"

"Guess not, but don't quote me on that. She did call the police, though."

"Gotta go before I piss my pants. Goddamn prostate must be the size of a tennis ball."

As he stood at the urinal, feeling blessed relief, Torch was thinking. *Hal raped his wife. I didn't even know he had a wife. Did they do a rape kit at the hospital?*

Torch went downstairs to the patrol division and asked to see the report. He stood, drumming his fingers on the counter, as they searched for it. He had left the urinal a little early and had buttoned his suit coat to hide the wet spot. He pushed up to the counter to keep that area from being in view. *Damn prostate, making a man piss his pants when he was fifty some years old. Women could pee a little and no one would know the difference. It was the same thing with being sexually excited. They could be as hot as an asphalt road in the desert and no one would know. But a man...he had to hide his excitement.* Torch shook his head and smiled to himself. *How the hell did I get off on this subject?*

It only took a moment to find the report. Luckily, it hadn't been filed yet.

Yes...yes...they had done a rape kit, and he might have his much-needed DNA.

Let's see, first he would secure the evidence, and then he needed to talk to the City Attorney about the legality of using it. Man, this could be the key. This could be big. He hadn't been this excited in a long, long time. "I need a copy," he told the clerk.

Torch left for his office with the information in hand. Right now though, he had another problem. He was hungry and it was time to go to Whitey's.

It was one thirty by the time he got to Whitey's and the noon crowd had thinned out a lot. Torch just took a stool at the counter.

"What's it going to be today, Torch?" The waitress leaned on her elbows and gave him a shot at her ample bosoms that had been around for at least forty of her years.

"Give me the special, Cassie."

"How's meatloaf hit you, Torch?"

"That's good; my guts can take anything today. Give me a cup of joe, too."

He looked around the place while he waited for his lunch, drinking his coffee and thinking to himself. *How many years had he been coming here? The same old dusty decorative dinner plates hanging on the walls. The old-fashioned cash register with its pop-up numbers. It had to be older than Whitey himself, and he was seventy, if he was a day.* He looked at the old-fashioned mug he was drinking out of, stained brown over the years. He had forgotten how long he had been coming here, but it seemed like a lifetime. One thing was for sure; when he retired he was going to miss it. He was eligible for retirement right now, but something had kept him from making the move. After this morning, he knew for sure what that something was.

He was down to just a few cigarettes a day now, but the one he lit as he left Whitey's was always the best smoke of the day. You know, maybe he would skip that City Attorney bullshit. Piss on it. Why not just go ask Hal's wife if she cared. She had to be more than a little pissed off at Hal right now. Her phone number was on the report. The more he thought about it, the more he knew that was exactly what he was going to do.

The family meeting on Wednesday morning, at the Halsworth's, had gone well with the exception of Becky's uncontrollable grief. She had felt very close to her dad…and his money. Ralph talked her down a little and they made some decisions—at least she and Ralph did. The funeral would be Saturday, at the big Baptist church in Minnetonka, where the folks had belonged for forty years. They had seldom gone, but they were great contributors. There would be a viewing the night before at the funeral home, and Mathew would be interned in the same cemetery as his parents.

Hal, on the other hand, was close-mouthed and seemed to be preoccupied. Anything was all right with him. He had other things on his mind. Things like the restraining order that had come from Stephanie's attorney late this last night. Things like the article in the paper that he, too, had seen; about the police reopening the Stacie Morrison case. New evidence, they said. What could they have found after all of these years? He hadn't thought about that incident himself, in years, and had conveniently forgotten about most of it. The statement he had made, in anger, to Stephanie when he was beating her, about her ending up in the river did, however, did come to mind. That had been a big mistake, and he had regretted it the moment he said it. He was almost sure she had been too far out of it to hear him, but maybe not. She was one tough bitch, that was for sure.

Had she called the cops and told them anything, despite his warnings? If she had filed charges against him, you would have thought they would have come for him by now. They knew damn well where he was, and it had been almost two days.

The family attorney had called and told them that Mathew had left a current will and he would review it with them right after the funeral. It was very involved.

Lamont had sat in his apartment for two days now. He knew Hal despised him, but beyond that, he just wanted to stay out of the way at such a difficult time. He had his own grief to deal with. He had been a faithful employee for nearly forty years, and right now, he had no idea what was going to happen to him. Mrs. Halsworth was so disabled now that it would not surprise him if the house was sold, and she was put into long-term care somewhere. Something else was going through his mind, however. He'd also seen the article in the paper about the Stacie Morrison case, and it had jogged his memory, too. Things were not always so clear from his drinking days, but he had remembered one thing. Those clothes, that bracelet, and that watch in young Hal's car that night.

They were advertising a ten thousand dollar reward. That could come in very handy to a poor homeless, out of work, black man. Besides, the only thing that had kept him from doing this a long time ago was Mathew Senior, and he was gone now.

He picked up the phone and called his niece, Clarice. She just might still have that bracelet and watch. Clarice's message center told him she was out of town until Sunday night but she would return his call then. *I can wait*, Lamont thought. *I have waited ten years. I can wait a few more days.*

Torch sat in his office chair, one hand on the phone, the other rubbing his forehead, trying to chase away the cobwebs that had seemed to wrap around his brain. He knew that calling Stephanie was the right thing to do; he just didn't know what to say, or how to say it to her. He looked at the clock across from his desk. Nine thirty a.m. Thursday morning; she should be up by now.

The phone rang twice before a sleepy voice answered, "Hello."

"Mrs. Halsworth?"

"Yes. This is Stephanie. Who's this?" She sounded brash and a little cranky.

"Stephanie, I'm sorry if I woke you. This is Torch Brennan from the Minneapolis Police Department."

"Look...Torch, is it?" She didn't wait for an answer. "I told you guys everything the other day. I have nothing more to say about this and I'm not going to file charges against him."

"No, no...listen, that's not what I'm calling about at all. It does concern your husband, but has nothing to do with what happened to you the other day. Can I come over and talk to you about this? I would just as soon not do this over the phone."

It was quiet for a moment. "When?"

"This afternoon would be nice if we could, Stephanie."

Stephanie's curiosity was up now. *What the hell else had Hal been up to?*

"Okay. Around two would work, I guess."

"See you at two. Let me confirm your address."

Torch had a meeting that would last until lunch and then, after that, he would head over.

Hal had found out some bits and pieces about his father's estate. There was a lot of money involved in his personal finance, and the company was going to be turned over to a nine-person Board of Directors for leadership, until Mathew's successor could be determined. This was not what Hal had expected. He was the lawyer in the family, and he had expected to succeed his father. He would, however, be one of the nine, so for the time being he would keep a low profile. As for the money he would inherit, he could use the cash infusion. Stephanie's spending sprees had left him nearly broke.

He was still concerned about what Stephanie had said, or not said, to the police, but he was not going to try talking to her. He had been up front with his brother and sister about their domestic problems, which Hal called irreconcilable. For now, he was going to live here at home and look after his mother.

Ralph was not so sure that Hal was speaking the truth about his concern for his mother, but Becky sided with him, so Ralph dropped the subject for the time being. He had enough on his plate right now as it was. Maybe after the funeral he would revisit the subject. He was still not giving up his newfound role as the family leader.

Torch checked the address against the piece of paper he had in his hand. This was the place all right. He walked up the sidewalk and rang the bell.

Even though Stephanie had tried to cover her bruises the best she could, she still looked beat up, but Torch didn't comment on it. She had made coffee, and after the introductions, they sat down at the kitchen table to talk. Hal was playing with a plastic truck, pushing it around the kitchen floor, making motor noises. Torch tried to make some kid talk with him, but the toddler appeared to not notice him.

"They are a lot of fun at this age, aren't they?"

Stephanie smiled. "Yes, too bad his father never noticed it."

"Speaking of his father…what's his status with you, right now?"

"I'll shoot the asshole if he comes back here, pardon my French."

"How well did you know Hal?" Torch asked.

"I was married to the asshole for two years. Well enough."

"Before that?"

"We knew each other for a few months before we got married, which was about long enough for him to knock me up."

"Ten years ago you didn't know him?"

"Ten years ago I was in high school."

"Stephanie, ten years ago your husband was arrested for suspicion in the abduction and murder of a girl here in Minneapolis. He was never indicted because we didn't have all of the evidence we needed. One of those things was his DNA profile."

"We still have a tissue sample from the dead fetus that was in that girl's body. If you will consent to giving us the sperm samples that we took from you the other day at the hospital, we might be able to make a match."

Stephanie had a slight smile on her face. "What if there is a match?"

"Then he is one step closer to going to jail for a long time, and some old people I know in Wisconsin, who lost their only daughter, can reach some closure."

She smiled. It was almost a cynical smile. "Let's go for it," she said. "Give me one of those cigarettes you've got in your pocket, Torch."

Stephanie poured coffee for both of them, and put some cookies on the table. "So when do you find out if it was him or not?"

"It's going to be a while, Stephanie. They have to send it to the FBI lab and I guess they're backed up quite a bit. For that reason, I have to ask you a favor."

"What's that, Torch?"

"Well, if Hal gets wind of this, I am not sure what he would do. He might run, and then again, he might come after you. It looks like he enjoys knocking you around and abusing you. We need to keep this quiet, kid." Torch paused for a minute to give it time to "sink in." Stephanie was feeling of the cast on her nose, and smiling, as that old "he who laughs last" cliché ran through her mind.

"I promise you, the police department is not going to say anything. By the way, is that why you didn't press charges? I did see you have a restraining order."

"It's not just me that I am afraid for." She looked down at Hal and tousled his hair.

"Let's do this," Torch said. "I am going to get a watch put on your place here for a while. Have you had the locks changed?"

"No. I'm not flush with money right now."

"Let me take care of that for you—the locks—not the money."

"What are you going to want in return?" It seemed like a terribly sarcastic answer to an honest attempt to help her out. Maybe he had taken it wrong. Torch almost came back with something, but at the last second thought better of it."

"Just a conviction, Stephanie, just some justice."

"Torch."

"Yes?"

She reached for his cigarette pack and shook out another one. She lit it, and blew a stream of smoke at the ceiling. "There's something else you should probably know. The other day, when Hal was trying to beat the shit out of me—I shouldn't say try, I guess he did—but anyway, he made a threat to me that might interest you. I think he thought I was unconscious, but I could still hear him. It meant nothing to me at the time, but now I see the relevancy."

"What was that?" Torch was being very attentive.

"He told me if I didn't do what he said; I would end up in the river, too."

Torch was floored. He just looked at Stephanie for a long time. In fact, his silence was making her uncomfortable, and she squirmed a little in her chair. A statement like that alone could get most people arrested, but he was not going to jump the gun this time.

"Would you testify to that?" he said."

She was thinking, while biting her top lip.

Torch interrupted her chain of thought. It was a decision he could get from her later. He could sense that, right now, she was terrified of Hal. "Let's talk more about that later. But don't you forget a word of what he said to you. Please."

He walked outside; this had been good, and he was proud that he had made the right decision in coming to see her. Now, to go pick up that rape kit and get over to the Coroner's Office.

CHAPTER TWENTY THREE

Charlie decided she would go to the funeral on Saturday, but she wasn't going to go to the viewing the night before. There was just too much time available at these affairs for people to talk and ask questions. She really didn't want to talk to anyone right now, or answer any questions. Not about Mathew, or her political ambitions.

She had shed the guilty feelings she had harbored of having anything at all to do with Mathew's demise. Charlie had concluded that, as rash as it seemed, if he had become that upset over her leaving for a life of her own, then he had it coming.

Her calendar was fast filling up, and the next couple of months were going to be a never-ending parade of meetings, rallies, and handshaking affairs. David had found a young man from St. Paul who had been hired to be her campaign manager. His name was Sid Gillman and although he was young, he was very experienced in campaigns, and a stickler for details. It seemed as if he was not just managing her campaign, he was in-effect, managing her life. She was fast learning about the ins and outs of politics.

Torch met with Dr. Lang to turn over the evidence kit. It had been sealed at the hospital to prevent contamination and Dr. Lang was being careful to make sure that integrity was maintained. Many a case had been lost because of sloppy police work.

He had also called the lock people to change Stephanie's door locks and issued an order for increased patrols in the area. The case had been put in a new folder and he was carefully going through the previous evidence, looking for things he might have overlooked. This was one case that was not going to be handed down to anyone. He would work this case himself.

Stephanie had her own lawyer now, and he was very busy. First order of business had been the restraining order. Right now, he was working on divorce proceedings and her share of the estate Hal had coming to him. They really were not sure how much that was, but he had found out the will would be read next week, and he intended to be there and represent his client. He had talked briefly with Ralph about it, and Ralph had referred him to the family attorney.

They had managed to get a loan for her until the proceeding would take place. The locks had been changed, and Stephanie had taken a big step to protect her and their son. She had purchased a .45 caliber automatic pistol, from a pawnshop just down the block, and the proprietor had given her a box of ammo with it, and encouraged her to go to a range somewhere and get familiar with it. "This is an awesome weapon for a small woman like you," he had told her. "Be careful."

The advice had fallen largely on deaf ears, however. She had been raised around guns, with four brothers and a father who hunted, and she knew all too well how to use them. Sitting on the edge of her bed, she slipped the loaded clip in and pulled back the slide and let it fall into place. The safety was on. It was locked, loaded and ready, and that was the way it would stay for now. The automatic felt heavy and cold in her hand, but at the same time, reassuring. It eased her fears somewhat. She stuffed it into her nightstand under some magazines.

The night of the wake was here, and the Halsworth family gathered to accept condolences and sympathy from friends and relatives. A steady stream of well-wishers filtered through the funeral home doors, all eager to get a last look at the man they felt had been indestructible, and an icon that had built the largest law firm in the upper Midwest.

Ralph took his post by the door and welcomed each of them, exchanging a few words and pleasantries. Many of them were business associates of Mathew's that were unknown to Ralph, but he welcomed them warmly, anyway. The only man who knew all of them stayed inconspicuously hidden away, in a corner of the room, seemingly trying to control the grief of his inconsolable sister; talking only to those who stumbled across him and Becky, and then only as few words as possible.

Hal wanted nothing to do with the whole wake, which he considered just another dog and pony show. At the same time, however, he was deeply disturbed. Not about his father's death, but about the police investigation into Stacie Morrison's death. He couldn't shake the thought from his head. Having the thought was one thing, but not being able to act on it was another. He was not used to feeling troubled like this. The more he dwelt on it, the more he was convinced that Stephanie had something to do with it. Something was going to have to be done about that, but he needed to be careful.

He had hoped for Stephanie to show up either tonight, or tomorrow, at the funeral. His son was, after all, Mathew Senior's grandson and namesake. Somewhere in his twisted, convoluted mind, he didn't think she could just ignore that. If she did show up, he was going to act low-key and repentant. Not that he expected her to forgive him for the mauling she had taken at his hands. Maybe, just maybe she would show up, for the sake of little Hal.

Mathew Halsworth Senior lay in the polished mahogany casket sitting on a small pedestal, surrounded by sprays of flowers and plants. A constant trickle of mourners passed by the body, some of them stopping to bow their heads and pray, and others' to examine the cards on the plants, while they talked in low murmurs.

Hal had stood there with the family when they first arrived. The time had been set aside for the immediate family, and he gazed down unemotionally at his father. His theory was that Becky was doing enough grieving for all of them. Ralph and his family seemed quite composed, but respectful.

Mother had been allowed to come and see the man she had married some forty years ago, but she didn't seem to see the significance of it all, and Ellie had taken her back home. Lamont drove them in, in Mathew's white Cadillac.

A few friends and family recognized and approached Hal with their sympathy, but he only smiled and shook their hands. For the most part, they took his reluctance to socialize as grief that he was having difficulty handling.

The day of the funeral dawned cool and wet; not the usual weather for August in Minnesota. It had rained hard during the night, but was calming down now to just a drizzle that was predicted to last the rest of the day.

Charlie put on a black pantsuit with a blue silk blouse. She dressed slowly and meticulously, with one eye on the clock. She didn't want to be there any earlier than necessary. She hadn't talked to the family since the call to Ralph the night of Mathew's death, and if all went well, she had no plans to do so again.

The church had a huge parking lot, and as late as she was, she ended up parking some distance away. Then she discovered she had forgotten to put her umbrella back in the car, and was forced to carry a newspaper over her head to keep her hair from getting drenched. It worked for her hair, but the rest of her was drenched. She slid into one of the last seats available, in the back of the church.

Charlie shivered as she sat listening to the soft organ music, while rainwater ran down her back and collected at the waist of her pants. The old woman beside her smiled, and moved away a little bit, in what could only be seen as an attempt to keep herself dry.

From her seat in the back of the church, she couldn't see anybody that she knew, just a sea of heads. *Oh well, last one in, first one out,* she thought.

The service was long and drawn out with eloquent eulogies from Mathew's many partners and friends. So long that the minister deliberately set his remarks aside, and appeared to condense the rest of the service. It was announced that the graveside ceremony would be held after the reception, hoping for a break in the weather that had worsened again.

The quick escape she had hoped for was thwarted, however, when the ushers dismissed people from the front to the back of the church. Charlie became one of the last to leave. The rain had not let up, and she stood on the steps, hoping for a break, but resigned to the fact that she was going to have to make a run for it. Most of the people had gone downstairs to the Fellowship Hall for a prepared luncheon.

Just as a bolt of lightning hit, not far away, and the ensuing thunder blast shook the ground, she took off for her car, almost at a sprint. She was drenched before she had gone twenty feet, and she realized that running only made it worse with all of her splashing, so Charlie slowed to a walk. She could only get so wet.

At last she found her car, and coming up from behind it, threw open the door and slid in. Hal was in the other seat.

Charlie was too startled to speak, and she reached over for the door handle she had just let go of, but Hal grabbed her upper arm in a vise-like grip.

"So you were going to hang me out to dry, were you, Charlie. You have a lot of balls, you know that? I read your letter to him and you know what? I think that was what killed him." He, too, was soaking wet, his hair hanging down across his face. His face showed how angry he really was, with his chin jutting out and his eyes with their piercing look. This was a side of him Charlie had seen many times before, and it scared her then as much as it was scaring her now. His voice was a low hiss, and his grip on her arm became tighter.

"Hal, stop it! You're hurting me."

He relaxed his grip a little, but didn't let go of her. "My father laid out a good plan for the firm that you rejected; a plan that would have been good for you, for the firm, and for me. He told me that you were essential to my making it at the firm. At first, I scoffed at that idea, but my better judgment tells me now that he was right."

She reached for his hand, and tried to pry his fingers loose, but he only gripped her tighter.

"There have been women in my past that have tried to ruin my life, and they failed, and you are not going to be the first." His voice was rising. "I promise you that, Charlie." He let go of her arm suddenly, realizing that his strong-arm tactics were sending the wrong message, to the wrong woman.

Now he was sounding conciliatory. "Look, I'm sorry, but this whole thing has my head spinning. Charlie…look…for the sake of all of us I am asking you to reconsider and come back. What do you say? We can make it work."

"Get out of my car, Hal." She reached for the ignition and started the engine. The windows inside were all fogging up and she was feeling closed in and scared.

Hal opened the door and stepped out, but stood by the side of the car, talking to her through the still open door.

"This is a big mistake on your part, Charlie. Wise up bitch," he screamed, "before it's too late!"

She hit the accelerator and took off, the door slamming shut as she drove off. In the rear view mirror she could see Hal standing in the parking lot, shaking his fist at her.

Charlie sat on the end of her bed. She had stripped off all of her wet clothes, and sat cross-legged on the bed wearing only a fluffy robe right now, trying to dry her hair with a Turkish towel. She should never have gone to the funeral, and she knew that now, but it was for Mathew that she went. Not the rest of his misfit family.

She was afraid of Hal, and tried to think about what she could do to ease her mind, but nothing seemed to fit right now. There was no end to what he was capable of doing. Maybe letting sleeping dogs lie was good advice sometimes, but she was not so sure this dog was going to stay asleep.

On Sunday evening, Lamont had sat in his favorite chair staring at the television, but not really watching it. His future with the Halsworth's was up for grabs, and he knew it. The decision had been made for Hal to live at home with his mother. Ralph had explained it to Lamont about an hour ago. Mathew Halsworth had always treated him right, and they had been become good friends. He was going to miss him terribly. But more than that, Mathew had protected Lamont from Hal, who hated him. Nothing good was going to come from this.

The week-old newspaper, with the article on the Stacie Morrison investigation, was on the table right next to his chair, the announcement circled in red pencil. He looked at his watch. She should be home by now.

He thought about what he was going to say and then, picking up the phone, dialed Clarice's number. The phone rang a number of times, but just before he was going to break the connection, she picked up.

"Hi, Clarice. How you doing?"

"Uncle Lamont. I'm doing great. I got your message—I just haven't had time to call you back yet."

Lamont chuckled. "You're a busy young lady, I know."

"What can I do you for you, Uncle?"

"Well, I don't know if you knew it, but Mathew Halsworth died last week."

"Oh, I am so sorry. You have worked there at his house a long time, haven't you?"

"I have, Clarice, but how much longer I am going to be working here is anybody's guess. My own guess says not long, but be that as it may, I have a question for you. Several years ago, I gave you a bracelet and a watch. Do you remember that?"

"I do, and I still have that bracelet somewhere around here. I wore the watch out."

"Honey, when I gave you those things, I was not aware how significant they were to something. I have thought about them over the years, but now I need to do something about them, or at least the bracelet, if that's what's left. I am a little ashamed of how I came by them, but now I think that I can redeem myself a little by getting that bracelet to the right people. I am not going to lie to you, Clarice, but right now that's all I can tell you."

"You're not in trouble, are you?" Her voice was filled with concern.

"I'm not sure, but the trouble will be far less than the trouble someone else might be in when I turn that bracelet over to the police."

Clarice was quiet for a second. "When do you want it back?"

"Well, I thought maybe tomorrow, if that's okay."

"Sure. Why don't you come over for supper? I haven't seen you for some time, anyway."

Lamont hung up the phone. He had one more call to make, but once again, he had to think about it. *How much was he going to say? Maybe he would just make an appointment to talk with them first. Maybe they weren't even interested in the bracelet, but there was an outside chance it could help them solve this crime and he might get some reward money. It was worth a try.*

Lamont dialed the number and listened to the voice mail message. "This is Torch Brennan of the Minneapolis Police, Homicide Division. I'm not here right now, but your message is very important to me. Please leave it at the tone and I will return your call as soon as possible."

Torch had deliberately posted his direct line in the newspaper ad. He was handling this himself...all the way.

Lamont cleared his throat before he started talking. "My name is Lamont Brown and I work for the Halsworth family. I saw your article in the paper, and I believe that I might have some evidence that would help you in the case you wrote about." He gave Torch his phone number.

Lamont was tired. It had been a long week and a long day, physically as well as emotionally. He walked to the window that looked down on the poolroom. It was going to be hard to leave all of this; he'd taken care of it for so long. The decision he'd made to go to the police hadn't been easy. It might mean leaving here and soon.

His eyes stopped wandering around the yard and focused on Hal, sitting in the pool area, drinking, ranting and raving. He saw him cut the lines with a razor blade and inhale the cocaine he had laid out on the bar top. Even though he couldn't hear him, he knew what he was saying and doing. Worse yet, he knew what he was really capable of doing, and that was all the more reason he had to go. There was nothing left for him here now but grief.

Hal was alone for the first time in a week, and right now he was drinking heavily, sitting in the poolroom and thinking about several things. He'd also made a trip downtown, found a dealer and bought some coke, and sucked up a couple of lines. Hal had nearly forgotten how good the stuff made him feel.

Hal wasn't used to fighting his own battles, or not getting his own way, and his frustration had reached the boiling point. Three things had him going right now. Charlie, Stephanie, and the Minneapolis Police.

As for Charlie, he was not going to push that subject right now. Maybe he had already pushed it too far. Tomorrow, there would be a board meeting and he would find out more about the firm's structure then. He was becoming more convinced that there had to be more than one Charlie in that firm, and after all, he was the heir apparent. Maybe this would play out all right in the end.

Stephanie. This was a bigger problem than he had realized. He had dodged a bullet when he assaulted her and she had not pressed charges. Yet, the big problem was going to come when she divorced him, and he was convinced she would do just that. His inheritance was going to be tapped heavily and he knew it. *No damn way was she getting one thin dime.* He threw his glass into the pool and walked over to the bar and grabbed a new one, filling it half full with scotch, and then throwing the empty decanter in the water, too. *The bitch had to go. She was the reason for the police investigation and he knew it. As for the police investigation, maybe he was getting excited over nothing. They hadn't tried to talk to him, had they? Maybe he would just jump that creek when he got there. He beat them once, didn't he? What was stopping him from beating those dumb cops again?*

Lamont walked into the pool area and approached Hal. He was slumped in an overstuffed chair, staring out of eyes that were only slits. "What the hell do you want, nigger?"

It had taken some courage to walk over here, and talk to Hal, but that comment made what he had to say so much easier.

"I came to say that I am quitting my job."

Hal stared at him. *I was going to fire the old bastard anyway*, he thought. *Now he is taking that pleasure away from me, isn't he?*

"You can't quit because I already fired your ass. I just forgot to tell you," he sneered at Lamont.

Lamont didn't know what to say, or if he should say anything right now. He turned to walk away, and the glass hit him in the middle of the back. It almost knocked the wind out of him, and he winced and grabbed a table for support.

He turned to look at Hal, who was getting up, unsteadily, from his seat. He pointed his forefinger at Lamont and shouted. "You pack your damn bags tonight and be out of here by morning, do you understand?"

"You are going to be sorry you treated me like this." Lamont had reached his breaking point and had some rage of his own to unload.

"What are you going to do, nigger?"

That was it. He had some pride left, and his anger was getting to a point where he had better leave before he said anything more. Lamont's voice was shaking. "Your past is going to come back to haunt you, Hal." He rushed from the room, ran across the parking area, up the stairs, and once in his apartment, he latched his door. He should have never said that last sentence.

Hal was really stewing now. *What the hell did he mean about his past was coming back to haunt him? Maybe he had been wrong about Stephanie. Maybe it was Lamont who had the evidence. It had been ten years, but he never forgot about the bag of clothing in the trunk of his car. Was it all there when he dumped it the next day?*

He shut off the lights in the poolroom and went up to his room. No more booze or coke tonight. He had to think this out.

The cocaine helped keep him awake but it mattered little. Lamont had to be gotten rid of, and it had to be tonight. Tomorrow, he might be gone. Hal dressed in a black sweater and blue jeans. The sweater was hot but he wanted to be as inconspicuous as he could be out there.

Lamont's apartment above the garage was dark when Hal crept through the darkened poolroom. He needed to get in the garage if this was going to work.

First, he needed to get his car out without waking Lamont. He pulled the cord on the garage door opener, and raised it by hand as quietly as he could. His car was parked in the last stall, the farthest away from Lamont's apartment. He slipped it into neutral, and pushed it out, free of the garage.

The only other car was his father's white Cadillac sedan. It was parked on the other end, next to the door which went into the enclosed stairwell that led to Lamont's apartment. He'd never seen the door at the top of this stairway closed. Lamont simply locked the lower door when he was gone. The lower door was locked this time, so Hal slipped his knife in the crack between the door and the frame, and pushed the striker back. The door had a closer on it but he held it open with the same wedge of wood that Lamont used for that purpose from time to time.

Then he went to the back wall of the garage, and took a coil of rope that was hanging on a hook there, and walking around to the outside entrance, crept up the stairs to the door. He made a loop and tied the rope to the doorknob, and then to the railing. This would prevent the door from being opened, as it opened in.

Back in the garage, he opened the door to the car and doused it down with gasoline, and placed the can back against the back wall where he had found it. He stood around the corner to protect himself, and threw a burning book of matches at the car. The first toss of the book missed, so he retrieved it and tried again. It went up with a huge whoosh from the gas fumes, and the fireball almost knocked Hal over. He ran through the building and pulled the garage door he had left open, down behind him.

There were only two windows to Lamont's apartment. A small ornate one, high in the entrance door, that no one could fit through, and the large, double, plate-glass window that overlooked the poolroom. Hal hid in the bushes and watched both. If Lamont did get out, he would have to go to plan B, but right now, he had no plan B. He would handle it, he was sure of that. He felt good for a change. He was back in the driver's seat and in control of his life again.

The smoke was now puffing from the soffits in the garage, and he could hear flames crackling behind the big doors. There was no sign of life on the upper level. He hoped Ellie was sleeping soundly in his mother's room on the far end of the house.

The first flames had broken through the roof, now turning the dark night brighter, and making shadows out of everything around the garage. He could feel the heat and the noise was getting worse, but there was still no sign of Lamont. How much longer before the neighbors or Ellie saw the fire? It was too risky to stay here any longer.

He ran through the poolroom, into the house and upstairs to his room, taking off everything but his underwear. Then he remembered the rope on the door.

"Ellie. Ellie," he was screaming as he came back down the stairs. "The garage is on fire. Call the Fire Department. Lamont...I need to get him out of there."

Ellie had come downstairs in her robe, and was now standing at the foot of the stairs. She ran to the phone to make the call.

Hal sprinted for the stairs. He could hear the flames inside of Lamont's apartment. Quickly, he untied the rope and threw it to the ground. As he turned to go back down the steps, the big window in Lamont's apartment blew out, and flames roared out and over the roof.

Ellie could see Hal, in his underwear, as he came back down the steps. He gathered up the rope and walked to the poolroom, carrying the rope with him.

"It's too late, Ellie," he cried. "That poor, poor, man...oh, my God, Ellie." He threw his arms around her and they both watched until the first fire units arrived.

CHAPTER TWENTY-FOUR

Torch was late getting into the office on Monday morning because he was in court—a place most homicide detectives learn to hate. Torch's take on the criminal justice system was that it was a lot like fishing—catch and release.

He had given some thought to calling in for messages when he woke up, but he was running late so the messages went by the wayside, along with breakfast.

Now, back from lunch at Whitey's, he was sitting at his desk, and he couldn't believe what he was hearing. He had been listening on the speakerphone, but he quickly switched it off when he heard the subject matter. For ten years this case had sat, going nowhere, and now for the first time he had someone calling him with information. The lab tests had been sent in for the DNA matches. Maybe he was finally going to be able to put this case in front of a grand jury.

He remembered Lamont, although it had been a long time ago. He was the man who had answered the door that day, when he had made his only trip out to the Halsworth estate to talk with Hal. Torch had a photographic memory. He remembered then having a gut feeling that Lamont wanted to say something more about Hal, but had been reluctant to do so.

The phone gave off some kind of squealing noise, and then an operator came on the line to ask what number he was calling. Torch recited the number Lamont had given him.

"I am sorry, sir, but that line has been damaged, and is no longer operational. If you want to call our maintenance and repair, they could probably be more specific about the problem."

"That's okay. Maybe I'll just drive out there. Thanks anyway."

Torch dug through the file. Somewhere in here was the address for the Halsworth home. Minnetonka. Yes, he remembered now. He grabbed the file and left, yelling to the receptionist that he wouldn't be back for a couple of hours.

It felt good to get out of the office, and it felt even better to be working on the case again. He looked down at the picture of Stacie, still clipped to the folder. *I'm not giving up, sweetheart, hang in there.* He rubbed her picture with his fingertips.

The first inkling he had, that something was wrong, was the red fire department squad parked in front of the house. That red car and the water that was still running down the driveway from somewhere in the back, said something was amiss.

From the front of the house you couldn't see the garage area so Torch, his curiosity getting the best of him, walked around the side of the house.

Two men in coveralls, with "**State Fire Marshal's Office**" stenciled across their backs, were sifting through what had been a rather large building, now reduced to ashes and some burnt timbers. A few whiffs of smoke still came from the rubble, and what was left of a car, and several pieces of lawn equipment. Basically, the only thing left standing was one end of the building with a set of stairs, seemingly holding the wall up.

One of the inspectors stopped what he was doing, straightened up, and walked out to meet Torch.

Torch offered his hand to the man, who was still trying to pull his dirty wet gloves off.

"Hi, there. I'm Torch Brennan from the Minneapolis Police. This is going to sound dumb, but it looks like you had a fire here."

"Hi, Torch. Rusty Tallon, State Fire Marshal's office. Yea, you can say that. They had a hell of a fire and quite a loss."

"No one hurt, I hope."

"Not from the fire department. There was a caretaker who lived above

206

the garage who died in the fire, and we're still looking for his next of kin, so not much information about him yet, that I can talk about. Whatcha looking for, or should I say, who yah looking for?"

"Lamont Brown." One look from the Inspector told Torch the answer. He fished in his coat pocket for his card and gave it to Rusty. "Was this an accidental fire?"

"Right now, we have no reason to think otherwise, but that could change. We just started going through things here. Why? Do you think someone had something to do with it?"

"Well, the man who died was important to us, but I can't get into that. Just let me know what you find out, will you. It could be part of something bigger."

"Sure…sure, we can do that."

Torch stared at the house as he walked away. *Was someone trying to get one step ahead of him in some kind of a deadly game? If so, he knew who that someone was.* Maybe it was time to call the Minnetonka Police. He picked up his cell phone and then, thinking better of it, put it back in his pocket. There was something else he wanted to check first. He had screwed up by being in a hurry ten years ago, and he needed to think things through here. No rush to judgment this time.

From his bedroom window, Hal had seen Torch arrive. He hadn't seen Torch since that interview at the police station a long time ago, but that was one face he would never forget.

Why is he here? This isn't in Minneapolis. He has no jurisdiction out here. He must have been coming here to see someone besides me because he never came to the door. Lamont…he was coming to see Lamont. That bastard was the squealer, after all. Well, tough shit detective, but your key witness is dead and gone.

Hal laughed to himself and lay back down on the bed. *Those dickheads out back, digging in the rubble, were not going to find anything. He had been too careful. Now to figure out what to do with Stephanie, but he had time on his side with her. Her legal moves were not going to happen overnight.*

Someone else was also looking out the window. Ellie hadn't seen Torch, but she was watching the fire investigators. She had contemplated going out and talking with them, but maybe she was just being foolish, and there was an explanation for why Hal's car had been out when the garage caught on fire. She had seen him put it in the garage earlier that evening, and he hadn't left the house, that she knew of. There was that, and what was up with that piece of rope, from that railing, he was so intent on saving. He seemed to have given up on rescuing Lamont from the fire pretty early on, but he almost died for that damn rope.

Melinda Halsworth had started coughing, so Ellie went over, and using a pillow, propped her up more in bed. She should think about getting them something to eat.

The only other person who knew about Clarice was Ralph, and when Ellie called and told him about the fire, he came right over. Both he and Hal walked around the pile of debris, while Hal tried to explain what had happened.

"I fell asleep in the poolroom, and then decided to go up to bed. I guess it was the sound of something blowing up that alerted me, and I rushed back down in my underwear, but it was going pretty good by then. I tried to get up the stairs to Lamont, but the flames and smoke were too much. Poor Lamont."

Ralph was only half interested in what Hal had to say. Hal lied so much you never knew whether to believe him or not. For now, he was going to give him the benefit of the doubt.

"I guess I better tell the police about his niece," Ralph said. "That's the only relative that I ever heard him talk about. Ellie said they were looking for next of kin."

Hal didn't answer him. Right now, he was filled with self-gratification for what he had accomplished. It had turned out better than he thought.

Clarice Brown put the phone down, and stood, crying. *Poor Lamont. He was her only uncle and about the only other relative she had in the world. He told her something bad was going to happen, because he could just feel it in his bones, but not this.* The coroner said they would release the body tomorrow. She'd never planned a funeral before and had no idea where to start.

She went into the bedroom and collapsed on the bed, sobbing. After a while, all cried out, she rolled over on her back and stared at the ceiling. She needed someone to help her with this, but whom?

Her eyes wandered to the top of her jewelry box, and she saw the bracelet he had called about the other day. It had been in the box for several years, but when Lamont called she had taken it out, just to make sure she still had it.

Clarice stood up, walked slowly to the dresser, and picked it up. She had never really looked closely at it, although she had had it in her possession for ten years. It was just a charm bracelet like young girls used to wear. There was one charm that looked like a scroll of some kind, but now she realized it was a diploma. It must have been for graduation. There was engraving on the back of the charm in very small letters *SM.1989. Who was S.M.?* She walked out into the kitchen and looked at the lamb chops she had gone out and purchased for supper tonight. Uncle Lamont loved lamb chops; she didn't, and she threw them in the garbage.

He said he wanted to get that bracelet to the police. *Which police? The police in Minnetonka, or some other police department?*

Maybe she should call the Minneapolis Police, and if they didn't know what she was talking about, well, maybe they would know who did want that bracelet. Maybe they would know who *S.M.* was. It was getting late and the sun was dying fast in the west. She would call first thing in the morning.

Rusty Talon and his sidekick had found three things they needed to check out more thoroughly. The fire had started in the Cadillac, but how? It certainly looked like it had started inside of it. The seat springs had been subjected to some tremendous heat, and the windows on the inside had blown outward. They needed to find out when it had been used last, and if there were smokers inside who might have left a burning cigarette in it.

Also, the door inside the garage that went up to Lamont's apartment seemed to have a deep char on both sides. It was almost as if it had been open sometime during the fire. It was a solid core wood door, and should have taken the heat from that fire for some time. The walls around it were sheet rocked with fireboard that would have held for an hour, and the door closer seemed to be operational. There was also a mark on the floor, about one and a half inches wide and three inches long, where the floor had been protected from the heat and soot by something. *Whatever it was burned up so it wasn't there now, but if he didn't miss his bet, it was a wood wedge that held that door open. Why would the man go to sleep with that door propped open?*

The last door opener on the overhead garage doors was also suspicious. It had been manually tripped, and not reset. Tomorrow, they were going to have to talk to the owners about his stuff. Also, tomorrow he had to call that Minneapolis cop. It was too late today.

On Monday morning, Earl Carver, a Hennepin County sheriff's deputy, was called in, and he and Rusty Talon went up to the house and asked to talk to whoever had been home during the fire. Since there had been a fatality, the Minnetonka Police Department had turned the investigation over to the county.

Ellie answered the door, and invited the officers inside.

Rusty made the introductions and explained why they wanted to talk to the occupants. Ellie listened quietly as he explained that there were some things about the fire that could be deemed suspicious and they needed to clear them up. They also needed to know more about Lamont's personal life.

"I didn't know Lamont that well," Ellie said. "He kept pretty much to himself. I do know that he had worked for the Halsworth's for many years; almost as long as they have lived here," she added. "He was always nice to me and congenial—the kind of man who seemed to like almost everybody."

"Almost everybody?" The deputy asked.

"Yes. He adored the Mr. and I think the feelings were mutual. He seemed to be very considerate of Mrs. Halsworth, and felt so sorry for her and what the disease has done to her. She has Alzheimer's, you know."

"I didn't." The deputy answered. "I'm sorry."

"As for the children, he never said too much about them, even though they had grown up around him. That is, except for Hal."

"Hal?" The deputy asked, looking around as if he was hiding somewhere.

"Yes, Hal. He is the youngest, and right now he is living here while he and his wife try to work through some problems. Lamont hated him. Don't ask me why, I don't know, but there were some deep-seated ill feelings there."

"Hal is where right now?"

"Work, I would guess. He works downtown in his late father's law firm. He is a lawyer of some kind or another. Would you gentleman like some coffee?" Ellie was not intimidated by the lawmen. In fact, she rather enjoyed the company. Taking care of Mrs. Halsworth was a boring job.

Rusty, who hadn't said a word yet except to introduce himself, shook his head no.

"I guess not, but thank you." The deputy continued looking at his notes for a second, and then asked, "Was Hal home the night of the fire?"

"Oh yes. He was the one who discovered it. I was sleeping in Mrs. Halsworth's room, which is on the other end of the house. If it had been up to me, the place would have burned down, and we wouldn't have seen it until the next morning."

"Did Hal wake you?"

"Yes, he woke me up and asked me to call the fire department."

"Then what did he do?"

"Well, he ran outside, saying he had to get Lamont out. I went to the kitchen to make the call so I wouldn't bother Melinda. That's Mrs. Halsworth."

Both men smiled and nodded.

"By the time I got out to the poolroom in the back, where I could see, Hal was running back down the steps from Lamont's apartment. He said it was too late and..." Ellie started to cry.

Rusty, who was doing nothing but listening, went over to comfort her. Sitting down on the sofa beside her, he put his arm around her and gave her his handkerchief.

The detective gave her a moment to compose herself, while he wrote some notes on his pad.

"Was Hal hurt or burned?"

"Hal wasn't in the fire." Ellie had a bewildered look on her tear-stained face.

"No. I know he wasn't in the fire. I just wondered if he got burned trying to rescue Lamont."

"No, he looked fine. He had only his underwear on, and they were white yet, I remember that."

"Tell me if you remember anything else. Now think about it, because this is important. Was the door at the top of the stairs closed or open when Hal came back down."

"Closed, I think. No, I'm not sure." Ellie seemed to be getting weary with the questions and the detective sensed it.

"Look, Ellie is it?"

She shook her head yes.

"We are going to leave you alone for now, but listen, here's my card and

211

if you think of anything that might have seemed strange or out of place, give me a call." He handed her a business card. "You've been very helpful and we want to thank you."

Once outside the door, Earl said to Rusty. "Let's go look at one more thing." The two of them walked back out to the pile of rubble.

"That door upstairs. Did it burn completely up?"

Rusty waded into the mess and pulled out what was left of the door. Just the bottom half of it with part of the frame still attached.

"Where's the knob?" The detective asked.

Rusty started moving things around again, and finally came up with the doorknob.

"Let me see that." Earl held out his hand.

He studied the blackened knob for a second, and then said. "This damn thing was locked from the inside. Where was the body found?"

"Well, the floor gave way so everything that was upstairs ended up down here, in with the garden tractors and tools. However, it did look like he never got out of bed. If you're done with me, Earl, I have to run." Rusty was peeling off his coveralls.

"Yes. Thanks, Rusty."

He wanted to talk with Hal, but decided to call him and have him come down to the station and make a statement, and he mentioned it to Rusty.

"Speaking of calling," Rusty said, "I have to call a Minneapolis detective that was out here yesterday."

"What did he want?" the detective asked.

"Just curious about the fire, I guess. He actually came out to talk with Lamont."

"Who was he?"

Rusty fished through a pile of business cards and handed Torch's card to Earl.

Earl smiled. "Hey, I know this guy. Mind if I call him?"

"No, not at all."

"Let's keep this scene secured for the time being, Rusty. We might have to do some more digging."

"Gotcha," said Rusty. "Here comes the housekeeper again, and I'm out of here."

Ellie was walking across the driveway towards the detective when she started talking to him. "I just wanted to say I did think of a couple of things I thought were strange. Maybe they mean something and maybe not."

"What were they, Ellie?"

"Well, Hal's car was not in the garage. It was sitting right outside of it. That last stall down there." She pointed in the general direction. "He moved it when the fire department got here."

"Was that unusual for it to be there?"

"No, but it had been in the garage when he went to bed. I remember looking outside about ten, and there was no car there, then. Hal was home all night and he never went anywhere else to my knowledge."

"You said you thought about a couple of things?"

"Yes. There was this rope that Hal had in his hands when he came back down the stairs, from his attempt to rescue Lamont. I just thought it was strange that, as upset as he was over Lamont being trapped in the fire and the building burning and all, that he would take the time to pick up a worthless piece of rope.

The detective smiled. "Thanks, Ellie. Who knows, it just might mean something."

CHAPTER TWENTY-FIVE

Torch was buried in paperwork when his phone rang. "Torch, Earl Carver from Hennepin County—how they hanging, man?"

"Earl," Torch laughed. "Things are looking up. What's happening today in that retirement job of yours?"

"Well, Torch, I just talked to Rusty Talon from the State Fire Marshal's office, and he asked me to call you and fill you in on what was going on out at the old Halsworth estate, where this fire was. You were kind of out of your jurisdiction, weren't you?"

"If I was interested in the fire I would have been. Actually, I went out there to speak with the man who died in the fire."

"About what, Torch?"

"He had some evidence he was going to turn over to me."

"Evidence relating to what?" It seemed almost funny, one detective grilling another.

"It's a long story, Earl, but it's an old cold case we just reactivated…a murder case. Hey, let me ask you a few questions, buddy. Was that fire an accident?"

"Don't know right now, but I will say it's suspicious. Buy me lunch and we can talk about it."

"Whitey's in an hour?" He looked at his watch it was eleven thirty.

"Shit, Torch, I'm not sure my guts can handle that."

"Then you buy, and we will talk."

"Whitey's it is."

The receptionist, walking by, handed him a couple of notes. The top one said, **call the Chief.** The next one said that a **Clarice Brown called and wondered if anyone was looking for a bracelet that might be evidence. If so, call Toni at the front desk.**

"Toni, Brennan here. What's this message about a Clarice Brown having a bracelet?"

"Hang on a minute, Torch." He could hear her rustling through papers.

"Torch, she called this morning and said she wasn't sure if she was calling the right police department or not, but her uncle apparently had died in a fire, and he had told her this bracelet he had given her was evidence in some crime, and he had to get it to the police, so I told her that I would spread the word and........."

"Hold on a second Toni, and take a breath. What was her name?"

"Clarice Brown." *Lamont Brown,* he thought.

"Give me her number please."

Toni gave Torch the number and he dialed it right away.

A soft pleasant voice answered, and said, "This is Clarice."

"Clarice, thanks for the call this morning. This is Torch Brennan. I'm a detective with the Minneapolis Police Department. You don't know how happy you have made me if you have that bracelet, and it is what I think it is."

"I wasn't sure which police department to call but being I live here in Minneapolis..."

"You called the right one, my dear, you called the right one. When can I meet you?"

"Well, I have to go to work right now, but I'll be home around five."

"Five is great, and your address is?"

"9600 Sheraton Circle. It's a condo over by Lake Calhoun."

"I'll find it, and thank you. See you then." He had to hurry to meet Earl at Whitey's. He could taste the meatloaf already.

Charlie hardly had a minute to call her own. From luncheons almost every day, to political rallies and campaigning in the evenings, her schedule was full. She had never in her wildest dreams thought that it would be this much work to run for an office. But the fever had caught her, and she was pushing ahead under a full head of steam. She was upbeat and enthusiastic. She had put the encounter with Hal, last Saturday, out of her mind for the time being. She just didn't have time to deal with that idiot right now.

Stephanie had picked herself a lawyer with a bone of his own to pick. His name was Rick Atelier, and he had worked for the Halsworth firm for many years, before being fired by Hal three months ago. She knew this, and she also knew he was a very good attorney when it came to divorce cases.

The divorce papers would be ready in a few days and they spelled out many reasons for the divorce, including persistent physical abuse. In the letter that was being sent to Hal, it more or less said that if he contested this fact, she would press assault charges for his latest attack. It also asked for full custody of little Hal with no visitation. And the real kicker, half of everything she and Hal owned, including his upcoming inheritance. Also, alimony and child support, until Hal was eighteen years old.

The police presence around her place had been dropped after the restraining order had been issued, but she had been told to keep a sharp eye out when she left the safety of her home, and to call immediately if Hal tried to get near her.

The whole thing was a vindictive game with her. She wanted to see Hal squirm. Every night, before she went to sleep, she slid open the drawer to her nightstand to make sure the nickel-plated forty five she had bought, stayed right at arm's length.

Torch and Earl spent the first few minutes getting caught up with old times before they got down to work.

"God, Torch! I get indigestion just smelling this place."

"You need to toughen up, Earl. You're just too used to that pansy ass food you guys eat when you're in those high paying jobs like you are. This shit will stick to your ribs, buddy."

"That's what I'm afraid of. That it will congeal into a rock hard mass, and some doctor will have to get his arm up my ass, and drill it out with a jackhammer." They laughed at their banter.

"Got the coroner's report back, Torch, and it seems that Lamont Brown died of smoke inhalation. There was no sign of drugs or alcohol in his system. No sign of any other trauma either, although there wasn't a lot left of him. Not sure, but we doubt he ever woke up. When his bed fell through the floor, things got tossed around pretty good."

Torch just sat back and wiped the gravy from his face. "Still think it might be an accidental fire?"

"No, we think the car was torched with some kind of an accelerant, but the hose jockeys who put the fire out, also washed away anything useful. Arson is hard enough to prove without losing any evidence that might be there. The door at the bottom of the steps from inside the garage was propped open, so somebody wanted that fire to get upstairs fast. Also, the housekeeper says that Hal Halsworth made some kind of an attempt to rescue Lamont, but came down the stairs saying there was too much smoke and fire to get in. We found that the door at the top of the stairs was never opened. The lock was still on and if it had been unlocked, or opened from the inside, it wouldn't be that way. There was enough of the door jam left to show it hadn't been forced. The window in the door was still intact. Hal also managed to rescue his car before he did that, and we believe it was before the fire started, and then he closed the door behind him."

Torch had a sly smile on his face. "You're dealing with a real bastard here, Earl. I know that from personal experience. Let me tell you a little bit about that."

Torch went on to explain the Stacie Morrison case. He told how they had reopened the case, and the new and old evidence they had. He also mentioned his meeting with Clarice tonight, regarding the bracelet, and how that might tie into both cases.

"You might have a better chance at putting this guy away for murder than we will," Earl said.

"Let's hope so," Torch said. "Not that I don't want him tried for the fire, too, but I want first dibs on him."

"Well, in the meantime, I am going to interview this guy tonight. Torch, you want to be there?"

"No. That would probably be a bad idea. He just might talk to you, and I know he is not going to talk with me around. I'm interested in what he says, though. Send me a transcript?"

"Sure, if I live that long." Earl belched and rounded his chest. "Let's get the hell out of here. This place will be a superfund hazmat cleanup case someday when they tear it down."

"What a pansy ass," Torch quipped, as their waitress approached the table. "Hey, tell Whitey that was the best today, darling." Torch stuffed a twenty in the top of her dress.

"You don't want to put things in there, Torch. It might fall through to the floor," she said, smiling.

Laughing, the two men walked outside and stood on the sidewalk in the bright afternoon sun. Traffic was light and the usual sounds of the city seemed to be subdued today.

"I have chased a lot of killers, Earl, but never one I wanted more than this one. I really don't want him prosecuted for the fire and murder the other night—I want to lock his ass up for what he did to this girl ten years ago," Torch said. He showed Earl Stacie's morgue picture.

Earl looked at the picture with a grimace on his face. "Can't blame you, Torch…can't blame you."

Hal was nervous about meeting with this Earl tonight, but he didn't want to show any signs that he was, or to appear the least bit defensive. He would go meet him, without a lawyer, and answer all of his questions to the best of his ability. After all, he was a lawyer himself, wasn't he, and a very good one despite what Charlie Malloy thought.

At seven p.m., with the address in hand, he walked into the Government Center, where he had been told he would meet with Earl Carver. Things at work had gone better than he thought they would today, and he was in a good mood and anxious to put all of this behind him.

Earl, along with a receptionist, was waiting for him when he walked in. Earl introduced himself and the receptionist, and offered Hal coffee or pop if he was thirsty. Hal said, "No thanks," and they all walked down a narrow hallway to a small windowless room with a table and four chairs. The room was empty, with the exception of the furniture and a cardboard box in the corner, full of old files.

The receptionist, Melissa, sat on the same side of the table next to Hal and Earl sat directly across from him. Melissa set up a voice recorder and showed

Hal how to speak directly into it, while Hal and Earl talked about the weather and the baseball team.

At last, with everything and everybody in place, Earl spoke first. "This meeting is taking place at the Government Center in downtown Minneapolis, as part of the ongoing investigation into the fire, and subsequent death of Lamont Brown of Minnetonka. The date today is August 17th 1999 and it is seven fifteen p.m. Present at this meeting tonight are Mathew Halsworth, who lives at the address of the fire, I, Earl Carver, and Melissa Tangin, from our office here. Hal, you are aware that this is being recorded, and you are here of your own free will, is that correct?"

"Yes," Hal replied.

"Hal, would you state your name and address."

Hal spoke softly, but with no hesitation. Melissa pushed the microphone closer and more directly in front of him, and Hal smiled at her. "Louder?" he asked her.

She smiled back at him. "Just a little."

"Hal, is this your principal residence, or were you just visiting?" Earl wasted no time with the questions. He was a seasoned interrogator, and knew that the more time you gave people who were being questioned, the more uncomfortable they got, and he wanted to keep the mood light.

"I grew up in that house. I haven't lived there much the last nine or ten years, but right now I am separated from my wife, and staying there with my mother for the time being."

"How long has that been going on? I'm sorry, Hal. I asked that poorly, and your home life is not in question here. Let me rephrase that. How long have you been staying there with your mother?"

"Just a couple of weeks."

"I take it you knew Lamont Brown well?"

"I grew up with him living in our home. He was a nice man, and yes, I was fond of him."

"Hal, the night of the fire, tell me, did you see Lamont that night?"

Hal thought for a second. "I don't believe I did. No, I'm quite sure I didn't."

"You were just relaxing around the house that night?"

"Yes, you might say that. I sat out in what we call the poolroom, behind the house. I watched some television and had a few drinks. I also spent some time in thought about my father's recent death."

"I'm sorry about that," said Earl. "Is that where you were when the fire started…in that same poolroom?"

"No, I had gone up to bed."

"Can you see, from your bedroom, the area where Lamont lived?"

"No, my bedroom is in the front of the house."

"What alerted you to the fire?"

"I heard an explosion of some sort out back, and I got up and went across the hall to another room and saw the whole thing going up."

"Then you did what?"

"I ran downstairs and alerted the housekeeper, who sleeps in the same room with my mother. My mother is handicapped."

Earl looked down at his notes, and turned the page, looking for something.

Melissa asked Hal once more, if he wanted anything to drink and he again declined, touching her shoulder and smiling at her.

."Once you alerted the housekeeper…Ellie…is that her name?"

"Yes."

"Once you called out to Ellie, then what did you do?"

"I told Ellie to call the fire department, and I ran outside and up the stairs to see if I could get Lamont out."

"That was not possible, huh?"

"No. When I looked through the little window in the door, all I could see was flames, and the knob was too hot to touch."

"So you never tried to open the door?"

"No." Hal looked a little defiant. "Would you at that point? You had to have been there."

Earl could sense something was going bad here, so he backtracked. "Sorry, Hal. No, I guess not, and I'm not questioning your judgment. It's got to be tough to be put in that position."

"It was tough. I liked Lamont, and there was nothing I could do for him. Not that I wouldn't have done something even if I didn't like him."

It was time to switch gears. "Hal, was your car in the garage when the fire started?"

Hal was quiet for a second. "No, just before I went to bed, I took it out.

I had some ideas about going to see some friends and then realized how late it was, and that I had drunk too much alcohol, so I just left it there and went back in."

"Was everything normal in the garage then?"

"I guess so." Hal shrugged his shoulders, and smiled again at Melissa. He had spent more time looking at her, than making eye contact with Earl.

"Was there a service door in the garage that you went through to get your car?" Hal frowned and gave him an inquisitive look.

"I'm sorry, the whole thing was in a collapsed heap when I saw it." Earl shrugged and held his hands out in front of him.

"Yes, there was a service door in the back, but I didn't use it. I used the keypad in the front."

Hal looked at his watch. "How much longer is this going to take? I have a meeting soon, with a client, and I would like to be on time."

"I think we have a pretty good idea what happened that night. You've been a great help. I guess if I have any other questions I know where to get ahold of you." Earl stood and held out his hand. "Thanks for coming in, Hal."

Melissa stood up, and holding her notepad to her chest, also shook Hal's hand.

Once outside, Hal tried to think of anything that he might have screwed up on, but he couldn't think of anything. He was confident he had performed admirably.

As for Earl, he had only one thing to hang his hat on as far as any inconsistencies. That was the unhooked garage door opener. He was going to have to have the technicians in the lab take a look at that. That and that damn rope Elli had talked about.

Torch sat on the leather couch in Clarice's apartment, while she handed him the bracelet she had gone to her bedroom to get.

"This is it, Mr. Brennan. It's been in my jewelry box for years. There was a watch that he gave me with this, also, but I wore it out and threw it away. I'm sorry if that was important."

"No, don't be, it wasn't…but this bracelet? This is very important to me. Did your uncle tell you where he got it?"

"No, but I have a feeling he took it from someone, or some place. He told me, the night before he died, that he was ashamed of how he'd come into possession of it, but he stopped short of explaining why."

Clarice let a tear slip out, and you could tell she was trying hard to control her emotions. "I'm sorry, I'm trying to put a funeral together for him, and I don't have much money, so this has all been difficult for me." She sat down beside Torch and took a tissue from the coffee table, blew her nose and wiped her eyes.

"Look Clarice, there is a reward if this solves a crime, and it just might. I will see that you get that reward. Your uncle was blessed to have a niece like you. I wish I would have known him; he seems like quite a man." Torch reached out and squeezed her shoulder, then turned his attention back to the bracelet.

"This is exactly as it was described to me, a long, long time ago, by the father of the young lady this belonged to." He turned around the scroll charm he was holding and read the inscription, **S.M. 1989**.

"What happened to her?" Clarice asked.

"She was murdered." Torch answered, and then realized what he had said, and seeing the expression on Clarice's face, quickly said, "Not by your uncle, my dear. I doubt he knew what he had here. I've been looking for it for a long time, and right now is just a good time to find it."

Torch stood up and took Clarice's hand in his. "I will be in touch, and thank you."

Outside in the car, Torch was now convinced he had been on the right track all along. He needed to call Earl and see how his conversation with Hal had gone. Tomorrow, he needed to take a trip to Wisconsin.

CHAPTER TWENTY SIX

Torch was meeting with Earl out at the fire scene this morning, and then he was heading to Wisconsin and a visit with Oscar. His heart was not in this fire scene crap, and especially since he had no jurisdiction there, anyway, but maybe two heads were going to be better than one on this investigation. Earl wanted him there, and it was hard to say, "No," to a fellow detective. If, by chance, they didn't get a murder indictment on Stacie's case, they needed to have this in their back pocket. All Torch hoped for was that this case would not be in the front pocket. He was going to have to have a talk with Earl. He wanted Hal's butt in court so bad, but he wanted him for Stacie's murder, first. He wasn't sure how Earl would react to this.

There were no cars in sight when he arrived at the Halsworth place, so he assumed that Hal was at work. He really didn't want to see Hal. Not yet, anyway. Torch walked through the rubble, and poked around inside a little bit while waiting for Earl to show up, not sure what he was looking for. He looked at his watch and checked the driveway impatiently as Earl was late, and he wanted to get on the road to Wisconsin. He picked up what was left of a chainsaw, and looked at how the heat had melted everything together. Fire was an awesome power.

Everything was so dirty and full of soot, and he wasn't really dressed for this, so he quickly waded out of the mess and went over and peeked through the glass into the poolroom. The pool was huge and the amenities inside were lavish. Torch marveled at how the rich and famous lived. *Where had he screwed up, to not be able to live like this?*

Then he heard gravel crunching, and a car coming up the drive. Turning around and looking up, he saw Earl's car coasting to a stop. *Better go give him some shit about being late,* he thought.

Just then, something caught his eye in the bushes, and he reached into the honeysuckle hedge and picked up a length of nylon anchor rope, about three-eighths of an inch in diameter. The rope was uncoiled so Torch started winding it around his hand to roll it up when he noticed a section, about a foot long, that seemed to be melted. *How did it get over here from the fire, or was it not related to this case?*

"Momma wouldn't let you get off this morning or what?" he hollered at Earl.

Earl laughed. "I wish that was the case. No, I had some car problems so had to trade vehicles. You know how that goes. Were you going to hang yourself with that, or what?" He pointed at the rope Torch was carrying.

"No, I found this in the bushes over here by the building, and look at this."

Torch showed Earl the melted section of the rope. For a second, Earl appeared to be daydreaming, and then he said, "You know, the other day when I was here with the fire inspector, that housekeeper talked to us for a few minutes and she mentioned something about Hal and a rope. What the hell was it she said? Hang on and let me get my notes."

He reached back in his car and came out with a yellow legal pad. "Yes, she said that when Hal came back down the stairs, after his failed attempt to rescue Lamont, he had a piece of rope with him and she thought that was odd. She also said when he came in the house to talk to her, he didn't have it."

"Earl, that door knob you picked up the other day. Where is it?"

"In a bag in the trunk. Let me get it."

He popped the trunk and came out with the scorched knob. "What do you want with this?"

"Let me see it." Torch took the knob and ran his hands around both sides of it, inside the knob. "You have your lab people look at this sticky shit, right here, and I bet it's from that rope. That's the outside part of that hardware." Torch handed the knob back to him.

"You mean this asshole had the door tied shut?"

"Bet you dinner at Whitey's."

Earl just smiled. "I'm not betting you that, but it does make sense. He said last night, 'the knob was too hot to touch,' when I asked him if he had opened the door. Well, this is two lies now. Not really two lies, but two things he got caught at."

"What was the other one?"

He claimed he used the keypad to open that last garage door to take his car out earlier in the evening."

"So?"

"That's the door that was mechanically tripped, Torch. It wouldn't have opened that way."

"Go easy on this, Earl. This guy screwed me over once, and he's dumb like a fox."

It was a nice drive out I-94 to Wisconsin. It had been a long time, but he still remembered the way as if it had been yesterday. He had called Todd yesterday, and he said they could meet at the farm, and they would ride into town and see Oscar together.

If there was a big change in the scenery passing his windows—it was the amount of development that had taken place in this border area over the last ten years. High on the hillsides, tracts of housing seemed to be going up everywhere, while down closer to the freeway, shopping centers and strip malls had gobbled up every piece of vacant land.

He tried to think of what he was going to say to Todd and Oscar that would be optimistic, but yet, not giving them the impression an arrest was a slam-dunk. He had failed in doing that once when it was far easier than it was now to get a conviction.

He had seen an article in the paper the other day about Charlene Malloy, who had been the lawyer for Hal back then, now running for County Attorney. It had seemed interesting to Torch because there was a chance if she got in, and she was proving to be very popular, that her office would be prosecuting the same person she had once been called on to defend. They'd bumped heads at a couple of trials since Hal was arrested, but he had to admit, he knew little about her.

Torch ran his fingers through his hair and shook his head slowly. *Oh what tangled webs we weave, when first we practice to deceive. No, he couldn't think of it like that. She was just being paid to do her job as a defense attorney back then, wrong as it seemed to the cops.* He made a mental note to try and contact her, and see what she thought about the whole deal. Then he made a second mental note…*be careful with this.*

Gradually, the countryside was rural again, with just a few towns and hamlets here and there. Simple people, living the good life in quiet areas where you could trust each other, and locks were for when you were not at home, if at all.

The exit to the service road to the farm loomed straight ahead, and he took his foot off the gas and signaled his turn. As he coasted down the ramp, his hand went to his jacket pocket just to make sure the bracelet was still there. This was one of many times he had checked on it since he left Minneapolis.

Wisconsin dairy country. The lush green landscape was dotted with farms, scattered in tiny wooded areas like little settlements. Here and there would be one with a newer house. But for the most part, there were a lot of old two-stories with countless dormers and white clapboard siding, reminiscent of the forties and fifties, and most of them needing painting.

Big red barns with long bow roofs, most of them covered with metal that reflected the August sun, overwhelmed the other structures. Tall blue metal silos stood alongside of them like silent sentries. Small red outbuildings seemed to be everywhere, finishing off the farmyards.

Herds of black and white Holstein dairy cows paused, and looked up at Torch as he drove by, slowly and methodically chewing, seemingly contented. Their tails continued to swish back and forth over their backs in a rhythmic pattern, keeping the bugs at bay. Young calves, standing beside their mothers, broke loose from time to time to kick up their heels and romp in the summer sun.

In the distance, he could see a tractor crawling slowly across a field of fresh hay, windrowing it for the balers. Corn, that was as high as a grown man, was everywhere; its heavy stalks forming an almost impenetrable barrier.

What a peaceful serene life compared to the rigors of the big city with its miles of concrete and asphalt. Speaking of asphalt, it ended abruptly, and the car seemed to be a little light in the back on the sandy gravel, swaying back and forth. Torch slowed his speed now, trying to remember the turn to the farm. His rear view mirror showed the huge cloud of dust he was raising behind him. He knew it was just past the church, and that was coming up on his right.

He had made good time and was about half an hour ahead of when he had expected to be here. Time enough to turn in to the churchyard, and go around to the back, where all of the monuments stood in the tiny cemetery.

Torch shut off the car, and just sat there for a moment with the door open. You could hear birds singing everywhere and smell the fresh-cut alfalfa just across the road. A cottontail rabbit was next to the church in the high grass, its nose twitching and its ears sticking straight up.

He remembered the day that they had buried Stacie here, in the rain. So many wet faces that day, but not from rain. He would always remember Oscar standing so stoically next to the grave, holding Thelma tightly in his stocky arm. His grief had been overwhelming, but he wouldn't show it.

Torch walked quietly to the corner where he remembered the grave was. He walked as if he was afraid that he would wake someone he shouldn't be waking, but actually, it was just his way to pay reverence to all who rested here.

The monument said simply, **Morrison**. It was a square gray granite block, simple in design. Under the name was a carving of an angel, its wings raised to heaven, its eyes looking down on the earth in front of it. In front of it, were two other granite blocks, set flat into the ground. The shiniest one said, **Thelma Kay. Wife and Mother. Jan.11 1926-December 27th 1998**.

Torch knelt in the grass next to the other plaque. **Stacie Marie. Beloved Daughter. June 12, 1969-December 24, 1989**. The plaque was already showing the rigors of time. Moss was growing around the edges of it and the sun had dulled its sheen.

His eyes were filling with tears. *He didn't cry at his own daughter's grave anymore, why was he crying here?* He took a deep breath and composed himself. *I cannot bring you back, Stacie, but I will bring you justice.*

He stood, and kissing his fingers, reached down and touched the stone. Then he turned and walked away.

Todd was waiting for him and they drove straight to town. This time, when he passed the church, he didn't look that way. He filled Todd in on what was happening as they drove down the dusty road. Torch showed him the bracelet and Todd looked it over carefully and said, "Yes, this was Stacie's. I never saw her without it. Dad will be very happy." Time had healed Todd's wounds, and if there was any vindictiveness left in him, he didn't show it.

They drove through the little town to a spot on the river about a mile north of town. There, on the river bank, stood a low brick building that seemed to stretch along the shoreline for several blocks. The yard was immaculate and several elderly people could be seen walking and lounging on its many paths. A sign by the drive simply said, **River Haven Senior Home**.

The door on the nearest end opened into a large gathering room, and several elderly people could be seen sitting by the windows that faced the water or watching television. Four silver-haired women were laughing and playing a game of cards. They stopped to look up, but quickly went back to their game. "He must be in his room," Todd said.

As they walked down the hall, Torch was taken with how homey the facility was. There was none of the urine smell, and institutional atmosphere, that was common to most nursing homes. It truly seemed like a group of people, just living together and enjoying each other's company in the twilight of their lives.

"I didn't tell him you were coming," Todd said. "Let's see if he recognizes you."

Oscar was sitting in a chair by his bed, reading his Bible, when the two men came in.

"Dad, I brought you company," said Todd.

Oscar looked up at both of them with a faint smile on his face. His once-sturdy muscular body had gone soft. The shoulders, that had once carried one hundred pound bags of feed, now drooped. The thick fingers that had hand-milked twenty head of cows twice a day, when he and Thelma had first started farming, now looked more like the hands of a piano player.

"Todd, you should have told me you were coming and we could have…" Oscar stared at Torch for a minute, and then broke into a big grin. "You're that police officer that came to see us when Stacie was killed. How nice that you would come and see me."

Torch sat down on the edge of the bed. "Oscar, I have something for you to look at. I told you we would find it, the day you called me so long ago, and we did." Torch laid the bracelet in Oscar's hands.

"Stacie's bracelet," he whispered. "Did you catch the person who took her life?"

"Not yet, but we are this close." Torch held his forefinger and thumb up, separated by about a quarter of an inch.

"We now have the bracelet, and we now have his DNA. Do you know what that is, Oscar?"

The old man shook his head yes, and smiled. "I watch a lot of television."

Torch laughed and patted him on the back. "As soon as the tests come back to us, with the DNA results we need, we will go to trial."

Oscar seemed confused for a moment. "Did he leave DNA on Stacie?"

"He left it in her, Oscar. You knew she was pregnant. That he had drugged and raped her a few weeks before he killed her? Well, that tiny tissue that was growing in her was frozen and kept in the police lab all this time, along with samples of Stacie's own DNA. When she was murdered, we could not have done these tests, but modern science has now made it possible."

Torch reached over and took both of the old man's hands in his. "It doesn't prove he killed her, but it does prove he had a reason to kill her. That is all we need."

"Who is this man?" Oscar looked up at Torch, with the question written all over his face.

"The same one we arrested last time. Only this time, we have all of the pieces to the puzzle. Last time, we just didn't have enough evidence."

"Dad, would you like to go for a ride?" Todd seemed to want to change the subject. "We could go to town for ice cream."

"That would be nice," he said.

They had hot chocolate sundaes and coffee at the local café. Then they took Oscar back, and went out to the farm. Todd stood in the farmyard, the summer wind blowing through his sandy hair. "Thanks, Torch, for going to see him."

"I will come and see him again when this is over, Todd. The pleasure will be all mine, believe me."

On the way home, it seemed to Torch that a small weight had been lifted from his shoulders. Now he had only to finish the job.

A name kept going through his mind, and for some reason, he could not let go of it. *Charlene Malloy. Yes, he had to call her.*

CHAPTER TWENTY-SEVEN

The days were getting shorter and fall was definitely upon them. The trees had turned an assortment of autumn colors, and then had lost their leaves for the year. The showy flowers, that had brightened the gardens and landscape all summer long, had since been nipped by the early frost. Now they were only a frozen reminder of the summer that once was.

Squirrels and other rodents were busy packing away supplies for winter. Many of the birds that had filled the air with their cheery songs had taken flight for their winter quarters.

Winter doesn't come easily in Minnesota, but when it does arrive, it can be brutal. Some years, however, there comes a period they call Indian summer, and this year they had been blessed with one of the best. The daytime temperatures hovered in the sixties, and people filled the parks and yards, trying to cram in one more day of outdoor fun.

In Wisconsin, the cornfields that were once too high to see over, were now just yellow chewed-up stubble on the black earth. Bales of hay were stacked in piles, covered by tarps and plastic; and those blue silos were filled to the top with winter feed. The cattle, now getting heavier with spring calves, lay on the southern hillsides in the sun's rays, chewing their cuds and soaking up the warmth. Those people, and the cows that had been around for a few winters, knew all too well that the long winter season, locked in the barn, could give you a super case of shack fever.

Charlie's election seemed to be all but a certainty. The polls had her far ahead of her opponent, and the election was only a week away. She was happy beyond her greatest expectations. Happy because, for the first time in her working life, she seemed to be in charge of her own destiny. She had, for so many years, been an indentured servant; at least it had felt that way. She was looking forward to a long career of serving the people of Hennepin County.

Charlie and Torch had met and talked in early September. At first, Charlie had been tentative. She was cautious for many reasons, but mostly because they had been adversaries so long. It wasn't easy to see each other on the same side of the fence. Cautious also, because Charlie was not the County Attorney yet, but it was looking better every day.

They discussed Hal and Stacie Morrison's case but only in passing. She knew that it had been reopened, and she also realized that if it came to trial, her office would be prosecuting it. There was no discussion about any information that she may have had that could be pertinent to the case—Torch knew better than to even ask. They did talk about some of the other cases they had worked on, and shared a laugh or two.

However, something in the back of both of their minds said, *we need to see each other again, and it has nothing to do with Hal Halsworth.* Maybe it had been Torch's "Nick Nolte" rugged looks and easy-going smile. Maybe it was Charlie's infectious laugh and bubbly personality. It was something that could not be explained, that was for sure.

Torch called her the first week in October and asked her if they could see each other again. No business, just to share a few drinks and talk about their lives. Charlie's better intuition said, "be careful," but she did say "yes." Actually, she had had more than a few daydreams about him. They would meet at Castillo's for supper, but it was to be a Dutch date, at Charlie's insistence.

Castillo's was an icon in downtown Minneapolis. Everybody who was anybody had, at some time in their lives, gone there to dine. From the uniformed valets who parked your car, to the elegant furnishings inside of the spacious dining room, the place reeked of class. But it could also be discreet, and Charlie knew that. The tables were placed in little alcoves, ensuring your privacy. With the election only a few weeks away, and her frustrated opponents looking for any dirt they could find, she wanted to be cautious.

Torch remembered being here only once before, with Evie. It had been right after she had gone into treatment, and he had brought her here as a birthday treat.

Charlie had been here many times, with clients that needed to be pampered and impressed. Also, several times with Mathew Halsworth when he had been impressed with her and she had been young and foolish…a part of her life she no longer wanted to think about.

Torch picked Charlie up at her apartment, right on time. She had had her bed full of discarded outfits before she decided on a red dress; with a shawl she had bought in Italy on one of her many trips with Mathew. The dress was conservative with a modest neckline and three quarter length sleeves. She carried only a small clutch that matched her shoes.

Torch had worn a black tailored suit, with an almost silver shirt, and a dark gray tie. He had a fresh haircut, new wingtip shoes, and had even dug out his Rolex watch, which he rarely wore.

"You clean up real nice," Charlie joked, as they drove away from her place.

Torch smiled at her remark. "I guess I really don't know what to say to that. Ladies like you are generally out of my league. I am glad you allowed me to share this evening with you."

"Thanks, Torch. If I wasn't comfortable with you, and just a wee bit attracted to you, I might not have."

It wasn't far to Castillo's, so they were there before they had much time to say anything else.

Hal had, more or less, crawled into a shell since his father's death. He kept a low profile at work, and stayed home with his mother at night. Stephanie's attorney filed a lien on his portion of the estate, which could be ready for distribution in a few weeks. It asked for half of everything, plus unspecified alimony and child support. The divorce papers had also been filed, and the restraining order was still in effect, so he kept his distance from her. They'd not spoken since the night he assaulted her.

As for Earl Carver, his case against Hal was flimsy, at best. The rope could have been put there for many reasons, and an examination of the railing showed no rope fibers or scuffs. Hal admitted bringing it back down the steps with him, and told Earl, "I have no reason for why I untied it and brought it down, and I don't know why it was there in the first place. I just did it, I guess."

As for the garage door opener, the collapse of the building could have caused it to trip. Hal stuck to his story that he used the keypad to get in a few hours before the fire. The cause of the fire was tied to the Cadillac, but no trace of accelerant was found except gasoline on the garage floor that could be explained by the two melted plastic cans, sitting in front of the car, that had burned.

Hal had a fire of his own, smoldering and festering inside of him. His hatred of Stephanie was growing each day. Something was going to have to be done with her. He had thought of a few scenarios, but they all seemed very risky, right now. The unknown evidence the police had on the Stacie Morrison case also bothered him no end. He had not heard or seen anything, lately, that would lead him to believe that they had made any progress, but he still didn't like the smell of things, and there was very little he could do about it.

Hal wasn't used to living like this. If he had a problem, he usually eliminated it or had his father take care of it. His hands were pretty much tied right now, and that was only making him more disturbed by the day.

They started out with a light white zinfandel and then switched to red Bordeaux to complement their veal cutlets. The ambience was impressive, and the food and wine so great. But above it all, the way they enjoyed each other's company made everything else seem insignificant. Torch had not laughed or enjoyed himself this much in years. His solitary lifestyle and the nature of his work left little room for happiness. Tonight, though, there had been no mention of work by either one of them.

Charlie was taken by Torch and she saw a side of him she never knew existed. He was clever and funny. He was also intelligent and compassionate. Charlie had been a defense attorney for too many years, and her bad attitude about the police was being radically changed tonight.

After their meal, they decided to walk and talk a little more. Torch drove her home and they walked the empty cobblestone sidewalks to a small park. They sat on a concrete bench, while Charlie fed the squirrels the rest of their leftover bread sticks. It was a small park with a pond in the middle, and although you couldn't see them from where they were sitting, you could hear the ducks and geese flapping their wings and talking with each other. It was a cool night, but not blustery. The sky was clear, and even in the glow of the city lights around them, the stars shone brightly.

"I am so excited to be turning a new page in my life, Torch. I haven't won the office yet, but it looks pretty good what with the elections only a week away. It has certainly been a new experience for me...this campaigning. I never thought I would like it, but I do."

"You are going to be a great County Attorney, Charlie and I, for one, will be glad to see you on the side of the law for a change."

For a second, Charlie had been a little offended by that statement, but then she realized that what Torch had said was true, and she smiled and pressed her hand into his. Her hand was soft and warm and the gesture made Torch slide over a little, on the bench, so their bodies were touching.

"What was it like to work for Mathew Halsworth?" Torch looked at her with small furrows of genuine concern in his brow.

For the moment, she seemed to be forming her answer as she thought. When she did speak, it was so softly he could barely hear her, but her eyes were locked on his in a serious gaze. "Torch, you will never know the things I had to do for that man, to be successful in that firm." She looked sad, and for a moment it was if she wanted to say more, but she didn't.

Torch put his arm around her. "Let's not talk about that anymore. Let's go have a nightcap."

Walking hand in hand, they went to Mollie's, a small bar just a block from Charlie's place. An hour ago, Charlie wouldn't have done even that small gesture of friendship, but things were changing. She wasn't sure why they were changing, but they were.

Torch ordered a Bud Light and Charlie had an orange juice with a touch of gin. The bar was nearly empty, with just a couple of grizzly old men at one end, nursing their beer and arguing about something. The lone bartender was wiping glasses with a dishtowel, while he watched television over his shoulder. He seemed to have tuned everything and everybody out. Honkytonk music was playing somewhere in the back, and you could smell something greasy cooking.

For some reason, they just didn't want the night to end, but as magical as it had been, Charlie felt she had so much more to learn about Torch before it went any farther. She also knew that being seen with a Minneapolis cop, right now, might not be sending the right message.

Torch, on the other hand, was just happy she had given him this opportunity, and he wasn't going to do anything to spoil it. They finished their drinks and he walked her home. While facing her, he took both of her hands in his. "I hope that you had a good time, Charlie. It's been so long since I dated; I hope I didn't make a fool of myself."

"I did have a good time Torch, and you were a prince. Thank you so much for a fun night." She leaned over and kissed him softly on the side of his mouth. "Goodnight, Torch."

He dropped her hands from his grasp. "Talk to you next week? By the way, you look beautiful tonight." He touched his forefinger to her nose.

"Please do, and thank you!" She turned and went into the house, with her heart racing.

The Monday before the election was a day Torch would never forget. He had a note on his desk to call Charlie, and he also had a note to call the lab. The DNA results he'd been waiting on were back from out east.

Hal's DNA was a perfect match with the fetal tissue from Stacie Morrison's body. There were only two possible men with that DNA—Hal and his brother, Ralph. Tomorrow, he would start putting the case in order, and then it would be time to move on it. He could have it in the County Attorney's Office by Friday. The City Attorney was going to help him with the preparation.

He dialed Charlie's number and it was busy so he left a message that said, "Tag, you're it. Call me at work."

The phone rang a minute later.

"Torch, hey, I just wanted to make sure you were going to be at my victory party tomorrow night."

"Will you have beer and food?"

"I will have everything your little heart desires, my friend. Beer, food and me, we will all be there."

"Beats what your opponent offered me," he joked. "Yes, I'll be there, and thanks for thinking of me."

"Lexington Hotel, Torch…around nine."

"Nine! I work the next day, counselor!"

"Take a nap, Torch."

"I can't sleep since I went out with you."

Charlie giggled. "Take a cold shower, Torch, and then take a nap. See you tomorrow. I've got another call coming in."

She stared at the phone. She had been confused, and a little befuddled, about Torch Brennan from the first time she had talked to him. But right now, she wanted nothing more than to be with him. Call it crazy, call it fascination, call it whatever you wanted to, she was falling for this man. Maybe that prayer she had been praying for so long was going to come true. She certainly hoped so.

CHAPTER TWENTY-EIGHT

Election Day dawned cold and windy. The weather forecast was for significant snow, but not until tomorrow. It was already snowing hard in Montana and moving this way.

The newspapers were calling for a record voter turnout, and for Charlie to win by ten percentage points. Her opponent had spent a ton of money in his bid to upset her, but it seemed to have had little effect. They had loved Bob Harris when he had been in office, and he had endorsed Charlie fully, promising everyone more of the same.

Charlie had been a fresh face in the political scene, and her credentials and her impeccable character were held with approbation by all who knew her. Her only dirty secrets had died, and were buried, with Mathew Halsworth.

The County Board had met last week and announced that whoever was the next County Attorney would take office immediately, and not wait until January. Bob Harris had resigned to pursue his own aspirations and they hadn't had a leader for three months now. There were a lot of cases that were being held in limbo because no one wanted to take responsibility for them. They needed a leader and they needed one now.

The polls opened at eight, and Charlie had her picture taken for the evening news on Channel Three, casting her ballot along with the Governor.

It wasn't staged because they both lived in the same district. Then she went home to wait. She tidied up the apartment and then went to get her hair fixed. All the people at the salon, where she had gone for years, avoided talking about the elections. They didn't want to jinx her.

Hal sat staring at the morning paper on his desk. He had put Charlie out of his mind for the last few days and now, there was her picture staring at him from the front page of the metro section, **Local Attorney is Front-Runner**.

He had read and reread it, and the more he thought about it, the more he didn't like it at all. For starters, he didn't like her, and wished that she had gotten her ass beat good so she would have no job. That would have served her right. *The damn traitor,* he thought. The worst part of this would be—if the Minneapolis police did have something on him and did press charges—this whole thing could end up in her office. Not a good thing, knowing what she knew about him. He should have done a better job of taking care of her at the funeral. It had been raining so hard no one would have seen them, and shit, he'd had a great alibi. He was in the church and no one saw him leave.

For right now though, he had bigger fish to fry. On Thursday, his father's estate was being divvied up. He had already seen the papers. One quarter to each of the three children, and one quarter put in trust for his mother's care. Each of the quarters tallied up to over fifty million dollars.

Stephanie was not going to get her hands on one cent of it. He had prepared a lawsuit that was going to be filed on Friday, challenging her claim to her half. It said that she had been married to Hal for less than three years, and the will had been made before that. Clearly, Mathew Halsworth did not intend for her to be part of it.

The second part of the suit challenged her claim for alimony. She was young, talented, and physically fit. She could work if she had to.

Hal had no problems with the child support and would not contest that.

He had no hopes of the suit being successful; that was not his intent. He just needed more time to plot how to get rid of her.

By ten thirty, the results were in, and Charlie had won in a landslide. Torch spoke with Charlie long enough to say, "Hi" and then he stayed in the background, watching her bask in her newfound glory. He was actually very happy for her, and wished he could pick her up and spin her around in a show of happiness, but he also understood the public image problem. Maybe later they could celebrate.

"Everybody listen, please." Charlie was standing on a small stage so she could see over the crowd, holding the microphone high in her hand and glowing like a June bride. "I just wanted to say thank you to all of you who worked so hard on my behalf. It is a great night for all of us, and it will be a great night for Hennepin County, I promise you that. I just received word that my opponent has conceded. I have also received word that Bob Harris is running ahead in his race. So let's party on."

A great round of applause went up from the jubilant crowd and shouts of "Charlie! Charlie!" She handed the microphone to an aide, and walked through the crowd, shaking hands and hugging friends.

Torch had seen Charlie approaching his table and stood to meet her. Several other people were crowding in, excitedly waiting their turn to congratulate her.

He wanted to pick her up and hug her. He wanted to feel her heart beating against his, when she was this happy, but he knew the rules right now.

"Congratulations, Charlie," he said, smiling broadly.

She shook his hand saying, "Thank you so much," and then, just that quickly, she had gone on to the others, leaving Torch standing there, with a key in his hand.

It was two-thirty when Charlie walked in the door, her shoes in her hand. Torch was sleeping on her couch. She walked as quietly as she could to the couch, and sat down beside him. She ran her hand through his graying blond hair. *What was there about this man that interested her so much?*

Torch looked up at her with a sleepy smile.

"Party over?" he asked.

Charlie shook her head yes. "Party's over, and now the work begins. I'm excited though, and anxious to get started."

"That's good, because I have some work for you."

"Hal Halsworth?" Charlie asked.

Torch nodded his head.

Charlie wanted to change the subject for now. "I hope that me giving you my apartment key didn't make you think you were going to get lucky tonight."

Torch smiled and squeezed her leg. "No, we couldn't even if we wanted to."

"Why is that?" Charlie asked.

"I think I have my period," Torch replied.

They both erupted in a fit of laughter. "I'll get you a blanket."

When she came back, Charlie covered Torch with the blanket and he held out his arms for her. She sat back down, and bending over, kissed him tenderly on the mouth. They parted for a moment, and then, their faces only inches apart, Torch put his hand to the back of her head and gently pulled her to him once more. The second kiss said it all.

Torch woke to the sound of bacon sizzling, and Charlie singing softly in the kitchen. He walked to the kitchen and poked his head around the corner. "Bathroom?" He asked quizzically.

"Through my bedroom, sleepyhead." She pointed. "There are clean towels in the linen if you want to shower, but hurry, breakfast is almost ready."

"You know, Charlie, I have this cabin up in Crow Wing County, by a small lake. It's probably dirty and dusty. I know I haven't been up there for a while. I thought maybe we could go up there this weekend, and get away for a little while, before you have to go to work?"

Charlie sat across from him at the table, both hands gripping her coffee cup while she peered over the top of it. She smiled softly, almost serenely. "I would like that, Torch. I would like that very much."

"Great, then let's plan on it." He stood and walked around the table; putting his hands on her shoulders, he bent down and kissed her. "I've got to run. I'm late already. Thank you for the bed and breakfast. You run a nice place here. But especially, thank you for caring for me. I do care for you. More than you know."

Charlie smiled, stood up and kissed him again. "Good luck with your period. I hope it's gone before the weekend."

Torch laughed and hugged her once more. "If I don't go now, I am going to have to take another shower. Goodbye."

Charlie sat at the table after he had left. She had never felt so much at peace with herself and the world. She had a new lease on life with her new job, and she now realized that she was in love with Torch Brennan, and he was in love with her.

Torch sat at his desk studying the outline he had made for the City Attorney, and ultimately, the County Attorney. It was still all circumstantial evidence, but it was overwhelming evidence, at least in his eyes. He had listed it in chronological order.

1. They had eyewitness testimony that put Hal and Stacie at the same party, and eyewitness testimony that he had taken her home sick.

2. There was her roommate's testimony that Stacie had come home from the party, sick and troubled. Unusual for her.

3. There was the phone call to Hal the night she had disappeared. He had explained it away, saying she was wishing him Merry Christmas. Why? She hardly knew him.

4. There was GHB in her body. Somebody had drugged her before her death, and that someone was Hal, when she had come to his apartment to confront him about her pregnancy.

5. She had not been sexually active. Her pregnancy had resulted from a one- time shot, indicative of a rape. Her conception date worked out to the night of the party.

6. The fetus carried Hal's DNA. His brother, the only other possibility, would be cleared before the trial.

7. Her clothes were found in a dumpster at a store that Hal had been at the day they were put there. The floor mat in the trunk of his car had been stained with human excrement.

8. Her jewelry turned up in the Halsworth gardener's hands, and he was going to explain "how" to police, when he mysteriously died.

Torch looked at the list again. *What was it he was missing? Oh yes, Stephanie's testimony, when Hal had told her she would end up in the river just like the other one.* He made that number nine.

He called the City Attorney's Office and asked to meet with him this afternoon. "Two p.m. would work." his secretary said.

Friday afternoon, Torch picked Charlie up and they headed for what he referred to as the north woods. The snow they had received earlier in the week had almost all melted, but as they headed north and it got colder, there

241

were banks of snow quite high along the highways, and the surrounding countryside was blanketed in white.

They had talked every day last week, like two teenagers filled with puppy love; but they hadn't seen each other since the night at Charlie's apartment. It was warm and cozy in the car, but not as warm as their feelings were for each other.

Charlie was mesmerized by the fields and the vast forestland scenery. She had seldom left the city unless it was to go to another city. They passed through many small towns and hamlets, and the farther north they got, the less frequent the towns appeared.

At long last, some three hours later, Torch turned off on a small country road where the pine trees and spruce trees formed an almost impenetrable barrier, and the road seemed as if they were in a tunnel of green trees covered with snow. They stopped once to wait for two deer to get out of the road, their red summer coats now almost entirely brown. Small clouds of vapor came from their noses, and they ran to find a break in the trees where they could escape these intruders.

At last, the tires squeaking in the few inches of snow that had not been plowed yet, they pulled into a much narrower road that snaked through the woods and came out in a small clearing. There sat a small log cabin, its roof covered with about a foot of fresh powder. In front of the cabin was a wide-open flat area that Charlie could only surmise was a lake.

They'd brought warm clothing and boots, and they dressed in the car before stepping out into a wintry wonderland that took Charlie's breath away. Not just in awe of the beauty of it all, but also from the cold bite in the air. The sun was just setting across the distant shore and was slowly disappearing behind the towering trees in front of it. This was as isolated from human life as she had ever been before, but she felt secure with the man she was falling in love with, and who was leading her to the cabin.

"It's so beautiful it takes your breath away, Torch."

"I love it here, Charlie, but I rarely get up here anymore with no one to share it with. My wife and I bought it twenty some years ago, and not much has changed."

They stomped the snow off their boots and went into the cabin. Charlie stood inside the door, taking it all in, while Torch went outside to get some firewood. There were actually three rooms inside…a kitchen, a bathroom, and the rest of the ground floor. On one end there was a large stone fireplace, and on the other end, there were steps that led up to a loft that overlooked it all. In front, a big picture window looked out over the frozen lake and the moonlight, reflecting off the snow, gave the image of being in a field of diamond dust.

Torch came in with a huge armful of wood and proceeded to get a fire going in the fireplace. Then, turning back to Charlie, who was still hugging herself to ward off the cold, he wrapped his arms around her, hugging her tightly and rubbing her back to warm her up. "It will warm up fast," he said.

While the fireplace roared and it got warmer by the minute, Charlie busied herself getting some coffee going, and heating up some stew Torch had dug out of a bag.

"I have to admit, I have no idea how to make coffee in this," she said, holding up a blue enameled coffeepot.

Torch laughed and came into the kitchen; he showed her how to pump water from the pitcher pump next to the sink. He found her a dented aluminum kettle, and using a knife, opened the can of stew for her. The little propane stove came to life, with the help of a farmer match, and they were in business.

There was a small leather couch that sat almost in front of the fireplace, and that was where they retired to eat their meal. The cabin had warmed up considerably, and Charlie sat in the corner of the couch, her feet tucked under her. Torch brought over their prepared food in what looked like pie tins, and they ate, hungrily. The coffee had grounds in it, and the stew had burnt to the bottom of the pan, but it still tasted so good.

From out of nowhere, Torch produced a bottle of wine and two plastic glasses.

The fire flickering in the fireplace was mirrored in the pools of Charlie's eyes, and she appeared hypnotized by the flames in front of her, and deep in thought. Both of them knew their relationship had passed the initial test with flying colors, and now it was time to go to the next plateau. Charlie was willing, but at the same time reluctant. Her body was saying yes, but her mind was saying, not so fast.

Torch put his arm around Charlie and drew her close. The soft kisses and cautious petting that had been characteristic of their growing affection for each other, the last few weeks, had suddenly became more brazen with each kiss. Hands began to roam to areas that were no longer sacred, or off-limits. With each new sensual discovery, their pulses increased and breathing accelerated. The clothing, that had hidden what they now wanted so badly to share, fast disappeared in a pile on the floor.

For Charlie, it was the first time in her life that sex seemed like a pleasurable act. It was all so strange to her. All those times with Mathew Halsworth had been a chore and nothing more. It had been devoid of any kind of pleasurable feeling and filled with pain and humiliation.

It all seemed so different. She was getting signals and urges from her body that she had never felt before. Torch was driving her to a near frenzy with his foreplay, and ladylike or not, she was taking this bull by the horn. She turned, facing him on the couch, knees straddling him, her bare back feeling the heat from the fireplace. Then she reached under her and brought them together as one. There was no pain, just a feeling of closeness and pleasure that made her moan in ecstasy.

For Torch, it had been a long time—way too long—and never with someone this willing. Their wet mouths moved in a wild rhythm with their all too eager bottoms emulating the same action. Charlie could not seem to get close enough. She was feeling something new; something so incredibly pleasurable, and nothing like anything that she had ever experienced before. It came in waves, one after another, and then she felt Torch's release, heard him groan, and they collapsed on their sides, facing each other, exhausted.

"Let's go upstairs," Torch whispered.

They climbed the stairs to the loft, Charlie going first, swaying her bare bottom seductively. By the time they arrived at the big iron bed that was covered in quilts, they were both more than ready again.

CHAPTER TWENTY-NINE

When Charlie awoke the next morning it was incredibly cold in the cabin and she pulled her head back under the covers. "Brrr...Torch, get up and make a fire, it's freezing in here."

"You weren't very cold last night, were you?" Torch quipped.

She reached behind him and pinched his bare bottom. "Ouch!" he exclaimed, without moving.

"Charlie leaned over him and brushed his lips with hers. "No, I wasn't, and neither were you."

He slid out of bed and crept down the stairs, wrapped in a blanket, looking for his clothing. *He didn't remember taking them off...or had he? He remembered taking someone's clothing off.*

When he had finished dressing, he looked up at the loft where Charlie stood, wrapped in a sheet. "Once you get that fire started, detective, why don't you come back up here for a while?" She opened the sheet for a moment.

Torch grinned. "You're insatiable, counselor."

After going snowshoeing across the lake that morning, they stayed in the cabin the rest of the day. Later, Torch drilled a hole in the ice, and both of them tried catching some pan fish, but they both got cold and gave it up. It was the first time in her life that Charlie had gone fishing.

Just before dark, they packed up for the trip home. Charlie had a meeting Sunday afternoon.

They had talked well into the night last night, between bouts of lovemaking, about their budding relationship. They both agreed it was something beautiful, but it had to be kept under wraps for the time being. Nothing was going to ruin this case for Torch and a relationship with the prosecutor could be construed as unethical. Charlie just listened in quiet agreement, preferring not to talk about the case at all. Torch knew she understood where he was coming from, and where he was going to go with it.

The ride back was a quiet one. They were both tired, but fulfilled and very happy. Charlie slept most of the way, with her head on Torch's shoulder.

On Monday morning, Charlie took over the reins of the County Attorney's Office. Most of the day was spent being introduced to all of the lawyers, paralegals, and clerks that worked in the department. It seemed like she shook as many hands that day as she had in the campaign.

By Wednesday, the City Attorney had things ready for the County Attorney's Office, and he and Torch met one last time to make sure they were on the same page. Since Charlie had just taken over the job, they decided that it would be better to wait until later in the week to file the papers.

The surviving heirs of Mathew Halsworth had gathered at the offices of Osmond Chambers, the family attorney who had handled the estate. There were two parts to the estate. The part that was to be liquidated— stocks, bonds, cash on hand, and some real estate. The other part— the office building downtown and the home. The office building downtown, and the firm, would be held in joint ownership by all three of the Halsworth children and could only be sold by a unanimous agreement to do so. Since the building was essential to the business, the firm and the building would remain as they were. The profits from the business would, yearly, be split three ways. The home would be maintained as long as Mrs. Halsworth was alive, and she would be cared for at that residence until such time as it was physically impossible by the effects of her ill health. After the parts of the estate had been liquidated, and after taxes, the sum of nineteen million three hundred dollars would be paid to each of the three children, and a similar amount would be held in trust for the care of Melinda Halsworth.

By court order, half of Mathew Halsworth Jr.'s inheritance would be held in trust until a ruling could be made as to the effect of Stephanie's claims on the estate. There had been a counter lawsuit filed by Hal, challenging her right to any of it, and that had to be settled, too. It could be some time before these things would be ruled upon. As for the child support she was asking for, he was paying that.

On Friday morning, Charlie received her first look at the case against Hal Halsworth, for the death of Stacie Morrison. The letter from the Minneapolis City Attorney's Office asked that the evidence they had outlined, be presented to the grand jury of Hennepin County, and that an indictment be issued against Mathew Halsworth Jr., for first-degree murder in the death of Stacie Morrison.

Charlie and Torch had spoken almost daily on the phone since she had taken office. On Wednesday night, Torch had enjoyed rib eyes on the grill at Charlie's, followed by a generous serving of Charlie for dessert.

She reached for the phone and dialed the Minneapolis City Attorney's Office. Then, having second thoughts, she quickly hung up and called Torch.

Torch, who had been in the middle of a heated argument with one of his detectives, mellowed out as soon as he recognized Charlie's voice.

"Hey buddy, I have some good news and some bad news. Which do you want to hear first?"

"Hit me with the good stuff, Charlie. I'm not sure I can handle the bad stuff right now. It's been a rough day." He waved the other man away from the conversation.

"Well, I went over the evidence you presented to us on the Stacie Morrison case and we will introduce it to the grand jury next week. I think it will fly, Torch."

"That's great, Charlie. This one has been a long time coming. Now give me the bad news."

"I will not prosecute this case myself, Torch. I know that's what you wanted, and believe me, for lots of reasons I do, too. However, my ties with the Halsworth family, and especially Hal, are going to come into question here, so I need to recuse myself. Listen though…your evidence is strong… especially the DNA. Even though it is all circumstantial, personally, I think it is overwhelming."

"Charlie, knowing what you know personally about young Halsworth, and without putting you on the spot, did he do this? Between you and me, dear."

"I would bet he did, Torch, but I have no smoking gun, and that is all I am going to say. Can we get together Sunday afternoon? I have two tickets to a play at the Orpheum if you're interested."

"Let's go for it," Torch said. "I miss you, Charlie."

"Miss you, too." Charlie said, and she quietly hung up the phone. She would be so glad when this was over and they could be more "out in the open" with their relationship.

Torch stood on Stephanie's doorstep and rang the bell. She looked surprised when she opened the door, but quickly recovered when she recognized him.

"You're the detective who helped me out, aren't you?"

"One and the same," Torch said. "Can I come in and talk to you about something?"

"Sure, hope you don't mind the mess. I'm painting the kitchen." Stephanie had her hair pulled into a ponytail. She had on blue jeans, and an old white shirt that had seen painting before.

"No. In fact, this will only take a minute. Has Hal left you alone?"

"I haven't seen the asshole since the night he beat the shit out of me and left."

"Was that the first time he had done that?" Torch was getting off-track, but he was trying to put her at ease.

She sat down and rubbed the back of her neck. "No, Mr. Brennan, it is not."

"Torch," he said. "Call me Torch." He pulled out a chair and turned it around so the back was facing the table, and then sat down, his arms folded in front of him on top of the chair back.

"Stephanie, you told the officers that came to help you that night that Hal had threatened you, and he told you that you could end up like the other one…in the river. Do you remember that? Do you remember telling me he said that?"

"How could I ever forget?"

"Would you testify to that in court? I asked you that before, and you never answered me."

She stared at Torch, while biting her top lip. "What the hell has he done now? Is this about that murder you talked about before?"

"I can't tell you much right now, kid, but it's bad, and he needs to be put away for a long time." Now, answer my question."

"Yes. Hell, yes! I'll do whatever I can to get rid of that bastard."

"Good, and as soon as I can, I will tell you the whole story."

Torch's pager buzzed, and he took it off his belt and looked at the screen. "Gotta run, kid. Thanks. I'll be in touch."

The show at the Orpheum was composed of a troop of Irish dancers traveling the country. They both enjoyed it immensely, with the folksy music and whirlwind dancing, but not as much as they enjoyed just being with each other. They had so much in common to talk about, but the real tie was a bond, binding them closer and closer together. A bond anchored in love and respect; it seemed to grow more each time they were together.

After the show, they walked down Hennepin Avenue, just enjoying the people and sights. It was cold and brisk out, but they didn't seem to notice the weather. Instead, they went to a small bistro for coffee, and made plans to spend Thanksgiving together in Florida. Torch had access to a condo on Clearwater Beach, just north of Tampa.

Back at Charlie's apartment, they talked well into the night. There was no lovemaking this time, just warm and friendly conversation, and an honest effort, on the part of both of them, to get to know each other as well as possible.

Hal became more unmanageable with each passing day. He rarely went into work, preferring to spend his time brooding and scheming in his room. With his newfound inherited funds, his drug habit was back, full blown, and this added to his unpredictable behavior. He knew something was up with the police department, and just today he had found out about the possible indictment. He was going to have to wait to see what the evidence was, but if Stephanie was a source, or a witness, she was going to have to be eliminated. How, and where, were the only questions left to be answered.

Hal had found out, long ago, that crimes committed with some forethought and planning had a good chance of not being solved. Yes, maybe the finger of the law would point his way, but in today's legal world you needed much more than that to get caught. He had gotten away with murder twice, and he'd get away with it again.

They sat as close together as possible, in the big silver bird, on their way to Tampa and some fun in the sun. They had had an early winter in Minnesota, and already people had their fill of it. On the day they left, it was snowing again and the temperature was in the low twenties.

"Look honey," Torch gestured out the window at the Chicago skyline below them.

Charlie smiled and squeezed his hand. "My parents came from Chicago. Someday, when we have time, we need to go and visit there."

Torch smiled softly. They had known each other for only a couple of months and the word "we" was finding itself in their conversation, more and more. They talked about the future as if it was a foregone conclusion that they would be together. The words they both wanted to hear each other say still remained unspoken, yet they both knew in their hearts they had found what they wanted.

The plane banked and headed southeast across Indiana and Kentucky. The ground below turned from snow white, to dirty brown, to green grass, and the low forested mountains of the southeast. Charlie leaned on Torch, her head on his shoulder, her eyes closed and just a hint of a serene satisfied smile on her lips. He could feel her breath faintly on his cheek. *Like angel kisses*, Torch thought.

He buried his nose in her soft hair. She smelled so good. It wasn't the soap or the fruity shampoo; it was a smell that was one of a kind. It dispersed from her in some kind of an aura, which seemed to have its very own atmosphere.

The squeal of the tires, as the big jet hit the runaway, jolted them both awake. They sat up and braced themselves as the pilot engaged the brakes, and brought the plane to a slow roll. People were gathering up their belongings, getting ready to disembark.

They squinted, and shaded their eyes from the bright Florida sun, as they boarded the shuttle to pick up their rented car. The temperature was in the eighties, the Florida heat soothing away the winter chill they had left behind.

It was just a short drive to the condo in Clearwater Beach, and they were there before they had time to acclimate. It was a one-story, Spanish style double home that looked out on the white sands of the gulf. The aqua blue waters stretched as far as the horizon before they disappeared, blending in with the clear blue skies.

"You make us some drinks, while I get my swimsuit on."

Torch changed quickly also, and with their drinks and some snacks in hand, they ran across the beach like calves out of the barn in springtime. Then they nestled down in a couple of oversized beach chairs, pushing their toes into the warm sand. Some hungry seagulls swooped and darted overhead, screeching and waiting for the first dropped snack, in a game they had played for ages.

"You're getting red already, Torch." Charlie filled the palm of her hand with lotion and rubbed it into his shoulders. It felt so good to touch his body. She kneaded his neck muscles in a mini massage, feeling him relax. Then, finished, she reached over and kissed him softly.

Torch took her hand in his. "Charlie, I am so happy when I am with you. All of the pressures, all of the craziness in this world, just seem to slip away and hide when I'm with you. I once knew another love, but this is so different, so special and it's that way because you are so special."

Charlie was staring out at the gulf, and slowly, a tear ran down her face.

"I'm sorry, sweetheart, if I said something to make you sad. I just wanted you to know how I felt."

Charlie turned to him and took her dark glasses off. Both of her eyes were brimming with tears. "Torch, I have lived a loveless life for many years, and then this happened. You came along and stole my heart. I'm in love with you, and these tears are tears of joy."

On Thanksgiving Day, they went out to a small family-style restaurant and had turkey dinner with all of the trimmings. They went souvenir shopping, and both came back in new hats and flip-flop sandals. They sipped large salty margaritas, as they walked along the narrow almost-empty sidewalks. A lot of the shops were closed, but a few of them saw it as an opportunity to stay open, and take advantage of the lack of competition.

Tomorrow they were going to take a harbor cruise that they signed up for at a small booth on a busy street corner, manned by a little old lady whose wrinkled face had seen way too much sun and too much of life. Torch pressed a couple of bills in her leathery hand and said, "Happy Thanksgiving."

"God bless," she said. The crooked smile from the toothless mouth said it all.

Their lovemaking was becoming refined, like a well-rehearsed play, and went on into the wee hours of the morning. Then they slept, exhausted, in each other's arms; neither one wanting to be the one to let go. They needed to share everything, even the very air they breathed.

Torch had one thing in mind and one thing only. He wanted to make Charlie crave their lovemaking, as much as he did, and to fall deeply in love with him along the way. She had told him about her earlier abuse at Mathew Senior's hands, and more accurately, at the end of his penis. Charlie had not been loved by him in any sense of the word. Rather, she was simply a depository for his lustful ways.

Torch understood how the female sensuality worked. He and Evie had worked on it, long and hard, back when times had been good. Now, he knew he had to change Charlie's phobias, and make it right in her mind, too. She needed to be taught the difference between lust and love. For once in his life, he was the teacher.

He needed not to have worked so hard at it if he had only known how Charlie was thinking. You see, Charlie was up to the top of her head in pure ecstasy, and she was fast falling for Torch in a big way.

The ride around the harbor the next day was done on a replica of a Spanish Galleon, complete with a one wooden-legged captain with a hook on his hand. Every so often, the cannons would fire and the smell of gunpowder would permeate the ship. Finally, getting sunburnt, they went below deck where a bar and snacks were available. They had margaritas that were so cold they seized your throat and took your breath away. Then they ate roast pig, on big fresh buns, with lots of napkins to wipe the grease from each other's faces.

That night they just stayed home on their patio and enjoyed one of the most spectacular sunsets they had ever seen. It had been the best weekend get-away either of them had ever had, and it seemed a shame it had to end.

It seemed that their love for each other grew with every passing moment, and late Saturday night, they lay on their sides facing each other after making love. "I wish you were mine forever," Torch said.

"I will be, Torch. Forever and a day, sweetheart. Forever and a day."

The plane ride home was filled with a sense of peace and tranquility. They had exhausted each other, both physically and mentally. The questions that had haunted both of them about each other's intentions had been answered and put away. They had made a commitment and a bond. Now, debilitated, they slept; Charlie's head on Torch's shoulder and Torch's head bouncing lightly against hers.

CHAPTER THIRTY

The indictment came down on Tuesday morning and Charlie made sure that it, and the warrant for Hal's arrest for first degree murder, were delivered directly to Torch's office.

For Torch, this was the culmination of his career. That gaping wound, that had been opened when Hal was set loose some ten years ago, was closing and he was confident that they would win this time.

Life, in general, was so much brighter right now. His love for Charlie, coupled with this victory in court, had him feeling euphoric. True, the trial would be the summit, and maybe his emotions were running ahead of the script, but Torch's whole life had been influenced by gut feelings, and he had a good one about this.

He made a phone call to the Minnetonka Police Department. Tonight, at about six p.m., he and two other Minneapolis police officers would make the arrest. They wanted Minnetonka police to stand by, right at the edge of the property.

They had chosen the time carefully. One thing they wanted to avoid was having a lot of people around when they made the arrest, so waiting until he got home was best. Charlie had told him that Hal always left work by four in the afternoon, preferring to start early and leave early. The only thing they hadn't planned on was Hal not going into work at all that day.

At noon, a Minneapolis plain-clothes officer took up a post outside of the residence in a plain brown Ford sedan. He immediately radioed back that Hal's car was still at the residence. With no garage now, his car had to sit outside. Torch radioed back. "If he takes off, follow him, and don't let him out of your sight."

Hal knew something was up. There had been the initial announcement in the newspapers reopening the investigation, and then nothing but quiet. That was unusual for the police. He had his own little snitch at the police department, but she was hard-pressed to find out anything, either. There were two people out there that could incriminate him, and that made him extremely nervous. He was hesitant to approach either of them right now, and he still had no proof they'd said anything.

His drug habit was out of control. With a never-ending supply of money, and no daddy to look over his shoulder, he had thrown caution to the winds. He had started to dabble in other drugs beside cocaine. Coke just wasn't doing it for him anymore, so he had tried some heroin, and tonight he was going to try some meth. These were dangerous drugs that could take him somewhere he might not want to be, but Hal wasn't thinking about that right now.

Ellie brought breakfast up to him this morning, and when he wouldn't open the door she left it outside, in the hallway, where it still sat untouched.

Hal had a three-day growth of beard stubble, and hadn't showered or changed his clothes in that same amount of time, either. His room was a mess of dirty clothes, empty food wrappers, and half-filled beer bottles. One of them had tipped over on the nightstand a few days ago, and now the wood was bleaching out and buckling up. The wastebasket beside his bed reeked from the vomit he had spewed in it and on it. In the bathroom, there was feces all over the inside of the stool and the floor, from the chronic diarrhea he was now suffering with.

Right now he was looking for his car keys, as he had to make a drug run. He found the keys and walked out his bedroom door, tripping over the breakfast dishes still sitting there. This infuriated Hal, and he kicked them all down the hallway. Ellie came out from the kitchen to see what all of the racket was, and Hal screamed at her.

"Ellie, clean up this damn mess and clean my room!" He was talking as he came down the stairs and Ellie was drying her hands on her apron, watching him warily.

"I'll be back in an hour or so. If anyone calls for me, tell them I'm sick. No wait, tell them to go to hell." He slammed the door as he left.

Ellie picked up the broken dishes and cautiously made her way up to his room. She took one look inside the room and then closed the door. She had put up with a lot of crap in her days, but this was too much. She was quitting.

The radio crackled in Torch's office. It was Levi, the stakeout cop. "Torch, he's on the move. Just left home and is going west on this road around the lake."

"Stay on his tail and keep me updated."

Levi was good at following people. He knew all of the tricks about staying back and letting other cars fall in behind the car you were following. Straying to the right from time to time he weaved in and out, peeking around the cars in front of him; just barely keeping Hal in sight, but never letting him completely out of his sight.

Torch was trying to formulate Plan B, if necessary. He really didn't want to apprehend him out in the open, but if it looked like he was on the run, it might be necessary.

He got Levi back on the radio. "What's happening now, Levi?"

"Well, it looks like he's heading back into the city. He's on the freeway heading east. Doesn't seem to be in a hurry and he's really not paying a lot of attention to things around him. "I should have put a GPS unit on his car last night, but it sat right out in the open under a yard light."

"Yea, that would have been nice, Levi, but right now I really don't think he has any idea we want him. He's probably just on an errand of some kind."

Approaching the Minneapolis loop, Hal skirted around it on I-94, and then took the Cedar Avenue exit back towards the loop. He was driving very slowly now, as if he was looking for someone or something. Suddenly, he pulled off and parked alongside the curb in front of some older storefronts, while talking on a cell phone.

Levi drove by him, keeping him in his rear view mirror. Two blocks up he turned right, made a U-turn, and headed back towards Hal, who was still sitting right where he had parked but was no longer talking on the phone. Levi spotted a small parking lot next to a deli and pulled in and parked. He walked back out to the sidewalk, peering at Hal's car, about a hundred feet away on the opposite side of the street.

A young black man was handing Hal a small rolled-up brown paper bag through the passenger window. Hal, in turn, gave him an envelope. Levi knew a drug deal when he saw it.

Hal headed back the way he had come, and it became evident to Levi that he was going back home.

Levi keyed the mike again. "Torch, I think he just went out and bought some drugs. He appears to be heading back home again."

Torch looked at his watch. It was nearly noon. Why wait any longer? Maybe he would just call the Minnetonka PD and tell them it was going down right now.

By the time Hal arrived back at the house, he had forgotten all about what he had told Ellie about cleaning up his room. He had one thing and one thing only on his mind—getting high. He rolled up his sleeve and stretched the rubber band tightly around his arm to get a vein to pop. Then he injected the heroin he had just cooked.

He slid off the bed and laid on the floor, leaning against the side of it, while the rush roared over him. He lay there for about twenty minutes until he started to slowly come around. He was barely aware of what was going on around him, but he did hear the squeal of tires on the cobblestones outside and car doors slamming.

Hal crawled to the window and looked out. There were two black and white squad cars and two plain sedans sitting outside.

"Asshole cops," he muttered, as he got unsteadily to his feet. He was going to go down and meet them; he didn't want them to see his room.

When he arrived at the bottom of the stairs, a flabbergasted Ellie was talking to Torch, and pointing upstairs. He didn't remember Torch, in his present stupor, or the two men with him.

"Look, I told you guys everything I knew about the fire, so why don't you leave us alone." Hal was reeling from side to side, and then it hit him. This wasn't the cops about the fire out back. This was the asshole that had tried to convict him a long time ago. He shivered, and crossed his arms, staring at Torch.

"You better have a damn good reason, or a warrant for breaking in here."

"I have both, Hal." Torch held the document in front of him so Hal could see it. "You are under arrest for the murder of Stacie Morrison. Hold your hands out." Hal turned to run, but the two men quickly subdued him and pinned him to the wall.

"Mathew Halsworth, I want you to understand that anything you say can and will be used against you in a court of law." Torch didn't need a card, he knew this one by heart, but never had the words sounded better. He finished the Miranda warning, enjoying every word, but he was wasting his breath. Just like ten years ago, Hal had clammed up and was not saying anything.

Ellie stood against the wall, her hands to her face, and then a commotion behind them caught everyone's attention. It was Melinda Halsworth, standing there in a long flowing white nightgown; her arms wide open as if she wanted to embrace someone.

"Mathew, is that you?" She was staring at Torch. Ellie ran to her and turned her around, moving her back towards her room. "Mathew, come to bed now. Where have you been, my love?"

The wheels of law were moving fast this time. The arraignment would be tomorrow at nine a.m.

Hal had used his one allowed phone call after his arrest to call the firm. They were the first words anybody had heard out of him since he was brought in.

Jack Salome, a prominent defense attorney with the firm, would be representing him. Torch had faced Salome many times in trials, and had seldom won, but this time it was going to be different.

Charlie appointed David Beverly, the Assistant County Attorney, to prosecute the case. Beverly was a sixty year old, well-seasoned and no-nonsense attorney. There wasn't much he hadn't seen or heard when it came to legal matters. He promised a vigorous prosecution of Hal Halsworth for the crimes he had been charged with.

He was impressed with the evidence that had been presented in the case, but asked Torch to dig deeper in a couple of areas. One was the fire and death at the house in Minnetonka. This had not been presented to the Assistant County Attorney, but Torch had mentioned it to him. A separate crime, to be sure, but it would all fit together in determining Hal's character. One other area to investigate more closely was his life with Stephanie. Despite the fact she had said she would testify, she was still holding things back, they were sure of that.

It was Beverly's strategy to show the court and the jury that, despite Hal's lack of a criminal record, he was incorrigible. That his life had been filled with crimes that he had escaped prosecution for, simply because of his status and his family's place in the legal community.

Hal's attorney, Jack Salome, issued a statement that they would have nothing more to say until after the arraignment, when they had a chance to see the evidence against him. For the time being, though, his client was innocent of any and all charges against him, and he was looking forward to clearing his name, once and for all, in a court of law.

Hal had said nothing since being arrested except to say, "If the police had anything to ask him, they could ask his attorney." For now, he sat on his bunk in his orange coveralls and stared at the floor. He was experiencing some withdrawal from the heavy drug usage he had put his body through the last few days. This made him extremely agitated and nervous. He appeared to be unable to concentrate on any one thought for more than a few seconds at a time, except thoughts of Stephanie.

Hal was convinced that, if anybody was helping the cops, it was her. This, with her claims to his money, left him no choice. She had to be dealt with. Jack Salome was coming to see him tonight and Hal had a plan.

Hal paced the tiny room while he talked to his attorney. "We have to have bail set, Jack. I cannot, and will not, stay here until the trial."

"Well, the judge will certainly have a lot to say about that, Hal. All we can do is try, but I'm not sure what will come of it. You do realize you have been charged with murder one, don't you? That is a charge they don't usually set bail for."

"You heard me, Jack. I want out of here. I don't care whose palm you have to grease or whose ass you have to kiss, you get me out of here."

"Well, the arraignment is in the morning so there's not a lot of time to do anything, but let's see what comes of it. Do you want me to ask for a postponement of the arraignment?"

"No! Just get me out of here. What part of that don't you understand?"

Jack shrugged his shoulders and started to put his coat on. "See you in the morning, Hal."

Hal didn't answer him, but sat down at the table and started to bang his head against the table top, until a deputy came and got him, and ushered him back to his cell.

Arraignments usually don't take a long time. It's just a time for the defendant to plead guilty, or not guilty, and a trial date is sometimes set. Judge Clarence Stevens was presiding over the arraignment.

Hal looked like he had been on a two-week bender. His eyes were rimmed with black shadows and he had a two-day growth of beard. His shoulders drooped and his lips were pressed together in a defiant grimace. He shuffled into the courtroom in his orange coveralls, his feet shackled and his hands cuffed in front of him. He stared at the carpet, choosing to not make eye contact with anyone.

He was ushered to the defendant's table, where Jack Salome sat waiting for him. It was at this point, and just before sitting down, he allowed himself a cursory look around. There was no one here that he recognized except Torch Brennan, who sat about halfway back on the defendant's side of the room.

"All rise. The Honorable Judge Clarence Stevens presiding." The judge came into the room in the flurry of a black gown and quickly took his seat.

"We are here today at this arraignment of Mathew Halsworth. You have been charged, Mr. Halsworth, with one count of murder in the first degree, contributing to the death of one Stacie Morrison on or about December 23, 1989. How do you plead?"

"My client pleads, 'not guilty,' your honor."

"Is there a reason your client cannot plead himself, Mr. Salome."

"No. He just asked me to plead for him."

The judge gave him a disgusted look, but said, "Very well."

"If that is your decision, Mr. Halsworth, you will be tried by a jury of your peers, in a trial in this court. I am sure, being an attorney, you understand what I am saying. No court date has been set yet, but one will be forthcoming. I would expect that the trial would be sometime this fall."

"Your honor," Jack Salome said, "I would like to discuss the issue of bail."

"Mr. Salome, you do understand that this is a first degree murder charge, and bail is rarely allowed for anyone under these circumstances."

"Yes, your honor. I do understand that this would be an exception to that rule. My client has been charged with this crime before and the charges were dropped for lack of evidence, just as they should be now. Be that as it may, Mr. Halsworth is no threat to flee. He has a business he needs to take care of, clients who need him, and a sick mother that he cares for. She would be under great stress without him to care for her."

The judge studied his papers for a moment. "Mr. Salome, I will take that under advisement and issue a ruling in a day or so. Until that happens, your client will remain incarcerated here in the county jail.

Does the prosecution wish to speak about this matter?" He looked over his reading glasses at David Beverly, who seemed to have been caught off-guard, and had not uttered a word during the whole proceedings.

"It is the prosecution's desire that this man not be released on bail, Your Honor. It isn't fleeing that is our greatest fear, but retaliation against witnesses. He is a violent man."

"That is a preposterous accusation that has no merit whatsoever," Salome retaliated.

Judge Stevens held up his hand. He had heard enough. "I will take that under advisement, too, Mr. Beverly. If there is no other business then, I will recess this matter for now. Court is adjourned."

Torch waited for Beverly on the front steps of the courthouse. "Dave, do you think he would allow bail for him?"

"I hope not, Torch, but there is little we can do about that except to voice our displeasure. That's up to the judge's discretion, and this judge can be very unpredictable. I'll be in touch, and I'll brief Ms. Malloy."

If only he knew what Ms. Malloy meant to him, Torch thought.

Torch was on the phone with Earl Carver, talking about the investigation into the fire at the Halsworth residence. Maybe they needed a second arrest.

"We have nothing that we could take to court, Torch. Yes, there was gasoline found at the scene of the fire, but there was a car with a potential full tank, and two six-gallon plastic cans that burned up in there. As for the melted rope on the doorknob, that is a red flag, but it's nothing you could hang your hat on. Sorry, Torch."

Torch scratched his head. Things were going good until today and now, well, he wasn't so sure of things anymore.

He had called Stephanie about talking more about her and Hal's relationship and she agreed, but not until Friday, two days away. She was going to be out of town.

Torch was meeting Charlie tonight for dinner. He needed a little confidence builder. They met at an out-of-the-way place in Woodbury, a suburb of St. Paul, and a place where they would probably not be recognized. Both of them hated having to sneak around. It made them feel like a couple of kids hiding from their parents. They chatted as they ate.

"Did Beverly tell you what Hal's lawyer said?" Torch asked. "He said Hal's mother was dependent on him, and for that reason, he needed bail to be set."

Charlie gave Torch a disgusted look, shaking her head. "Yes, and what a bunch of crap that is. I checked with their housekeeper and she told me Hal had not visited his mother in weeks, even though they live in the same house. The housekeeper went on to say that she has assumed full responsibility for Hal's mother, but she also said she has given her two weeks' notice and she is leaving. When I asked why, she refused to comment, just saying she was afraid of him."

"Everybody seems to be afraid of this asshole." Torch replied.

"As for his business commitments," Charlie went on, "People that I know over there told me he hasn't been in to work for two weeks, except to make token appearances. He's telling them he is still too upset over his father's death and his mother's health." I left a call for Judge Stevens but he hasn't returned it. I doubt that he wants any more information from us anyway, that we can't substantiate any better than this."

They sat in Charlie's car for a while and just held hands. Charlie turned to lock eyes with him. "Torch, I want you so badly. My thoughts keep going back to the trip we took to Florida, the fun we had, and how much I love you."

"Let's go to Chicago this weekend," Torch said. "My treat. I have a buddy that lives there that has this big house and he would love the company."

"Can't, Torch. I have to work this weekend, but let's go the next weekend and maybe we can make it for three days. I would love to see Chicago again."

"When I was a little girl, I always dreamed that someday I would find my special person, my 'knight in shining armor,' as cliché as it sounds. I remember lying in my bed at night, hugging my pillow, and fantasizing how nice it would be to hold him, caress him and make love to him. I didn't even know what love was back then, but I knew I wanted it. Now that I have met you and experienced it, I know how really special it is."

"There are some dreams I have had to let go of. Children, a home in the burbs, and President of the P.T.A. Things like that. I guess I never thought that my life would be two-thirds over before it all happened. Mathew Halsworth ruined my best years. I envy you that you were able to accomplish some of these things before you met me. Now I just want to make you happy for the rest of your life."

"I love you, too, Charlie. You're a very special lady. Yes, I did have that happy home 'in the burbs' as you call it. I had a wonderful little girl, and for a while, a loving wife. Then I lost it all, Charlie, and believe me, the pain of that overshadowed all the good that I'd achieved. That's why my biggest fear right now is that I will wake up and find out this has all been a dream, and you will be gone. Be with me forever, sweetheart?" Torch kissed her softly.

"For all of eternity, Torch."

On Wednesday morning, Judge Stevens summoned both lawyers to his chambers for a ten a.m. meeting. He had made a decision on the bail request.

Both lawyers sat in soft leather chairs, facing the judge who was reclining in his, minus the usual robe. He was dressed casually, in a sweater and brown khaki slacks, with a pencil perched on top of his ear and his reading glasses sitting precariously on the end of his nose.

"Gentleman, I am going to get right to the point as I have only a few minutes. This will not be a win—win situation, but it will make it hard for Mr. Halsworth if he has any ideas of leaving town. I am going to allow bail in the amount of five million dollars.

Beverly stammered as he tried to find the right words to express his disappointment, but Judge Stevens cut him off. "That is my decision and it is final. Now if you will excuse me, I have court in five minutes."

CHAPTER THIRTY-ONE

By three in the afternoon, Hal walked out of jail, not exactly a free man, but at least a relieved man; and at about the same time Torch found out about the whole thing from Beverly.

There was little they could do about it, so Beverly just asked the judge for as speedy a trial as possible. The judge, in turn, said he would do his best to set it up soon, maybe as early as springtime. The court docket was packed with drug-related cases.

Speaking of drugs, that was the first thing Hal headed for as soon as he arrived home. His room was a haze of smoke from cooking drugs, and right now he was spaced out—way out. He had no more patience for dealing with people who were trying to ruin his life. First and foremost of these was Stephanie. Hal appeared deep in thought. *No matter what happened to her, he would be suspected. With no friends he could trust, it was going to be hard to set up any kind of an alibi. The best he could do was make sure there were no witnesses and no evidence. They could think whatever they wanted to. They still had to prove it.*

Charlie was the other problem. He would not have much of a chance in

her court and he knew it. She was going to wish she had not screwed with Hal,
County Attorney or not.

Hal was too stoned to do anything about it tonight, but tomorrow night, Stephanie and the child were going to disappear forever. His money would all be his, and she would play no part in a trial against him. Now he just had to figure out how. This would be a night to make plans. That is, between bouts of anesthetizing himself.

His high was fading, so he sat up on the edge of the bed and started to cook a new batch. He pulled the lace curtain back to look outside. It was three in the morning and outside his window it was a damp and spooky quiet. *The kind of night that belongs to the devil.* Then he laughed. *Maybe I am the devil, or at least his right hand man.*

The yard light that shined all of the time had burned out, adding to the darkness that enveloped the big yard. He was going to have to find somebody to take care of the place, now that Lamont was gone. Hal giggled when he thought about Lamont. *Stupid black dope. Never knew when to keep his mouth shut, and didn't know enough to mind his own damn business. Well, you can tell everybody your secrets wherever you are now, Lamont. No one back here gives a shit, anymore.*

He quickly pulled the curtains shut, as he was sure he saw shadows behind the trees out on the lawn. *He was being watched, wasn't he?* Hal was extremely agitated right now, and didn't know if he was hallucinating, or if there really was someone out there.

He lay back on the bed and held a pillow over his head. He better get some rest, he had a big day tomorrow.

Stephanie arrived home about nine on Thursday night. She and her sister had gone to Vegas for two days, and their mother had taken care of Hal. Hal had fallen asleep in the car on the drive home and she put him to bed right away. She felt of his forehead as he looked a little flushed, but he didn't seem warm. She wound up a little music box on his dresser, and shutting off the light, went down the hall to her room.

Hal had been on her mind the last few days. She knew he was mad at her and the police had arrested him. That made her uneasy, but at least he was locked up, and she hoped it was for a long time.

She undressed slowly by the foot of her bed, and then went into the bathroom and started the shower. They had stayed up late in Vegas both nights, and she was tired.

The warm water felt so good she stayed in it until the tank went dry. Then she put on a fresh gown and checked on Hal once more. He was sleeping soundly.

The bed felt so good, and it was only moments before she fell asleep, thinking about her meeting in the morning with Torch.

Hal had slept until the middle of the day on Thursday, and then he had gone downstairs to see his mother. He had laid off the drugs so far today, so his mind was quite lucid. Ellie was in the kitchen cutting vegetables, and although she had been aware he was home, she was still surprised to see him.

"How's mother?" he asked.

"She's as well as can be expected. Hal, we need to talk about her. I will only be here for another week, and you are either going to have to find someone to care for her, or put her in a home someplace."

"Look Ellie, I know I have not been the easiest person to be around the last few weeks, but if you will give me another chance, I think we can work something out. Maybe a nice raise would help."

"No, Hal, I gave you my reasons for leaving, and besides that, I already have a new job."

Hal stood with his hands on the countertop, staring at her across from him. His face was thick with whisker stubble and she could smell his body odor way across the kitchen. He appeared to be chewing something, although there was nothing in his mouth but his tongue.

The look he was giving her right now scared her, and Ellie figured she had better not say anything more.

Suddenly, Hal whirled and went out the back door. Ellie went to the window to see if she could see him. He had picked up a large dead branch, and he was viciously beating on a hedgerow. Spittle was flying from his mouth and he was screaming something but she could not hear him.

And you wonder why I'm quitting?

Hal came back in and went up to his room, slamming the door behind him. He would deal with Ellie after tonight. She was no longer useful to him, nor was his mother.

Hal smoked some pot, and snorted some more coke, but went easy on it.

He needed to have his wits about him. He would leave for Stephanie's around midnight. Right now he just needed a little something to relax him.

It was one fifteen in the morning when Hal awoke. For a second, he had to sit on the edge of the bed and put the upcoming events in order. It was no time to screw up.

First and foremost, he had to leave here without Ellie knowing it. If and when the cops came, she would be his alibi.

Second, he needed a weapon. There was no way he could drug Stephanie like he drugged Stacie. The thought of Stacie lying on that bed, dead and naked, brought an urging to his groin. It had been a while, and maybe he would give old Stephanie a poke in the whiskers when he got done with her. *Just a little goodbye touch.*

Hal had backed off on the boy. If he stayed sleeping he would leave him alone. He was too young to be a witness, but if he woke up, then he and momma were going out together.

He went to the bathroom and cleaned up a little, putting on a fresh white shirt, a sport coat and blue jeans. Hal primped in the mirror over the dresser. Damn, he still looked good, despite all he had been through.

Satisfied he had thought of everything, Hal crept down the stairs and went into the kitchen and selected a long-handled kitchen knife. He wrapped it in a towel and let himself out the back, but not before he looked in on his mother and Ellie, who both appeared to be sleeping soundly.

Hal had left his car on the top of the hill, pointed down the driveway. He gave it a slight shove and it started rolling down the grade. He jumped in and steered it until it glided to a stop a safe distance from the house. Then he carefully started it and drove quietly away.

He turned down the dash lights so anybody looking in would only see a shadow of a driver. Tonight, the night belonged to him. Tonight, things would be made better for him. Tonight, the people who had made life miserable for him were going to get theirs.

On the passenger seat, written on a notepaper, was Charlie's address. He had been there before, a long time ago. He remembered that it was a townhouse that looked just like her neighbors, and he could ill afford to get in the wrong unit. Unlike Stephanie's place, he didn't have a key. It might take a while to decide how best to get in, but when he did, Charlie was going to wish he hadn't. Lying beside the note was the towel, hiding its deadly weapon.

Stephanie's building was dark but there was a faint glow coming from the kitchen, which faced the road. It was just that damn nightlight she always left on.

Hal walked down the sidewalk, about half a block, to get his thoughts straight one last time. He was determined, but still tentative.

He was going to go straight to the bedroom, grab her by the hair, slit her throat and leave. He didn't want to see her face as she died, and he no longer wanted to have sex with her. Maybe when he got done here and went on to Charlie's, he would do her before he killed her. His dad thought she was a good lay, so she couldn't be all bad. It would be the ultimate insult he could give her.

Hal's car was parked across the street from the townhouse, next to the curb. When he reached the end of the block he turned, crossed the street, and came back on the other side of the street. The car window was down and Hal reached inside for the towel and its baggage. There was no one around and the street was deserted. There were no lights on in the other units. It was now or never.

Hal reached into his pocket for his door key and walked briskly across the street.

His heart was racing, but deep inside of him was a fervent desire to get this over with. There was no turning back now. Standing on the top step, he looked up and down the street once more but there was no one to be seen. *No, wait, a car was coming.*

The headlights bathed the entire street as the car slowly entered the complex, slowed even more, and then pulled into a driveway about three doors down. An obviously intoxicated man and woman got out, and supporting each other, stumbled to the doorway and disappeared inside. Hal had stepped off the step while they passed and he remained there in the bushes for a few seconds, holding his hand over his mouth to conceal the vapor from his breath in the cold December air. When he was assured they were in, and not coming back out, he jumped back up on the step and inserted his key. It fit but it wouldn't turn.

Infuriated, he tried the key several times, but it was no use. *Bitch changed the locks did she? Locked me out of my own damn house. Well, you have pissed me off one time too many little girl, and now you are going to pay.*

Hal smashed the sidelight window with his elbow, and in one motion reached in and turned the lock. The door opened wide.

Stephanie was in a deep sleep, but not too deep to realize what was happening. She heard the sound of breaking glass. She had rehearsed this scenario many times in her fearful thoughts.

It was Hal and she knew it. This was the moment of truth she had just known was going to happen.

She felt the cold blast of air coming down the hallway and knew the outside door was open. Sliding out of bed, Stephanie reached into the nightstand for the forty-five automatic. The gun felt heavier than she remembered it, the blue steel felt ice cold in her hand. It was locked and loaded, she was assured of that.

She could hear the intruder in the kitchen, opening drawers and looking for something. She had to act fast. She moved quickly and quietly, around the room to the door, and looked toward the kitchen. She could still hear him and then she heard a hideous laugh and she knew for sure it was Hal, and he had come to harm her.

Once inside the house, Hal realized that the towel he was carrying had nothing in it. The knife must have slid out in the bushes, and there was no time to go back. Stephanie had knives, too. *What a fitting end—to kill her with her own knife.*

The first drawer he opened held only silverware. The second drawer was full of towels. *It had been a while, where the hell did she keep them? She had a block full of knives. That's right; they sat on the corner by the stove.*

Hal crept around the center island. In the near darkness, he could barely make out the counter from the glowing numerals on the stovetop. The only other light was the tiny yellow nightlight behind him.

He found the block of knives and now his hands felt of the handles, looking for the biggest knife. The first one he pulled out was too small; the second one was a cleaver.

Then he pulled out a knife about ten inches long. Hal ran his finger down the edge of it and it felt sharp. *Enough screwing around—let's get this over with.*

Stephanie was going through the door to Hal's room when Hal stepped into the hallway. His focus was on her bedroom door and he didn't see the fleeing shadow behind him. She reached into the crib, and picked up the sleeping toddler, praying that he would stay quiet.

He moaned softly but went back to sleep. She had to hold him with one arm as she had the heavy pistol in the other hand. The door to his closet was open and she backed into it and slid to the floor. Her heart was racing, her chin trembling, and her hands were shaking. She had never been so afraid in all of her life. In her daydreams she had rehearsed this so many times, knowing that it could come to this, but never really thinking that it would, and never did she think it would be this terrifying. She could only pray that he would find her room empty and leave.

When Stephanie had slid out of the bed, the bedclothes had remained unopened. The body pillow she slept with was a discernible hump in the bed. Hal could see it clearly in the red glow from the bedside clock. The knife slashed again and again into the pillow, and then Hal realized that it was not the object of his hostility.

He screamed in rage and spun around. He ran to the door and turned on the light switch. The door to the walk-in closet and the bathroom door were both closed. Hal, grinning with a maniacal sneer, approached the bathroom.

"Come out, you little bitch, and get what you have coming to you."

Stephanie had heard his voice in that tone only once before, and that was the night he had raped and assaulted her on the kitchen floor. The memories of that night flashed back to her, and suddenly, she wasn't afraid anymore. Her hands quit shaking, her breathing slowed, and she felt a strange calm in this sea of hostility. *No, Hal, you bastard, you come here and get what you have coming to you.*

She had laid the toddler down on the floor, and now she stood, holding the gun in front of her face with both hands. No longer fearing Hal, and almost wishing he would show his face before she once again lost her nerve.

Both the bathroom and the closet were empty and Hal whirled and ran to the bedroom doorway. The light from the bedroom was spilling into the hallway, illuminating him from behind. From the half-opened closet door, Stephanie was looking at the face of a mad demented man.

"Now you both die, bitch," he hissed. "I didn't want to harm the boy, but if you insist on hiding with him, well, that's your choice."

He had the knife raised over his head; the light from behind him glittering off the polished stainless blade. He was at the doorway when she pulled the trigger.

The explosion from the gun was deafening. The recoil jerked the pistol backwards, hitting Stephanie in the forehead and opening up a gash an inch wide. Blood was spilling down her face and in her eyes. Little Hal was screaming, terrified. The small closet was filled with smoke and an acidic smell of blood and gunpowder.

The bullet tore into Hal just below his heart, tearing through his stomach and exiting just above his right kidney, leaving a ragged hole the size of a tennis ball in his back. A stream of blood and gore exited with it, and splattered the white hallway walls. Hal stumbled, but did not go down. His open mouth was mouthing words but all that came out was a loud guttural groan. His right hand still held the knife at his side; his left hand was balled up pressing into the wound in front of him. A mixture of blood, stomach contents and bits of rib bones oozed out over his fist.

Hal staggered forward. He had not seen Stephanie in the dark room, but now she stepped from the closet, and closed the door behind her on the screaming child. He didn't need to see his father die like this.

She had gone from a defensive mode to an offensive mode. Strangely calm, her bloody face showed only a grim determination to rid her, and the world, of this evil despicable man.

Hal staggered forward one more step, leaning against the hallway wall, and raised the knife again. For a second, their eyes locked, and then she raised the gun once more and pulled the trigger.

This time, the bullet hit Hal just above his nose and his brain exploded out the back of his skull, spraying the walls once more. He crumpled into a heap in the doorway.

She stood and watched his body for a couple of minutes, the smoking gun still held in front of her. A pool of blood was forming under his head. His chest heaved one last time and then went still.

Stephanie dropped the pistol, and opening the closet door, picked up the terrified toddler. Shielding his eyes with the blanket he had been wrapped in, she skirted the body in front of her, and rushed down the hall and into the kitchen.

She picked up the phone to call 911, and then set it back down. She put Hal into his high chair and went back into the bedroom and got her purse. There, in the side pocket, was the card Torch had given her. She dialed his number.

CHAPTER THIRTY-TWO

It took a second before Torch realized who the terrified woman was on the other end of the line. For one thing, he was half asleep and had no idea who he was talking to. Then he recognized her voice.

"Stephanie, what's the matter?"

"It's Hal," she sobbed. "He tried to kill me, Torch, just like I said he would."

"Where is he now and where are you?" Torch was standing beside his bed now, wide awake. He fumbled for the lamp switch.

"He's in the hallway, Torch. He's dead."

He could hear the baby screaming in the background.

"Look, Stephanie. Get out of that house. Take the baby and go to your car, and lock the doors. I'll call a squad from here, and I will be over as soon as I can."

When Torch arrived, there were two black and whites and an ambulance sitting in front of the house. Stephanie was sitting in the back of one of the squads, holding Hal, and staring out the window, crying. Torch slid in beside her. He held her for a few minutes until things settled down, and then he asked a female officer to stay with her while he checked things out inside the house. "We can talk later," he said to her.

Inside the house, the crime lab people were setting up shop and both of them nodded to Torch as he entered. His eyes followed the trail of carnage through the house, taking in each and every detail. There was the glass littering the kitchen floor from the sidelight window that had been broken. It had obviously been broken from outside. Two drawers in the cabinets were open, and a small knife and meat cleaver were lying on the countertop.

As he walked through the doorway to the hallway going to the bedrooms, the odor of death permeated the air. It was a mixture of blood, vomit, and human excrement coming from the walls, the floor, and the crumpled body lying in the hallway in a congealing pool of blood.

He entered the master bedroom first. The bedclothes were ripped and torn and chunks of foam littered the floor and the bed from the shredded pillow. On a chair beside the bed was a pair of women's jeans and some underclothes. Everything else seemed to be in order. Torch tried to imagine what went on in here. He must have caught her in bed or did he? She had a cut on her forehead but apparently was all right otherwise. He would hear her story in a few minutes. First, he needed to see the scene.

He walked slowly from the bedroom, trying to be careful not to step in any of the gore. He looked behind him and there were two bullet holes in the wall. The shots had to have come from the other bedroom. He carefully skirted by Hal's body.

In the child's room, the gun lay on the floor in front of the open closet. One spent shell was on the closet floor and the other one was out in the middle of the room. The gun appeared ready to fire. There were some drops of blood on the closet floor.

Torch had seen enough in here. He stopped long enough to do a cursory exam of Hal's body. Two gunshot wounds. One in the lower chest and one in the face. Most of the back of Hal's head was open and he was looking at brain tissue and bloody remnants of bone and hair. *Hell of a gun*, Torch thought.

He walked back out and stood on the stoop for a moment. He didn't have to tell the lab people how to do their job; they'd done it hundreds of times before. He was looking for Hal's car.

On the opposite side of the street, about halfway down the block, was a white Lexus sedan—out of place and unoccupied.

The car was unlocked, the keys in the ignition, and it was empty except for a sheet of paper lying on the front seat. Torch reached in the open window and picked up the paper.

It simply said **4368 Belmont Court**. That was Charlie's address. The bastard was going there next, Torch just knew it. He folded the paper and put it in his shirt pocket. Then he called Charlie to make sure she was all right.

"I'm fine, Torch," the sleepy voice said, "What's wrong?"

"I'll fill you in in a little bit, kid. Come down to my office, if you can." He closed the phone.

The first stop for Stephanie was at the county hospital to get her forehead stitched, and then she met Torch at the police station for the interview. His maternal grandmother had picked up Hal.

Torch conducted the interview in his office, along with lots of doughnuts and coffee. An officer at the scene had retrieved her clothes and purse, and she had changed at the hospital.

"I have to record this, Stephanie, and there will be some kind of an investigation. It's required at a fatal scene, but I can assure you it's just a formality and it will be justifiable homicide. Now I want you to tell me step-by-step what happened, from beginning to end."

They sat on the same side of the desk together. Torch was trying to make things as easy and informal as he could for her. She had three staples holding the cut in her forehead together.

"He did that to you?"

Stephanie smiled. "No, the gun kicked back and smacked me."

"That was quite a cannon you bought there. We'll need to keep that for a while."

"You can keep it forever. I never want to see it again."

Torch smiled and squeezed her shoulder. "Tell me what happened."

Stephanie's story fit the scene like a well-rehearsed script. She left nothing out, and when she was finished, she looked at Torch and said, "That's the God's awful truth."

"I believe you kid," he said.

"I wish that it wouldn't have come to this, Torch. I'm just not cut out to kill people, no matter how bad they are."

"Few of us are, kid. But it was you or him, and maybe more people. Who knows who else he might have killed." Torch thought of the note in his shirt pocket. *Yes, Hal was out to kill anyone who was going to put him in jail. Maybe even me.*

"Grab your jacket and I'll take you to your mother's. It will be a couple of days before they are done at your house. We can take care of getting someone to clean it and fix the window."

There was a knock at the door. It was Charlie and one of the detectives.

"Torch, I just wanted you to know we found another knife at the scene. Talked to the housekeeper out at the Halsworth estate and she said it came from there. I told her Hal was dead. She shrugged her shoulders and said, 'she wasn't surprised'."

Thanks Bud. Torch was looking past him at Charlie, who stood smiling in the background. Stephanie stood beside him, somewhat bewildered by all of the activity.

"Charlie, this is Stephanie, and she just saved you a lot of work. Stephanie, this is Charlene Malloy, the County Attorney."

Charlie smiled sheepishly. "I just heard all about your ordeal. I hope you will be all right."

"Got time to ride with us?" Torch asked."

"I do have some extra time, detective. My biggest case just got cancelled."

EPILOGUE

Stephanie was very happy. The courts had found her justified in the killing of Hal, and no charges had been filed. In fact, she had become a hero in the eyes of some women's advocacy groups, but she turned down all offers to talk about it.

She had inherited Hal's entire share of the estate, and was rich beyond her wildest dreams. But, yearning for a more simple life, she had started a small gift shop in a small town just outside of the cities. Behind it sat a new home she had just moved into last week. She was a resilient woman, and the horrors of the past had been all but deleted from her memory. All except for an old police detective she could never forget.

Oscar seemed more at peace as he lived out the last days of his life in the nursing home. He had never been a vengeful man. Had Hal been found guilty in a court of law, and apologized for his deeds, it might have been a better ending, at least for Oscar. Now, he reasoned, Hal would never hurt anyone again.

Melinda Halsworth now lived in a nursing home across the lake. Her days were filled with empty thoughts. She no longer knew anybody or was aware of the world around her. All of the frightening things in this world had vanished along with the good things. She now existed from moment to moment, each memory fleeing as fast as it came.

It was the following spring and Charlie sat on the end of the dock, as she and Torch had just driven out to the lake. She had kicked her shoes off and it felt good to dangle her feet in the cold water. Out on the lake, a pair of loons chased each other around and around in a noisy mating ritual. Their shrill cries echoed over the blue waters, and into the forests around, as if there were speakers hidden in the foliage.

"Spring is a time for lovers, isn't it, Torch. Everywhere you look…birds and animals are building nests and pairing up. It's like God is recreating his world once more; giving the earth and all of us a fresh start."

Torch reached over and took her hand and brought her fingers to his mouth. He kissed the new diamond ring that sparkled in the spring sunlight. "It is a time for lovers, sweetheart, but there is a difference between us and those loons. We have found each other and our chase and mating ritual is over."

The End